What People Are Saying about the Left Behind Series

"This is the most successful Christian-fiction series ever."
—**Publishers Weekly**

"Tim LaHaye and Jerry B. Jenkins . . . are doing for Christian fiction what John Grisham did for courtroom thrillers."
—**TIME**

"The authors' style continues to be thoroughly captivating and keeps the reader glued to the book, wondering what will happen next. And it leaves the reader hungry for more."
—**Christian Retailing**

"Combines Tom Clancy–like suspense with touches of romance, high-tech flash and Biblical references."
—**The New York Times**

"It's not your mama's Christian fiction anymore."
—**The Dallas Morning News**

"Wildly popular—and highly controversial."
—**USA Today**

"Christian thriller. Prophecy-based fiction. Juiced-up morality tale. Call it what you like, the Left Behind series . . . now has a label its creators could never have predicted: blockbuster success."
—**Entertainment Weekly**

Tyndale House products by
Tim LaHaye and Jerry B. Jenkins

The Left Behind® book series
Left Behind®
Tribulation Force
Nicolae
Soul Harvest
Apollyon
Assassins
The Indwelling
The Mark
Desecration
The Remnant
Armageddon
Glorious Appearing
Coming Soon: Prequel and Sequel

Other Left Behind® products
Left Behind®: The Kids
Devotionals
Calendars
Abridged audio products
Dramatic audio products
Graphic novels
Gift books
and more . . .

Other Tyndale House books by
Tim LaHaye and Jerry B. Jenkins
Perhaps Today
Are We Living in the End Times?

For the latest information on individual products, release dates,
and future projects, visit www.leftbehind.com

Tyndale House books by Tim LaHaye	Tyndale House books by Jerry B. Jenkins
How to Be Happy Though Married	*Soon*
Spirit-Controlled Temperament	*Silenced*
Transformed Temperaments	
Why You Act the Way You Do	

APOCALYPSE
BURNING

BASED ON THE BEST-SELLING
LEFT BEHIND® SERIES

BEST-SELLING AUTHOR
MEL ODOM

TYNDALE HOUSE PUBLISHERS, INC.
WHEATON, ILLINOIS

Library of Congress Cataloging-in-Publication

Odom, Mel.
  Apocalypse burning / Mel Odom.
    p. cm. — (Apocalypse series)
  ISBN 1-4143-0033-6 (sc)
  1. Rapture (Christian eschatology)—Fiction. 2. End of the world—Fiction. I. Title.
  PS3565.D53A853 2004
  813'.54—dc22   2004010711

Printed in the United States of America

07 06 05 04
5   4   3   2   1

United States 75th Army Rangers Temporary Post
Sanliurfa, Turkey
Local Time 1422 Hours

"Help me! Please, God, send someone to help me! My wife! They took my wife!"

The agonized and fearful cry jerked First Sergeant Samuel Adams "Goose" Gander from the mental paralysis that had gripped him for the last several moments. The early afternoon sun blazed over Sanliurfa, beating down on the city with an unrelenting heat. Shimmering blasts of ovenlike air radiated from the shattered buildings surrounding him and the hard-baked asphalt beneath his boots. Sweat soaked Goose's BDUs and ran down his face from beneath his Kevlar helmet. The helmet shaded his eyes and would deflect most bullets and shrapnel, but right now it felt like a stewpot slowly parboiling his brain. Sand stuck to his chin and burned his eyes. The coppery taste of his own blood still lined his mouth, a souvenir from the fight he'd just had with Icarus.

Goose still stood in the alley where minutes ago he had first fought, then talked with the man he knew only as Icarus, the rogue CIA agent that Special Agent-in-Charge Alexander Cody and Ranger Captain Cal Remington had scoured Sanliurfa to find. Despite their desperate efforts, neither had been able to locate their target.

Goose, however, had encountered the fugitive on three different occasions. On two of those occasions, Icarus had sought Goose out. The rogue agent had staged the circumstances of those events so that Goose had had no choice but to let him walk away. The third time, at their meeting in this place, Goose had discovered by accident where

Icarus was hiding. He'd forcibly taken the rogue agent into custody. But he hadn't remanded Icarus over to Remington, Goose's commanding officer.

Though he and Remington disagreed on the matter of Icarus—as they had on many other things over the long years of their association in the military—Remington was Goose's good friend and a brother in arms.

But in the end Goose hadn't held Icarus. He'd allowed him to slip free. Now Icarus was gone, once more loose to pursue whatever mission drove him to remain within Sanliurfa's boundaries despite the dangers of the Syrian army, poised to attack the city, and the presence of his hunters Remington and Cody. If any of his pursuers caught up with him, Icarus's odds of survival, Goose knew, were essentially zero.

Goose also knew that he should be in hot pursuit of the rogue agent. But it appeared that chasing Icarus wasn't an option just now. Something else was going down, and Goose couldn't ignore the plea for help. He was a soldier, and soldiers defended those who couldn't defend themselves. In Sanliurfa, there were a number of defenseless.

"Help me! Someone help me! For the love of God!"

Goose stared toward the mouth of the alley, tracking the plea for help. He automatically slid his M-4A1 assault rifle from his shoulder and canted the weapon so the barrel pointed down and the butt rested on but not against his right shoulder under his chin. Four inches shorter than the M16s that infantrymen had carried in past wars, the M-4A1's design lent itself to close-quarter combat. Today's battlefields moved increasingly in the direction of urban warfare rather than open terrain. The weapons the Rangers carried reflected that.

A man in brown khaki shorts, hiking boots, and a gray shirt staggered in front of the alley mouth. He appeared thirty-something, balding and sunburned. Blood poured down the side of his face from a wound at the top of his head. Crimson lines ran down his chin and neck, disappearing into his shirt. His battered features were red and raw. Swollen bruises almost closed one eye.

"Sir." Goose kept his voice strong but neutral. The man jerked away and covered his head with one arm.

Peering fearfully under his forearm with his one good eye, the man looked at Goose. "You are American."

"Yes, sir," Goose replied. The wounded man stood partially behind Goose's Humvee, hiding as well as he could. Goose had driven into the alley to have his confrontation privately with Icarus. But right now the man was using the Humvee as cover. Goose cleared his throat, searching for the right words to get through to this man. "I'm First Sergeant Gander. With the United States Army 75th Rangers from Fort Benning, Georgia." His words were tinged with a southern accent, acquired courtesy of Waycross, Georgia, where Goose had been born and raised.

"Thank God," the man said. "Thank God." He started down the alley but almost fell over a loose hunk of debris from the nearby bomb-blasted buildings. Syrian artillery hadn't hit this part of the city as extensively as it had in other sections, but fallen debris still blocked the alley behind Goose.

"Sir," Goose said in a sterner voice, "stay where you are."

The man gaped at Goose but halted where he was.

Over the past few days, the Sanliurfan citizens and visitors had quickly learned to obey commands given by the three armies that currently held positions within the city. In addition to the Syrian threat looming outside the city's borders, the strange anomaly that had ripped away what most experts agreed was at least a third of the world's population had left people everywhere confused, paranoid, and afraid. No one knew if the disappearances would start up again, or who might disappear next.

"What?" the man shouted.

"Stay where you are," Goose repeated. "I don't know you."

During the past few days, the Rangers as well as the United Nations Peacekeeping teams and the Turkish army had learned that Syria's blatant and unprovoked attack on Turkey and the subsequent invasion had inspired a number of local terrorists to start ratcheting up their own campaigns to make political and religious statements. Most of those campaigns concentrated on raising the body count. Several soldiers of all three armies, various Sanliurfan citizens, and some innocent tourists trapped in this mess had paid the price for the terrorists' convictions.

The man stopped. "*Mon Dieu!* This is insane! I need help! My wife needs help! Do you not understand? They have her! They *took* her!"

Goose listened, straining his ears for any sounds of a struggle or confrontation. Distant vehicle noises and the roars of earthmoving equipment used to clear the primary streets and reinforce fighting positions, none of them nearby, created a constant aural backdrop over the city. He blinked stinging sweat from his eyes. He was edgy from not sleeping for more than twenty-four hours, and even the last sleep he'd managed hadn't been uninterrupted for more than an hour and a half at a time.

"You have *got* to help her." The man leaned heavily against the alley wall, as if the realization that he would have to win Goose over was almost too much to bear. Blood continued to thread down the side of his face and neck. His injured eye seemed to close a little more with each frantic heartbeat. "I do not know what they will do to her. Please."

"Your wife was taken?" Goose asked.

"*Oui.*" There was no mistaking the pain in the man's eyes.

"Who are you?"

"I am Jean Arnaud," the man replied. "I am a university professor in Paris." He named the school, but his French was so rapid Goose couldn't understand him. "I have papers." He reached for his shirt breast pocket with trembling hands that left bloodstains in their wake. "I was here in Sanliurfa on a sabbatical with my wife, Giselle. They took Giselle. You *must* help her." His fingers fumbled with the pocket and barely got the papers out.

Trusting his instincts that the man was telling the truth as well as the physical evidence of the beating Jean Arnaud had obviously undergone, Goose lowered his weapon but didn't put it away as he approached the man. If someone had kidnapped the woman, time was already working against a rescue effort. Sanliurfa, with its hodgepodge of architecture and hundreds of years of history, was a rabbit warren of hiding places.

Goose gestured to the Hummer. "Get in."

Arnaud hesitated just for a moment.

Grabbing the man by his arm, Goose pulled Arnaud into motion. He escorted the man to the passenger side of the Hummer and shoved him into the seat.

Goose jogged around to the driver's side, limping a little on his bad knee, and slid behind the wheel. Starting the Hummer's engine, he tagged the communications headset he wore to open a channel, then pulled the pencil mike to the corner of his mouth.

"Base," Goose said. "This is Phoenix Leader."

"Base reads you five by five, Phoenix Leader," the calm male voice responded.

"I need a com network for an immediate SAR op and access to soldiers at this twenty." Goose gave his location, then looked over his shoulder and backed the Hummer out into the street.

"A SAR, Phoenix Leader?"

"Affirmative," Goose replied. The call for a search-and-rescue team drew immediate attention, especially after the Syrian attack that had taken place the previous night. The city and the Rangers were still picking up the pieces from that. "The SAR target is a civilian, not one of our own."

"Understood, Phoenix Leader. Go to two-one for your network. I'll get a detail assembled for the SAR."

Goose flicked the headset to channel 21 and looked at Arnaud as the Hummer rolled to a stop in the middle of the street. "Which way?"

Arnaud looked around for a moment. His face was pale and anxious. Indecision weighed heavily on him. "There." He pointed to the right. "Giselle and I were in a little café. They ambushed us in the alley. They robbed us and took Giselle. I thought they were going to kill me."

Maybe they thought they had, Goose told himself, looking at the damage that Arnaud suffered. He put the Hummer into forward gear and let off the clutch, feeling another twinge of agony from his knee.

For the past few years he'd been careful with his left knee. He'd been wounded during a firefight in the first Iraq War, barely getting by on medical reports after extensive surgical repairs, because the doctors had known he was a dedicated soldier and wanted to muster out with a full pension, and because he'd always been able to handle the load. The crisis in Turkey was slowly eroding his physical ability to function. He needed rest but he wasn't getting it. The cortisone shots he'd used in the past to block the pain weren't working as effectively here, thanks to the continual stress and strain of constant use; even though the shots provided some relief, they didn't help the knee heal.

"Who took your wife?" Goose asked.

Arnaud shook his head miserably. "I do not know." He continued on in French.

"Sir, I don't understand what you're saying," Goose interrupted. He spoke just enough French to order a meal from a restaurant, and the man's rapid pace made comprehending him impossible. Goose's mind was still whirling from all the secrets that Icarus had revealed during the past few minutes.

"I was drawn to you, First Sergeant," Icarus had said. *"By something greater than myself. I know that now. There's a reason we've been put in each other's path."*

Goose gripped the Hummer's steering wheel harder. He knew how Arnaud felt, how the panic and helplessness slammed through the man. He forced himself to focus.

Shaking, Arnaud made a visible attempt to control himself. "The men, First Sergeant, they were not known to me. They are Bedouin, *oui?* Very probably traders. Scavengers." He glanced around, half out of his seat as he craned his neck to peer into buildings and down alleys. "You can see any number of them in the city. They come. They go. Some of them take what they can from the wreckage of the city. Others bring supplies into Sanliurfa. By any other name, most of them are still looters, taking profit from the hardships the rest of us have gone through. Now they have taken my wife."

Goose knew about the Bedouin. With the military satellite reconnaissance systems presently off-line in the Middle East, the nomadic people were a major conduit of information for the military forces currently hunkered down in Sanliurfa. The Bedouins existed as they always had, by trading and scavenging and taking whatever they could find. The Syrian assault on Turkey had proven a boon to the Bedouins, allowing them to capture prizes to own and to trade that they might never have gotten legally. According to news reports Goose had seen, several of the Bedouin tribes had started caches of war booty in the caves in the surrounding mountains.

"When was your wife taken?" Goose felt compassion run through him for this man. He hadn't seen his own wife in months, but if anyone ever tried to harm Megan, ever tried to take her away against her will—

God took Chris.

The thought rattled through Goose's mind, making him feel hollow and helpless, stripping away his confidence. The fact that God had taken Chris during the Rapture had been part of the message Icarus had delivered. *"Your son,"* Icarus had said in a quiet voice, *"is safe. God came and took your son up as He took all the other children."*

Goose couldn't allow himself to believe everything Icarus had stated. If he did, he had to give up on ever seeing his five-year-old son again.

In this life.

That possibility ripped at Goose's mind. He didn't have a faith strong enough to allow him to accept that. He'd tried, but he couldn't believe God would do that. Not to the point that he could give everything—his hopes and his fears—over to Him. Goose didn't know how a person did that.

Bill Townsend, his good friend and a devout Christian who had always talked about the end times and the fact that the Rapture might happen any day, had disappeared during the anomaly. If Bill were here, Goose was certain his friend would tell him that he'd see Chris again. At the end of the seven years of Tribulation. If he wasn't one of those who would die long before the end of that time.

But Goose couldn't help hanging on to the possibility that all those disappearances had been man-made—or even, though the concept strained his credulity, of extraterrestrial origins—and that he could somehow find a way to reverse those disappearances and bring those people—*bring Chris*—back. God wouldn't take his son away from him. The God Goose wanted to believe in couldn't be capable of that kind of cruelty.

"Over there." Arnaud pointed toward a small café and brought Goose's focus back to the present op. "I asked the people inside the café for help, but no one would help me."

That didn't surprise Goose. Most people who had remained in Sanliurfa after the mass exodus that came on the heels of the SCUD missile launch had stayed because they believed they would prosper, that Turkish reinforcements would arrive at any moment—which wasn't going to happen—and push the Syrians back. Or they simply didn't have anywhere else to go. The ragged crowds at any local café were probably a lot more interested in avoiding trouble than in looking for it.

"Were you dealing with the Bedouin?" Goose asked, peering along the street.

"No. I did not see them until they attacked us in the alley. They were waiting for us."

"Why did they attack you?"

Arnaud shook his head. "They robbed us. They took Giselle." He swallowed hard. "I have heard that some of the Bedouin have been stealing European and American women from the city." His voice broke. "I was told those Bedouin sell the women they kidnap."

Goose had known about the white slavery problems in the area before the Syrian attack. Women serving in the armed forces—in the United Nations Peacekeeping effort as well as in the Ranger support teams—had received warnings about the issue.

"Giselle and I were trying to find someone to help us get out of the city." He turned back to Goose and looked guilty. "For a time we believed that the combined militaries here would be able to hold off the Syrians. But after the attack last night, we could no longer hold out any such hope. I am sorry."

Goose met the man's gaze. "I understand." Last night's attacks had only continued the assaults the Syrians launched against the city. And those attacks, Goose knew, would continue to come.

Sanliurfa was a keystone for the Syrian aggression. If the Syrian military could secure this city, they could stage attacks elsewhere. Their second logical target was Diyarbakir City to the east. If that city fell, the Iraqi rebels who still fought American intervention in their country might be inspired to rise up and join with the Syrians, creating threats on two fronts for Turkey.

Sanliurfa, after time enough for the U.S. and Turkish military to shore up defenses and build an offensive line, was considered an acceptable loss by the Allied forces. In fact, the American and Turkish commands considered every soldier in the city an acceptable loss if it came to it. The military commanders of both countries as well as the United Nations feared that the Turkish-Syrian conflict—it wasn't officially referred to as a war yet—could ignite a conflagration in the Middle East.

Throughout the history of humankind, and certainly since the creation of Israel in 1948, the Middle East had been a powder keg waiting to be touched off. With Chaim Rosenzweig's discovery of the chemical fertilizer that had turned the Israeli deserts into lush farmlands and pulled the nation into a time of bountiful wealth, the enmity felt by the Arab countries of the Middle East toward Israel had increased.

Even Russia had felt threatened by Israel's newfound wealth. The former Soviets had launched an attack against the country. But only minutes before the jet fighters reached their targets, the Russian aircraft fell to the ground or imploded in the sky. Like the disappearances only days ago, no one knew the cause of that event. That sudden defeat of the Russian air force had come about as mysteriously as the massive disappearances that had occurred around the globe.

Goose pulled his thoughts away from that event. Thinking about that led right back to the unsettling conversation he'd had with Icarus. *"God came and took your son up as He took all the other children."*

For a moment, Goose remembered the peace that had settled over him as he'd almost come to accept that thought. But he hadn't been able to swallow it, and in the end that peaceful feeling had retreated. Maybe Bill Townsend could have believed that God had taken those people, but Goose couldn't. He wouldn't believe it, either, not until he had proof.

Goose was a good man. He believed in God as best he could, and he acknowledged Christ as his personal Savior. But Goose was also a fighter, a practical man used to meeting problems head-on, a man who resolved situations, problems, and the evils that men could do to one another. He believed more in himself and in finding a way to reverse the effects of the disappearances than he believed in divine intervention in the world.

"Phoenix Leader," a man's voice crackled over the headset. "This is Sergeant Clay of Echo Company. We're responding to your SAR request."

"Acknowledged, Sergeant," Goose responded. Sergeant Thomas Clay of E Company was a solid soldier and a good man. "Glad to have you. How many strong are you?"

"Seven. Myself and six. Base says others are on their way here. We're still spread out and dealing with the problems left over from last night. We're coming from the north, closing in on your twenty."

"Affirmative," Goose responded. "Base, are you there?"

"Base is here."

"Can I get a helo attached to the SAR?"

"I'll check, Phoenix Leader."

Goose stared along the streets. A number of alleys spread out through the area, all of them filled with hiding places. He hoped the Bedouin kidnappers hadn't taken their prey and ducked into hiding. He wasn't looking forward to playing cat and mouse with them in the debris-strewn streets and bombed-out buildings.

"Who are we looking for?" Clay asked.

Goose looked at Arnaud. "Have you got a picture of your wife?"

Arnaud pulled his wallet out and flipped it open. He showed Goose a picture of himself and a younger woman. "This is Giselle."

"Her name is Giselle Arnaud," Goose said, jerking his attention back to the alleys. "She's French. I'm with her husband. He says she was taken by a group of Bedouins after they were robbed." He glanced at Arnaud. "Does she speak English?"

"*Mais oui*," Arnaud answered. "She is very fluent in five languages. That is her specialty at university. She is also a teacher."

"Giselle speaks English," Goose said, glancing back at the picture of the couple standing in front of a flowered archway that existed only in some photographer's studio. "She's a little over five feet tall. Dark hair down to her shoulders. Dark eyes. Thirties. She's wearing—" He looked at Arnaud.

"A red sleeveless blouse," Arnaud said. "Tan pants. Walking shoes."

Arnaud, Goose realized, was a man who paid attention. The description made Goose feel guilty. He couldn't remember what his wife had worn the last time he'd seen her. Megan had come to the airfield to see him off as she always had since they'd been married. He'd seen her, remembered her brave smile even though the separation hurt her, but he didn't remember what she was wearing. With a pang, he realized he couldn't remember what Chris had been wearing the last time he'd seen him either.

Mechanically swallowing the lump in his throat, Goose passed the information along. Just as he finished, Arnaud stood up in the seat and threw his arm out.

"There, Sergeant! She is back there! I saw them!" Arnaud shouted. "You must back up!"

Before Goose could say anything, Arnaud leaped from the Hummer. Goose made a frantic grab for the man but missed him. By the time Goose braked the Hummer, the worried husband was already rushing toward the last alley they had passed.

"Sergeant," Goose spoke over the headset as he pushed himself from the Hummer and dropped into the street. The impact cracked through his injured knee, but he ignored the pain and kept moving.

"Here, Phoenix," Clay responded.

"We've got a possible ID on the SAR target." Goose checked the street signs and relayed his location.

"Acknowledged, Phoenix," Clay said. "We're only a few blocks away."

Goose ran, favoring his left knee and feeling the pain lance all the way up his side to detonate in the left side of his brain. It was projected pain. He recognized the sensation from years of dealing with the injury. He held the M-4A1 in both hands, high across his chest to keep his lower body clear.

A car that had been following the Hummer honked impatiently. With all the debris in the street, there was little room to pass. The earthmovers had worked only to clear a vehicle-wide path, not two lanes. A few pedestrians, all of them civilians, stopped to stare at Goose as he ran.

At the mouth of the alley, Arnaud shouted, "Giselle! Giselle!" He started forward again. Before he'd taken his second step, he jerked and spun to his right. Pain etched his features, popping even his swollen eye slightly open with surprise.

The flat crack of the rifle report reached Goose's ears just before Arnaud hit the ground. The echoes of the shot rumbled in the narrow alley between the three-story buildings. Chunks of rock jumped up from the street as three more rounds landed near the fallen man but miraculously did not touch him. Arnaud scrabbled weakly to right himself. Blood darkened his shirt on his upper chest.

Moving quickly, Goose slammed into position with his back against the building to the right of the alley mouth. He pushed his weapon vertical, then curled around to peer down the alley.

A group of Bedouin men, all dressed in flowing robes and burnooses, hurried along the alley nearly eighty yards away. Goose saw that three of the eleven Bedouin carried a woman whose appearance matched the picture Arnaud had shown him. The Bedouin closest to their position racked the slide back on the heavy-caliber rifle he carried, then took deliberate aim at Arnaud.

"I've got targets at my twenty. Shots fired." Goose lifted the M-4A1 to his left shoulder, switching hands easily because he'd trained himself to be ambidextrous with the assault rifle, and got himself into a straight line with the weapon. He leaned his shoulder into the building, kept both eyes open to view the battle zone, looked through the scope with his left eye while his right took in everything, swapping fields of vision inside his head, and squeezed the trigger.

The 5.56mm round caught the Bedouin in the center of his chest just before he fired again. Driven back by the tumbling bullet, the Bedouin fired his weapon into the air, knocking stone chips from the second floor of the building.

Staying locked on his target, Goose drove a second and third round into the center of the Bedouin's upper body, wanting to make sure his opponent was down. Switching to his right eye, he picked up his second target: a man turning to bring up his rifle.

Goose knew the sound of his weapon firing had alerted the other Bedouins to his position—and not just to his position, but also to his nationality—but there had been no way around that. The M-4A1's sharp report was a lot different than the heavier detonation of the Russian SKS chambered in 7.62mm carried by the Syrians. Flicking his vision back to his left eye between heartbeats, Goose centered the crosshairs above the Bedouin's rifle, almost looking down his opponent's barrel, then squeezed the trigger.

The M-4A1 chugged against Goose's shoulder almost recoil-free, but a spray of stone splinters and dust blinded him almost immediately as the Bedouin's bullet struck the wall in front of him. Withdrawing, Goose kept himself from instinctively trying to wipe the stone grit from his eyes. Rubbing at them now might scratch one of his eyes, or even both of them. He looked down, letting the tears come naturally to wash the grit and dust from his eyes.

Footsteps pounded down the alley toward Goose.

Arnaud lifted his head, eyes big with fear. "They are coming," he whispered in a hoarse, panicked croak. "Giselle." He tried to crawl but couldn't move.

His vision still partially blurred and his tears cool on his face, Goose swung around the corner again. He slid the fire selector to three-round-burst mode, then centered the rifle at the lead Bedouin's waist and squeezed the trigger. He rode the slight recoil up and to the right, stitching the man from hip to shoulder in two three-round bursts and knocking him back.

The assault rifle rode naturally, carrying over to the second man in the alley. Goose squeezed the trigger again, holding the weapon steady and putting a three-round burst into the center of his chest.

As this target went down, Goose saw that his initial round at the second man in the alley had sprawled another man out. Four men were down. Seven were up and moving. Giselle Arnaud remained among them.

Moving quickly, Goose hooked the fingers of his left hand in the back of Arnaud's shirt and dragged the man clear of the alley's mouth. From Goose's quick look at the man, he noted that the wound in his shoulder wasn't life threatening.

Goose took a compress from his field medkit and covered the wound. "Hold this on your chest," he ordered. "Tight. Slow the bleeding."

"My wife," Arnaud whispered. "Giselle—"

"We're going to get her," Goose said and hoped that he told the man the truth. "But you need to take care of yourself." He pushed himself up, feeling the weakness in his bad knee, then positioned himself at the corner of the alley again. He swapped magazines in his weapon, shuffling the partially spent one to the back of his LCE.

The Bedouins ran for the other end of the alley.

"Sergeant Clay," Goose called over the headset.

"Here," Clay responded immediately. "We heard gunshots over your headset."

"There was an exchange," Goose said. "Four Bedouin are down. Seven remain viable. They do have the woman. She's alive. Let's keep her that way."

"Affirmative," Clay replied. "We're on top of your twenty now."

"Base," Goose said, pushing himself forward into the alley.

"Base is here, Phoenix Leader."

"I need a medical team here."

"Already en route."

"What about air support?" Goose passed the first two men in the alley's mouth.

"Negative. The captain doesn't see the need to risk a helo at this time."

Not for a civilian, Goose thought, feeling angry with Remington. At the same time, though, he recognized that Remington's reluctance was good military strategy. Helicopters were hard to come by in these tough times. They were a limited resource not meant for squandering. Plenty of civilians had taken refuge throughout the city, too afraid to brave the open expanse back to Ankara, Turkey's capital to the north and west. As far as Remington was concerned, they weren't his problem. Only holding this line against a superior force of invading Syrians mattered.

"Affirmative, Base." Goose kept going, watching as the Bedouin juked into another alley to the east. "Clay, our targets broke east. Along an alley."

"Acknowledged," Clay replied.

"I see them," another Ranger said.

Gunfire broke out in a steady staccato roar.

"Keep the woman clear." Goose broke into a run, passing the final two Bedouin bodies, then positioned himself beside the alley the group had disappeared into.

Gunfire continued, filling the air with harsh cracks and accompanying echoes.

"They're turning back," Clay said. "Coming back your way, Leader. Two more are down. Five remain."

"Understood." Goose glanced around the corner. The other end of the alley was too far to reach, and he didn't want to expose Arnaud to enemy fire again. "What about the woman?"

"She's alive. We picked targets we could take without endangering her."

Goose flattened himself against the building. "Come up quick, Sergeant. I'm about to be in the middle of them. They've caught me exposed."

"Understood," Clay said. "Look over your shoulder when it goes down. That'll be us."

Footsteps pounded the asphalt, drawing closer. Hoarse shouts in a language Goose couldn't understand punctuated the sporadic weapon blasts. Despite the Kevlar armor he wore, he knew he might die in the coming encounter.

Will I see Chris if I do, God? I believe in You, but I don't believe You took my child away from me. I don't believe those disappearances were by Your hand. I don't believe that was the Rapture. I refuse to believe that. But if I die right here and right now, please let me see my boy again and know that he is all right.

Then the first Bedouin broke from the alley, coming into view and passing Goose all in the same instant.

Goose let the man go and prayed that the man would not notice him. Another followed. The three Bedouin carrying the kidnapped woman brought up the rear.

Settling into the moment, knowing surprise was his greatest weapon, Goose shot the first of the three men through the head, aiming for the base of his skull as he passed. The bullets severed the spinal cord and the vagus nerve, destroying all motor control immediately. He dropped like a rock, causing the two men following him to stumble and fall and drop Giselle.

Goose spun, switching the fire selector to full-auto, and opened up on the two Bedouin farther down the alley. He emptied the magazine in less than two seconds, not even enough time for the two survivors to recover from their fall.

Dropping the assault rifle, Goose swept his M9 pistol from his hip, thumbed the safety off, and aimed at the nearest fallen Bedouin, who pulled a pistol from beneath his robe and pushed himself up.

Giselle Arnaud lay on the asphalt. Ropes bound her wrists and ankles. Blood trickled down her hands, evidence of her struggles to free herself. A gag tied around her head prevented her from crying out, but tears spilled down her cheeks, leaving tracks on her dusty face. Her bruised and dirty features were twisted with fright.

Goose looked away from the woman, locating his targets. He put a bullet through the nearest Bedouin's face. He followed up with two more through the man's chest as he fell. Near the woman's head, the other Bedouin rose with a pistol in his hand, firing as he stood.

Bullets slammed into Goose's chest armor. One of them caught his helmet, bouncing his head to one side. He remained on task. He wasn't dead and he had a job to finish. He fired the M9 at the Bedouin, hitting the man's chest and working up in case the man wore body armor beneath the robe.

As the Bedouin fell away, Goose spotted Sergeant Clay and his Ranger squad coming down the alley, throwing themselves forward and taking up positions as the men behind raced up to move into new positions.

Gunfire opened up behind Goose, letting him know the two men farther down the alley weren't dead. He dropped and covered the kidnapped woman with his own body, lending her the protection of the body armor he wore as Clay and his men reached the alley mouth.

The M-4A1s blazed on full-auto for a few seconds. When they stopped, Goose doubted any of the Bedouin remained alive. Clay ordered his men into new positions, securing the alley in a standard two-by-two deployment.

Looking down at the woman, Goose knew immediately that something was wrong. Her face was slack and still. Fear still showed there, but nothing moved. He saw his own reflection in her glassy eyes.

"No," Goose said hoarsely. Over the past few days, he'd seen too many dead not to know what he was probably looking at. He pushed himself up.

The woman didn't move.

"Goose," Clay said, striding toward him.

"*Giselle!*" Arnaud called from the alley's end. "Where is my wife?" He continued in French.

Stunned, Goose gazed at the dark spot in the center of Giselle Arnaud's red blouse. The spot was not spreading. She wasn't bleeding. That meant her heart no longer pumped.

Laying his pistol down, Goose tore the woman's blouse open. The wound was a jagged mess of torn flesh, but—

"There's no penetration here," Clay said as he hunkered down beside Goose. "She caught a ricochet. The bullet was too spent to break through her sternum. Deflected from bone."

"She's not breathing," a young Ranger said.

"The bullet stopped her heart," Goose said, stripping his helmet off. "Impact caught her between heartbeats, stopped her heart. She's got a chance." *God, please let there be a chance.* "Help me start CPR."

"Giselle!" Arnaud called, sounding closer. "*Mon Dieu!* What has happened to my poor wife? What are you doing? Sergeant? Sergeant, answer me!"

Glancing over his shoulder, Goose spotted Arnaud only a few feet away now. "Corporal," Goose ordered, "keep that man back."

The corporal stepped forward to block Arnaud. The man tried to fight his way past him, but the corporal wrapped his arms around the man and prevented him from walking closer.

Clay tilted the woman's head back and opened her airway. "No obstruction."

Ignoring the biting pain in his knee, Goose straddled the woman and put his hands, one on top of the other, over the bloody wound. He leaned forward and heaved, applying pressure in short impacts, rolling his shoulders to use his weight.

"All right," Goose said, "breathe for her."

Clay did, putting his mouth over the woman's, ignoring the standard operating procedure of using safety gear to prevent spreading possible disease. The woman's life hung by a thread and they knew it. They had no time to drag out the gear.

Arnaud wept in the background, calling out his wife's name.

"Break," Goose said.

When Clay pulled back, Goose curled his right hand into a fist and struck the woman's sternum, hoping to create enough shock to start her stilled heart. Then he settled into the rhythm again, putting his shoulders and his weight into the effort.

"C'mon," Goose said, keeping count in his head. "C'mon. You can do this. You aren't gone yet. You've got a lot of living to do." But he wondered how much time had passed since her heart had stalled. After four minutes without a heartbeat, brain damage usually occurred.

He leaned back and let Clay breathe for her again, barely managing the panic that filled him. Everything swirled in his mind, running together in a blur that threatened to overwhelm him. Chris was gone. He was stranded in a war-torn country with no true hope of survival. He would probably never see Megan or Joey again. And this woman whom he'd risked so much to save wasn't breathing.

It was more than Goose could bear.

This woman was going to die on him, caught by a ricochet that should never have happened.

Clay broke away. Goose straddled the woman again, locking his hands together over her heart and pushing, hoping to revive that fist-sized clump of muscle that was the engine for the human body.

If God had raptured the world, if He had taken the children, then why had He left so many other people behind? Why would He take all the children? Why would He take Chris?

God wouldn't, Goose told himself. God hadn't done those things. The God he believed in wouldn't do something like that. Someone else caused the disappearances. Someone else took Chris. If God had done those things, there would be some kind of sign, some—

Miraculously, Goose felt the woman's heart suddenly flutter under his hands. In disbelief, he drew his hands back and pressed his ear to her chest.

Her heartbeat was erratic at first but quickly settled into a strong rhythm.

"Hey," Clay said excitedly, "she's breathing! She's breathing on her own. You got her back, First Sergeant. You got her back."

Tiredly, giving in to the pain in his knee, Goose moved away from the woman and stood. He stared down at her.

A moment passed before she opened her eyes and tried to sit up.

"Easy," Clay said, restraining her with a hand to her shoulder.

"Let me go!" Arnaud demanded, struggling more fiercely now. "Let me *go!*"

Goose nodded to the corporal, who released Arnaud.

The man dropped to the ground beside his wife. "Ah, Giselle! I thought you were lost to me!"

The woman looked at her husband, then at Goose. "I thought I was. I'm sure for a time I was dead. I was outside my body, standing here in this alley looking down at myself and you and these men. I was so scared. I was screaming for you, but you could not hear me. I thought I would never see you again. I felt like I was drifting away. Like fog giving way to the morning sun." She shook her head and smiled. "Then I saw the angel."

"Angel?" Arnaud seemed startled. "There was no angel."

"There was," the woman insisted. "There *is.* I saw it. The angel was at the sergeant's shoulder as he worked to start my heart. The angel told me everything was going to be all right, that it wasn't my time yet, that the sergeant was going to save me. Then the angel leaned down and touched my heart, and it started."

Goose didn't believe a word of it. The woman had gone through considerable trauma. It wasn't surprising that she'd imagined the angel.

But she looked at Goose with wide, awestruck eyes. "It's true, Sergeant. Believe it or not, but you have an angel at your shoulder. I saw it. I see it still."

"Yes, ma'am," Goose said politely, but he knew the woman must have been hallucinating. There could be no other explanation. Accepting that an angel had stood at his side meant accepting the supernatural. And that meant accepting that the Rapture had taken place, that everyone left on the planet was doomed to seven years of war and death, that a newly elected Romanian president named Nicolae Carpathia was the Antichrist even now rising to power to bury the world in deceit and treachery.

And that Goose would never see Chris again.

Goose couldn't believe any of that. He wouldn't allow himself to believe that.

Because if he believed it, it meant that his son was lost to him.

❀ ❀ ❀

Hazel's Café
Marbury, Alabama
Local Time 0915 Hours

Eating breakfast in Hazel's Café was like stepping back in time.

Chaplain Delroy Harte got a definite feeling of déjà vu as he sat across the table from Deputy Walter Purcell in one of the back booths. The rustic decor, cobbled together from farming and ranching equipment; from NASCAR's licensed hats, mugs, and posters; and from local high school sports equipment, looked exactly as it had when he'd eaten there with his father when Delroy had been first a boy and later a young man.

At a few minutes past nine in the morning, the café held mostly late starters and farmers and ranchers who'd already put in a half day's work and wanted to take a break in each other's company for an hour or two before getting back to the full day's work waiting for them. The smell of fried sausage, ham, and beefsteak mixed with the scents of fresh-baked rolls, plain and sweet, eggs done a half-dozen different ways, and grilled onions.

But many of the people gathered here had come so they wouldn't be alone. Their need for company resonated within these walls. Fear etched their faces and kept their conversations to a bare handful of words thrown among them as they watched the two televisions, one on each side of the café. Both sets were tuned to news stations.

Delroy's heart went out to the frightened people, but he knew he had no words of comfort for them. He made himself look past them. They would be all right. Either they would help themselves or someone would help them. He had no business feeling like he could.

Not after the way he'd spent last night.

Delroy had arrived in the graveyard outside Marbury where his son was buried. Lance Corporal Terrence David Harte had died in action five years ago and had returned home to be buried here. After following Captain Mark Falkirk's orders to leave USS *Wasp*, Delroy's ship, and making the trek to speak to the Joint Chiefs in the Pentagon regarding his belief that God had raptured the world, the chaplain had requested leave to attend to personal business. With the confusion going on regarding military action and the need to defend the United States, Delroy's request had received authorization.

In the cemetery last night, Delroy had started digging up his son's casket, wanting to discover if Terrence's body had been taken to heaven, if he had truly known God in his short life. Or if—like his father—he'd been left behind. Before he'd reached the casket, Delroy had realized that if he dug his son up and discovered the truth, his faith would be in jeopardy. If Terrence's body was still in that hole in the ground, Delroy didn't know if he would ever be able to believe again. And if Terrence's body was gone, true faith would be impossible because Delroy would know that God existed.

And people were supposed to go to God in faith. That was one thing Delroy's daddy, Josiah Harte, had taught him.

Overcome by doubt and fear and frustration, Delroy had turned from digging and been confronted by the demon he had first seen in Washington, D.C., days ago. They had fought, Delroy and the demon, and it had shown him the unforgettable image of Terrence—his body torn and broken by the conflict he'd died in—trying in vain to break out of the coffin.

When at last the demon had disappeared, Delroy had passed out, unable to leave the cemetery where his son and his daddy lay in their eternal slumber. Deputy Walter Purcell had found Delroy lying in the rain and mud. The big deputy had taken Delroy to the hospital in Marbury and little more than an hour ago got him released. Now he was taking Delroy to breakfast.

"Lotta memories in this place?" Walter stirred grape jelly into his scrambled eggs, then spooned the mixture onto a biscuit.

"Aye," Delroy answered. They'd only gotten their food a few minutes ago. Getting out of the hospital had taken longer than expected. With a third of the patients and more than that from the staff disappearing, the hospital struggled to get everything done. Even with the disappearances, the hospital still needed to bill the insurance companies.

"You grew up here." Walter blew on his coffee, then took a sip.

"Aye. That I did." Delroy waited for the other shoe to drop. From his observation of Walter, he knew the man wasn't one to beat around the bush for long.

The egg-and-jelly biscuit had disappeared, but Walter was just getting started. Like a craftsman, he cut his ham into sections. The metal knife and fork rasped with quick strokes. His plate was piled high with sausage gravy and biscuits, fried onions and hash browns, bacon, and pancakes.

"Are you going to drop the other shoe?" Delroy asked. "Or are you going to just let it hang there?"

Walter chewed his ham, swallowed, and washed it down with coffee. He eyed Delroy directly. "You been around Yankees maybe a little too long. Too direct. Maybe you've forgotten how to maintain a conversation before you get to the ugly parts of it. Around here, we kind of take things a bit slower. Use conversation and a meal to get to know each other a bit before we get down to it. That way you can still seal a deal with a handshake."

"I was just wondering what you had in mind, Deputy."

Walter wiped his mouth with his napkin. "My ulterior motive, you mean."

"That'll do," Delroy said.

Narrowing his eyes in irritation, Walter asked, "You always been this suspicious?"

"No."

"Well then, you should get away from it. It ain't becomin'."

Embarrassment stung Delroy and turned his face hot.

Walter returned his attention to his plate. "I say anything to you that makes you think I got some ulterior motive?"

"Not yet."

The deputy shook his head. "I ain't got but a couple things I want to make sure of." He counted them off on his thick, blunt fingers while maintaining his hold on the knife and fork. "One: that you ain't gonna hurt nobody in my county."

"That's not going to happen."

"Well, now since I only just met you—and not under the best of circumstance, I might add—I don't know that, do I?" Walter's gaze was fierce.

"I'm not going to hurt anyone here."

"I found you at your son's grave site," Walter went on. "You wasn't exactly plumb on the bob when I found you. You looked like you'd been beat near to death, and that's the flat-out gospel." He mopped his plate with a biscuit, picking up bacon grease, jelly, eggs, and gravy. "Then I did some checking around. Found out you were from here. Found out your daddy was a preachin' man. Found out he was killed—"

"He was murdered," Delroy said, and was surprised at how hollow his voice sounded in his ears.

Walter nodded. "They never caught the man who did it, did they?"

"No."

"But they figured they knew who it was."

Delroy remained quiet and still. His chest suddenly felt so tight he couldn't breathe.

"Man named Clarence Floyd was the man Sheriff Dobbs thought killed your daddy," Walter said.

"Where are you going with this, Deputy?"

"Walter. Call me Walter. I told you that."

Delroy waited.

Walter sighed and shifted his equipment belt. "Ain't no way but the hard way with you is there? Shoulda known that from all them knots on your face."

"Now who's being unbecoming?"

Frowning, Walter said, "I blame you. Yes, sir, I do. It's like you bring out the worst in me."

Delroy let the accusation hang between them. Anger stirred restlessly within him. He forced himself to breathe out. *Give me patience, Lord. This here's a good man, and I've got no cause to make his life any more complicated than it already is.* Slowly, the anger fizzled out. He broke the eye contact with the deputy and reached for his fork.

"I'm sorry," Walter said. "I shouldn't have said that."

"It's all right. I'm pretty sure I had it coming." Delroy broke open a biscuit, added butter and grape jelly, and ate.

"Biscuits still as good as you remember?" Walter asked.

"Melt in your mouth," Delroy answered. For a time, they ate in silence.

Delroy watched the news and saw fitful bursts of information regarding the military effort in Sanliurfa. More interviews with Nicolae Carpathia, the Romanian president scheduled to speak at the General Assembly of the United Nations in New York City, spun across both televisions.

"Reason I asked you about Clarence Floyd," Walter said.

Delroy looked at him.

"Three years ago," Walter said, eyes level and steady, "Floyd moved back to Marbury. He lives here now."

The news slammed into Delroy.

"You didn't know that, did you?" Walter asked.

Delroy didn't try to lie. He knew his angry disbelief had been too strong. "No."

"I didn't think you did. But if you're gonna stay here a couple days, chances are you'd probably find out once folks in town figure out who you are."

Delroy sat quiet and still. His father's murder had happened over thirty years ago, but the grief and anger over the act had never truly dimmed. If he hadn't been so worn out emotionally from last night, he didn't know what he might have done.

"Why did he come back?" Delroy asked when he could talk again.

Walter studied him, then scooped up more jelly and scrambled eggs to spread on a biscuit. "He just come home. Like you, I suppose. Wasn't nowhere else to go, maybe. His life, it ain't been like yours. He doesn't have no navy career, no calling to keep him busy. He's just a mean seventy-three-year-old man who's afraid of dying."

"You've seen him?"

"Not today," Walter said. "But I have. I take a look through Sheriff Dobbs' cold-case files from time to time. When Floyd moved back into his folks' home, I looked him up." He ate the biscuit. "Wasn't nothing ever brought up against him regarding your daddy's murder."

"His father paid off the judge."

Walter shrugged. "That wasn't ever proved either."

"That's what happened."

"That may be. I can't say. But one thing I gotta tell you, Chaplain Harte. As long as you're around here, I don't want you seeing Clarence Floyd. Now normally, the city, why that's the police chief's concern. But what with everything going on that's been going on, the sheriff's department and the police department are working on a share-and-share-alike basis. We help each other out because we know most of the same folks around here. I brought you into town, and I decided to release you on your own recognizance. That makes me somewhat responsible for you."

Delroy sat back for a moment. "This breakfast isn't turning out the way I thought it was going to."

"No, sir." Walter nodded. "I expect not. Usually these eggs settle on my stomach better'n they are right now. From what I see of you, you're a good man. Just a little lost right now. In my experience, that's when men make bad decisions that can haunt them the rest of their lives. I ain't here to save Floyd's neck so much as I am to save yours."

Delroy didn't speak, didn't really know what he would have said if he had been so inclined.

"You can believe that or not," Walter said. "But something you can take to the bank is this: If you go out of your way to cause problems for Floyd, I'll lock you up so fast it will make your head spin."

"All right," Delroy said.

"Another thing," Walter went on. "I made some phone calls while I was out and about waiting to get the doc's report on you. As it turns out, your wife Glenda is still in town."

Surprise pushed Delroy's outrage and pain aside. "Glenda is here? She didn't . . . leave with the others?"

"No, sir. She didn't leave. She's here."

The world grew silent and still and as cold as a January morning. Delroy couldn't breathe for a moment. Then he heard the blood roar in his ears as his heart chugged through another beat.

"Does she . . ." Delroy's voice failed him.

"Know that you're here?" Walter shook his head. "Not that I know of. I ain't one to go around jacking my jaws about everything. The doctors and nurses at the hospital ain't connected you with Glenda. As a matter of fact, I doubt they even know her."

"You said the floor nurse knew my name."

"Yes, sir. She did. But she don't know Glenda. She knew stories about your daddy. I also asked her to keep things quiet. She will."

"Thank you for that. I don't know how Glenda would react to knowing I was in town."

"You wasn't planning on stopping in and seeing her?"

"No," Delroy admitted, and he felt guilty at once. "All my plans ended at the graveyard."

"You thinking about stopping in and seeing her now?"

"No." Delroy's answer was immediate.

"You two divorced? 'Cause that's not the way I heard it was."

"Not divorced. At least, not that I know of."

"She's still carrying your name."

Delroy knew that was how Glenda was. She'd married him all those years ago, and she'd told him she'd wear his name for the rest of her life.

"You mind me asking what it is that's come between you two?" Walter asked.

"I do mind."

"Too bad. I'm asking anyway. Things I've heard about Glenda Harte are all good. I wouldn't stand for hearing that any harm's come to that woman because I made a mistake about somebody else."

Delroy thought about getting up and walking out of the café. His eyes darted to the door.

"Leaving wouldn't do you any good," Walter continued in a level voice. "I brought you to breakfast because I thought we might talk things out like men."

"What's gone on or is going on between my . . . wife and me is none of your business."

Walter sighed and rubbed his face. "Chaplain Harte, you're carrying around more grief and anger and confusion than any man I've ever met in my life. Or at the very least, any man I've met in a good many years. And in my line of business I've met no few men like that. So I consider myself a pretty good judge of another man's disposition. Maybe that's conceit on my part, but I've paid my dues for that one. Now, we're gonna get straight with each other this morning, or I'm gonna bust you and take you in to get some psychiatric help. I ain't gonna have no loose cannon roaming around this county I swore to protect and defend."

"I'm not here to hurt anyone."

Walter held up a hand. "Ain't nothing wrong with my hearing. I look like a man gone hard of hearing?"

Delroy said, "No."

"My wife's the only one accuses me of that, and that's 'cause I don't jump up ever' time she wants me to do something on her honey-do list. But I'm good at law enforcement. I get so I ain't, I'll lay it down immediately." Walter blew on his coffee and sipped it. "Now if I lock you up, it ain't but one short phone call to the navy. Bet if I told whoever was at the other end of that line that one of their officers was down here acting squirrelly, you'd be back wherever it is you belong in a New York minute." He brushed biscuit crumbs and gravy from his mustache with his napkin. "Are you reading me now, Chaplain?"

"Aye," Delroy responded. "Loud and clear."

"Good. That's real good. 'Cause that's the last thing I want to do. I don't think that's what will get things done for you here." Walter leaned back a little.

"My son's death separated my wife and me," Delroy said.

"I heard your son passed during military action."

Delroy nodded, having to force himself to move.

"Your wife couldn't get over it?" Walter asked. "I've seen people like that. People that couldn't make peace with a loss. Took me a long time to meet eye to eye with God over the loss of my own boy. I still don't think it was right, and maybe I stepped away from Him some. I faulted Him a lot for a long time. Maybe that's part of why I'm still here."

Shame burned Delroy's features. It was hard to admit everything, but at least he felt that he and Deputy Walter Purcell shared something in common.

"It wasn't my wife that couldn't get past it," Delroy said in a low, soft voice. He thought of Terrence lying in that muddy grave, the ground above him all torn up where Delroy had tried to dig down to him. "It was me. I couldn't get past the death of my son."

Walter stared at Delroy for a long time. Then the big man leaned forward and put a hand on Delroy's shoulder. "It's a powerful hard thing to get past. And it's mighty confusing because you just don't feel right about moving on through it."

"I know. I've given a lot of people that speech over the years." Delroy felt cold and empty inside. "Glenda faltered. I saw her. And I tried to comfort her. That gave me something to do, gave me the chance to turn away from my own pain and anger." He stopped, lost in the memory and unable to go on.

"Then she started to come around," Walter said quietly. "She started healing."

"Aye."

"And you resented her for it."

Delroy tried to speak but couldn't.

"It's an easy thing to do, Chaplain," Walter said.

"Not for me," Delroy said fiercely. "Never once did I ever think I would resent Glenda for anything. I took a vow before God to cherish her always. I didn't." His voice broke, betraying the strong emotion that vibrated inside him. "I was supposed to be stronger than that. My father raised me up to be stronger than that."

"Your daddy," Walter stated gently, "wasn't there. And it wasn't him asked to give up a son, Delroy. It was you. You were entitled to your grief. Still are. I ain't finding no fault with that."

Delroy brushed tears from his eyes before they could fall; then he willed them to stop. "Not five years of grief." He kept his voice flat and neutral. "I'm being selfish. I just—I just don't know how to stop. It wasn't supposed to be like this."

"You're human. Ain't nothing wrong with being human. Just hard wearin' from time to time." Walter shifted. "I seen men what didn't care about nothin'. Seen 'em on battlefields and I seen 'em in law enforcement. Some of them men even wore badges now and again, and that was real hard to witness and not do nothing."

"I'm a navy chaplain," Delroy said. "A preacher's son. My father taught me my faith."

Walter was quiet for a time. "One thing I learned through losing my own son: God's grace is never known to you till after the fact. Sometimes, I suppose, it ain't gonna be known till you're in the hereafter. I still struggle with my own belief, but I believe God is there. Just haven't figured out my own relationship with Him. I guess that's why I'm still here. I look around this town, Reverend, and I see a lot of good folks stuck in much the same boat."

"Pretty good Christians." Captain Mark Falkirk's final words aboard *Wasp's* flight deck echoed in Delroy's mind: *"The most dangerous man on this planet is the person who believes he is a pretty good Christian."*

"That's as good a term for it as any other," Walter said. "Good people that, for whatever reason, just didn't make the final cut. Now, I believe the world was raptured. I'm sure you do too. So that means we got a limited time to make a difference. Not just in our lives, but in the lives of others. Me, I'm a man what's always stood on the right of things. Straight and narrow. That's how I've lived 'er. When I could. And I could most of the time."

Delroy met the other man's gaze with difficulty.

"Now, I usually ain't one to go around taking chances," Walter continued. "Before all this happened, before I started opening up my Bible and reading Revelation, why if I'd come across you in that graveyard, found out the man who murdered your daddy and your ex-wife was living in this town, I'd have had you locked up for observation in two shakes of a lamb's tail. Just to keep the peace."

"I would never hurt Glenda," Delroy said. "I give you my word on that."

"And now I believe you about that. But you see, I know she's got her own grief she's dealing with. She didn't just lose her son; she lost her husband, and weren't none of that her fault. Might be her that started something, and I'd end up with the same problem."

The deputy's words cut through Delroy. He couldn't imagine Glenda doing something like that. But after what he'd done, after what they'd both suffered— *No. She still wouldn't do anything like that. The deputy just doesn't know her.*

"I know how she probably feels," Walter said. "Because that's how my own wife felt. I know that 'cause she cared enough about me to get riled up and tell me about it over and over. Till I owned up to it and pulled my head back on straight." He sipped his coffee. "Now, it ain't been easy, but I worked at it. Still do." He held his left forefinger and thumb about an inch apart. "Little bit ever' day. Reckon I always will. And as long as I have to, I'll see that it gets done."

Delroy glanced out the big window overlooking the street in front of the café. Sluggish morning traffic passed by only occasionally.

"I can't go see my wife," Delroy said.

"Wasn't suggesting that you do. In fact, I'm thinking it might be better for the both of you to wait until you get your head together."

"I can't guarantee that will happen either."

"Didn't expect you to. The kind of changes you're gonna have to make are gonna take years."

Years. The word sounded like a prison sentence to Delroy.

"But I will remind you of one thing," Walter said. "These changes you gotta make? You're running out of time. Way I read my Bible, there's only—"

"Seven years," Delroy said.

Walter nodded. "Less than that already. Figured you'd know. Don't help with the clock ticking, but I guess that's how it's gotta be."

"It's hard to care."

"Yes, sir. I expect it is. But you listen to me, Chaplain. Whatever chance you got of seeing your boy again—whole, hale, and hearty— why it's through the sacrifice Jesus made to take our sins on and the grace of God Almighty that you're gonna get it done. The way I figure it, you still got His work ahead of you."

"There's a reason I didn't go back to my ship," Delroy said. "I don't belong there. Those men are involved in a war zone. There are chaplains aboard *Wasp* that can do what they need done. I'm not the rock they need."

He felt guilty when he said that. He'd signed on to take care of those responsibilities. For the last five years, though, he'd hidden aboard *Wasp* more than he had attended to God's work. The Lord had been given lip service and short shrift. *And if that won't send a chaplain straight to hell, I don't know what will.*

"Wasn't talking about you taking care of nobody else," Walter said, breaking into Delroy's thoughts. "I was talking about you taking care of your own self. Man's drowning, why he's gotta make sure he's safe enough to save ever'body else. It's always been that way."

Delroy waited for a moment, then asked the question he didn't want to ask but he couldn't leave it alone. "What am I going to do if I'm not strong enough to save myself?"

"You'll cross that bridge when you get to it. Just take one step at a time for right now. That's plenty fast enough."

"That's not an answer."

Walter shrugged. "Onliest answer I got. And the way you get started on that is to finish that breakfast. They go to a lot of trouble to fix a good plate here, and ain't fitting for them to throw it out because you're denying your appetite. You gotta eat and keep your strength up. You're a military man, Chaplain. You eat what's put before you to keep yourself fit because that's part of a soldier's standing orders. Right now, God and the navy own you, and you'd best see that they get their investment back."

Delroy worked to turn off his feelings, his doubts, and his fears and concentrated on his plate. He got both jobs partially done. When he pushed the plate back, food remained but Walter Purcell seemed satisfied.

"Settle up the check," Walter said, grabbing his hat from the table. "I'll give you a ride."

Delroy paid the bill, left a generous tip, and joined the deputy outside the café. The wind blew cold and clean from the north, but it carried a taint of woodsmoke and burned rubber.

"Hotel's not gonna have you," Walter said as they climbed into his cruiser.

"Why?" Delroy asked.

"Because I ain't taking you there. I got a room in back of the house I can let you use for a few days." Walter cranked the engine over. "Till you figure out what you're gonna do."

"So I'm under house arrest."

"I wouldn't call it that."

"What if I want a hotel room?"

Walter looked at him. "You gonna insult my hospitality?"

Delroy didn't know what to say. Walter Purcell surprised him at every turn.

"You wasn't listening back in the café when I told you I had a couple of things I wanted to make sure of." Walter put the transmission in gear and pulled out of the parking lot into the street.

"You didn't want me to see Clarence Floyd and Glenda. I got that."

Walter nodded. "Yep. You heard that right enough. I don't aim to see you hurt nobody in my town." He paused and shifted gears. "But I also want to make sure you don't hurt yourself either."

"I wouldn't do that."

"Says the man who looks like he shoved his face into a wood chipper."

Delroy remained silent as he looked over the town. So many things seemed different, but so much of the area looked the same. Memories of his father played inside his head. He remembered the rough feel of his father's hand holding his when he was small, and the smell of his father's cologne when he was older.

Lord, I was wrong to come here. I was wrong to test You. I don't know what I'm supposed to do, but this is the wrong place to do it. My daddy's all over this town. I'm going to see him everywhere I go.

He knew he'd be trapped into remembering Terrence as well. Delroy had brought his family to Marbury often to visit his mother. Terrence had played in the same park he had, had spent time in his father's church after the new preacher had taken over, had eaten breakfasts in Hazel's Café.

"You okay?" Walter asked.

"Aye," Delroy answered.

"You ask me, that sounded a tad weak."

"Regretting coming here."

Walter nodded and pulled to a stop at the red light. "I can see how you'd feel that way right now."

"I do appreciate your hospitality, Walter. There aren't many men who'd do what you've done."

"No, sir. I expect not. A few days ago, before all them people disappeared, I wouldn't have done it." Walter glanced at Delroy and grinned. "I called my wife, told her I was bringing you home. She thinks I've lost my mind."

"Then why are you doing it?"

"Because it feels right." Walter shrugged and looked a little embarrassed. "Kinda following my heart on this one. And way I feel, I don't think I could walk away if I wanted to." He looked at Delroy. "Why'd you take me up on it?"

"I had a choice?"

"You coulda made me make that call. Coulda spent the night in jail and probably got you a navy escort out of here first thing in the morning."

"I could still slip out the window tonight."

Walter laughed. "Maybe we're both fools then, Chaplain."

"Call me Delroy. Chaplain . . . just doesn't feel right at the moment."

"Fair enough, Delroy."

"I'll probably trouble you for the bed today and tonight," Delroy said. "More than likely, I'll make a phone call to the navy tonight and be gone first light if I can get a rental car."

"What about your missus?"

Delroy shook his head. "I've made enough mistakes coming here. I don't need to make one more. And that one would be a big one." He laid his head back on the headrest and closed his eyes, shutting out the familiar streets and all the painful memories.

Just get me free of this town, Lord, Delroy prayed. He hoped God was listening, but he didn't know if He was. *No, it's not that you don't know; it's that you don't believe, Delroy. You call this one fair and square.* He wanted to cry but he lacked the strength and he knew it would do no good. He kept his eyes closed good and tight.

Then he grew aware of how long the car was sitting at the red light. No red light lasted that long. Delroy lifted his head and peered forward. The light was still red. To his left, Walter Purcell sat patiently with both hands on the steering wheel. If he noticed the passage of time, the deputy gave no indication.

The growling pop of a loud exhaust suddenly thundered into Delroy's ears. The side mirror showed the approach of a yellow-and-red Harley-Davidson motorcycle. The lone rider, dressed in scarred black leather, kicked his feet out as the motorcycle drew even with the cruiser.

Drawn by the noise and the closeness of the motorcycle, Delroy looked at the rider.

He was young and blond, his bare arms and neck covered with tattoos. He wore wraparound mirror sunglasses. As Delroy watched, the rider's skin switched from tan and tattoos to a hint of reptilian scales.

The rider grinned. Somehow his voice carried over the thunder of the cycle's exhaust. "Glad to see you're hanging around here, Preacher." The thing glanced over his shoulder and made a show of taking in the town. "Lotta people here to hurt. And as long as you're around, I get to hurt them." He smiled, bright and cruel and cold. "I have to admit, playing with you has become more exciting than I thought it would be. You're being stubborn, but that just makes the chase better." He twisted the accelerator and revved the engine, cracking ominous thunder all around them. "But in the end, I'm going to bring you down. Your faith is weak."

Delroy fumbled for the door lock and pushed the button down.

The thing on the motorcycle laughed uproariously. He made a pistol of his thumb and forefinger and shot Delroy with it.

"Are you all right?"

Surprised by the deputy's voice, Delroy turned to look at Walter.

"I said, are you all right?" Walter asked again. He nodded at the lock. "You afraid of falling out?"

Delroy glanced back at the side of the cruiser, only then realizing the sound of the throbbing engine had disappeared. The street beside him was empty.

United States of America.
Fort Benning, Georgia
Local Time 0941 Hours

Megan pulled Goose's pickup truck to a halt in front of the counseling center where she worked during the day. She felt guilty about getting here late. Anger at Major Augustus Trimble, commanding officer of the chaplains at the post, still pounded her temples.

She had confronted the major in his office only a short time ago. Megan had wanted Trimble to acknowledge that the Rapture had happened and start classes for the young people on the base that would explain what was going to happen during the coming seven years of the Tribulation.

Trimble had refused, had shouted her down, and had her escorted from his office. Megan hadn't gone graciously, but she had gone.

Maybe Trimble hadn't come around in his faith to the Lord, but she had. Somewhere up there, she knew Chris was in heaven with God and would be safe from all the coming savagery. It was a lot to be thankful for. However, she wasn't convinced that God cared much about the present situation she was in.

Gerry Fletcher had been a child in her care. As one of the civilian counselors for the post, Megan saw a number of children and teenagers who had problems with drugs, alcohol, and emotional trauma. Gerry's problem had been his father, Private Boyd Fletcher, who had a history of violent behavior.

The night of the Rapture, Gerry had been in the post ER with Megan, recovering from his latest session of abuse from his father. Megan had made the choice—against hospital, counseling, and military policy—to not inform the parents. She and the hospital staff had hoped that she could convince Gerry to testify against his father this time and break free of the cycle of abuse.

Instead, Gerry had ended up on top of a building in an attempt to commit suicide. He'd fallen by mistake, though, and Megan had barely managed to get hold of him. But that respite lasted only seconds. Despite Megan's best efforts, Gerry had slipped from her, plummeting to certain doom.

But halfway down, Gerry had been raptured. He'd never had to endure the horrible death from the four-story plummet. His empty clothing had landed on the pavement below.

But no one believed that Megan had truly dropped the boy. They believed that she had faked the fall.

"Boyd Fletcher retained a civilian attorney who is waiting in the wings for the deposition of the provost marshal's case against you," Lieutenant Doug Benbow informed her.

"A civilian attorney?" Megan paid only a little attention to the young lieutenant sitting next to her in the truck. He was currently assigned to act as her military legal representative in the matter of the dereliction of duty charges against her regarding Gerry Fletcher.

"Yes, ma'am."

"Why would he want a civilian attorney?" Megan asked, knowing there was something she'd missed.

"Megan." Benbow frowned a little as he looked at her. "Have you heard a word I've said on the trip over here?"

It hadn't been Megan's idea to bring him along. But when Benbow had seen how upset she'd been after leaving Trimble's office, he had volunteered to accompany her. He was planning to catch a ride to his office in one of the jeeps ferrying people back and forth across the post. He'd said he hoped that the time would give them the opportunity to talk.

He'd talked, Megan realized. She just hadn't listened. Her mind had been too full of the things she needed to do for the kids she cared for. If Trimble and the post chaplains—at least the ones who believed in the Rapture and the coming Tribulation, which not even all Christian churches believed in—wouldn't teach the kids about the trials and horrors ahead, she had to make other arrangements to take care of her young charges.

"I was listening, Lieutenant." Megan felt defensive and she hated that. "I heard a word or two. Now and then. Sometimes complete sentences. I just didn't get the whole civilian-attorney part." She switched the truck's ignition off. The engine died and left the cab full of strained silence and distant noise muted by the glass. "I'm listening now."

"Not including last night," Benbow said, "how much rest have you been getting?"

"Enough," Megan replied.

Benbow gave her that familiar earnest look that reminded her he was nearly ten years younger than she was.

"*Nearly* enough," she amended.

"I think we're talking more in the *not nearly* enough range," Benbow said. "In fact, I believe we're more in the red-line range here. The drop-dead-can't-make-another-move red-line range."

"I'll get more rest when things slow down." Megan glanced at her watch, hoping Benbow would take the hint.

"Things," Benbow said in a measured voice, "are not going to slow down soon. If they ever slow down again. You're going to have to slow down."

"Look, Lieutenant—"

"Doug. Please. I'm trying to talk to you as a person, Megan. As a friend. Maybe a few days of knowing you don't seem like a lot, but they've been extremely hectic days. I've seen you at your best." Benbow paused. "And I've seen you at your worst."

Megan knew that. Sometimes in order to talk to her about the impending military court investigation, Benbow had ended up helping her prepare meals, do laundry, and babysit. He'd wedged snippets of conversation between her counseling sessions and all the emergencies that seemed to be hers to deal with. He'd also, on more than one occasion, gotten roped into making supply runs for her.

"You are a friend. I appreciate what you're doing," Megan said. *But what you're doing barely even touches the big picture of what's going on.* She didn't say that because she didn't want to take away from any of the tremendous effort Doug had made on her behalf to get the charges dropped. She knew he'd been doing that. And not only because she'd signed off on the paperwork.

Benbow sighed. "We've reached the point where you've got to do more than just appreciate what I'm doing. You're going to have to start listening and acting on the advice and guidance I'm giving. You've got a lot riding on this, Megan."

"I wasn't derelict in my duty that night," Megan said. She still remembered how cold the air had been on top of that building as she'd tried to talk Gerry Fletcher down. She'd never really realized how long a four-story drop was until that night. The boy had gone up because he'd blamed himself for the trouble his father was in. He was wrong, of course, but he'd been following the program of self-blame his father had instilled in him as a child.

He was still a child, Megan told herself. *He was only eleven years old.* Barely old enough to understand all the guilt and persecution his father had heaped on him, and way too young to carry it.

"I know you weren't derelict," Benbow said. "You were protecting Gerry Fletcher from his father."

"That's right," Megan said. "If this . . . situation . . . goes to court, I can bury Boyd Fletcher in reports citing his abuse of his son."

"Fine," Benbow said. "Now that I have your full and complete attention, let's roll with that. Let me take the opposing counsel's viewpoint for a moment. Please bear with me."

"I can do the opposing counsel's position for you: Why didn't I make recommendations that Gerry Fletcher be taken from the home?" Megan frowned. That question kept coming up during their discussions.

Benbow nodded. "Exactly."

"I don't see what difference that makes."

"Because the opposing military counsel will use your failure to act to his own advantage," Benbow explained. "And to Boyd Fletcher's. Which will enable Fletcher's attorney to use that information as well."

After hearing how Trimble had twisted everything she'd said in his office around to suit his own needs, Megan suddenly found herself more attentive than usual to Benbow's words. Over the past few days, she had convinced herself that nothing would come of the provost marshal's investigation. After all, why single out Gerry's disappearance from among the millions of disappearances worldwide? But the threat of legal action hadn't gone away. It was still headed right at her, with a rumble that was starting to resemble that of an inbound freight train.

Benbow hadn't told her she was in denial about the situation, and she didn't really think she was, but the possibility of getting fired from her position as counselor or even jailed because the act was directed against a military person just hadn't seemed real to her. The kids she helped needed that help. Surely the base commander had to realize that.

"How can he use that?" Megan asked.

"You're being investigated for being derelict in your duty. If you take the stand and talk about Boyd Fletcher's abuse of his son, or

allow documents concerning those events to surface during the hearing, the opposing counsel is going to use them to show that you've
got a history of being derelict in your duty. He's going to convince the
jury that you should have acted prior to the night in question. He's
going to say that your dereliction of duty started long before the night
you climbed up onto that building with Gerry Fletcher."

"The decision to remove a child from a home has some heavy repercussions for the family as well as the counselor. I felt that taking
Gerry from his family would have been more detrimental to him than
letting him stay."

"More detrimental than getting beaten?"

"There had been only one incident at that time."

"But others followed?"

"Yes. By then," Megan said, remembering the situation with helpless frustration, "Gerry had locked into a pattern of lying to protect
his father. I would have had to tear down his stories before I could
have helped him."

"Wouldn't that have been the right thing to do?"

"I would have lost his trust. And, yes, that would have affected
everything."

"Was the situation at Gerry's home then a matter of life or death?"

"I didn't think so."

"What about the night in question? The night you willfully didn't
tell Boyd Fletcher his son was in the hospital."

"I wasn't sure then, but I knew something had to be done. Things
had been escalating, but a lot of time had passed since the last violent
incident. That night I didn't feel that the situation had gotten completely out of control until Boyd Fletcher showed up drunk at the hospital and Gerry climbed up on that building."

"You weren't certain what your course of action would be when
you arrived at the hospital?"

"No. I was working my way through the situation."

"Megan, the jury judging you is going to be made up of men—
maybe a few women, God willing, because they hopefully know what
it's like to be a mom or an aunt or a big sister—who live on a daily basis prepared to make life-or-death decisions between heartbeats. Pull
the trigger; don't pull the trigger. And with everything going on in the
world right now, those men are tuned directly into that mind-set:
Take charge and make a difference. They may very well feel that you
didn't take appropriate action. That 'working your way through a situation' wasn't what was needed to save Gerry."

"Because I didn't take Gerry out of his home?"

"Exactly."

"Then why wouldn't they blame Boyd Fletcher? He's the one who created the situation. He came into the ER in a drunken rampage that night. It took two MPs to subdue him, and both of them had to be treated for injuries. Gerry was scared of his father. That's why he ran and that's why he ended up on that building."

"They *will* blame Boyd Fletcher," Benbow agreed. "But they'll only blame him for his part in this. Trust me, Boyd Fletcher isn't going to get off scot-free in the eyes of the military men he serves with. At least, not with most of them. And probably not with the army. I'm willing to bet his career is over, one way or another. But that court and that jury are going to hold you accountable too, Megan."

"For what?"

Without flinching, Doug answered, "For allowing the situation to come to that. For not notifying the parents their son was in the ER. For failure to act."

"I *was* acting."

"You just told me you didn't know what your course of action was going to be."

"That's ridiculous." Megan had to rein in her anger before she exploded all over the young lieutenant.

Benbow held up both his hands in supplication. "Easy. I'm just pointing things out. Better now than on the stand in a courtroom, don't you think?"

Megan took a deep breath and nodded.

"There's a lot of blame to pass around on this," Benbow said. "The people who are going to serve as your jury are soldiers, not counselors. Their world is more black and white than yours. Their whole existence is keyed into things that they can do and can't do. And they know exactly what those things are every minute of every day. If they don't know, they can ask. Usually before they have to ask, someone has already told them. If things change, if situations change, they're told that, too. It's easy for them to forget that a lot of us have to make decisions for ourselves. And that we're fallible."

"I did everything I could do. Keeping Gerry with me that night, that was part of what I could do."

"Keeping him there without telling his parents he was in the hospital was dereliction of duty. They had a right to know. You were derelict in that regard. So was the hospital. But none of the hospital staff involved are available to press charges against. Boyd Fletcher is after you. His statement says he feels that Gerry's stay there, without his knowledge, was directly your responsibility."

"In a way, it was," Megan said. "Over the last few weeks, I couldn't get his mother to come forward about the abuse issues, but I hoped I could talk Gerry into telling the truth that night. Then we could have acted."

Benbow nodded agreeably. "We can't start with that night because that depends too much on your testimony. The jury may see that as prejudiced."

"Prejudiced?"

"They may think you're trying to cover your own complicity in this." Benbow shook his head. "We have to lead the jury up to that point. We have to start before then to develop the history you were acting on. We're going to have to train those people to think like counselors, to understand what the constraints of your job are, and to put them into context with the situation that night."

Megan felt familiar frustration. She knew most counselors dealt with that feeling on a daily basis. So many things should be simple when dealing with clients, but they weren't because many individuals didn't want to deal with those issues and had long since built up personal support groups among family and friends to help them avoid those issues.

She let out a long breath. "All right. I can see where you're coming from."

"Not me. Where Boyd Fletcher and opposing counsel are going to be coming from. That's a big difference. You need to keep that in mind. I'm on your side, Megan."

"I know."

"Prior to that night, did you feel Gerry was in danger in his home?"

"Yes."

"Then why didn't you have him removed from the home?"

"For two reasons."

"Two is good," Benbow said, smiling a little. "I'd prefer a dozen, but I'll settle for two. It's twice as good as one."

"Primarily," Megan said, "I didn't try to have Gerry removed from the home because—before that night—I felt like we had the situation under control."

"'We?'"

"The family and I. And the counseling office."

"Other counselors were aware of the situation in the Fletcher household?"

"Yes. We always have a peer we can use as a sounding board."

Benbow nodded. "What do you mean when you say you felt you had the Fletcher situation 'under control'?"

"I'd been seeing Gerry for fourteen months. Since PFC Boyd Fletcher got transferred to Fort Benning. During that time, Gerry ended up in the hospital twice. The first time was nine months ago. His ribs were heavily bruised."

Benbow reached into his uniform pocket, took out a spiral-bound deck of index cards, and flipped through them. "On June sixteenth of last year. The injury was due to a fall."

"That's what Gerry said."

"And that's what the attending physician put on the report."

Megan scowled. "The attending physician was Dr. Henry Plunkett. He was on short time. Less than three months to go before retirement. He'd been military all his life. Putting Gerry's story down as Gerry relayed it was the path of least resistance. He didn't want to rock the boat." She paused. "And truth to tell, I didn't push him hard."

"Why?"

"At that point, I didn't have enough history with the family to make a charge stick." Megan took a breath and tried to keep the frustration at bay. The effort was harder than normal because her encounter with Trimble kept coloring her thinking. "In a domestic situation like this, you have to be careful how you handle things. If you push too early with not enough information, you can wreck the case forever and always."

"Because the defendant can prove a case for prejudice on the part of the counselor."

"Exactly." Megan was surprised, and it must have showed.

Benbow gave her a small smile. "A situation like this wasn't exactly something we covered in law school. I've been doing my homework."

"Yes, it seems that you have," Megan commented. She felt a little better. Lieutenant Doug Benbow was new to Fort Benning and new to his legal profession, but he seemed surprisingly thorough.

"But on June sixteenth you didn't believe Gerry's story about falling was the truth."

"Helen Cordell—"

"The night-shift supervisor of the counseling center?"

"Yes. She was." Helen and her husband had vanished in the disappearances. Megan's friendship with the woman had been deep and had spanned several years. She missed Helen terribly.

"She's gone. One of the vanished."

Megan felt a stab of pain at how casually those words rolled off Benbow's tongue. That was how so many people who had been left behind had categorized those who had disappeared. *The vanished.* Like it was some kind of terminal illness the rest of them were lucky not to have gotten infected with.

If they only knew the truth.

For a moment, Megan wondered what it would have been like to arrive in heaven with Chris. He would have been so full of wonder, the way he was when they went to the zoo or the park or the mall. Almost any place. His eyes had constantly made the world new to her. She almost felt his small hand in hers, and her hand clutched at his reflexively. Only he wasn't there. Tears burned the back of her eyes.

"Are you all right?" Benbow asked. Worry creased his forehead.

"I'm fine." Megan's voice sounded tight. "Like you said, last night was a long night."

Benbow nodded, but he didn't look overly certain. "Maybe we could postpone this to another time."

"I can't guarantee when that time would be."

"All right." The lieutenant referred to his notes again. "Helen Cordell told you something about the bruising on Gerry's ribs the first time he was admitted to the emergency room here at the fort hospital."

"She told me that she didn't believe Gerry had gotten hurt during a fall down a flight of stairs."

"Why?"

"Because the injury looked like the result of multiple impacts— and the bruising wasn't consistent with impact with stairs."

"What do you mean?"

"Helen believed after observing the injury that the bruising was caused by repeated punches. Unfortunately, the bruising was old enough and so heavily massed that knuckle imprints didn't show up."

Benbow's brows drew together and he didn't look happy.

"Doug," Megan said, "Gerry's life was hard in some respects."

"Yeah. I know that from your reports, and from what you've told me there were problems."

"The reports don't tell the whole truth. His problem was that his father has an anger-management issue. Whenever Boyd Fletcher got mad at the army or at his wife—whom he suspected of being unfaithful—or came home in a bad mood, Gerry was the one who paid the price."

"It's hard for me to imagine a full-grown man beating up a kid."

"I don't have to imagine it. Over the years I've counseled kids who have had problems like that. Gerry Fletcher's situation wasn't unique."

"But you didn't have enough evidence to act."

"No," Megan confirmed. "Not then."

"Gerry wouldn't admit that his father hit him?"

"No."

Benbow shifted, bringing out a pen and making notes on the index cards. "You followed up with the family?"

"No."

Benbow looked at her.

"There was no just cause," Megan explained. "No real proof. Only suspicion, and you've got to have a lot more than that to perform in any manner that might suggest accusation. I suggested that I see Gerry again. Just as a follow-up because he seemed apprehensive. I said that maybe the move to Fort Benning wasn't agreeing with him. But when I tried to set up a time later, Boyd Fletcher declined."

"And he could do that?"

"Yes. He's Gerry's father, and no charges had been filed."

"You couldn't do anything about that?"

"No."

Benbow referred to his notes. "Gerry came into the hospital on three other occasions."

"Before his arm was broken, yes."

"We'll get to the broken arm. I want to discuss the other visits where similar instances of bruising were reported."

"All of those visits weren't for medical attention for his injuries. They occurred when Gerry went in for routine medical care—for a vaccination or a flu shot or a round of antibiotics for a cold. On those three occasions you're talking about, the attending physician made notes that Gerry had 'suspicious bruising.'"

"Suspicious bruising?"

"Yes."

"Did you view the bruises?"

"No. I couldn't. The physicians didn't ask me to. I only found out about them later. There are all kinds of privacy issues to consider in a case like this."

"What did you do when you found out about this suspicious bruising?"

"I was able to schedule counseling time with Gerry."

"Did you see the bruising then?"

"No."

"Then how were you able to schedule time? Especially if his parents didn't agree to counseling sessions. Which, I'm guessing, Boyd Fletcher didn't."

"He didn't. I had to go over his head. I suggested to the physician each time that we might want to interview Gerry for possible depressive episodes that might trigger repeated self-inflicted injuries."

Benbow pursed his lips. "I really wish we had gone over this before."

"Why?"

Tapping his pen against the index cards, he answered, "Because if there's paperwork around that documents your belief that Gerry Fletcher was hurting himself because of depression, it's going to look bad for us."

"He wasn't depressed," Megan said. "He was scared. I only used that as a wedge to get inside the family."

"Okay, but it may come back to haunt us. And that brings us to another issue. To the jury, it's going to look like you were tampering with the evidence. Setting Boyd Fletcher up to fall. The jury may view the case as tainted from that point on."

"Boyd Fletcher was *beating* his son." Megan couldn't believe what she was hearing. "It was the only thing I had to use."

"I understand that. Really, I do. I know that you did the best you could, Megan. I *know* that. But what I also know is that the opposing counsel is going to have a field day with the ammunition you're inadvertently giving him."

Megan took a deep breath and released it. "If you're thinking that maybe this case is getting shaky and you want out, Lieutenant, all you have to do is say so."

Benbow looked at her in surprise. "That isn't what I'm saying."

"It sounds like it from here."

"Megan, I'm on your side. I believe in you." Benbow's voice softened. "I wish I had more time to prepare, that's all."

His meaning wormed through her angry, conflicted thoughts. "They've set the preliminary hearing?"

"Yes."

"When?"

"Three days from now."

"What?" Megan struggled for a moment to remember what day it was. "We're going to start on Monday?" Saying that seemed to make the whole ordeal even more fearful.

"Yes."

She took a deep breath.

"Scared?" Benbow asked.

"Oh, yeah. Terrified. I really thought you'd have been able to quash this thing before now."

"I tried. It just won't go away." Benbow hesitated.

"Say it," Megan said. "You've already thought it."

He looked at her.

"Body language," Megan said. "I'm a trained counselor, remember?"

"I suppose so." Benbow wiped at his face tiredly. "This should have gone away, Megan. Really, the charges should have been dropped. The provost marshal's office should have conducted a cursory investigation, churned some paper, and left you alone."

"Then why isn't that happening?"

"Because General Braddock can't let the situation go away now."

"Why not now? What's changed?"

"Boyd Fletcher's new attorney won't let the general drop the charges."

"This new attorney is going to be involved with the hearing?"

"No."

"Then what?"

"Boyd Fletcher's new attorney is a civil suit lawyer who specializes in claims against the military."

"Civil suit?" Slowly, with terrifying certainty, Megan understood the ramifications of the attorney's chosen venue.

"Yes. Fletcher's attorney plans on suing you *and* the army, Megan. It's not part of the criminal trial the military is putting you through. He's going to sue you for damages for the time Gerry was held at the hospital without his parents' knowledge."

"Why?"

"Because the army has deep pockets," Benbow stated. "Fletcher's specialist, an Atlanta attorney named Arthur Flynn, has been successful in a number of cases against the military."

Megan thought she remembered the man's name from the news, but she couldn't recall the story or stories.

"Flynn's got a big interest in the army's case against you. General

Braddock can't let the provost marshal's office dismiss your case because it will look like the post is trying to cover up wrongdoing on their part."

"Then why press charges against me?" Megan asked. "If they find me guilty, won't that make them guilty, too?"

"Not necessarily." Benbow shifted, looking terribly young and uncomfortable. "If they find you guilty of dereliction of duty and move on to prove that you were unfit that night, the army can possibly distance themselves from you. They can show good faith that they are dealing with the fact that you were unfit for your job and that they dealt with the matter as soon as it reached their attention. That might be enough to keep the army, Fort Benning, and—probably most of all—General Braddock out of the legal storm that's headed this way."

"That's what General Braddock wants to do? Distance his post from me?"

"That's what I've been told."

"Not exactly an exhibition of loyalty, is it?"

Benbow sighed. "No." He paused. "The thinking is that you're civilian, Megan. Not military personnel. You're an acceptable loss. The military is all about acceptable losses."

"What about the 'never leave a man behind' way of thinking?"

"General Braddock doesn't feel that applies to you."

"So what happens if this attorney Flynn successfully sues me?"

"Let's not think that way."

"I have to."

Benbow hesitated. "If Fletcher wins his suit against you, you and Goose could lose everything. The retirement you guys have put back. Property you own. And if he gets a judgment against you, you could end up paying him for the rest of your lives."

Megan tried to understand all the ramifications. How could everything she and Goose had worked for be taken from them so easily? It wasn't fair. But she knew judgments like that happened. She'd seen court cases in the news where events had gone exactly as Benbow was describing them.

Only those people deserved what they got. Didn't they? Megan forced herself to calm down. "Even if Fletcher got all that, Goose and I aren't rich. There's some money, enough to make our lives comfortable, but not enough to interest somebody like this Flynn."

"Flynn considers you a stepping-stone. If he gets a judgment against you, he gets a shot at the army. He's going to try to prove that the post was culpable in the civil matter as well. If Fort Benning hasn't built a strong enough case against you, he might make it stick."

"And if Flynn is successful against me and the army? What does he get?"

"I don't know." Benbow shrugged. "That's what everyone at the post—and higher up in the military circles—is concerned about. With the present hysteria in the country, with so many people feeling that the disappearances are somehow related to what the American military has done globally, or with President Fitzhugh's current political stance, a civilian jury could find against Fort Benning. It's possible they could grant the Fletchers hundreds of thousands or millions of dollars in damages." Benbow paused. "I've heard a rumor that Flynn is willing to settle out of court for one hundred million dollars."

Disbelief swept through Megan with paralyzing force. "Because I kept Gerry Fletcher in the hospital without his parents' knowledge— for an hour?"

"It was," Benbow said, "the last hour they would have spent with their son."

"They didn't know that then." Pain replaced the disbelief as she gazed at the young lieutenant. "*I* didn't know that then. I spent the last hour when I could have been playing with my youngest son try- ing to help Gerry."

"I know that."

"I gave up that time with Chris." Saying her son's name somehow made Boyd Fletcher's case against her even more hideous. Megan made a fist and pressed it against her mouth in an attempt to control her warring emotions. "I kissed my baby good night and left him. He didn't want me to go."

Chris's voice haunted her. "*I'm just going to sleep for a little while, Mommy, so you can come and get me soon.*" Sweet and delicate, despite the fact that he hadn't wanted to be left in the care center, Chris had curled up, closed his eyes, and pretended to be fast asleep.

Megan felt her heart break all over again. "I'm never going to see my baby again in this world."

"You don't know that," Benbow said. "A lot of people are working on what caused the disappearances. Maybe those people, maybe your son, can be brought back."

Shaking her head, Megan said, "They're not coming back. Ever." Her eyes burned with unshed tears. "See? You don't even understand what's happened."

"Nobody does," Benbow agreed. "Not yet, anyway. But we will."

Megan wanted to curse and scream. That was something she hadn't often done. She was so mad and so hurt she trembled and thought she was going to be sick. Jerking her gaze from Benbow, trying desperately to remember that although he wore that uniform, he wasn't really part of the vast machine presently arrayed against her, she peered through the truck's windshield.

Is that what this is coming to, God? she demanded. *Is this what You want to do? To tear me completely down? Because if that's what You're all set to do, it's working. How much do You think I have left to give? How much more do You think I can take?* She tightened her grip on the steering wheel and tried to hold the tears back. But she couldn't.

"Megan—," Benbow began.

"*Don't,* Lieutenant," Megan said in a hoarse voice. "Not one word. Not till I'm ready."

He nodded and sat still on his side of the pickup.

Megan struggled to keep from crying. She shook with the effort. Her face grew hot and wet. Her vision blurred. She smelled Goose all around her. Then she cursed him for being gone, for not being here when she needed him so much. It was unfair, she knew, but she couldn't help herself. She faulted him for not being here to help her through the court situation, for not being here to help find Joey, and—most of all—for not being here to help her grieve over Chris's disappearance.

It's not Goose's fault, God. It's Yours. You're doing this. I don't know what I did that was this wrong, so wrong that I deserved this. But I believed in You. Over these past few days, I've come to lean on You in ways I never before imagined. Now You're going to do this to me? to my family? Is this what I get for trusting You? You're not being fair!

Gradually, Megan emptied of tears. She didn't regain control of herself so much as she just ran out of emotion of any kind. She felt dead inside. Her eyes were swollen and puffy in the grayed-out reflection of herself she saw in the windshield.

All those brave words she'd spoken in Trimble's office about seeing Chris again didn't mean a thing. She knew that now. More than anything, she feared she would never see her baby again. God had given her no reason to believe that. She wasn't asking for proof, just the ability to believe as best she could in peace.

Now she wasn't even being given that illusion.

Megan wiped her face with her shirttail. She didn't look at Benbow. "You haven't mentioned whether General Braddock's people are offering a deal."

Benbow didn't say anything.

"Are they?" Megan looked at the young lieutenant.

Obviously torn, Benbow hesitated. "I was approached. Off the record. This morning after the provost marshal's office received the reports on Leslie Hollister."

"What does Leslie Hollister have to do with Gerry Fletcher?"

"The provost marshal plans to tie the two together to strengthen the case against you." Benbow spoke quietly. "They're going to use what happened last night to Leslie Hollister against you, Megan."

Megan was stunned speechless.

"The reports—and I haven't seen them yet—indicate that you persuaded the Hollister girl that she was just dreaming, that the whole sequence of events she was going through—including the disappearance of her mother—was a figment of her imagination."

"I was trying to get her to relax. If I could have gotten her to lie down, she would have gone to sleep. She was out on her feet. Instead—instead—" Megan heard the sharp report of the gunshot echoing in her memory, then saw all the blood and smelled the cordite of the expended round.

Benbow nodded. "The provost marshal's office isn't choosing to see things that way."

Megan found her voice with difficulty. "And neither is General Braddock."

"No. He's not."

"How are they going to present what happened?"

Shifting uncomfortably in the seat, Benbow said, "Worst-case scenario? They're going to say that you tried to convince Leslie Hollister to commit suicide."

"That's insane." Megan couldn't believe it. "Why would I do something like that?"

Benbow hesitated only a moment. "The provost marshal's office is prepared to make the case that you did that because you're suicidal yourself."

"That's not true."

"They're going to say that you tried to get Leslie Hollister to commit suicide so you could box yourself in with your own self-destruction. That you wanted to get your own personal life so tense that you could see only suicide as an option. You didn't want to give yourself an out."

"They think I want to kill myself?"

Benbow looked at her earnestly. "Megan, I know you. I know that you're going through a tough time, but I know—in my heart—that you're not suicidal. I don't think they really believe that either, but they're going to use it. If the provost marshal's office at least makes a case that will question not only your ability to do your job but also your mental state, they can better separate themselves from any kind of civil repercussions."

"What motive would I possibly have for killing myself?"

Benbow pursed his lips and exhaled. "They're going to say that it's because of the loss of your son. They're prepared to say that you've been stressed for some time—which accounts for the ill-advised decision to keep Gerry Fletcher from his parents. They're going to say that losing your son pushed you over the edge."

Anger burned through Megan. "They're going to—going to use *Chris*—" She couldn't go on. When she did, her voice was coarse, as if it had been sandblasted. "They're going to use my little boy like that?" Her voice grew steadily tighter, ending up as a squeak. "They can't do that!"

"I'm sorry, Megan. But you need to know what you're going to face. If we go to court."

"*If* we go to court?"

"You have a choice."

"What choice?"

"The deal from the provost marshal's office."

Megan waited, swallowing hard. Her mind whirled. Thoughts chased themselves, and none of them made any sense. She was crying again, despite the fact that she'd thought herself drained of tears. Everything Benbow was saying was so . . . so . . . unbelievable. None of this could be real. *God, please don't let this be real.*

"They want you to admit culpability in the Gerry Fletcher matter," Benbow said. "Say that you were willful in dereliction of duty. Because of the personal agenda you have against Boyd Fletcher."

"I was trying to save Gerry."

"No one has to save Gerry now," Benbow stated gently. "He's gone, Megan. Wherever he is, he's no longer part of this."

"But they're going to use my baby against me. And he's not—he's not here either."

"Megan, I'm sorry. But, yes, they're prepared to do exactly that."

Megan forced herself to think, forced herself to breathe, and maybe she even forced herself to live in that moment. "What happens if I agree to that?"

"The provost marshal's office recommends leniency. The downside is that you'll be left completely exposed to Boyd Fletcher's civil suit."

Megan whispered, "Goose and I could lose everything we've worked for."

"Probably. If Boyd Fletcher wants to pursue the civil suit."

"He will."

"I think so too." Benbow let out a breath. "I've never met a more vindictive man."

"You've met Boyd Fletcher?"

Benbow nodded. "I wanted to see if I could reason with him. That didn't happen."

"Goose and I will lose everything, but the army will be clear." Megan's tears dried as the anger inside her turned cold and burned away the feelings of helplessness.

"That's what General Braddock is hoping."

"That's insane."

"It's the best shot they have of walking away from this thing."

The anger grew stronger, pushing aside the frustration and helpless feeling. *Is that how it's going to be, God? I'm supposed to help myself because You don't care?* She was angry with God and Goose and Joey and Benbow, mad at everyone who was supposed to be here to help her but was somehow MIA.

"What do I get out of this?" Megan asked.

The question caught Benbow off guard. He hesitated. "They'll drop the charges."

"Only because I admitted guilt for those charges. There's nothing in that for me."

"They'll agree not to come after you, Megan. They won't press criminal charges. You won't take the risk of losing your counselor's license."

"I don't think anyone would be inclined to hire me after I admitted guilt in something like this. It's not the kind of thing you want on a résumé."

"I don't know."

"*I* wouldn't hire me," Megan said.

"You also won't be looking at any jail time."

"Jail time?" That surprised Megan for a moment. No one had mentioned jail time.

"This is the military," Benbow said. "There is the possibility that you would have to serve out a sentence. Probably no more than a few months, but more time could be involved."

"Because I didn't tell Gerry Fletcher's parents that he was in the ER that night?"

"No. I was told that if they had to prosecute you for the Fletcher case, they'll come after you for Leslie Hollister on a follow-up investigation. They may even press charges for second-degree attempted murder."

Megan felt trapped. No matter which way she turned, things only got worse. "What would you do?"

"Megan, I'm not facing a trial here."

Taking another breath, somehow getting calmer by the heartbeat, Megan said, "If I decide to fight them, will you represent me to the best of your ability?"

"If you decide to do that, it's not going to be easy."

"That wasn't the question, Lieutenant." Megan made her voice hard. "Your career is going to be at risk in this too. I know that. I want to know if you'll stick with me. And how far you're willing to go."

Benbow looked clear eyed and competent, like the kind of guy who would take a bullet for a friend. Like the kind of soldier Goose would be proud of. "Yes, ma'am," he declared. "I'll stick with you. Every inch of the way."

"Fine. Then you take a message to the provost marshal's office and General Braddock for me. Tell them if they're going to hang me out to dry, use my baby against me, and put me through hell so they can protect themselves, tell them that I'm going to take them with me."

"I really don't think we should respond in such an inflammatory manner."

"Do you have a nice way of putting it?"

Benbow shook his head. "No, ma'am."

"Then you tell them. Just like I told you. I don't want them to get the mistaken idea they can change my mind."

"Yes, ma'am."

Megan gathered her purse and her portfolio. "I've got to go. I've got a job and I've got kids depending on me. If you need anything else, let me know. I'll make time for you. If these people want a fight, they're going to get one."

"Yes, ma'am."

Megan let herself out of the truck and turned her steps toward the counseling center. *Okay, God, if You're not going to stand up and be counted, I'll do it myself. And if You think You can break me, then do it. I've got to fight to survive. And maybe I have to fight even You. I don't know.*

You haven't given me many options here. But I'm not going to give up. Do You hear me? I'm not just going to lie down and die. That's not in me. I hope You understand that. If not, I guess that's just one more reason You've abandoned me.

Riding in the passenger seat of the Ranger Special Operations Vehicle, Captain Cal Remington stared out at the city he'd been ordered to hold no matter what the cost, while the U.S. Rangers, the U.N. forces, and the Turkish army shored up the next line of defense against the coming Syrian invasion. The fact that these combined troops had survived this long was nothing less than amazing. The only good thing about it, Remington told himself, is that *amazing* looks good on a military résumé.

But he hated the idea that he'd been assigned to a mission he had no hope of winning. Losing wasn't an option in Remington's personal or professional plans. He didn't compromise, either. In his opinion, compromise was the first step toward acknowledging an upcoming loss. Accepting the inevitability of a loss was intolerable and unacceptable to him. He believed that there was always a way out if a soldier looked for it. There was always a way to win.

Although dawn was just a pale smear of pink and gold against the indigo sky to the east, Sanliurfa was awake. As far as Cal Remington could tell, the city never slept anymore. Occasionally it passed out for fitful rest or unconsciousness that passed for sleep, but mostly the city lay awake and fearful in the night. No one relaxed.

During the day, all the people in the city had to work constantly just to maintain some crumbling level of survival. At least during the day they didn't have to worry about turning on lights that could be seen and used as targets by the Syrian military. Also, if Syrian aircraft chose to stage another air strike, the air force in Sanliurfa could scramble in time to meet them, driving up the Syrian cost of such a venture. Their SCUD missile use had dropped after Allied forces had deployed Patriot antimissile systems along the front lines. The Patriots weren't exactly the highest of high-tech systems these days—but then neither were the SCUDs. And when Syrian artillery squads got close enough to launch, they were also close enough to the battle lines to become targets.

For the last fifteen and a half hours, Sanliurfa's defenders had kept the Syrian aggressors and their terrorist allies, who were looking to rack up trophy kills fast, at a stalemate.

Remington wanted to change that, wanted to take the fight back to the Syrians and keep them off guard. He figured such an attack would buy them more time. He'd already put all the key people into play that he needed to make the necessary changes. However, the plan he had in mind would require sacrifices.

Cal Remington didn't mind sacrifices. At least he didn't mind them up to a point. He'd sacrificed others now and again to further his own ambitions and for the good of the units he'd commanded. Therefore, he could understand the orders he was presently under, but he also counted himself clever enough to survive those orders.

He knew First Sergeant Gander wouldn't deal with the compromises that would have to be made. Goose was the most uncompromising man Remington had ever met. That was both Goose's greatest strength and his worst weakness.

When Goose had a viable plan of action laid out before him, there was not a better soldier in the field. But when things went ugly and sacrifices had to be made, Goose hesitated before making those choices. Only after fighting against all odds, fighting until he finally realized he was going to lose even more if he didn't back away, only then would Goose make the necessary sacrifices and get out.

That was why Goose would never have made it through OCS. Or, if he had gotten through Officer Candidate School, Remington felt certain Goose would have never risen through the ranks.

Goose was hard as nails, but when it came to his men, he was soft. Too soft.

The RSOV slowed to allow an earthmover to trundle across the street ahead. All the heavy construction equipment in the city had been rounded up, and operators for all of the machines had been selected from the ranks of all three military contingents. As soon as the all-clear echoed over the radio links fifteen and a half hours ago, work had begun to clear the bombed, congested streets so the supply runs could be made and fall-back positions within the city could be reinforced.

"Talon. This is Smoke." Corporal Dean Hardin's voice carried clearly over the encrypted channel of Remington's headset.

"Go, Smoke," Remington replied.

"Just wanted you to know we're in position, sir."

"Affirmative. I'm en route. Hold our interviewee in place."

"Understood, sir. But this guy, he's getting antsy."

"If you have to put a pistol to his head, get it done."

Hardin's reply was instant and crisp. "Will do."

"Outstanding," Remington said. He knew his irritation sounded in his voice.

The earthmover cleared the street. The private put the RSOV back into gear and sped around the big machine. The earthmover lowered the box blade and scooped up a pile of broken rock and mortar from the street. The thunder of the engine and the crash and crunch of the broken rock bombarded Remington's hearing as they passed.

The parks and garden areas of downtown Sanliurfa mostly looked like someone had torched Eden. Several areas still smoldered, covered in piles of debris where the construction teams had dumped broken chunks of buildings and burned-out vehicles. In other places, surplus tents stood out under trees. Remington knew vast numbers of Sanliurfa's people were living in the streets in makeshift homes like these. It seemed they thought that the Syrians would rather target buildings than open areas with their missiles and aircraft attacks, though how they could believe that with all the smoking evidence to the contrary, Remington didn't know.

Only a few blocks farther on, Remington spotted the huge tent area where Corporal Joseph Baker kept his makeshift church running 24/7. Acidic anger burned through the Ranger captain's stomach as he realized the church had grown even larger since the last time he'd seen it.

When the Rangers had first arrived in Sanliurfa, the stories about the freak earthquake that had broken the Syrian pursuit of the Allied retreating border troops just as they were about to overwhelm them had captured the immediate attention of the media and the locals, not to mention a good percentage of the Allied troops. Remington still didn't know what had triggered Corporal Baker's decision to lead the troops trapped there in saying the Twenty-third Psalm. But he had. And in that moment, after the earthquake wiped out the first of the Syrian armor, Corporal Baker had become a man of mythic proportions in far too many people's minds.

The talk in Sanliurfa was that Corporal Joseph Baker had God's ear.

Remington didn't like it. Not one bit.

Even before the retreat from the border had begun, Baker had baptized soldiers from all three armies as well as media personnel, Turkish citizens, and nomadic traders. He'd been out there in that stinking river for hours. Remington still caught occasional video bites of the event on the news channels.

The baptisms had continued even after their arrival in Sanliurfa, as more soldiers came forward to give themselves to God, followed by a goodly chunk of the city's civilian populace, who heard of the man of God who could lead them to salvation, even in a war zone. Baker and the men who believed in him—some of them military chaplains!—had dragged under the makeshift church tent a metal tank that held enough water to dunk a man deep enough to baptize him.

Remington thought the whole process was nothing more than religious mumbo jumbo. As far as he was concerned, baptism was simply a get-out-of-jail-free card for losers convinced they were about to die.

The Ranger captain had never been baptized. Nor had he ever wanted to be baptized. He didn't believe in God. He believed in himself.

So far, he'd managed his life so that believing in God hadn't been necessary. Anything Remington wanted, he went out and got for himself. So far, nothing he had ever wanted had been completely out of his reach or his ability to change his circumstances so that whatever he wanted became available. The instant he started believing in something outside of himself, some higher power, Remington knew his life would be over. What point was there in believing in God in a world where man made the rules? He figured he might as well believe in luck. And he did. In his own luck.

As the RSOV passed the tent, now offering supplies, light medical treatment, and care to wounded soldiers as well as to any civilians who needed help, Remington got a glimpse inside. Soldiers wearing Ranger uniforms, marine uniforms, U.N. uniforms, and Turkish army uniforms knelt together on the ground with their heads bowed and their weapons within easy reach. Civilians knelt beside them.

The lion shall lie down with the lamb. The thought came unbidden to Remington. He was irritated that the biblical phrase should even occur to him. Religion was not his deal. All his life, all he'd ever had to believe in was himself. And in the military, all the belief in the world wouldn't save a man from superior weapons or superior tactics. All these people thinking about God were wasting time they should have been using to develop plans of action. The Syrians were coming. If there was a God, He'd shown no sign of stopping it.

Surprisingly, Baker wasn't at the pulpit that someone had fashioned from ammo crates covered with a sheet of plywood. One of the Ranger chaplains stood there leading the prayer as another man dunked a soldier into the large metal water container. A line of men obviously waiting their turn for a dunking stood to one side of the container.

The religious convictions of Baker's followers had created friction among the Rangers as well as among the other military units. Most of those who were baptized by Baker or one of the chaplains seemed to believe that they were somehow divinely protected. Remington had seen one instance himself, though he noticed that those men died just as readily as any other soldier in his command.

But their belief in the hereafter—that they were going to survive somewhere else even if they were killed in the city they held on to by the skin of their teeth and bled dry to keep—offended other soldiers. Remington believed that having someone constantly in the next trench harping about saving his immortal soul simply reminded a fighting man that he could be dead in the next heartbeat.

And where do you go once you are dead?

Remington hated that the question was even formed in his mind. Death would catch him someday, but until that moment he intended to live like he was going to live forever. He wouldn't allow himself to get distracted by Baker or his converts. They were all idiots, all soldiers too weak to face death and spit in its eye. They were spineless.

Turning away from the tent, Remington made a mental note to check on Corporal Joseph Baker's hours. Maybe there was a way to cut into Baker's free time even more. That'd disrupt the church schedule. Then Remington focused his thoughts on his upcoming meeting. If everything worked well, he'd have a chance to strike back at the Syrians within the next few days, maybe even the next few hours.

And maybe he'd be able to work out his situation with First Sergeant Samuel Adams "Goose" Gander at the same time. After all, the holding position in Sanliurfa was all about acceptable losses. Somebody was going to have to take them. And Remington knew just who he was going to toss into the next desperate situation.

✼ ✼ ✼

United States 75th Army Rangers Temporary Post
Sanliurfa, Turkey
Local Time 0611 Hours

"First Sergeant."

Startled, totally engrossed in what he was reading and struggling to make sense of, Goose looked up from the Bible. His mind reeled from the prophecies contained in the book of Revelation, partly because of how huge and sweeping they were, and partly because he had trouble understanding many of them.

Corporal Joseph Baker stood in the doorway of the makeshift barracks. At six feet eight inches tall and built like a Kodiak bear, the corporal was both a threatening and an awe-inspiring man. His face was round beneath his blond crew cut, and his china blue eyes held innocence as well as fatigue. Bruises from the fighting he'd survived still marked his face, but they were green and yellow with age now. He wore BDUs and carried an M-4A1. He hung his helmet by its strap over one broad shoulder.

Goose dragged his feet from the small cot and dropped them to the floor. He wore his boots, though he had taken the time to change his socks. Going without his boots wasn't something he was prepared to do, but, as a soldier, he knew fresh socks meant he had less chance of catching athlete's foot or some other bacterial infection. In a battle zone, an infantryman without healthy feet was only one quick step away from being a dead man.

"Corporal," Goose said in greeting.

The building the Ranger contingent was using now as their barracks had been a grain mill for a hundred years or more. Located near the heart of the city, because Sanliurfa had been around in one incarnation or another for hundreds of years, the mill offered the Rangers a good central location from which to deploy troops.

The Rangers bunked in the basement. There were no windows—one of its greatest advantages in the current situation—so light came from electric lanterns and torches run by generators. The noise from those generators constantly hammered and chugged to create a solid racket that underscored every conversation. But the building's walls were a couple feet thick and offered a lot of protection against the artillery shelling the military expected to resume once the Syrians took up their assault on the city in earnest again.

The sweet smell of the milled grain accumulated through the centuries thickened the air to the point that men with asthma or sinus conditions hadn't been able to stand it. Fine particles floated in the air, filled every nook and cranny, and coated every surface. Goose knew that grain dust could be explosive, and though he'd been assured by the demolition guys that the concentrations in the basement weren't anywhere high enough to be dangerous, he still worried.

Dozens of beds were spread over the basement floor, but all of them were organized to provide aisles for rapid evac if the troops were called into a firefight.

The Rangers didn't really rest in this room, Goose knew. The men collapsed, passed out, and gave in to fatigue or injury. Most of them sleeping or lying in the beds now bore light wounds. These wounded were just the tip of the iceberg. The hospitals overflowed with more critically wounded. To Goose it didn't seem like an hour could go by without somebody—soldier or citizen—succumbing to his wounds.

They were bleeding to death slowly in Sanliurfa, and Goose knew it.

So the mill basement wasn't a place of rest or hope. It was a staging area, where men took brief respite and hoped and prayed they and their friends weren't going to be the next to die. The healthy Rangers occupied the few bars or restaurants open throughout the city. At least those places provided his men with a comforting façade, a place where they could pretend for a moment that everything was going to be all right.

Goose had taken to splitting his time between the bars, the taverns, and the temporary barracks. As a first sergeant, he pushed himself to maintain a high profile. Other soldiers leaned on his ability to keep himself up and going. He felt frayed and ragged now, and his interpretation of the book of Revelation was building a solid fear in his heart and mind. It wasn't his only source of unease, either. Goose's talk with Icarus and his decision to let the man go remained constantly in the first sergeant's thoughts.

"Am I interrupting you?" Baker asked.

"No," Goose replied. "I'm due back in the field at 0700."

Remington had issued standing orders that every man was supposed to be in the rack for five hours a day until the next round of Syrian attacks. That wasn't enough sleep to keep a warrior healthy or sane, but it was something.

"Have you slept?" Baker entered the room and nodded hello to several of the men who called out to him.

Other men, Goose noted, rolled over in their beds and turned away from Baker. The corporal was something of a messiah and a pariah these days. His church was one of the only areas that didn't move on a regular basis.

Remington had objected to the permanent placement of the tent church but hadn't chosen to fight a battle over it yet. Baker's argument for staying put was that the soldiers and the citizens stranded in Sanliurfa needed to know the location of the church. And he had a point, Goose figured. Word of Baker's ministry had spread throughout the city by word of mouth, although a few stories about him had aired on the media.

"I've slept some," Goose answered.

"Should I try to speak with you at another time?"

"Now's as good a time as any. What do you need?"

Baker glanced around and picked up a folding chair that looked incredibly small compared to his massive bulk. "I don't need anything, First Sergeant. But I've noticed you coming around more than normal. I thought perhaps you might need something."

Goose considered that. He'd wanted to talk to Baker after finishing up with Icarus the previous day, but there hadn't been time. Baker had been assigned to help clear debris because he had been a heavy-equipment operator prior to his army career. The loud earthmovers hadn't provided Goose a chance to discuss anything that was on his mind. Later, Baker had gone directly to his church and joined the service.

"I saw you," Baker said, "at the church. You came in, stayed for a while, then left."

Goose nodded. The church hadn't been the place to talk either. Unable to relax, Goose had borrowed a Bible from one of the ammo lockers Baker had established for people to share the Word of God. He'd felt guilty that he didn't carry a Bible of his own.

When Goose had first joined the military, Wes Gander—his father—had packed one into his things without telling him. His dad had also added a half-dozen decks of playing cards, a memory book filled with pictures, a cribbage board, an extra pack of underwear and two extra packs of socks. Wes Gander had always been a caretaker. He'd been a Green Beret in Vietnam during some of the hottest parts of the war. He'd been the first to tell Goose about the importance of dry socks, even if a man couldn't get clean ones.

"I thought maybe you had something on your mind," Baker said.

Goose did, but he didn't know how to approach the subject.

Upon further reflection, Icarus's statements about Nicolae Carpathia being the Antichrist had seemed too far-fetched to even speak about. Carpathia was all over the news yesterday and today, so it was no surprise that Icarus had chosen the Romanian president to fixate on.

Icarus hadn't been in any better shape than Goose was. The man hadn't had any sleep for days, was suffering from wounds he'd received at the hands of the vengeful PKK terrorists, and was paranoid from being hunted by the CIA and by Remington's handpicked dirty-tricks squad. The man was hallucinating, obviously trying to find a way to make sense of everything that was happening to him.

"It's nothing that can't wait," Goose said.

Baker nodded, then pointed his chin at the Bible Goose held. "Reading?"

"Yeah." Goose marked his place in Revelation, closed the Bible, and put it on the bed beside him.

"You developed a sudden interest?" Baker asked.

"Maybe." Goose hesitated. "We're in the middle of the country where all of this took place."

"Most of the Old Testament, sure." Baker indicated the Bible. "May I?"

Uncomfortable with the attention Baker was paying to his new-found interest, Goose said, "Yeah."

Baker scooped the Bible up in one huge paw. He flicked the golden sash that marked Goose's place. "Revelation."

Goose really didn't want to get into this discussion. Too many questions and challenges crowded his mind. He needed to remain focused on the mission.

"This part of the Bible, First Sergeant, happens everywhere. Not just in Turkey."

"I know."

Baker replaced the Bible on the bed. "That particular book is one that has puzzled sages and laymen for centuries."

"I can understand how," Goose admitted. "The reading goes pretty hard."

"There's a basic precept in the book of Revelation that people forget."

"What's that?"

"God didn't lay out the end times so everyone could understand them. Those words are warnings, signs, portents. They are not a concrete blueprint of what's going to happen and what a man should do about it. They're guideposts for choosing how to live, and they're not meant to be clear. God wants you to have to work at it. He wants you to read it and think about it. Prophecy is like that. Like John says in Revelation 1:3: 'Blessed is he who reads and those who hear the words of this prophecy, and keep those things which are written in it; for the time is near.'"

"There's that question of belief," Goose said. "My daddy talked about that a lot."

Interest flickered in Baker's eyes. "Your father was a preacher?"

"No. He was a soldier, and after that he was a lot of things. Never found a true calling after the military, but we made do with the odd jobs he held. One of the things he spent a lot of time at, even though it didn't pay, was teaching Sunday school. I learned a lot about the Bible and about God while I spent time with him." Goose glanced at the Bible. "I wish now that I'd paid better attention."

"Why? So you'd know what heaven is going to be like?"

Goose thought of Chris and silently hoped that was where his young son was. "Nah. I don't think that's meant for us to know. The book of Revelation isn't exactly a tour guide of heaven. It's more focused on the troubles here on earth."

"Yeah. Revelation describes things that are yet to come to us humans. The good things and the bad things. It talks a little about heaven, but mostly it concerns itself with what comes after the Rapture."

Nodding, Goose said, "I never really noticed that before when I read it. I thought the message was always about what you could look forward to in heaven."

"No. It's a war map for the final battles with Satan and his minions." Baker shifted and the chair creaked threateningly. "I've been talking about Revelation quite a lot in my services."

"I've heard some of it," Goose admitted.

"But you weren't drawn into it enough to join in discussion?"

"I've had my own war to fight here. It's kept me busy."

Baker picked up the Bible again. "And now?"

Goose took in a deep breath and released it. He knew he couldn't tell Baker anything but the truth. "Now I'm beginning to think that the war I'm fighting and the war that's described in Revelation may be the same conflict."

"Does that scare you?"

"Yeah," Goose said without hesitation. "It scares me a lot."

"Because you're afraid of dying and losing your immortal soul?"

"That, too. But mostly I'm concerned about the guys that I keep sending into battle. I'm afraid that most of them don't know what's truly at risk."

"To begin with, First Sergeant, I don't see you *sending* anyone into battle. You *lead* your men. That's why you're respected." Baker paused. "If anything, we were poised on the edge of all these conflicts—and I'm talking about the one described in the book of Revelation as well—and we got drawn into the eye of it. At least, we're in the eye of the storm brewing in the Middle East."

"It's not the first time biblical history was made here with all-out war. You read the Old Testament," Goose said, "and you find that a lot of wars, a lot of the people who fought them in the Bible, came from right here, and they fought and died right here. This land has been a biblical battlefield almost from its beginning."

"That's the reason these countries are called the Holy Lands." Baker shifted again. "Modern science and the Word of God differ on a lot of issues. If you study your Bible and pay attention to the sciences, you'll find that out quickly. But one thing—one of many things, actually—that they both agree on is that civilization started near here."

"The Tigris and Euphrates Rivers." The answer came easily to mind from all the history classes Goose had taken in high school.

"Exactly. Sanliurfa has its history in the Bible as well. Abraham was born here. Several other prophets named in the Bible were drawn here at one time or another. That's why the locals call Sanliurfa 'The City of Prophets.'"

"I knew that," Goose said. "But I didn't know it until we got here and I heard it on the news." He looked at Baker, feeling increasingly uncomfortable about the corporal's interest. He wanted to tell Baker about Icarus and about the claims the rogue CIA agent had made. But Baker had come here; Goose hadn't sought Baker out. It followed that Baker wanted something from Goose. "You didn't come here to discuss ancient history. What *do* you need?"

Baker looked puzzled. "I don't understand."

"You came here for a reason, Corporal. Maybe we'd better get to it."

Shaking his head, Baker said, "No. I'm not due back till 0700 myself. I'd intended to speak to more of the men at the church, to allay their fears as much as I can." The big man was silent, and his tiredness showed on his face. "They carry on as best they can, but they feel they're hovering on the brink of disaster."

Goose didn't comment. Every professional fighting man—from

U.S. troops to U.N. military to Turkish army—knew that the Syrians were gathering strength for a final push against the city. And anybody with any knowledge of military tactics and the concentration of resources on both sides of the line was pretty sure which side was going to win. It didn't take a genius right now to predict that the Syrians' chances of rolling over them were pretty good.

"The men are afraid," Baker said.

"I know."

"They see how we're burying our dead here," Baker said. "They know that those fallen warriors aren't going home to families so those people can grieve more properly. That knowledge is putting more pressure on our warriors to survive."

"We're marking the graves," Goose said. "Later, when we get this thing cleaned up, the military will return for those bodies and bring them home."

"That time—if it ever comes—is a long way off. They know that."

Goose knew that too. With all the disappearances and the outbreak of so much violence, the American military was seriously undermanned.

"Once Syria invades this country, even if they hold only Sanliurfa and the southern part of Turkey, it'll be years before we take these lands back. If we ever do."

Goose remained silent. He knew other Rangers in the room were listening to the conversation. He didn't want that fact discussed here because it would drive down morale, but he wouldn't lie about the eventuality either.

"I came here this morning because I felt a . . . need . . . to speak with you," Baker said.

"What do you need?"

Baker shook his head. "It's not about what *I* need or the church needs, First Sergeant. I felt called here to find out what *you* needed."

Goose stared at him.

"More and more these past days," Baker said, "I've been getting strong feelings about things I'm supposed to do. I'm paying attention to those feelings."

"What things?" Goose was thinking maybe he needed to alert Captain Remington that they could have a problem on their hands. So far, none of Baker's churchgoers had caused any serious problems. Sure, there had been occasional fights between soldiers concerning religious issues, but they fought over meals and postings as well.

"There's nothing wrong with me, First Sergeant. Believe me."

Goose's doubts in Baker's psychological stability cleared up instantly, once he looked in his eyes. He *did* believe the big corporal, but he couldn't for the life of him understand why. These were battlefield conditions. Soldiers got stressed and had mental breakdowns. Even when they survived, a lot of them had to work through differing levels of post-traumatic stress syndrome. That fact was part of a professional warrior's life. But he'd never seen a saner man than Baker was right now.

"I don't know what prompted me to come here to see you," Baker said, shrugging. "Maybe it was the fact that since yesterday I've noticed you coming by at least a half-dozen times. At the church and at my postings. It seemed reasonable to think that you wanted to talk to me. However, I was willing to wait. I didn't think it was my place to seek you out."

"But you did."

"That changed twenty minutes ago." Baker smiled. "I could no longer put off speaking with you. The . . . feeling . . . got too strong. I didn't even have a clue what we might talk about. Not until I saw you with that Bible in your hands."

"I was just reading, trying to relax." And that wasn't an out-and-out lie. Goose *had* been struggling to relax. How could he not, knowing what he did about the involvement of the Rangers and what was truly at risk in the battle for Sanliurfa?

"The book of Revelation, with all its prophecies of doom, isn't the most relaxing reading material," Baker said.

Goose hesitated. "No, it's not. But that wasn't exactly a lie. I wanted to know more about what was coming, what things are going to be like after the Rapture."

"Because you think it's already happened?"

Think, Goose thought to himself. *Not believe. World of difference.* He said, "I've had to admit to myself that it's possible."

Baker looked Goose in the eye. "I know your son was one of those who disappeared, First Sergeant, and I hate reminding you of the pain I know you must feel, but you need to remember that loss in order to give you a better understanding of what you're going through."

Baker was poking at what it felt like to lose Chris. Anger surged up inside Goose. He barely managed to grab on to it and throttle it back down before it escaped him and he did something he'd regret.

Baker was definitely stepping across the line when he brought Chris up.

"All those people who disappeared," Baker said, "your son among them, where do you think they went?"

Goose slowly shook his head. "I don't know." *Facts,* he reminded himself, *deal in facts.* The fact was that he had hoped Icarus would help him find a way to bring those people—and Chris—back from wherever they had gone. But Icarus had pointed Goose to the Bible, to the book of Revelation, and to what had to be the only answer.

"That many people," Baker said, "and *all* of the children. Those facts alone are staggering. Think what it means."

Goose kept his silence.

"Your friend Bill Townsend was among those who disappeared," Baker said. "You know what kind of man he was: a believer. I visited with Bill on a number of occasions."

Goose didn't know that.

"Bill tried to help me get my faith back," Baker said. "But after my wife and my child were killed in an awful car wreck, I felt bereft of God. I felt certain that He had deserted me and no longer cared about me." The big man's eyes shone with unshed tears. "But that day in the river when I was asked to baptize John Taylor, then after him all those men who came forward, when I was able to hold up the RSOV that had fallen from the mountain path, and finally when the earthquake came and washed the Syrian armored units away, I knew God cared."

Seated there in the makeshift barracks, Goose heard again the familiar lines of the Twenty-third Psalm.

"God saved us that day, First Sergeant," Baker said with childlike intensity.

One of the nearby Rangers cursed, then said, "Why'd God save us, Baker? So we could end up as targets in a shooting gallery for the Syrian army?"

Other men joined in, some of them supporting the cutting remark the Ranger had offered, while others argued with them.

The first speaker pushed himself up from his bed and crossed toward Baker. He was tall and lean and carried his assault rifle over one shoulder. A bloodstained bandage covered his right cheek. Another covered his right eye.

"In case you ain't exactly got a clue as to what's going on," the soldier said, "we ain't exactly saved. If I'da asked God to save me, I'da sure asked Him to move me right on outta this place. Or at least to keep the Syrian army from breathing down the back of my shirt."

Goose recognized the man with difficulty. Covered in layers of fatigue and dirt, the military men were starting to look alike.

Vaughn Turner was a redneck from East Texas. He was an aggressive soldier, following in the footsteps of a military father, but he had a problem with being too outspoken.

"I know what's going on," Baker said. "I've got a clearer idea of what's going on than you do."

Turner cursed again.

"Private." Goose stood up. His voice assumed the tough no-nonsense tone of a trained sergeant. He felt the familiar and painful throb in his knee.

Conversation in the barracks came to a swift halt.

Turner realized the change at once. He pulled himself together, coming to attention. "Yes, First Sergeant."

"You want to tell me if my eyesight's failing, Private?" Goose barked. "Because I see one more stripe on that man's shoulder than I see on yours."

"No, First Sergeant." Turner kept his eyes forward but couldn't keep all the anger from his tone. "Your eyesight is fine, First Sergeant."

"Outstanding," Goose replied, pulling his arms behind him and stepping up to the private. "I guess I can put off that visit to my optometrist then."

"Yes, First Sergeant."

"You still owe your unit rack time," Goose said, sticking his face within inches of Turner's and watching the younger man pull back. "Your fellow Rangers expect to have a well-rested fighting machine at their side the next time they step into a post with you."

"Yes, First Sergeant."

"Then I expect you to deliver on that."

"Yes, First Sergeant." Turner whipped a salute up immediately. "Permission to return to my rack, First Sergeant."

"Granted, Private." Goose returned the salute.

Turner about-faced and flopped back into his bed.

Glancing back at Baker, Goose said, "This isn't the place for this conversation."

Baker looked at Goose. "Maybe we could finish it somewhere else."

More than anything, Goose wanted to tell Baker no, that he was finished with the conversation. He wanted to be finished with all the confusion and the pain. He wanted to put that Bible down and never pick it up again.

But he couldn't. Icarus's conversation rolled through his mind like a ship at sea, tossing and turning and twisting at the mercy of an unrelenting storm. Even as he stood there, he thought of another media piece on Romanian President Nicolae Carpathia's stunning presentation at the United Nations in New York City.

The Antichrist.

Icarus's accusation echoed in his head. The memory of it wouldn't go away.

According to the book of Revelation, everything over the next seven years, minus a few days if the Rapture had truly happened, would turn on events controlled by the Antichrist. Using deceit and fear, the Antichrist would pull most of the world into turmoil and away from God, away from the redemption offered by Jesus Christ when He had died for the sins of anyone who would seek His Father through Him.

"You feel the pull too, don't you, First Sergeant?" Baker asked in a quiet voice.

Goose looked at the man. He wanted to deny the words, but he couldn't. "There are things," Goose said hesitantly, "that I need to know."

Baker smiled gently. "I understand. I see that in you, First Sergeant. Come on. There's a small shop not far from here. We can get coffee there."

Goose picked up his gear, slid his helmet onto his head, and looked at the Bible that Baker held out to him.

"Take it, First Sergeant," Baker urged. "You're going to need His Word. The time we have ahead of us is not going to be easy. You'll need everything you can get. But mostly you'll need to know what's coming."

Aware that most of the men in the barracks were watching him, aware too that how he reacted to Baker was going to set the tone for stories that were told among the soldiers throughout the city, Goose hesitated. Then he was immediately ashamed. His father had never been ashamed of his beliefs. His dad had never stopped questioning things that happened that he thought should not have.

Goose took the Bible and found a place for it in his chest pack as he followed Baker out of the room.

✵ ✵ ✵

United States 75th Army Rangers Temporary Post
Sanliurfa, Turkey
Local Time 0617 Hours

Descending the steep wooden steps into the cellar, Captain Cal
Remington ran his flashlight beam around its stone walls. The space
beneath the burned-out shell of a family-owned restaurant was larger
than he'd expected, but the low ceiling took away some of that sense
of space.

"Captain," Dean Hardin called out of the darkness. "Over here."

An electric torch flared to life and illuminated the dogleg turn to
the left. The harsh white light also illuminated Hardin and three
other Rangers standing around a man in a nomad's robes and
burnoose seated in a straight-backed wooden chair.

Hardin and the Rangers wore full combat dress stained by dust
and hard use. They all had NVGs—night-vision goggles—as well, so
they could see in the dark cellar.

Remington's flashlight was probably blinding his men. He flicked
it off and opened his eyes wide so they would more quickly adjust to
the light.

The man in the chair looked frightened. Blood flowed from his
swollen nose into his mustache and beard. His right eye was closed,
and his cheek was discolored and scraped from some kind of abrasive
impact. Despite the lines of pain and fear on his face, he was young,
maybe in his midtwenties. His swarthy skin and exotic attire made
Remington place him as one of the locals.

The cellar floor was hard-packed earth. The room smelled like an
open grave, a scent Remington knew from personal experience, but
had trace odors of sprouted potatoes and rancid flour mixed in with
the rot. Naked wooden beams shored up the hardwood floor above
the cellar. Shelves in various states of disrepair occupied the space in
the center of the room.

Remington figured that the restaurant had fallen on hard times
years ago. But it had survived, only to be bombed out by Syrian artillery. Hardin had found the place and used it for his own purposes.
Remington had been around the corporal long enough to know not
to ask what all of those purposes were. He looked at the man seated in
the chair.

"Please," the man said fearfully, "I have done nothing. I swear to you. I have done nothing. You must let me go. I will sing your praises to Allah."

Even under the circumstances, the man's English was pretty good.

"Who is he?" Remington asked.

"Abu," Hardin answered. "Got a last name I can't pronounce."

"Alam," Abu said. "I am Abu Alam. I am nobody. A gnat on a camel's rump. I assure you, sir, whatever was done was not done by me. I offer you a thousand apologies."

"You're sure this is the guy?" Remington asked. He already knew what Hardin's answer would be, but sometimes it helped to throw more fear a captive's way.

"Yeah." Hardin spat tobacco juice between his boots, then covered it over with dirt he scraped from the floor. "I've been trading with him over the last few days. Almost since we got here. Reason I noticed him, he was selling used American goods and making change with American currency." He spat again. "You know, Captain, we left a lotta dead men behind us when we retreated from the border."

Surprise lit Abu's face. "Those things! Those things—" He stood up from the chair.

Moving inhumanly fast, Hardin slapped the man back into the chair. Abu hit with enough force that he would have fallen over backward if Hardin hadn't put a foot on the chair's seat between the man's legs and pushed the chair back down.

Abu covered his face with his hands and screamed. Unfortunately for him, his shriek wouldn't penetrate the massive stone-lined walls. Besides being a place that guards wouldn't go, it was the reason Hardin had selected the place.

"Abu," Remington said.

The man stared at Hardin fearfully.

Opening the flap on his holster, Remington took out his sidearm and shoved the barrel against Abu's forehead, resting it between his eyes. Hardin and the other Rangers stepped back. Their hands automatically went to their assault rifles. If Abu tried to reach for the pistol, Remington knew his Rangers would kill the prisoner before he could even close his fingers on the weapon.

"No," Remington ordered as Abu's eyes widened and he started to move.

Abu froze. He sucked in a rattling breath.

"Now do I have your attention?" Remington asked. He pushed so hard against the pistol grip that the barrel of the gun was beginning to bruise Abu's flesh.

"Yes," Abu whispered.

"The minute I lose your attention," Remington said, "the minute I know you're lying to me, I'm going to pull this trigger and walk away from here." He paused, letting his words have their effect. "Do we have an understanding?"

"Yes." Tears slid from Abu's eyes and mixed with the blood on his face.

"Corporal Hardin," Remington said.

"Yes, sir."

"How do you think Abu came by those American supplies and the American money?"

"Two options, sir," Hardin responded. "Either he took those things from the American dead we left behind—which makes him a carrion feeder who needs to be eliminated—or he got those goods trading with the Syrians who took them from our dead, which makes him a danger to our men who needs to be eliminated."

"Abu?" Remington asked.

"Yes?"

"Where did you get the money and the items?"

Abu swallowed hard. "From trading, Captain."

"Trading with who?"

"Other traders. Men the corporal has traded with besides myself."

Remington knew Hardin always connected with the local black market whenever they were in the field. The Ranger captain also suspected Hardin managed illegal enterprises in the United States as well. Until Goose had caught Hardin stealing from a dead marine after the planes and helos had dropped from the sky the day of the disappearances, Hardin had always stayed one step ahead of any legal entanglements. A lot of Hardin's luck these past few years, though, had been due to Remington interceding on Hardin's behalf.

"What about the Syrians?" Remington asked. "Have you been trading with them as well? The Syrian military?"

Hopelessness filled Abu's sad eyes. "Yes, Captain. Yes, I have."

"Good," Remington said. "I'm not going to ask if you stripped the corpses of American fighting men to take their goods."

Desperately, Abu tried not to show his evident relief.

Remington filed the information away, though. If Abu had been on hand to steal from the dead military men, he'd been working the trade routes often.

"I'm not even going to ask if you've been giving the Syrian military information about our operations here," Remington said.

If he hadn't been in obvious pain from the beatings he'd gotten, Abu would have looked ecstatic. "Thank you, Captain. You are most gracious and wise."

"What I am going to ask you for," Remington said in a calm, level voice, "is information about the Syrian hard sites."

Abu started to speak.

Remington cut the man off, talking slowly and softly. "One lie, Abu. Just one. And they won't find enough of your skull to drink out of."

"Captain, I have not been everywhere among the Syrians." Abu swallowed again.

"But you have been among them?"

"Yes."

Remington reached into the pocket of his BDUs and took out a folded map. "Do you know how to read a map?",

"Yes. Though I am no scholar."

"I don't need a scholar," Remington replied. "I just need a guy who can speak and point. You can do that, right?"

Abu nodded. Nervously, he wiped at the blood streaking his face. He only succeeded in smearing it.

Remington shook the map open with one hand, using his other hand to keep the M9 in place against Abu's forehead. "The Syrians have a fuel dump. A place where they're stockpiling gasoline and diesel to supply the armor they're pushing north."

The existence of the supply line was a no-brainer. The distance between the Syrian-based command post and Sanliurfa necessitated a new staging point, as did the fact that the Americans and Turks and U.N. forces had booby-trapped their own fuel stores in the city. When the order was given to evacuate Sanliurfa, Remington would make sure that no fuel would remain in the city, even if he had to leave the city burning like Nero's Rome. He didn't plan to leave any useful equipment behind either. He knew his enemy would be unwilling to place their supply lines in plain sight of a potential fly-by discovery by an American or Turkish pilot. The Syrian command would want their fuel stores hidden.

Remington placed his thumb on his pistol's hammer and rolled it back. The clicks as it locked into place sounded ominous in the quiet cellar.

"I'm thinking," Remington said, "that there are caves out there in the mountains that the Syrians are using. Either to the west or the east of the route they're using to get to Sanliurfa."

"Caves," Abu said. "Yes, there are many caves."

"Have you seen the fuel stores?" Remington's plan was thin, but if successful—even though there would be "acceptable losses"—his plan would net the defenders of Sanliurfa a few more days' grace. The present military engagement could turn around in minutes if he could buy enough time to convince Turkey and the U.S. to invest more troops in the Sanliurfa theater of operations.

Abu licked blood from his lips. "I know where the Syrian fuel stores are, Captain."

Remington held out the map, careful not to occlude Hardin's field of fire. "Show me."

With a trembling hand, Abu shoved a forefinger at the topographical map. "There."

Looking at the map and estimating the distance, Remington saw that the Syrians were west of the road into Sanliurfa. "Are the fuel stores in caves there?"

"Yes. But that is not all that is there, Captain." Abu shivered. "There are also the ruins of a city."

Remington examined the map again. "There's no city on the map."

"Captain, several cities in this part of Turkey died out hundreds and even thousands of years ago. This place is a very old place. I am told some of the first cities in the world were here." Abu shrugged. "Only Allah knows if this is true. But I do know the bones of an ancient city are there. The Syrian dogs have dug hiding places in that dead city to store their gasoline and diesel."

Lowering the map, Remington looked at the man.

Abu held his gaze fearfully. He licked his lips again. "Please, Captain, I swear in Allah's name that I am only telling you the truth."

After waiting a beat, Remington said, "I believe you."

Relief flooded through Abu. He almost collapsed in the chair. "Thank you, Captain. You will not regret this."

"No," Remington said. "I won't regret it." He pocketed the map, holstered his pistol, and walked away from the man. "Hardin."

"Yes, sir?"

"Make certain I don't regret this." Remington thought his voice sounded cold and distant and alien even in his own ears.

"Yes, sir."

Silhouetted by the electric torch behind him, Remington saw the long black shadows on the stone wall in front of him, saw the shadow of the man seated in the chair and Hardin's shadow as he stepped forward with his assault rifle ready. In that instant, Abu must have realized that he was the only one outside of the Rangers who knew Remington was planning to target the Syrian fuel depot. He traded with the Syrians. Releasing him was out of the question. How could Remington trust the man to keep his silence?

"No! Captain! Please! I beg you! Cap—"

A quick burst of gunfire hammered Remington's ears as he started up the wooden steps. The muzzle flash momentarily erased the shadows on the wall to his left, even as the bullets permanently erased Abu Alam. When the shadows returned, the dead man's shadow was missing. Only the shadow of the empty chair stood between the Rangers.

"Thank you, Corporal," Remington said without turning around.

"Yes, sir," Hardin said.

"Stay here until we make arrangements to get rid of the body."

"Yes, sir."

Outside the burned-out husk of the building, Remington slid his sunglasses back on. He tried to control the nausea that squirmed through his stomach, but he failed. The image of Abu's shadow getting eradicated by the muzzle flash from the M-4A1 bounced around inside his skull like a pinball. Sour bile tainted the back of Remington's throat. He managed to hold off the worst of it until he reached the alley; then he bent forward and threw up.

The gut-churning purging left him weak, shaking, and lightheaded, but the feeling soon passed. He hadn't wanted Hardin to see that reaction in him. The sickness over one more meaningless death was a weakness in himself, and Remington hated it. But he'd had no other course of action. He had to hold the city. The Joint Chiefs had trapped him into taking the steps he had.

During his years as an officer, he'd seen men die horrific deaths. He had found their bodies after violent passings. But he had never so cold-bloodedly ordered an execution. There had been times when he'd had a chance to take a person alive, and he'd given orders not to risk his men, but he'd never had a man killed who had been so defenseless.

This time, though, he'd walked into that cellar knowing he was going to leave a dead man behind. He hadn't thought it would bother him. He had told himself that it wouldn't. He was only doing what he had to do, and he expected himself to do it.

The life lost in that cellar could save the lives of dozens—maybe hundreds—of the men in his command. He forced himself to remember that. He wasn't a murderer. He was a man in command accepting the responsibility of that command. An officer who accepted the burden of keeping his men alive and able to fight. Abu had to die so that his men had a chance to live.

And also so that he had a chance to win with the losing hand he'd been dealt by the powers that be. In the game of war, losers died. Winners lived and got to fight another day. And they had a chance at glory. Captain Cal Remington didn't intend to blow his chance.

His stomach spasmed again but nothing came up. He felt certain there was nothing left to lose. He cursed his weakness. It wasn't like he'd had a choice in whether or not to kill Abu. The Joint Chiefs had pushed him into killing. They'd sat back on their duffs and played war games, sacrificing *his* unit because they were afraid to risk what they were ordering the Rangers to put on the line every minute of every hour of every day that the 75th occupied the city.

He wiped his mouth with a handkerchief, then turned and walked back toward the waiting RSOV out of sight around the corner. A quick scan of the street showed him no one was around to witness his loss of control.

He thought about Corporal Dean Hardin waiting down in the cellar so patiently with the dead man. Hardin didn't act like killing the man had meant anything to him, hadn't even flinched when Remington had told him it would be necessary.

There was still, Remington knew, a huge difference between himself and Hardin, but the Ranger captain didn't know if that was a good thing or a bad thing. He only knew that the difference existed.

Remington was glad he had men in his command like Hardin, men who would see every nasty job done that needed doing and wouldn't hesitate about getting it done. Goose and men like him— which most of the Rangers tended to be with their sense of fair play and honor, even on terror-ravaged battlefields fighting enemies fueled by insane rage and selfish fear—wouldn't do what Hardin had done.

Of course, the upside of that was that Remington would never have to worry that Goose or those men would start up an illegal enterprise that might come up and bite their captain on his nether regions. Unlike Hardin.

Remington buttoned the flap over his pistol holster as he turned the corner in front of the burned-out shell that had once housed the restaurant. He pushed all thought of Abu and the man's execution from his mind. Maybe in the quiet of night that memory would return, but he knew why things had to happen the way they did. He'd stepped over the line, but he could live with it because it was for a good reason.

The RSOV's driver stood at the front of the vehicle smoking a cigarette and holding his assault rifle in one hand. His attention was focused on a midnight-blue Mercedes sports coupe idling in the street beside the Ranger vehicle.

Remington's adrenaline spiked as his gaze swept the luxury car. No one was supposed to be here. Certainly not some media geek with a camera. He scanned the nearby rooftops, wondering if Hardin or his team had somehow tipped off one of the broadcast groups. With the dead man in the cellar, the Ranger captain knew his career might end in the next few seconds.

Taking a deep breath, Remington pushed the throbbing fear from his mind. He was in control. No matter what, he was going to stay in control. He continued forward.

Black-tinted windows masked from Remington's view whoever sat inside the blue Mercedes. The German engine ran so quietly it couldn't be heard over the distant noises of the city, the vehicular traffic as well as the earthmovers. A helicopter buzzed overhead, but the pilot gave no indication of interest in the Mercedes.

A chill ghosted through Remington as he surveyed the vehicle and looked for clues about its origin. The vehicle gave the air of being an alien creature plopped down in the middle of the city's ruins. It looked too complete and too powerful to be touched by the vagaries of the war that had left Sanliurfa broken and shattered. The vanity plate on its front bumper read DEALZ.

"Captain Remington." The RSOV driver caught sight of Remington and wheeled around. He flicked the cigarette from his fingertips, crushed it underfoot, and stood immediately at attention. He snapped off a quick salute.

Remington returned the salute. "At ease, Private."

"Yes, sir."

"We have company," Remington observed.

"Yes, sir. A man to see you, sir."

"What man?" Remington never broke stride, but his hand drifted down to the holstered M9. No one had known in advance that he was going to be at the restaurant other than Hardin's handpicked crew. The driver hadn't known before Remington had given him instructions. Until Hardin and his team got rid of Abu's body, Remington couldn't afford to be tied to this site.

"The man didn't give his name, sir," the private answered.

"You didn't ask, Private?"

The private hesitated as if confused. "I confronted him, sir. I asked his name. That's SOP. He told me he didn't have to give me his name. He said that you would understand."

The statement made no sense to Remington. Getting names of people in a secure area was one of the first things a soldier working a post did—standard operating procedure.

"What does he want?" Remington asked.

"To speak with you, sir."

"Why?"

The private shook his head and looked lost. "I don't know, sir." His brow wrinkled in frustration. "I know I should have asked. I was going to ask. But he told me everything was going to be all right." A perplexed look twisted his features. "I guess—I guess that I believed him, sir."

Closer to the Mercedes now, Remington peered at the black glass and wondered who would be stupid enough to drive a Mercedes sports coupe into a war zone. He wondered even more how the car had stayed in showroom condition. Dust hadn't even settled on the midnight blue exterior. The finish gleamed like fresh-poured metal. Only Remington's reflection showed in the black-tinted window that was as shiny and nonreflective as oil pumped from a deep well.

Then the passenger window rolled down, sliding easily in its grooved channel, like the smoothly articulated movement of a trained athlete. Remington's reflection melted away and revealed the man sitting behind the steering wheel.

"Captain Remington," the man called out in a thick accent. The man had a shaved head and a rounded goatee of rich copper hair. His complexion was pale, as blemish-free as young, clean bone. Wraparound sunglasses hid the man's eyes. He wore a charcoal, pin-striped suit that fitted him as if it was tailor-made. In fact, Remington was pretty sure it had been.

"Do I know you?" Remington asked.

The man grinned, splitting the goatee and creating dimples in both cheeks. He didn't look older than twentysomething.

"No. You don't know me yet, Captain Remington," the man said. "But you'll be glad you met me."

Remembering the vanity plate on the front of the car, Remington said, "If this is a sales pitch, I'm not interested." He walked behind the RSOV and up to the passenger seat, standing between the Ranger vehicle and the Mercedes.

"Not a sales pitch," the man promised. "A deal."

"I'm not interested in any deals either."

The man leaned across the seat toward the open window. "I think you'll be interested in this one, Captain." He paused. "I guarantee you that it will be much better than the deal you gave Abu Alam just now."

Anxiety ripped through Remington like a Bouncing Betty land mine. The initial surprise leaped up at him just as the deadly booby trap was designed to do, then shattered into a thousand screaming pieces that ran throughout his mind.

Dropping his hand to his hip, Remington drew the M9 pistol, thumbed off the safety, and pointed the weapon at the driver of the Mercedes.

Still grinning, showing no fear at all, the man lifted his hands before him in surrender. Black driving gloves encased his hands.

"I assure you, Captain, you have no need for weapons. Or for violence of any kind."

Wary, knowing he was somehow trapped, that Hardin hadn't been as circumspect in his delivery of Abu Alam as he'd thought, Remington held the pistol in a Weaver stance, left hand cupped under the right. He rolled the hammer back with his thumb. The menacing click of the action was louder than the Mercedes' engine.

"I'm a friend, Captain," the man said.

"I know all my friends' names," Remington said. "It's a short list." He glanced around at the building rooftops, thinking that maybe the guy wasn't a media person after all and that the Mercedes was a decoy to catch him off guard.

"There's no one else here, Captain," the man said. "Just us. I give you my word on that."

"Private," Remington said to his driver.

"Sir."

"Secure this vehicle."

"Yes, sir." The private moved forward with his M-4A1 at the ready.

"I want the driver out, facedown on the ground."

"Yes, sir."

"If he resists, shoot him."

"Yes, sir."

Annoyance colored the Mercedes driver's face. "Really, Captain, this isn't at all necessary."

"Who sent you here?" Remington demanded.

"A friend." The man shrugged slightly. "I was a bit hasty in calling myself a friend of yours. I see that now. You're obviously a very careful man. But after we get to know each other, I know that we will be friends."

"Are you with the media?" Remington asked.

"No. But I do have a rather unique relationship with the media. I have . . . talents that they find useful, and that I find helpful in strategizing my other labors."

The private set up on the driver's side door. He reached for the latch but the door wouldn't open. Instead, seemingly of its own volition, the driver's window slid down.

"Private Horgan," the driver said in a calm voice.

"Yes, sir," Horgan responded. The private halted, frozen in his tracks.

"Your presence here won't be necessary. Return to your vehicle and await the captain there."

The private stood for a moment longer, then shook his head. Without a word, he lowered his weapon, turned, and walked back toward the RSOV.

"Private," Remington called. "*Private*. Follow the orders I gave you."

Horgan kept walking.

"Private, I gave you a command." Incredulous, Remington watched the private return to the RSOV and take his seat behind the wheel. Horgan sat still and silent and peered straight ahead as if oblivious to everything going on around him.

"Captain."

Turning to face the man in the Mercedes, Remington asked, "What did you do to him?"

"Merely convinced him that I'm not a threat to him. Or to you. I was able to do that because I am not a threat to you or to him. He knows the truth. I only wish I could convince you as easily." The man opened his hands and smiled again. "Please, Captain, time presses all of us. I've got a number of things to accomplish today."

Remington wanted to do nothing more than squeeze the M9's trigger and put a bullet through the man's smiling face. But he couldn't. As yet, the man had only shown some kind of hypnotic effect over Private Horgan. Probably the man had already given the private a hypnotic suggestion before Remington had ever returned to the RSOV. Maybe he'd even received a mind-control drug through brief physical contact. The man driving the Mercedes wore gloves, and Remington knew that the CIA and DARPA had experimented with all kinds of mind-control weapons over the years.

If Hardin were here, Remington would have ordered the corporal to shoot the man and be done with it. But he wasn't the corporal, and he had yet to kill a man in cold blood.

At least you haven't killed one with your own hands, a voice whispered inside his head.

Remington felt guilty. He slipped his finger from the M9's trigger. "I'm going to walk away. I suggest you put that vehicle in drive and go."

"I can't, Captain Remington. I've been assigned to help you."

"Who are you?"

"Felix," the man said. "You can call me Felix. It's a name that will serve as well as any other, and I've gone by that name before."

"All right, Felix, I want you to go away now." Remington kept the pistol pointed.

Shaking his head regretfully, Felix said, "I don't know what I'm going to have to do to convince you that I've been sent here to help you, Captain. We're on the same side."

"What side would that be?" Remington couldn't help thinking that the mind-control Private Horgan was evidently under was something CIA Section Chief Alexander Cody would have access to. Was Felix one of Cody's agents who hadn't been seen before?

"Ah," Felix said, nodding in understanding. "Paranoia. Do you know what causes paranoia, Captain?"

"I know what the business end of this 9mm pistol causes," Remington responded. "You're about to get that experience firsthand. I wouldn't bet on living through it."

"Paranoia," Felix went on, obviously not feeling threatened at all, "is simply a discomfort that comes about when you don't think you have control of a situation." He waved at the war zone around them. "You're standing in the greatest moment of paranoia in your life."

Even Remington couldn't argue that point.

"I'm here to help you," Felix said smoothly. "A good friend of yours asked me to come to you."

"Who?"

"Nicolae Carpathia." Felix grinned.

"Carpathia?" Remington was confused. "I barely met the man over a couple videoconferences."

"Nicolae has taken a special interest in you. He knows the kind of man you are, and the kind of man you are capable of becoming. Abu Alam's fate is proof of that." Felix paused, giving the Ranger captain a measuring glance. "I have to admit, when he first told me of you, I wasn't too impressed. However, he insisted you could be of use."

"Nobody," Remington said, "uses me."

"Pardon me, Captain. That isn't at all what I intended to say. What I meant to say was that dear Nicolae insisted you were an asset worth developing. A relationship worth pursuing. You are a man who can . . . become so much if you're only given the chance to follow your true nature."

Remington was certain he didn't like that any better. But he was stuck and didn't know what to do. Felix had implied that he knew what had happened to Abu Alam in the basement. Even if he didn't know the real truth, Felix could at least tie Abu Alam to Remington if anyone came looking. The media people had traded with the Arabs as well as with the Syrians.

One thing the newspeople would descend on like ravenous vultures was any story concerning improper actions of an American officer on foreign soil. Remington's cold-blooded murder of a civilian would seize newspaper headlines and television and radio sound bites. Even though Hardin had pulled the trigger, it was Remington's game, and he knew it. By the time the case came before the military courts and into the public eye, everyone would have forgotten that Abu Alam had to die to save the lives of the military personnel caught in Sanliurfa between a rock and a hard place.

Even if Remington managed to survive the holding action in the city, despite being critically shorthanded and facing the best that the Syrian army could throw at him, he would still be facing a court martial and probably a prison sentence. There would be no glory, no medals, and no career advancement for him. He wouldn't have a career at all.

Despite himself, Remington lowered the weapon and listened.

"Your action against Abu Alam was justified, Captain," Felix said gently. "Unfortunately, not everyone will understand that. Especially if they should learn of his unfortunate demise at the hands of your men. But then . . . not everyone is here where you are, are they? They're not having to make the decisions you're faced with."

"No," Remington said, knowing that Felix understood exactly the kind of situation he was in and the overwhelming odds he faced.

"You want to change your stance here in this city," Felix said. "Become less of the victim and more of the aggressor. Less of the lamb and more of the lion."

Remington's answer was immediate. "Yes."

"I can give you the means to do that."

"How?"

"You still don't have satellite reconnaissance."

"I did."

"I can give it back."

"For how long? Carpathia saw fit to take that away once."

Felix frowned. "President Carpathia is juggling a great many things at the moment."

"I know. I've seen him in the news." Remington envied the Romanian president his successes. The man appeared to be a consummate politician. He'd come from nowhere to immense power. He'd gained ground during the most trying of times. Things could not have gone better for Carpathia if he'd planned the disappearances himself. It was like he'd been standing ready, waiting for them.

"Nicolae's work at the United Nations is progressing better than he had hoped." Felix gestured with his hands. "May I put my arms down? I'm getting tired. I've done my best to put your fears to rest."

Remington nodded but he didn't put the M9 away. He didn't like how the other man just assumed everything would go his way. But at the moment things couldn't go any other way. The Ranger captain didn't intend to shoot the man. Not yet, anyway. However, he didn't intend to trust him yet, either.

Felix lowered his arms, placing his hands on the steering wheel so they were in plain sight. "Would it surprise you to learn that President Carpathia is going to be offered the position of secretary-general of the United Nations?"

That did surprise Remington. Despite the outstanding showing Carpathia had made at the General Assembly in New York only hours ago, no one had mentioned anything about the Romanian president taking a position within the United Nations. On the other hand, such a move didn't seem that far-fetched in light of Carpathia's universal acceptance by the people there, or by the media's reaction to him.

"It's true," Felix went on. "The announcement will be made in two days. Mwangati Ngumo, the president of Botswana and present secretary-general, is going to announce that he is stepping down. Ngumo is going to suggest that Nicolae take his place and put the matter to a vote."

Remington was stunned. How could Carpathia guarantee or even arrange all of that?

"Nicolae will become the secretary-general to the United Nations," Felix said. "No force in this world can keep that from happening."

The sincerity and certainty of the man's words swept over Remington with conviction. Slowly, he holstered the weapon. "If Carpathia is becoming secretary-general, why would he be interested in me?"

"Because he has plans, Captain. Huge plans. Wonderful plans." Felix stared at Remington and smiled. "But plans require people to put them into effect and to keep them moving. Nicolae wants you to be part of those plans and part of that movement."

"How?"

"Nicolae plans to revamp the Security Council," Felix said. "As secretary-general, Nicolae is going to ask for unilateral disarmament among the member nations."

"That will never happen."

Felix's smile grew wider. "All around the world, Captain Remington, people are afraid. They fear the disappearances, but they also fear each other. And they fear the primitive sides of themselves and others that will lash out in the coming darkness. They are ready to listen to a calm voice that will lead them out of the darkness. Nicolae has that voice."

Remembering the way Carpathia had conducted himself in the media interviews and how much airtime he was getting, Remington doubted there was a person left in the world who didn't know who the Romanian president was. Carpathia had also made great inroads into world politics.

If it was true that Carpathia was about to close the deal on the position of secretary-general of the United Nations, how far could the man go? The possibilities were staggering.

"You believe Nicolae can do this, don't you?" Felix asked.

"It's not possible," Remington stated. He shook his head. No matter how much the media idolized the man, the steps Felix was describing were too big, too different from anything that had ever gone on before.

"But it is possible," Felix said softly. "Not just possible. It *will* happen. The nations of the world will lay down their arms and let Nicolae assume leadership of a one-world peacekeeping force. He will guide them all into times of peace and prosperity that the world has never before seen." He paused, smiling. "Nicolae has the power, Captain Remington. You've seen it in him."

Thinking back on all those press conferences, Remington knew that Carpathia did have that kind of power. No one had ever seen a man like him.

"Nicolae wants you to be part of that coming empire," Felix said.

Empire. Remington liked the sound of that. "Why?"

Felix shrugged. "Because he has talked with you and he liked you. He said the two of you had kindred spirits. He admires the way you desire responsibility for the leadership of others. That is a natural thing for a man gifted with your vision and your abilities. He said all you need is someone in power who could recognize that in you."

Remington accepted that, thinking it was high time someone saw those qualities in him.

"When Nicolae calls his army together," Felix said, "he wants men who can be leaders. He wants you. And in order to have you, you must survive your present situation. He wants you to achieve the glory that is your due."

"I have a plan to strike back against the Syrians," Remington said, wanting to share what he had developed. "I know how to buy time for the people here, maybe convince the Joint Chiefs that we can hold Sanliurfa."

"Nicolae will help you," Felix said. "First through me, then through public support of your efforts here. Everything will come together. But sacrifices will have to be made."

"I'll make them," Remington said.

"You will," Felix told him, flashing a confident smile. "Abu Alam was only the first of many. The way will be costly, but your efforts and those sacrifices will take you to those things you most desire in this world." He paused. "Let me help you. Let Nicolae help you."

Remington hesitated only an instant. "All right."

*   *   *

United States 75th Army Rangers Temporary Post
Sanliurfa, Turkey
Local Time 0639 Hours

"You have to remember that I'm still studying everything I can about the Tribulation." Corporal Joseph Baker sighed regretfully. "I'm embarrassed to tell you that I'm lacking several of the books that would help me in researching these times. During the years I stepped away from God, after I lost my family, I let many things go."

"Losing your wife and child like that," Goose said, "had to have been hard."

Baker nodded. "It was, First Sergeant, but I should have been stronger. My faith should have been stronger. I was brought up in the Lord, and I should have stayed there. But I was weak."

Goose remembered how he berated God over Chris's disappearance, and how he continued to have his doubts about whether the Rapture really occurred or whether God cared about him. "It's not easy."

Baker looked at him, started to object, then obviously remembered that Goose had been through similar circumstances. The big corporal nodded. "It's not easy. I don't think it's supposed to be."

"Letting go?" Goose was surprised at how tight and hoarse his voice got. Talking like this disturbed him, like the end of the world was at hand. Like there was no way Chris would be returned to him.

"Believing," Baker said. "If believing was easy, everyone would believe. There would have been no one left behind when the Rapture occurred."

"Why would God make believing hard?"

"That's the point," Baker said. "God makes faith easy. Jesus shed His blood to save us so that we would know everlasting life. That's all we have to believe. Nothing else. All we need is belief the size of a mustard seed. But even that little thing seems beyond most people." He took a deep, shuddering breath. "So simple a belief was beyond me for a time. Satan makes believing hard. God offers us a world beyond this one, a world of wonders that we can only begin to imagine. Eternal life. Constant happiness. No one who lives here can imagine such things. Moreover, Satan dwells here, in this world that we think we know and understand. Satan exerts his influence here in this place, and many believe in the evil that the Great Deceiver shows them and calls truth. But this place, First Sergeant, this is the real illusion."

Goose straightened his leg and tried to find a comfortable position for his throbbing knee. His eyes felt grainy and he knew the three hours of sleep he'd managed before Baker had come to him wouldn't be enough to get him through the coming day.

They sat at a table in the back of the small coffee shop Baker had suggested. The windows facing the street were stripped of their glass, victims of one Syrian attack or another. The owner and his wife prepared breads and coffee in the back using a bricked wood oven that the man's father had built nearly forty years ago.

Before the Syrians had invaded, the coffee shop had also offered pizza, a concession to foreign tourists. Without electricity, meats and soft cheeses quickly spoiled. But the traditional menu was basically unchanged. The family who owned the coffee shop made their breads on a daily basis. The flour was from stockpiled stores. They used milk and eggs from the goat and chickens they kept penned out in a small lot behind the building.

Normally the family—the husband, wife, and three small children who had vanished—lived in the upstairs portion of the shop, but lately the times weren't normal. During the nights, the husband and wife now slept in the cellar below the shop. On good nights, when they felt the military holding the city was in control of things, they slept on the floor of the shop, where they could watch their possessions better. They wouldn't leave, Baker had said, because they wouldn't desert the city until they had their children back—or knew that they would never return.

"I hope you find peace concerning your own son," Baker said to Goose.

"I do too," Goose said. He tried not to say anything more, but he couldn't help himself. His anger at God was too strong. "Taking Chris like that, if that is what happened—"

"The Rapture *did* occur, First Sergeant. That is the cornerstone of the rest of your belief, and the building block to the peace with God that you seek."

Goose nodded and breathed out slowly, striving to control himself. He tried to speak, then had to try again. "It doesn't make sense."

"That God would take the children?"

"Yes."

Baker shook his head. "I disagree. I think it makes perfect sense. God cherishes the innocence of children. So He reached down and removed them from harm's way. Every good general would do that for a civilian population, and God is preparing for the final battles against the Great Deceiver."

"But He took them from *us*," Goose said. "He took my son from *me*." Goose could feel tears threatening to fall, and he held them back by sheer willpower.

"Do you truly blame God for this?"

"Yes," Goose replied without hesitation. "Who else is there to blame?"

"Satan."

"Satan didn't take my son."

"No," Baker said agreeably, "and aren't you glad that Satan didn't? Have you ever thought about what Chris's life would be like right

now if he were still here with us? How terrified and vulnerable he
would be?"

For the first time, Goose realized the truth of that. Chris was safely
out of the line of fire from the greatest enemy mankind had ever
known and struggled to deny. He was safe; he was with God. Forever.

Pain threatened to bring back the tears at that thought.

"So you see?" Baker asked.

"I still don't want to accept it. I miss my son. Chris was safe back at
Fort Benning."

"Was he?"

"Yes. I've talked with Megan." Actually, now that he thought
about it, Goose hadn't been able to talk to her for days. Phone communications had been spotty. Few military men had been able to get
in touch with their families. "Things are confused at the post, just like
the things we've seen on television, but everyone there is safe, including my stepson, Joey."

"Things there are safe *for now*. The world isn't going to get better.
Cataclysmic events lie ahead of us. Many people will perish." Baker
sipped his coffee. He glanced at the bread on the small plate in front
of Goose. "You need to eat, First Sergeant."

"I'm not hungry."

"Eat anyway."

Reluctantly, knowing he would need his strength, Goose turned
his attention to the bread. Despite the primitive conditions, it was
good.

"The time has come for the world as we know it to end," Baker
said. "That was written in the Bible more than two thousand years
ago. We weren't told all of the details of God's plans for battle, but we
were told some of them."

"Seven years, right?" Goose asked. "That's how long the Tribulation will last before there's an end to everything?"

"Yes. God took the children and raptured His church to get them
out of harm's way. A soldier protects those who cannot protect themselves."

"Bill Townsend was a soldier," Goose pointed out. "He vanished.
We could have used him here." *I could have used him here.* Goose immediately felt selfish, but he also knew he was right. "There were a lot
of good soldiers among the missing men that we could use now."

"Bill and those others earned their places in heaven, First Sergeant. You can't begrudge them that. They knew the Lord better than
we did before the world changed so much for the rest of us."

"I don't begrudge them that. But I wish they were here."

"Those of us who were left behind," Baker said, "we have to learn to fight our own battles. We must come to our beliefs truly and without holding back. Many people—if not most—who were left behind will not survive these next seven years." He paused. "You saw the dead children in Glitter City? And the bodies of the children who were killed in the SCUD attack launched on this city?"

The images of the small corpses flooded Goose's mind. He remembered that one of the first tasks Baker had volunteered for when they had reached Sanliurfa was the comfort crew. Those men had prepared mass graves to empty the city of the dead. They had taken the dead from their loved ones, gathered broken, gory corpses, and buried them with as much honor and dignity as possible under the circumstances. Baker had served prominently among those teams.

"Yes," Goose said. "I remember. I won't forget them."

"Nor should you." Baker looked at him. "But for the grace of God, soon you could be burying your own son as so many of these families have done."

The thought hammered Goose, making him feel shamed and agonized at the same time. "I know," he whispered.

"The sad thing is, First Sergeant, you have another son that wasn't so blessed. You still have a son who's at risk in this world, and that is a frightening thing."

Goose thought of Joey. The last he'd heard, Joey had left the house after an argument with Megan. With the phones out, he didn't know if Joey had returned. Or even if Joey was able to return. Baker was right. Joey was still at risk.

"Chris is gone from you," Baker said, "lifted on high by God Himself. Thank God in your prayers that you didn't have to bury him."

"I know." Goose let out a tense breath. "I just wish that all of this was easier to accept."

"Don't wish for that, First Sergeant. *Pray* for it. God will answer those who call on Him. Read Psalm 145:18."

Goose nodded.

"Now, as to what we can know and guess of the Tribulation," Baker went on. "We know that those left behind will be tested for seven years. At this point, I can only tell you about the first twenty-one months. I could guess at the rest of it, but I don't want to do that."

"Nearly two years' worth of battle plans," Goose said. "I can live with that. As of right now, we're still going day-to-day here."

"During these first twenty-one months," Baker said, "we're going to witness miracles and cataclysms known as the seven Seal Judgments. And according to the book of Revelation, the next twenty-one months will be filled with the seven Trumpet Judgments."

"I know a little about the Seals," Goose said. "Those have been talked about a lot outside of the Bible."

Baker nodded. "Before those begin, though, the Antichrist will rise to power. He will promise peace and find a way to unite the world. Many people will fall for the great lie the Antichrist spins because, during the time of fear and confusion that is upon us now, they will want to believe that someone knows exactly what to do. They will seek a leader, and the Antichrist will be swept into position by that need."

"And someone here in this world that we think we know and understand is easier to believe in than in God."

"Exactly. You see the problem."

"Bad intel," Goose said. "Wouldn't it be easier if Jesus just returned now?"

"Or if we'd all been raptured?"

"Yes."

Baker leaned forward. "Not all of us were deserving, First Sergeant. Staying here, dealing with the terrible things going on in this world, this is the course set before us by God Himself. We will be tested and forced to look inside ourselves to find our faith. It just has to be."

"I have a problem with that, too," Goose said.

"Many people who come late to their faith are going to struggle with that concept. If things could be any other way, they already would be. This is what we have to deal with. Just like we have to deal with being stuck in Sanliurfa."

"If God loves us, why didn't He just take us as we are?"

"God does love us," Baker said. "That's why we have this second chance to get it right. And all the reason in the world to do so because there will be nothing left here to cling to."

"I wouldn't abandon people."

"As a person or as a Ranger?"

"As either."

"But we left men behind at the Turkish-Syrian border during the retreat. They fell and we kept going."

"We couldn't stop."

"No," Baker agreed. "And those men became 'acceptable losses.'"

"So that's what we are in God's eyes? Acceptable losses?"

"No."

"Then what happens to those who die now?"

Baker took a deep breath. "That will be between those people and God, First Sergeant. In my heart and according to Scripture I have read, I believe that He will be merciful and accept them and only turn away those who truly deny Him. But our faith wasn't as strong as those who left us. So we owe this world a death. Regretfully, that death will probably be even more horrible than we have ever imagined for ourselves."

Fear thudded through Goose as he thought about Megan and Joey. If Baker was right, if the world was going to end in seven more years, they would have to die then. *If not before. God, You can't allow that to happen. You took Chris. I can't live through losing them too. I swear to You I can't.*

"What are we supposed to do here?" Goose asked. He was a soldier. Soldiers were supposed to do something to protect innocents. "During this seven years? Especially if so many are going to die?"

"Those of use left behind are going to get right with God," Baker said. "We no longer have a choice, and we won't be able to disbelieve any longer. Those of us who are strong enough will help the weaker ones to survive and to better understand everything they are facing. That will be our mission." The big corporal spread his hands. "I'm doing that now with my church, and you're doing that now by questioning God and this world and your place in it."

"I'm a soldier, not a preacher."

"You're a witness. As you become stronger in your faith—and I believe you will, First Sergeant—others will watch you and follow your lead. I believe you have a large part to play in the coming battle for the souls of those left behind."

A big yellow bulldozer stained by dust and blackened by fire damage rolled through the street. A cargo truck filled with soldiers carrying shovels as well as assault rifles rolled along in the bulldozer's wake. The bright morning sunlight already promised a long, hot day.

For a long time, Goose considered what he should say. He had told Baker most of what Icarus had told him, that the man had confirmed that the world had been raptured and they now faced the Tribulation.

"I was also told the identity of the Antichrist," Goose said.

Interest showed on Baker's bruised face. "By this man you talked to? Icarus?"

"Yes." Goose had hesitated only a short time before revealing part of Icarus's story to Baker early in their conversation. For some reason, it was easy to trust the big man. That impulse to talk to Baker chafed at Goose. If there was anyone in the city whom he should have told, it should have been Cal Remington.

They had been friends for seventeen years, brothers in blood, with trust and friendship forged on battlefields. And, as commanding officer of the Rangers posted there in Sanliurfa, Remington should have been the one to decide to whom the information was disseminated, how much would be told, and what weight would be given to Icarus's claims.

"Do you believe him?"

"I think so." Goose hesitated. "I mean, it could be. Have you heard of Nicolae Carpathia?"

A sour look darkened Baker's round face. "I was already considering Carpathia for the role of Antichrist."

"Why?"

"Because of his sudden rise to prominence on the world scene and his interest in the United Nations. Although U.N. Peacekeeping forces have been somewhat ineffectual throughout the world since they were first set up, the fact remains that the U.N. is a worldwide organization. Many connections across international borders are already in place." Baker spread his hands. "Do you know about Carpathia's history in Romania?"

"Just what I caught in the news."

"Apparently, Carpathia skyrocketed to power in Romania."

"I'd heard something about that. The previous president stepped down."

"The day before the attack by the Syrians and the Rapture occurred," Baker acknowledged.

"That doesn't mean anything."

"Perhaps not. But if we are going to look at Nicolae Carpathia as the potential Antichrist, let's consider everything he's done." Baker ticked off points on his fingers. "Becoming a rich man; stepping up to become an investor in international business; buying out several companies and making one out of them—as he did with OneWorld NewsNet; choosing to set himself up as a spokesperson for international concerns and getting a lot of attention for doing so; getting elected as a national leader in his home country; accepting the presidency of that country that was more or less handed to him, then using that position to immediately take advantage of a chance to speak before a world body like the United Nations. Those things aren't on the agendas of most people. Or even goals other people would be able to accomplish."

Goose thought about that. "No. But it almost sounds . . . right. From what I've seen in the news, the guy has deserved everything he's gotten. He's worked hard and he's . . . deserving. I can't think of a better way to put it."

"Exactly the way it should be for the Antichrist to come to power in plain sight of everyone, as the Bible foretells," Baker agreed. "If I hadn't been looking for signs of the Antichrist, I probably wouldn't have given Carpathia a second glance. But I was looking for signs."

"What does the Antichrist do besides unite the world?"

"You make that sound like unifying this world is an easy task. That's something that has eluded statesmen for decades, even in spite of all the advances in modern communication."

"If the Antichrist is going to get it done in twenty-one months or less, it might not be easy," Goose said, "but it's going to be quick."

"It will be quick," Baker agreed. "Look at how quickly Carpathia has already stepped into the limelight with the United Nations. The Antichrist's coming is signified by a white horse."

"The First Seal," Goose said, remembering what he'd read in the sixth chapter of Revelation.

"Yes. He will achieve world peace and unification in one to three months."

The timeline blew Goose away. "After all of this, after all the vanishings, the Antichrist is going to be able to pull the world together in a way that decades of politics hasn't been able to do?"

"Not after all of this," Baker said. "*Because* of it. If the Rapture had not occurred, if times were not this confusing, he would not be able to come to power. But just as quickly, once the Antichrist's true goals become apparent to some, a world war will consume the nations of the earth. That is represented by a red horse."

"War," Goose said.

"Yes. Three rulers from the south—I've not yet been able to ascertain who those people and what the nations will be—will oppose the Antichrist. Millions will die in that war."

Goose winced at the thought. Even after everything he'd seen in Sanliurfa, he wasn't so dead inside that he couldn't experience dread at those coming times.

"After that, the third Seal Judgment, a black horse, will usher in famine. From what I've read, the famine will last two to three months. More of those left behind will die."

"Then the fourth Seal," Goose said. "The pale horse. Pestilence and plague."

Baker nodded. "At the end of the first year, or shortly thereafter, a quarter of the world's present population will have perished."

The thought was staggering.

"Those things, First Sergeant," Baker said, "are the horrors that God has spared your child from. Chris will not suffer the war or the famine or the plague that could have ended his life so painfully."

Goose felt humbled, regretting—at least for the moment—that he'd ever thought that Chris should have remained on the earth with him. He was being selfish. In this instant—*Please, God, help me to understand and remember why You did what You did*—he understood what his son had been saved from.

"Millions will die during the fifth Seal Judgment," Baker explained. "When the sixth Seal Judgment takes place, God will cause an earthquake that creates devastation that reaches around the globe. Every living person will feel His wrath over the murder of His saints."

In his mind, Goose watched the mountain tumble again to save the retreating American, U.N., and Turkish forces from the advancing horde of Syrian armor only a few days ago. No one had ever found a scientific reason for the mountain to fall at that precise moment. But there was no doubt that the earthquake had spared hundreds of lives.

"All of this in twenty-one months," Goose whispered, overcome by the magnitude of the coming events.

"Yes," Baker replied. "The seventh Seal will bring about the beginning of the next twenty-one-month period, the time of the seven Trumpet Judgments." He shook his head. "I'm still trying to decipher all those portents and omens. I will, but it will take time."

Goose shifted his leg again, feeling the pain gnawing at his knee. "Time may not be something we have, Corporal. The Syrians are no doubt preparing their next assault, and it could be the final one. We don't have much left to give."

"We have time," Baker pointed out in a soft voice. "Seven years. All of that the worst period mankind has ever seen. If we survive it, we will witness the Glorious Appearing of Christ."

Glancing at his watch, Goose saw that the time was seven minutes till seven. The number resonated within him.

"Perhaps you and I won't see the end of those seven years or the Second Coming," Baker said, "but we need to prepare as many of the others as we can so they may prepare yet others."

Goose pushed himself up, favoring his injured knee. "It's almost

0700. We'd better get to it. Today we'll dig in a little deeper, hold on a little harder, and try to make it through whatever the Syrians have waiting for us."

Baker stood as well. "I hope this talk has helped ease your mind, First Sergeant."

"All the prophecies of terror and death coming to claim the world?" Goose shook his head. "It's hard to face all that, Corporal. Not and feel easy about anything."

"At least you know there is a plan in place."

Goose nodded and drained his coffee. He placed the empty cup back on the table. "I just wish I had known that God was going to take the children like that."

"Why?"

Goose looked at the other man as he pulled his rifle over his shoulder, then clapped his helmet on his head. "It would have been easier."

"What would?"

"If I had known that God was going to take my son from me, that the end of the world was so near, I wouldn't have brought Chris into this world." Goose was surprised at how tight his voice got and how much he instantly regretted what he'd said. He could barely remember the world before Chris, and it was almost impossible to imagine the world now without him. He hadn't been thinking, just speaking with the pain in his heart instead of the love.

Baker dropped a hand on Goose's shoulder. "God blessed you with your son, First Sergeant. Never lose sight of that. For the few short years you had your son, you were shown God's love." He paused. "Without Chris in your life, you would not have become the man you are today. You would not have become the man God needs now to help others learn what is going on. Try to keep that in mind."

Goose swallowed hard and choked his anger back. "It's not that easy. I want to be angry. I want Chris back, more than I want to understand."

"I'll pray for you."

"Thank you."

"And keep something else in mind, First Sergeant," Baker said.

Goose looked at the man.

"Just remember that when your tour of duty is finished in this world—" Baker smiled through his own tears—"you have a son waiting to welcome you into his arms again in the next. God blessed me with that understanding. I keep that close to my heart every day. Most of us are going to die at some point in this conflict. We're all on short time. There will be few veterans of this war left in this world at the end."

Goose nodded, then turned toward the door. The first thing he noticed was the sudden blackness that filled the sky. Amazed, he walked out of the coffee shop, drawn into the rubble-strewn street as were so many others. They all gazed at the sky in awe and fear. It was hard not to think that anything ominous didn't have to do with the Syrians poised to sack the city as they had so many times in the past.

For a moment, Goose thought the dark sky was from a dust storm blowing in from the south. Turkey had a few of those, and the extra dust, dirt, debris, and particulate matter blown into the atmosphere by the SCUDs, bombs, and artillery added to the already considerable problem.

But the dark masses swirling against the blue sky weren't dust clouds. Goose smelled the thick, cloying odor of fresh rain coming. The scent caught him as it always did, tickling his nose and tightening his lungs for the briefest of moments. The wind whipped through the street, picking up litter and papers and shingles and sending them scurrying. A chill chased the wind. In seconds, the heat index had dropped ten or fifteen degrees.

The coffee-shop owner, a middle-aged man with sad eyes and a large mustache, joined Goose and Baker on the street. He spoke his native language, then caught himself and said, "I'm sorry. I was just commenting on the rain. It seldom rains this time of year, and usually only a light shower or two when it does. Not a storm like this promises to be."

Goose nodded. "The weather reports I looked at last night didn't forecast any rain."

The wind plucked at Goose's clothing. The primitive feeling that he'd always experienced but never understood filled Goose. Storms excited him, left him on the edge of breathless and vibrating with energy. Megan and Wes Gander had never understood Goose's fascination, and would often come out to him as he watched a storm, telling him that he would be safer inside.

But Chris had viewed storms with the same intensity that Goose did. Although his son had watched the wind and the lightning and listened to the peal of thunder coursing across the heavens while safely held in Goose's arms, Chris had loved the storms as much as Goose did.

Lightning blazed across the dark mass of clouds. In the same instant, rain fell. Thick, fat drops marked the street and the surrounding sidewalks and patios like tracer fire. The drops formed miniature craters in the thick layers of dust and dirt that coated the street. Then the sky opened up and the deluge began.

His spirits pulsing within him, his mood lightened by the storm, Goose pulled his helmet off and tilted his face up to the sky. Wind tousled his hair and rain pocked his features, cold and hard and heavy as .50-cal rounds. Before his next drawn breath, the rain became a solid curtain that pounded the city.

"Never," the owner said, retreating to the open doorway of his coffee shop with both hands over his head, "have I seen such a thing as this. I have lived here all my life, and there has never been a storm like this."

Goose weathered the storm, feeling the cleansing power of it. But the rain meant something else too. A smile lit his face as he turned to Baker.

"What?" Baker asked.

"It's raining," Goose stated simply.

Evidently caught up in the infectious nature of Goose's joy, Baker smiled back. He shook his head in confusion. "I don't understand."

"There's a lot of dirt between here and the Syrian outpost," Goose said. "A lot more between that and Aleppo, from where the Syrian army transports are getting staged."

"So?"

"If it rains long enough, all that dirt's going to turn into mud." Goose pulled his helmet back on, already drenched in his BDUs but not minding. "Syria needs tanks, APCs, and heavy artillery to take this city. They can't move those through mud. At least, they won't want to because they'll be sitting ducks for the limited air force we have here. Even if they didn't worry about being attacked, mud is hard on tracked vehicles. Mechanic crews will be working repairs and teardowns the whole way."

Understanding dawned on Baker's face. He held his hands up to the sky, letting the rain strike his palms. "We're being given some time to heal. Praise God."

"Pray that it keeps raining," Goose advised. "I've got to find Captain Remington." If the rain held, it was going to change a lot of their strategy. He prayed that it would and took comfort in the raindrops drumming the street around him as he flagged down a jeep. Whatever the reason, the Rangers were being given a chance. And Goose intended to make the most of that chance.

"Can't sleep?"

Sitting in a patio chair in her backyard, looking out over the fort and play set that her son would never enjoy again, Megan glanced back toward the voice.

Jenny, one of the young girls living at Camp Gander, stood in the doorway. She looked tired and disheveled in a pair of sweatpants and a T-shirt she had borrowed from Megan.

"No," Megan admitted.

"You know," Jenny said, "I'll bet the doctor's office might have something you can take to help you relax."

"I've thought about it," Megan admitted. "A couple of the other counselors suggested the same thing. But I need to keep a clear head."

"They've got stuff that can do that too."

"I'll wait. I can't keep up this pace forever. I'll drop soon enough."

"True," Jenny said. "But it would be nice if you dropped somewhere short of the emergency room."

Megan offered a smile. "I'll try."

Nodding toward the phone, Jenny asked, "Did you call Goose?"

"I tried. There's some kind of storm that's blown into southern Turkey unexpectedly and is interfering with the phone lines." *God, please let that be it. Don't let Sanliurfa have fallen.* Megan glanced at the small television that had been brought out to the patio area. With all the teens in the house, it was hard to hear the reporters at times. Bringing the set outside had been a compromise she could live with.

"I've been watching the news but there's not much coming out of Sanliurfa right now."

"I know. All the news on every channel seems to be centered on Nicolae Carpathia. He's kind of shaking things up. Mind if I join you?"

"The last I saw you, you were asleep on the couch."

"Well, that didn't last as long as I'd hoped." Jenny crossed the patio and sat in the chair beside Megan. "Lieutenant Benbow called earlier."

"Oh?"

Jenny nodded. "While you were at the commissary."

The trips to the commissary were on a daily basis. At present, the commissary was staying open twenty-four hours a day to meet the needs of the base population and because they'd finally been able to get enough employees to cover all the shifts.

"I would have told you earlier," Jenny apologized, "except I fell asleep on the couch before you got back."

"Did he want me to return his call?"

"No. He asked how you were doing. Whether you were resting or taking time to work on the notes he'd asked you to make."

Megan gestured to the legal pad on the patio table. The top page was still blank. She couldn't seem to marshal her thoughts regarding Gerry Fletcher. "I'm trying."

"I asked him what was going on, but he wouldn't tell me. He just asked me to help you out if I could. So I'm going to ask you what's going on."

Megan hesitated.

"Don't shut me out, Megan," Jenny said. "I know you could use a friend right now. God knows I've been there plenty of times myself."

Taking a deep breath, Megan said, "All right, but we're going to need coffee for this."

"Not coffee. Hot chocolate. Coffee will keep you wired but hot chocolate may get you to unwind. I've got some in a thermos." Jenny vanished into the house and returned in a moment with the thermos, two cups, and two pieces of pumpkin roll. The orange bread wrapped around a creamy white filling.

"So this is what I smelled earlier."

"Yeah. It smells and tastes like it's hard to make, but it's really simple. Just have to do it in stages. The hardest part is keeping the pumpkin bread from tearing when you unroll it and reroll it."

Megan cut a piece off and ate it. "Cream-cheese filling?"

Jenny nodded. "You know what makes it even better?"

"What?"

"I'm going to lie to you and tell you it's all calorie-free." Jenny grinned, her smile white in the night's shadow.

Despite the somber mood, the fatigue and the anxiety, Megan laughed. They ate in silence for a while, then slowly, Megan told Jenny about the civil lawyer Boyd Fletcher had gotten and all the pressure that was coming down on Fort Benning, which in turn was coming down on her.

"That's ridiculous," Jenny said after they'd finished the dessert and Megan had completed the sketch of the day's events. "Can't Lieutenant Benbow get this case tossed out? I mean, it's not like you took Gerry away from his parents. God did that."

"Lieutenant Benbow says that General Braddock doesn't want the post vulnerable to a civil suit."

"So they sacrifice you."

"Yes."

"What are you going to do?"

"Fight," Megan answered.

"But you're risking the charges the army could bring against you."

"Yes, I am."

"You could lose."

"Yes."

Jenny peered at her with concern. "You could go to jail."

"Possibly."

"Then why risk it?"

Megan placed her fork on the empty plate. "Because I can't get any more scared than I already am, Jenny. That's what Braddock was trying to do to me today. Scare me into accepting the deal they've offered. I can't do that. If I did, I would be turning away from everything Goose and I have worked for. We didn't come this far in our lives to not go the distance. *I* haven't gone through everything I've gone through in my life and my career to start backing down. I've fought for myself before, and I'll fight for myself now."

Taking a deep breath, Jenny said, "If it were me, I'd be scared."

"I am scared. That's the point. If I don't fight back, I'm going to have to live scared for a long time. I did that after my divorce from Joey's dad. I was afraid of everything. But for the most part, I was afraid of the mistakes I was going to make. Mistakes with Joey. Mistakes with finances. Mistakes with my career." Megan shook her head. "I can't do that. I can't be afraid like that. Not again. Not for something I believe in."

"Do you think maybe you could reason with the Fletchers? get them to drop the civil charges? Maybe if they did that, the provost marshal would drop his."

"Benbow doesn't think the Fletchers will do that. Neither do I." Megan sipped her hot chocolate. "The bottom line is, Boyd Fletcher never cared about his son. Gerry was redheaded, something neither Boyd nor Tonya is. Boyd told Gerry on a number of occasions that he didn't even believe Gerry was his."

"Did he really believe that?"

"Sometimes. I think Boyd Fletcher mostly thought that when he wanted to distance himself from Gerry more."

"That's horrible."

Megan nodded. "Gerry didn't have a good life. He was a good kid, a bright kid. He should have had better."

"But you can't bring any of that into the trial?"

"I'm the one on trial here," Megan said. "Not the Fletchers. Benbow has reminded me of that a lot. Even if I somehow manage to get that past history introduced into court, there's a good chance it will work against me."

"Because you didn't do anything then."

"Right."

"That's so stupid."

"But that's where it is."

"So what are you going to do?"

"Hope. Pray. Trust Benbow to do his job well." Megan sighed. "I don't have much control over how the court case is going to go."

"However it goes," Jenny said, "I just want you to know that I'll be there for you."

"I appreciate that." Megan wrapped her arms around herself as the sudden chill of the night embraced her. "I just wish I could talk to Goose and let him know what's going on. And I wish that Joey would come home. Or that I knew for certain he was all right."

"I do too. I still feel a lot of why he isn't here now is my fault. He was really angry with me when he left."

"It wasn't you. If Joey was angry with anyone, it was probably me. He's been angry for a long time. Thinking back on it now, I see that. But I thought I was handling everything all right. I was just hoping that when Goose finished with his tour in Turkey everything would be all right."

"He'll be back."

"I hope so. Until then, I've got to deal with what's on my plate here." Megan looked west, in the direction of Columbus. "I can't go out there looking for him."

Jenny took a deep breath. "I could."

"Where would you start?"

"I don't know."

"Do you know any of his friends' names?"

"No. Just the people at the Kettle O' Fish."

"Is that restaurant open?"

"I don't think so. I tried to call, to let them know where I am because I'm going to need a job when I get off-post again. All I get is the answering machine telling me there are too many messages in the box."

"I hadn't thought of calling there. I didn't even think about Joey trying to show up for work."

"I did. When you're on your own, the next paycheck is always something you're concerned with."

"You'd be better at tracking Joey down than I would. I don't think like he does. But it's safer for you here. Even if you found Joey, I know how stubborn he can be. He won't come home until he's ready."

"You're probably right."

"I've been praying for God to look out for him. I'll keep doing that, and I'll try to be patient. As long as nothing happens to him, I believe he'll be back. I've seen a lot of kids run away from home. You can't bring them back at this age and make them stay. That's up to them."

"I know. I just wish I could help."

Megan was silent for a moment, her mind racing. "There's something else I could use your help on."

"What?"

"That book you were reading about the end times—the Rapture and the Tribulation—I read it last night."

"What did you think?"

"I think you were right. I think that what that book talks about is going to happen. *Is* happening."

Jenny nodded. "The whole Antichrist thing is creepy. Thinking that a guy like that can just step into power and control the whole world for a while."

"Look at what Hitler did in Germany in World War II," Megan said. "Before the war, Germany's economy was flattened. The people lived under horrible conditions. They wanted change, wanted someone to come along and change their lives. Hitler did that. Even before the disappearances a lot of people—here and around the world—were looking for someone like that. Someone to take responsibility for an unstable economy, to tell them job layoffs would never touch them, to tell them how to avoid losing their jobs, their homes, and their families." She nodded toward the TV, which was muted but still broadcasting. An image of thronging crowds protesting in the streets of Los Angeles filled the screen. "People are more scared now after everything that has happened. They're scared all around the world."

"Nicolae Carpathia could be who we need to keep the Antichrist from power," Jenny said. "Have you seen that guy and listened to him?"

"Yes." Despite her own problems and worrying over her son and husband, Megan *had* noticed the young Romanian president in the news. Cameras and the media were kind to Carpathia, generating interest immediately. "He leaves quite an impression."

"He's the kind of guy you want to believe in," Jenny agreed. "And his background. All those things he's done to improve his own country and now his plans to help out here and across the globe. If Nicolae Carpathia could get enough backing, maybe the Antichrist part would never happen."

Megan shook her head. "I think you've got to believe everything the writer says in that end-times book. You can't just pick the good from the bad." She paused. "I told you I was going to talk to Major Augustus Trimble this morning, but I didn't tell you why." She took a deep breath. "These kids I'm responsible for are scared, Jenny. Just as scared as we are. And just as confused. They've got just as many questions. The problem is, nobody's answering those questions. I told Trimble that I believed we were post-Rapture and into the Tribulation."

"And he already knew that?"

"He basically told me I was crazy."

"You're kidding. And he's the top chaplain at the post? How can that guy not see what's going on?"

"He's convinced that there's a military reason for all the disappearances. I went there to ask him to get some of the chaplains to start teaching classes about the Tribulation to the kids. They need to know what's going on. They need to know what to expect and what they're going to have to do."

"But the chaplains aren't going to do that?"

"Trimble's not going to ask them to."

"You could ask them."

Megan shook her head. "Without Trimble supporting it, I don't think I'd get far. This is the military we're talking about. Nobody wants to break rank and file, or buck the chain of command. Trimble's negative answer pretty much covered anyone else."

"So what do you want from me?"

"In addition to counseling," Megan said, "I'm going to start teaching about the Tribulation. What I understand of it, anyway. I'm going to get copies of as many of those books as I can get my hands on, and I'm going to put them in the hands of the kids I know are natural leaders. Kids who will talk to the other kids and help them work through this. If you don't mind, I'd like you to start doing the same thing with some of the kids here at the house. When you have time. If you think you can. I know it's asking a lot."

Jenny thought about it. "I'd be happy to do it, but I don't know how good I'll be."

"If you're good enough to start those kids asking questions and searching through those books, you'll have done everything I could have hoped."

"Not everyone we talk to is going to understand or even believe—"

"But if we can get a few kids talking, we can make this information spread," Megan finished. "They're looking for answers, Jenny. Maybe we can't give them all of the answers, but we can at least point them in the right direction. They can help each other. And us."

"Maybe, but you've got another problem."

Megan raised an inquisitive eyebrow.

"Trimble's not going to like you stepping onto his turf."

Nodding, Megan said, "I thought about that, and I have to admit that made me hesitate. For all of two seconds. Jenny, that man is a jerk. He's pompous and he's arrogant, and he's afraid of making a mistake. Maybe doing this will light a fire under him. He can decide if he wants to be part of the fire or stand there and get burned."

❄ ❄ ❄

United States 75th Army Rangers Temporary Post
Sanliurfa, Turkey
Local Time 0717 Hours

The two privates standing in front of the temporary command post in the basement of a government office building near the center of the city stepped forward and confronted Goose. They held their assault rifles at the ready.

"Privates," Goose said, looking from one man to the other. They stood under an overhang and were protected from the continuing deluge that slapped into the street behind the first sergeant. He stood soaked to the skin from his brief trip across the street.

"I'm sorry, First Sergeant," Private Malone said. "Captain Remington's orders. No one in or out unless they're cleared by security."

"Including me?" Goose asked. He'd never been stopped at the door before.

"Yes, First Sergeant."

Goose knew Remington was still ticked off about the whole Icarus snafu, because the captain hadn't been in direct contact with him for hours. Remington had only checked in then to let Goose know he wasn't pleased with the base-recovery speed or the fact that Corporal Baker's church attendance was growing. Both were issues that Goose had little control over.

Shutting Goose out of ops was behavior Remington had exhibited before. This increased distance between them served as a silent reminder that they were officer and first sergeant now instead of equals and an official notice that Remington didn't like having his authority questioned or negated in any fashion. If Remington discovered that Goose actually talked with Icarus, the first sergeant knew the captain would have him up on charges immediately. Goose refused to worry now because he knew that when Remington needed him, all would be forgiven. The only option at the moment was waiting it out.

Besides that, there wasn't much Remington could plan or strategize that would surprise Goose. Most of Remington's actions were dictated by the amount of damage the Syrians had caused during their latest attack. During the recovery briefing, Goose had organized most of the mission and tasking lists himself, only passing them through Remington's office for the rubber-stamp treatment.

The few changes the captain had wanted had been cosmetic things, timing issues, or inconsequential items that served only to remind Goose who was in charge. Remington hadn't wanted to deal with the day-to-day nuts and bolts of command. Goose knew the captain was striving to find some way to come out a winner. That was Remington's nature, and that was what made him an excellent officer.

"Check the clearance," Goose ordered. He turned from the privates and peered out at the street.

Rain drummed the broken concrete and poured into the gutters. The streets flooded quickly because Sanliurfa wasn't designed to handle this amount of precipitation. A cargo truck sped by, and its tires whistled wetly as they plowed through standing water.

Private Malone talked quickly into his headset, identifying Goose and letting the security detail know Goose wanted to see the captain. A moment later, the security teams inside the building cleared Goose.

After he entered the door, a two-man security team met Goose. They flanked him without talking as he headed for the stairwell to the left that led to the underground basement where the command post nerve center was set up.

As he glanced around the open area of the office building's main lobby, Goose saw that security in all the areas had been stepped up. All the security personnel were Rangers. No one had notified him that security for the ops center was being bumped up.

He took the stairwell down, wishing he'd taken the elevator, but he was too proud to favor his injured knee like that. He gritted his teeth against the throbbing pain and kept the knee in motion.

The office building was one of the newest constructions. It had leased space to companies and corporations all over the world. Those companies and corporations had been some of the first to evacuate Sanliurfa after the first wave of SCUDs.

The basement area had been designed to withstand terrorist attacks and even operate cut off from the rest of the city for a time. Auxiliary generators kept the power on to the belowground offices even in times of power outages.

Goose and the privates' footsteps echoed in the hallway as he followed the familiar path to the command post's nerve center. When he entered the room, Goose was surprised at the amount of activity. Evidently Remington had called all three shifts in.

The large room was darkened except for the pale, glowing light of dozens of computer screens on desks as well as on walls. As Goose's gaze swept the monitors, he noted instantly that many of the op techs were watching satellite pictures of the area around and north of the Turkish-Syrian border. Ordnance tape held thick, fat serpents' coils of cables together and fastened to the tiled floor.

"When did we get satellite access back?" Goose asked.

"I'm sorry, First Sergeant," one of the two privates accompanying Goose replied, "but we're not at liberty to discuss anything happening here at this time. Captain's orders. We're on a communications blackout with the rest of the military. Our guys as well. Everything in this area operates on a need-to-know basis. So far, you're not cleared for that knowledge."

So we've got satellite access and we're not telling the U.N. Peacekeeping force's commanding officer or Colonel Mkchian of the Turkish army, Goose thought, and immediately felt uneasy. When those two men discovered that Remington had somehow gotten access to a satellite array, Goose knew the relationships among the three military teams were going to be strained. The strategy wasn't the wisest in the present situation because the secret could divide loyalties, but Goose knew Remington had chosen to play it that way because the captain kept to-tal control. Remington worked to keep control of everything he was involved with.

The Ranger captain stood at the back of the room in front of a huge wall screen. When Remington's cybernetic ops teams had first hit Sanliurfa, they'd made the rounds among the computer stores and shops and salvaged every bit of equipment they could, adding to what they already carried and replacing what they'd had to abandon at the border. In hours, they'd cobbled together a nerve center that looked like it could have managed space-shuttle launches.

Remington was talking to a man in civilian clothes. At first Goose thought the man might be one of Cody's CIA operatives. Goose's stomach clenched, and his mind filled with questions as he consid-ered the possibility that Remington was working with the CIA. That might explain the satellite access. Goose couldn't help wondering if the CIA had finally caught up to Icarus and if the rogue agent had told Cody and his people that he had told Goose everything.

When the man turned to face Goose, the first sergeant saw some-thing predatory in the man's gaze. Even standing there in Kevlar with his assault rifle and sidearm, Goose felt more vulnerable than he had on the battlefield. The man was tall and bald and broad. A mustache and goatee marked his Middle Eastern features. But his clothing was expensive, a European suit that hadn't come off the rack. A dangling earring in the shape of an upside-down pointed star hung from his left ear.

The man smiled at Goose, but there was nothing friendly about the expression. The first sergeant almost felt like he'd been threat-ened.

"Captain," one of the privates said just before they came to a stop a few feet from Remington. "First Sergeant Gander reporting, sir."

Reading the situation, Goose remained at attention. He watched as the scenes shifted on a rotating basis every few seconds. The big screen was divided into eight sections, all of them showing Syrian armor and troop movements.

"At ease, First Sergeant," Remington said.

"Yes, sir," Goose responded. "Thank you, sir."

The two privates took three steps back, but never left Goose unattended.

"What brings you here, First Sergeant?" Remington asked.

"The rain, sir." Goose felt foolish as soon as he gave the answer. He'd wanted to say more, but his instant read of the captain's mood had shut down his enthusiasm. Also, the guilt for having talked to Icarus behind the captain's back and telling Baker about it came fullblown to the surface.

"You came here to tell me it's raining?" Remington waved a hand toward the computer screens. "I know it's raining, First Sergeant. I can tell you all of the immediate vicinities where it is raining. In just a few seconds, I can tell you where it is not raining."

Goose tried to ignore the biting sarcasm embedded in each word the captain spoke. "With the rain, Captain, I doubt very much that the Syrians will move their armored cav units."

"No, First Sergeant, they are not moving. Nor do they show any signs of moving until this rain stops. I've already confirmed that." Remington waved to the screens where Syrian T-62 and T-72 tanks sat alongside BTR-60 APCs and artillery field pieces covered by tarps and tied to stakes hammered in the ground.

Goose tried not to let the cold distance in Remington's tone throw him. "I thought we might discuss possible strategies for taking advantage of this reprieve, sir."

"That's commendable, First Sergeant," Remington said, "but I was already starting to plan those strategies forty-two minutes ago when I learned the unexpected storm front was gathering."

"We have satellite access again, sir?" Goose asked.

"I do." Remington nodded.

"I wasn't aware that the U.S. satellites were back online. The media people still seem pretty much out of the loop and don't have access to these connections."

"The U.S. satellites are not back online, First Sergeant."

Goose thought about that. The mil-sat systems the Rangers presently tied into were part of the same system that supported the American media efforts. If he wasn't using those, that meant Remington had an outside source for the feeds on the screens.

"You have feeds," Goose stated.

Remington turned and looked at Goose. "Yes, I do, First Sergeant. And I'm considering my options at this point. With the Syrian cav units temporarily immobilized, I intend to capitalize on their weakness. We are a Ranger unit. We specialize in hit-and-git strikes when the time comes. At present, I am identifying targets and examining possible courses of action."

"Yes, sir."

"When I find something you'll be useful for, First Sergeant, I'll send for you."

Even in the darkness, Goose felt heat fill his face. "Yes, sir." OCS might have placed bars on Remington's shoulders and taught him about diplomacy, command history, and how to conduct himself in the upper tiers of the military, but Goose knew he was as well-informed about tactics, weapons, men, and materials as Remington was. The only thing the captain had over him at the moment was access to enemy intel.

Remington turned from Goose. "You can also discontinue the need for weather reports, First Sergeant. Although I appreciate your zeal, I'd rather get them the modern way."

Something's going on, Goose realized. He'd rarely seen Remington so cold and contained. Although their relationship was sometimes rocky, as all relationships got at times, Goose could count on the fingers of one hand when Remington had gone out of his way to pull rank so harshly. And the captain never pulled rank in front of other members of the team unless dressing Goose down was an object lesson to the others and put them all on notice, uniting them and letting them know that their fates depended on how well they served their captain.

"Don't you have ops you should be overseeing, First Sergeant?" Remington asked, shifting his attention back in Goose's direction.

"Yes, sir." Goose pulled his right arm up in a salute.

Remington cut him a brief salute and turned away.

Dismissed abruptly, knowing Remington had stopped just short of being insulting, Goose performed a sharp about-face that set his knee to screaming. He managed three steps before Remington called for him.

"First Sergeant Gander."

Goose turned, on the defensive at once and feeling helpless. When they were sergeants together, Goose had taken offense at the smug tone of superiority Remington often evidenced. The captain had better diction, was totally comfortable at a general's black-tie

affair, and had master's degrees in history and political science—
from college courses taken while he was a sergeant and aiming for
general—to fill in the lulls in conversation.

During the seventeen years of their association, Goose had never
felt intimidated by Remington when it came to the hands-on grunt
work of soldiering. Only in the occasional social circles or around
women had Goose felt somewhat at a loss. Remington could be the
life of the party, and he always had two or three good-looking women
hanging around him.

"It has come to my attention that the void left by the death of First
Lieutenant Tarver as my executive officer in the chain of command
has yet to be filled," Remington said, facing Goose again.

"Yes, sir." Goose also knew that the captain hadn't had a single
problem using him as executive officer. They'd worked together as a
team for years. They knew each other's moves. None of the lieutenants available to replace the XO had that kind of knowledge.

"I've rectified that by placing Lieutenant Perrin as my XO as of this
morning."

Goose knew Perrin and didn't care for the man. Nick Perrin was
twenty-nine years old and had come into the military as an officer out
of college. The fact that he hadn't advanced past lieutenant in five
years spoke volumes. However, Perrin was devious and smart as a
weasel, making him one of Remington's immediate selections for the
group of hard cases the captain kept for ops that didn't run exactly by
the book.

"Understood, sir," Goose said.

Remington waited, probably thinking that Goose might want to
comment on the selection.

Goose wanted to comment but knew that the effort would do no
good. The fact that Remington had selected Perrin out of three other
lieutenant choices within the Rangers spoke volumes. Perrin had
been chosen for two reasons that Goose could see. One reason was to
get back at Goose because Remington knew Goose didn't approve of
the lieutenant, and the other was to make certain Remington could
operate any questionable activities in plain view without meeting
Perrin on the sly. That didn't mean that Remington's black ops would
take place aboveboard, but Perrin's constant presence wasn't going to
be questioned.

"Comments, First Sergeant?" Remington invited.

Goose knew better than to bite. "No, sir. I understand, sir. I'll be
awaiting your orders or Lieutenant Perrin's, sir."

Remington stared at Goose as if somewhat dissatisfied with the easy capitulation on his first sergeant's part. Or maybe the captain was more unhappy and uncertain of his friend's acceptance of another superior officer that he knew wasn't as skilled as he was. If that was true, Goose knew, then Remington had forgotten that all sergeants had a history of dealing with "superior" officers that weren't.

"Is there anything else, sir?" Goose asked.

Remington's jaw tightened. He wasn't happy about Goose's relaxed demeanor about the change in the chain of command. Goose knew that he was supposed to take the change as an insult, but at the same time he knew getting out from under Remington's direct supervision would give him the necessary time to see to his troops, their needs, and their morale. That was where sergeants operated best to command the units and missions they were in charge of. Sergeants were trained to act and think for themselves.

He'd also have more time to pursue the questions his talk with Icarus had raised.

"No, First Sergeant, there isn't. You're dismissed."

Remington turned so abruptly that Goose could only salute the captain's back. Goose did that, setting the example for the enlisted men in the room. No matter what else happened in the field, in his personal life, or between Remington and him, Goose prided himself on being a professional soldier.

He did another about-face and left the command center. This time he made it all the way to the door without being called back.

As he stepped out into the driving rain still flooding Sanliurfa's streets, Goose knew that Remington was planning something. The captain's nature prevented him from simply lying back and awaiting the Syrians' next move. Waiting wasn't one of Remington's strong suits.

Thinking along those lines, remembering the screen images of the stagnant Syrian army huddled down under the rain, remembering Remington's comment about the Rangers being a hit-and-git strike force, Goose figured the captain would field a special ops team with orders to exact a pound of flesh from the opposing army.

While awaiting the captain's orders—or possibly Lieutenant Perrin's—Goose decided he would put together and ready a team who could deploy for such an engagement. The trick was not to let the captain know Goose was already working on the same agenda. A good first sergeant always anticipated his commanding officer's orders and stood ready in such a manner that the CO still thought a mission was his own idea.

"Seriously, love, we've got to stop meeting like this."

"Yeah, yeah, yeah," Danielle Vinchenzo growled irritably as she scrambled into Sid Wright's rented Land Rover. She shook off the nylon hoodie she'd donned hoping to keep her hair dry. There were no plans to shoot any additional TV footage at the moment, but she knew that could change in a heartbeat, depending on whether the Syrians stood by the apparent rainout going on. Water from the drenched hoodie splashed all over the seats.

Sid said, "Do be careful with the upholstery."

"You're kidding, right?" Danielle asked as she shifted the tote bag that carried her extra makeup, tape recorders, and digital camera.

"I don't like having my things wet. Nor do I care to have this vehicle in any worse shape than it is."

"This is a rental, Sid. Nothing to get emotional about. If you want to get fussy about things, I'd talk to whoever put those bullet holes in the right rear quarter panel."

"I would have, except at the time I didn't feel like hanging around for the matching bullet hole between my eyes." Sid took his foot off the brake and rolled into the sparse traffic moving slowly through the rain.

That surprised Danielle. "Someone tried to shoot you? While you were in the car?" She hadn't heard about any skirmishes with the Syrian army during the night. Things had been unusually quiet, which meant—judging from past experience—that the situation was about to turn ugly again.

"Yes." Sid drove with both hands on the wheel and a cigarette hanging between his lips. "You're not the only one stringing news stories out of the city, love."

"So what did you have?" Danielle asked.

Sid glanced askance at her. "I should tell you? The princess of the Sanliurfan airwaves?"

"They aren't calling me that."

Sid gave her a look.

"No. Really. They aren't calling me that on the other networks."

"Not *on* the other networks," Sid admitted after a moment, "but some of the other reporters—poor souls who were evidently born without one flicker of human compassion, people who would probably not allow the use of the computer and satellite phone to a rival who was racking up story after story for the international market—"

"Other reporters are calling me that?"

Sid shrugged. "Yes, love. And some rather repugnant names I won't, out of my own vaunted sense of civility, repeat for your delicate ears."

"My ears aren't all that delicate."

"Yes, well, I'm a gentleman, you see."

"A true gentleman would dress in a fresh shirt and not use the one that has lipstick stains." Danielle touched his collar.

"Lipstick? Truly?"

"Truly," Danielle said. "See? I can be compassionate. I could have let you go out among your peers with evidence of your debauchery quite literally hanging around your neck. As a further show of compassion, I won't mention said debauchery or lipstick to anyone."

"You are one of a kind," Sid admitted. He reached up for the rearview mirror and turned it to check his reflection. The lipstick was bright, bubblegum pink and stood out dramatically against his white shirt collar. "Oh. Well, there is a glaring bit of evidence, I suppose. I wasn't near my luggage when this . . . happened."

"You ask me," Danielle said, "that doesn't look accidental at all."

Sid ignored her barbed comment. "Or when I got your call at this dreadful hour. After seven o'clock in the morning and rain pouring straight down, I assure you they've put this war on hold at least for a bit. No soldier wants to fight in the rain. Especially an infantry with a heavy armor assist. Planes won't even be flying much today. You should have taken this opportunity to catch up on your sleep."

"Someone I know wasn't sleeping. Bubblegum pink lipstick?"

Sid dabbed at the lipstick with a handkerchief but succeeded only in smearing the color. "I'm sure there's another name for it. An exotic name, I'd wager."

"Who wears bubblegum pink lipstick?" Danielle's natural curiosity got the better of her.

"A gentleman never tells."

"How young was she?"

"Above the age of consent." Sid gave up on the rescue of the collar. "I must say I don't care for your insinuation."

"You're the one wearing bright pink lipstick. I'll feel free to insinuate away."

"I'm also the one with the computer and satellite phone you wish to borrow. *Again.* For unknown and nefarious reasons."

"You wish." Danielle still felt antsy. Mystic had told her he/she/they would be in touch with her in three or four hours. Almost eighteen hours had gone by since she'd talked with the computer hacker. She had contacted Sid Wright on two other occasions to check her e-mail. "So tell me about the bullet holes."

"I should keep you in suspense," Sid groused. "As you have been doing the whole time you've been using my equipment."

"I asked out of politeness," Danielle protested.

"Politeness?"

"Yes. Either it's a story that you've already broken and you're champing at the bit to tell it, or it's a story still in progress and you're champing at the bit to tell me it's secret, stupendous, and you can't tell me about it."

"So, according to you, either way I'm to exhibit equestrian behavior."

"An equestrian is a rider, not a horse," Danielle said. "The word you want is *equine.* I'm suggesting you're exhibiting equine behavior."

"I know what I'm talking about," Sid growled. "I'm sure you're mistaken about the word choice. I'm English. We invented the language. You people mutilated it."

"Only because the English can't spell."

Sid cursed.

"What happened to all those gentlemanly habits you were talking about only moments ago?" Danielle asked.

"I reserve them for ladies of breeding."

"Young ladies who wear bubblegum pink lipstick."

"You do make it hard for a man to do you a favor, love."

"The bullet holes," Danielle prompted.

"Ah yes. Well, the young lady I was with last night was helping me follow up on a lead I'd been pursuing." Sid glanced at Danielle. "You never said where we were going."

"Achmed's," Danielle replied. Every time she borrowed Sid's equipment she insisted they park in a different area. She also kept an eye peeled to make certain none of her OneWorld NewsNet coworkers trailed her. Achmed ran an open market that was still operating.

"Fine. I know where it is. The man brews a decent pot of tea when properly motivated."

"The lead you were pursuing."

"An interesting story, I think. If anything comes of it, which I doubt." Sid turned the corner near a building that had been hit more than once by Syrian artillery. Mounds of broken rock and mortar filled the lower floor where earthmovers had shoved the debris back into the building. "According to my sources, one of the independent merchants, a man named Abu Alam, was kidnapped at gunpoint yesterday afternoon."

"In Sanliurfa?"

"No. Curiously, he seems to have been taken from his group somewhere between this city and the Syrians' front line."

"He's been trading at both ends of the battlefield. I've heard of him."

"Presumably." Sid nodded and took another puff from his cigarette. "I think Abu Alam had his hand in just about every morally bankrupt way to make a profit that has taken shape in this area, before and after the conflict began. I've also been told that he's kidnapped American and European women who were trapped here in Sanliurfa and sold them to the Syrians."

"Is there any truth to that?"

"I believe so, love. Can't have been very many or the stories would be further spread. Plus, Abu Alam tends not to leave anyone behind to bear witness against him when he conducts his little slavery operation. With the ravaged state of this city, I'm sure it's quite easy to hide a few murders."

"Sounds like a guy with a lot of enemies," Danielle commented.

"Oh, Abu Alam does indeed have enemies. But he also has some loyal supporters who are doing their best to find him. He's family, you see. The Bedouin take their family very seriously."

"The bullet holes."

"Exactly. I was just pursuing an interview. His people told me to go away. I didn't. So they opened fire and shot the Land Rover to show me they meant business. I'm certain they would have shot me, and the young lady next." Sid looked at her. "Believe me when I say there's nothing that cuts across a language barrier like gunfire pointed in your direction."

"You left."

Sid nodded. "In the straightest route possible and with all available speed."

Even despite her driving interest in Mystic and why the hacker hadn't contacted her, Danielle was drawn into the story. "Who grabbed Abu Alam?"

"I didn't say anyone grabbed him."

Danielle wrinkled her nose at him. "C'mon. I'm a big reporter girl now. I know bubblegum pink lipstick when I see it, and I know that you wouldn't be pursuing a story about a black marketer getting nabbed by one of his rivals in the middle of a war zone. The story has a more interesting twist to it than that. If you find out one of the military units has acted on a vendetta or taken improprieties to rob Abu Alam, you'd have a zinger of a story."

Sid laughed. "You have gotten quite erudite in these matters, haven't you, dear?"

"Yes. So give."

"The lead I was following was given to me by a rather disreputable Eastern European man who's been dealing with scavengers in the city. He hires people to break into empty houses and businesses and take anything of value. They load those valuables—including electronics, household appliances, and furniture—onto trucks—which are also stolen, by the way—and ship them north."

Danielle was sickened. She'd heard stories about men like that who were doing exactly that kind of theft. The military forces couldn't stop them because the efforts to shore up the city's defenses took all their time. They were geared for protecting Sanliurfa from the army of predators outside the city walls rather than the handful inside.

"The interesting wrinkle in the story this man gave me," Sid said, "is the tale of the only survivor of the attack that left six of Abu Alam's people dead outside the city. The lingering casualty hung on only long enough to give this story to his mates."

"Okay. I'm interested."

"The story is," Sid said in a quiet voice barely audible over the Land Rover's engine, "that the people who kidnapped Abu Alam and killed his people were American soldiers."

Danielle thought about that. Her quick mind flew through the variables. "That leaves the army Rangers, the marines, and the American soldiers serving with the U.N. Peacekeeping effort."

"And all of those chaps have been busy since the attack the night before." Sid threw his cigarette out the window. "It's interesting that you divided the Rangers and the marines. I hadn't thought to do that. But I had thought of the American soldiers serving with the U.N."

"The Rangers and marines have different agendas," Danielle said. "Similar, but different. They still maintain their own gear and identity inside the Ranger temporary barracks." She pointed at the corner ahead. "There's Achmed's."

"So it is." Sid pulled to a stop in the alley beside the marketplace. He killed the engine and waited.

"Uh-uh," Danielle said.

"I was sleeping when you called," Sid said in a grudging tone. "I don't really feel like walking around the marketplace. Or trudging outside and getting drenched."

"Sid."

The British reporter threw his hands up in mock surrender. "All right. All right." He got out and closed the door, pulling his jacket up over his head. The sound of the pouring rain invaded the Land Rover's cab. "Would you like anything?"

Danielle had to read his lips through the rain-spattered window. "Bagel. Cream cheese. Coffee."

"Can't promise. We've had all those power outages. But I'll see what I can do." Sid turned and hurried away through the rain.

Working quickly, Danielle hooked up the satellite phone and the notebook computer. She brought the Internet online and scooted over to the mail drop she used to contact Mystic.

Muckraker:>R U THERE?

The cursor blinked at her.

Muckraker:>R U THERE?

She waited long minutes. Her breath started to fog up the window. Paranoia caused her to glance up several times as people hurried by. The marketplace was enclosed and the business was already brisk. The supply of fresh goods often didn't meet the demands of the people living in the city.

A moment later the mail-drop screen shifted radically. Panicked, knowing that the change could have been caused by someone hacking into the transmission, Danielle almost shut the link down.

Then the cursor jerked into quick motion.

Mystic:>I'M HERE.

Muckraker:>YOU HAD ME WORRIED.

Mystic:>YOU HAD REASON TO BE WORRIED. WHOEVER THESE GUYS ARE, THEY'RE GOOD.

The statement screamed at Danielle, and for the first time she realized that she didn't know who was at the other end of this connection. Someone had killed her friend Lizuca Carutasu in cold blood, stalking her through the cybercafé and shooting her down without remorse.

Muckraker:>HOW DO I KNOW YOU'RE WHO YOU'RE SUPPOSED TO BE?

Mystic:>LOL. PARANOIA. YOU GOTTA LOVE PARANOIA. IT'S ONE OF THE MOST ADDICTIVE THINGS OUT THERE WHEN YOU LIVE AND DIE ON THE NET.

Muckraker:>MAKE ME A BELIEVER.

Mystic:>NOW THERE'S A LOADED COMMAND. A BELIEVER IN WHAT?

Muckraker:>YOU.

Mystic:>HEY, I'M TIRED AND THINGS HAVEN'T GONE EXACTLY THE WAY I'D THOUGHT. THOSE GUYS YOU SENT ME AFTER FOUND ONE OF MY CUTOUTS. IF I WASN'T AS SMART AS I AM, THEY MIGHT HAVE HAD ME.

Muckraker:>IF I DON'T HAVE SOME CONFIRMATION IN THE NEXT TWO SECONDS, I'M GONE.

Mystic:>WOW. AND I THOUGHT I WAS THE PARANOID ONE.

Danielle made no reply. Tension built up in her. If it wasn't Mystic at the other end of the connection, someone could already be tracking her back to Sid Wright's computer. Granted, the sat phone made success at finding her improbable, but not impossible. All the trackers needed were two sets of gear so they could triangulate her position.

She thought about Sid's story concerning Abu Alam, the black market dealer who might have been kidnapped by American soldiers. In a city full of strangers and warriors, whom was she supposed to trust? Not too surprisingly, Sergeant Goose Gander came to mind. Now he was a man she'd believe in, and she knew she didn't want to do that unless she had to.

Mystic:>OK. YOU REMEMBER THE FIRST CARTOON I SENT YOU? THE ONE WITH THE WINTER THEME?

Muckraker:>YES.

Mystic:>NAME THE STRIP.

Muckraker:>YOU'RE THE ONE PROVING YOURSELF.

Mystic:>YOU NAME THE STRIP AND I'LL DESCRIBE THE SCENE.

Danielle hesitated only a moment:>CALVIN AND HOBBES.

Mystic:>AND THE SCENE WAS THE TRAFFIC ACCIDENT IN-VOLVING THE SNOWMEN.

Danielle smiled a little in spite of the tension. The one-panel joke had been one of her favorite Calvin and Hobbes strips. The two characters had sculpted a group of surprised and frightened snowmen and snowwomen gathered around the parked family car, and another snowman lay on the ground partially under the car as if it had been run over.

Muckraker:>I GUESS WE'RE BOTH WHO WE SAY WE ARE. DID YOU GET THE INFORMATION ON THE GUY IN THE PICTURE?

Mystic:>YES. THIS GUY HAS A REAL HISTORY. AND HE'S DEFI-NITELY A BAD GUY. YOUR EMPLOYER HAD A TON OF INFORMA-TION ON HIM.

Muckraker:>YOU SAID YOU ALMOST GOT CAUGHT.

Mystic:>I'M GOOD. REAL GOOD. I WAS SNOOPING AROUND YOUR EMPLOYER'S FILES. SOMEONE WORKING INTERNET SE-CURITY TUMBLED TO ME, ALMOST GOT ME AND FRIED MY MA-CHINE. BEFORE I KNEW IT, SOMEONE WAS AT THE DOOR OF THE LOCATION OF THE CUTOUT I WAS USING. HE BROKE IN-SIDE AND HAD A GUN IN HIS HANDS.

The story immediately reminded Danielle of what had happened to Lizuca. How fast did these people operate?

Muckraker:>YOU'RE IN ROMANIA?

Mystic:>NO. I'M NOT TELLING YOU WHERE I AM. BUT THE CUTOUT WAS IN AUSTRALIA.

Muckraker:>WHAT'S A CUTOUT?

Mystic:>A FALSE ADDRESS. I'VE GOT A FEW OF THEM. IN AUS-TRALIA, THE CUTOUT WAS AN APARTMENT I KEEP RENTED WITH A COMPUTER SYSTEM THAT I CAN ACCESS FROM OTHER PLACES. PEOPLE TRACE BACK WHAT I'M DOING. IF THEY'RE GOOD ENOUGH, THEY GO TO AUSTRALIA. OR WHEREVER THE CUTOUT IS THAT I'M USING FOR THAT PARTICULAR JOB. BE-FORE THEY CAN TRACK ME FROM THERE, I'M GONE AND THE HARD DRIVE IS CHURNING ITS WAY INTO OBLIVION. I FIGURED AUSTRALIA WAS FAR ENOUGH AWAY NO ONE COULD GET THERE. I MAKE IT A HABIT TO WORK AT LEAST A HEMISPHERE AWAY FROM THE TARGET SITE. I WAS WRONG.

Danielle considered that.

Mystic:>IF THEY HAVE PEOPLE STATIONED IN SYDNEY, AUS-
TRALIA, I HAVE TO START WONDERING WHERE THEY *DON'T*
HAVE PEOPLE.

Danielle couldn't believe the information. How big was Alexander Cody's organization?

Muckraker:>GUY WHO BROKE INTO YOUR CUTOUT WAS CIA?

Mystic:>DON'T KNOW. HAVEN'T IDENTIFIED HIM YET. GOT A
PICTURE, THOUGH.

Muckraker:>HOW'D YOU GET THE PIC?

Mystic:>GOT THE CUTOUT SET UP WITH A PC CAMERA. GUY
BROKE IN AND I GOT HIM IN ACTION.

Muckraker:>NO ONE TRACKED YOU BACK FROM THAT COM-
PUTER?

Mystic:> NO. IF THEY HAD, I HONESTLY DON'T THINK I'D BE
HERE NOW. THAT GUY IN SYDNEY CAME IN READY TO KILL
SOMEBODY.

Muckraker:>ARE YOU GOING TO WORK ON IDENTIFYING
THE GUY WHO BROKE INTO THE AUSTRALIA APARTMENT?

Mystic:> WE'LL SEE. LIKE I SAID, THESE GUYS ARE GOOD AND
THEIR ORGANIZATION IS HUGE IF THEY'VE GOT PEOPLE ON
THE PAYROLL IN AUSTRALIA. I DON'T KNOW HOW MUCH OF
THIS I WANT TO TAKE ON. WAIT. I TAKE THAT BACK. I ONLY
WANT TO TAKE ON AS MUCH AS WHAT WON'T GET ME KILLED.
I'M *REALLY* CURIOUS NOW. STILL GOTTA FIGURE OUT WHERE
THE LINE IS ON THAT.

Muckraker:>WHO'S THE GUY IN THE PIC I SENT YOU?

Mystic:>HIS NAME IS ALEXANDER CODY. HE *IS* CIA. SECTION
CHIEF. IN THAT CAPACITY HE HAS SOME FREEDOM TO MAKE
CALLS OF HIS OWN AND NOBODY WATCHES TOO CLOSELY.
THIS GUY IS SOME PIECE OF WORK, I HAVE TO TELL YOU. BAD,
BAD MAN. YOU WANT TO STAY AWAY FROM HIM.

Danielle didn't know if that was possible.

Mystic:>ALSO FOUND OUT CODY WORKS FOR YOUR EM-
PLOYER.

Muckraker:>???

Mystic:>FOUND PAYOFFS LISTED IN YOUR EMPLOYER'S
FILES. THAT'S PROBABLY WHAT GOT YOUR FRIEND KILLED.
SOMEONE IN YOUR EMPLOYER'S OFFICE WAS COVERING UP A
TRAIL. GOT COPIES OF THE PAYOFFS, BUT EVEN AS I WAS
DOWNLOADING THEM, SOMEONE WAS COMING RIGHT BE-
HIND ME TURNING THEM INTO WHIFFLE DUST.

Muckraker:>WHIFFLE DUST?

Mystic:>GEEK-SPEAK. WHIFFLE DUST = ELIMINATION. I'M
SURE THE RECORDS DON'T EXIST ANYMORE. TWO OF THE
BANKS USED TO HANDLE THE MONEY TRANSACTIONS ARE
CONTROLLED BY YOUR EMPLOYER THROUGH INVESTMENTS
AND SHARE HOLDINGS. RUSSIAN BANKS. LOTTA UNDER-THE-
TABLE BUSINESS DEALINGS AND MONEY LAUNDERING FLOW
THROUGH RUSSIAN BANKS BECAUSE YOU CAN'T SUBPOENA
THE RECORDS FROM THE RUSSIANS. TURNED UP THE NAMES
OF TWO MAJOR PLAYERS IN SHADY DEALINGS THAT ARE CON-
NECTED WITH YOUR EMPLOYER: JOSHUA TODD-COTHRAN
AND JONATHAN STONAGAL.

Danielle knew both men from news stories. Todd-Cothran was a
British financier. Stonagal was from old money America. Both
Stonagal and Todd-Cothran had histories of questionable business
practices that included allegations of strong-arm techniques and cor-
porate spying.

Mystic:>THERE ARE OTHER PEOPLE, BUT TODD-COTHRAN
AND STONAGAL ARE THE BIG BOYS IN THE BUNCH.

Muckraker:>YOU HAVE COPIES OF THOSE REPORTS?

Mystic:>CAN'T PROVE THOSE REPORTS EVER EXISTED EVEN
WITH WHAT I MIGHT HAVE HAD. THAT'S THE PROBLEM WITH
DOWNLOADED FILES: YOU CAN'T PROVE THAT YOU DIDN'T
CREATE THEM YOURSELF. GOTTA CATCH THE FILES AT THE SITE
OR ON A HARD DRIVE OR ON A REDUNDANCY SYSTEM SOME-
WHERE. AND THE FILES I WAS LOOKING AT WERE COPIED ONTO
THE HARD DRIVE IN SYDNEY. I DIDN'T GET THE CHANCE TO
MOVE THEM TO MY SYSTEM HERE WHEN I NUKED THAT SYSTEM.

Muckraker:>WHAT IS CODY DOING IN SANLIURFA NOW?

Mystic:>NOTHING IN THE FILES TO INDICATE THAT. THE CIA
FILES—I BROKE INTO THEM TOO—SHOW CODY IS ON THE
SCENE THERE TRYING TO TRACK DOWN A ROGUE AGENT.

Muckraker:>ROGUE AGENT?

Mystic:>SOME GUY CODE-NAMED ICARUS. DID UNDER-
COVER STUFF. INFILTRATED THE PKK. A KURDISH TERRORIST
GROUP. DIDN'T KNOW THAT TILL I SEARCHED THE NET.

Leaning back in the Land Rover's bucket seat, Danielle thought
about that. She remembered how she'd seen Goose guarding the
room in the temporary hospital. Cody had confronted him; then
Captain Remington had stepped in and taken charge from both of
them. Cody hadn't been happy about that.

Did Remington have the rogue CIA agent?

Then she also remembered how Sergeant Gander had spirited away one of the men from the building the terrorists had used as bait to attack the American soldiers. Who was that man?

Okay, Danielle told herself, *take a deep breath. You're obviously onto a huge story here.* Then, in the same moment, she realized the downside. One of the people she would be investigating was Nicolae Carpathia. If the story was legit and Carpathia was involved in illegal activities—and *if* she was able to break the story—her career at OneWorld NewsNet was finished.

It only took memory of Lizuca Carutasu's cold-blooded killing to remind Danielle that she was out for more than just a story.

Muckraker:>WHAT KIND OF WORK HAS CODY DONE FOR CARPATHIA?

Mystic:>FILES ARE KIND OF SPOTTY AT BEST. BUT I WAS READING BETWEEN THE LINES. IF I'M RIGHT, CODY HAS BEEN HELPING CARPATHIA FOR YEARS. DOING ODD JOBS. GETTING INFORMATION ON PEOPLE, BLACKMAILING PEOPLE. THERE'S EVEN THE POSSIBILITY THAT CARPATHIA, OR SOMEONE CLOSE TO HIM, HIRED CODY TO MURDER A BUSINESS RIVAL SEVEN YEARS AGO. I ALSO READ ENOUGH TO KNOW THAT CARPATHIA'S APPOINTMENT TO THE PRESIDENCY OF ROMANIA WASN'T AS EASY AS THE PRESS RELAYS THE STORY. A LOT OF THINGS WENT ON BEHIND THE SCENES THEN. REAL GUERRILLA TACTICS. PEOPLE VANISHED AND TURNED UP DEAD.

Muckraker:>CAN YOU GET THIS INFORMATION TO ME?

Mystic:>WE'RE TALKING ABOUT A BIG FILE HERE. YOU'RE ON DIAL-UP. I CAN TELL BY THE PING. IT WOULD TAKE HOURS, MAYBE DAYS, TO GET ALL OF THIS TO YOU.

Danielle thought about that. Sid wouldn't let her have his computer and phone for hours. And she wouldn't leave the computer alone while it was downloading if she took it. She also couldn't be away from OneWorld NewsNet for that amount of time.

Other media agencies had satellite burst transmission capabilities. OneWorld NewsNet did, but she definitely couldn't use their computers to receive the data Mystic had. Not if it implicated Nicolae Carpathia. And she wasn't really happy about trusting other news agencies. If any of them, including Sid Wright, got an indication of the story she was sitting on, they would be all over it.

Muckraker:>LET ME GET BACK TO YOU. I MAY HAVE A WAY TO GET ACCESS TO A FASTER CONNECTION.

Mystic:>TIME FRAME?

Muckraker:>DON'T KNOW. I'VE GOT TO DO A LOT OF CON-VINCING BEFORE I CAN SELL THIS.

Reluctantly, Danielle closed the computer down and disconnected the sat phone. She took a couple deep breaths and thought about Sergeant Gander. Goose already knew about the CIA angle, but did he know it all? Would he want to know?

If things got dangerous, she also knew that the first sergeant was one of those guys who would stick till the bitter end of something. She'd already seen him doing that.

She blew out her breath. On the other hand, if this story was as risky as she believed it was, did she have any right endangering him by telling him everything Mystic had discovered?

Could she even trust Mystic?

Glumly, Danielle stared at her gray reflection in the foggy windshield. Mystic had been right about one thing: Paranoia was definitely addictive.

Shackleton Heights
Marbury, Alabama
Local Time 0928 Hours

"Area still look that familiar to you, Chaplain?"

"Aye. It does. Like it was just yesterday when I was here." Delroy Harte sat in the passenger seat of the sheriff's cruiser and peered out at the small, quiet neighborhood of Shackleton Heights. Usually Saturday mornings in that neighborhood were more active, filled with kids and noise and the sound of spring flower gardens being tilled. None of that was going on today. "You'd think after five years things would change."

"Oh, now there's probably been some changes. A few more folks with dish TV. Newer cars. But you're right, of course; there probably ain't been many changes."

Deputy Walter Purcell drove, one hand on the wheel and the other holding a cup of take-out coffee in a Styrofoam container from Hazel's Café. Today Walter had insisted on buying breakfast that morning before taking Delroy to the car-rental lot.

He'd also decided to take the long way there. The neighborhood tour through Shackleton Heights was part of the price of getting the taxicab service, he'd said. The car lot they were going to didn't open till noon, and driving was better than cooling his heels waiting to make certain Delroy was safely on his way.

For his part, Delroy didn't mind the side trip. After arriving at the Purcell home yesterday morning, he'd met Clarice, Walter's wife, visited for a while, then sacked out in the back bedroom of the small house. If he could have remained conscious, the navy chaplain supposed he would have felt more than a little guilty about crashing the home as he had. But Walter Purcell was an insistent man and wouldn't take no for an answer.

Delroy had roused at dinnertime, called to the table by Walter, and spent an unbelievably enjoyable evening talking to Walter and Clarice, a quiet, reserved woman who at first didn't seem to match up well with Walter. Walter came across as rough and gruff but was meek and mild around his wife, obviously loving her very much. Clarice and Walter had done the dinner dishes together, and it had reminded Delroy of evenings he'd spent at home with Glenda.

Not too surprisingly, the after-dinner talk drifted to the subject of the disappearances. Clarice had surprised Delroy by announcing that she felt certain the Rapture had occurred and that God had called His church home. Knowing he was a navy chaplain, she had asked Delroy his opinion on the matter. Delroy had quietly agreed with her but didn't offer further elaboration because he hadn't felt worthy enough to try to interpret God's Word. He couldn't do it with Walter sitting there, knowing the deputy had seen him digging up his own son's grave, giving evidence of his own fears and doubts.

Later that evening, Delroy had made a phone call to a car dealer Walter had suggested, confirmed the existence of a rental—though the price was exorbitant—and secured it through his credit card. He'd also tried to contact the USS *Wasp* last night and this morning, but to no avail. He'd wanted to leave word with Captain Falkirk that he was heading to Norfolk, Virginia—*Wasp*'s homeport—and hoped to hook up with a ship or a plane headed to Turkey. Men and materials, as many as could be found, were being routed to the Mediterranean Sea to support the Turkish defense, but the military was feeding teams on several fronts as national defenses were shored up and martial law still ruled in some of the larger metropolitan areas around the country.

After watching the news, the three of them trying desperately to keep up on what was happening in the world, Clarice had treated Walter and Delroy to huge wedges of deep-dish apple pie with home-made ice cream out on the back veranda. They'd stayed up till 2 A.M.

Absolutely stuffed and feeling guilty, Delroy had bid the couple good night and returned to his borrowed bed. His dreams had been haunted all night by images of his father pounding at the pulpit as he preached to his congregation in the small church where Delroy had grown up.

"Depends on where you're living," Walter said in that straight-forward way he had, still talking about the changing neighborhoods.

"At least, that's what I've always found out. Cities what's got money to spend—or can put a hand in somebody else's pocket and get money to spend—why, they do a lot of changing. Neighborhoods that get bought up by one outfit or another, they do a lot of changing. It's 'cause money's being pumped into them areas, you see. But here in this part of Marbury, why, folks are pretty much set in their ways and mostly happy with what they've got. Or, leastways, not so unhappy that they'll move on into the city proper." He glanced around. "Though now and again one of 'em will kill another, or steal from another, or do bodily harm to another. It ain't paradise."

"No. It never was." Delroy looked at the white wooden houses with their red and brown and green roofs. Most of the houses were forty and fifty years old, usually packed with three small bedrooms and a bath and a half. They were houses built for the middle class during an exodus to get out of the growing metropolis back in the '50s and '60s. Over the years, that middle class had changed, sliding more toward poverty and the same problems that had plagued them in the inner-urban areas they'd come from.

Shackleton Heights had its beginning back when Marbury was young, and the new suburb had never quite recovered from its days of infamy. In the early 1800s, the area had been a separate town, smaller than Marbury, and it had been named Shackle Town. For forty years, till slavery was abolished at the end of the Civil War, Shackle Town had provided auction blocks for slaves and a way of rough living for hard men who preferred that. At the turn of the twentieth century, a riot had broken out and the small town had burned to the ground.

The people who lived in Shackleton Heights now were mostly black, and generally they worked shifts at factories, fast-food restaurants in the metro area, or on construction projects that were usually state sponsored. They were men and women, young and old, who held jobs to make ends meet rather than spending time in careers to keep up with the rest of the world. Those who worked for themselves tended to do so seven days a week and from can-see to cain't-see.

Trees lined the small, narrow streets. Cars parked at the curb congested traffic. More than a few of those cars sat up on blocks or were in various stages of being cannibalized for parts. Porches that had gone crooked with age and neglect sometimes held defunct washers and dryers and refrigerators, small graveyards of dead appliances that the city wouldn't take and the inhabitants couldn't afford to have hauled off.

"Did you live here long?" Walter asked.

"All my life," Delroy answered, only then realizing that Walter hadn't wandered into the neighborhood by accident. Delroy had learned there were few things accidental about Deputy Walter Purcell, despite his easygoing manner and abrupt nature. He'd known exactly where he was taking Delroy. "Till I went away to college. If I hadn't gotten a basketball scholarship to Alabama State, I might never have made it out of town."

"Well, do you miss it?" As always, Walter was blunt and to the point.

"Surprisingly, I have on occasion. Shipboard life is close like this neighborhood is. Maybe that's why I fit into the navy so easily." Delroy wondered what Walter's objective was for bringing him through the old neighborhood. The chaplain didn't doubt that the deputy had one, but he didn't know what it was.

"Was your daddy from here?" Walter paused at a stop sign.

"From farther out of town," Delroy said. "But from this area, aye. My mother lived in Marbury all her life."

"Was your wife from here?" Walter made the turn and approached the elementary school where Delroy had attended as a child. The buildings sat empty and forlorn.

"Glenda is from Montgomery." Delroy had trouble referring to her as his wife since he hadn't talked to her in so long. "She was born there. We met in college. She was bound and determined to change me and the world."

Delroy's heart ached as he saw the empty swings and soccer field at the elementary school. A handful of women, young and middle-aged, walked through the empty schoolyards. He didn't know if they were teachers missing students or mothers missing their sons and daughters. How could anyone live in a world without children?

Walter laughed. "Did she?"

"Change me? Aye. That she did. She took a rough, prideful young boy, turned him into a man, and guided him through the navy, prodded at him till he finished college and rose from the ranks to make officer grade, and backed him every step of the way."

"It's surprising that since you been gone she didn't move back to Montgomery instead of hanging around here as she has." Walter realized he'd spoken too quickly and held up a hand in apology. "Me and my big mouth."

"I don't know why she stayed," Delroy admitted. "I bought a house here, after Terrence got to be school-age, and Glenda didn't feel comfortable living on base. She'd always wanted a home in a small town. Both of us felt Montgomery was just too big to raise Terrence in. After Terrence . . . passed and I didn't handle things well, I don't know why she stayed."

"Well, maybe she just feels at home here. For all its faults and lacks, Marbury is a good town."

Delroy watched the houses. Few people were outside, but the ones who were in their yards or driveways glanced in the cruiser's direction with nervous apprehension.

"These people are scared," Delroy said before he knew he was going to speak.

"Yes, sir," Walter said, nodding. "They are that. And it might surprise you to know they been scared for a while." He glanced back at the neighborhood. "This end of town, well, it had fallen on hard times even before these last few days." He looked at Delroy. "Bet you didn't have crack cocaine in these streets when you was growing up."

"No—" Delroy shook his head—"we didn't." His daddy had lectured on the evils of marijuana from time to time even back then, though.

"Well, sir, they have it now." Walter tore open the lid on his Styrofoam cup. "You missed out on the gangbanger shootings too."

"Here?" Delroy couldn't believe it. Back when he was a boy, no drugs had been in the streets, and the most violence that was ever done was at the high school basketball courts and football fields when rival schools met. Even when Terrence had been a boy, things hadn't been truly bad.

"Yes, sir," Walter replied. "Here. Right in this neighborhood." He glanced around. "What you're looking at, this here's a part of the city that's well on its way to dying."

Delroy looked out on the neighborhood and felt a great sadness. The condition of the houses and the decrepit cars bore mute testimony to the truth of the deputy's words. "My daddy would never have allowed this to happen."

"Not meaning to take anything away from your daddy," Walter said, "but he might not have been able to help what this place has become through economic hardship and neglect. Then again, I hear your daddy was a man strong in his faith. A hard-knuckled man when it came to that too. But those have turned into some mean streets out there. There's stabbings and shootings. Robberies and burglaries. Fathers battling sons, and half the time they don't know each other until the police or the deputies pull 'em apart and introduce 'em to one another."

Delroy wondered how a place that looked so familiar could sound so alien. When they halted at another stop sign, Delroy spotted the Domino Parlor sandwiched between a cleaners and a Qwik-Mart. A battered pickup was parked out front. Three old black men, their hair iron gray in the morning light, leaned against the truck and talked, evidently waiting for the Domino Parlor to open.

"I was listening to Clarice and you talking last night," Walter said.

"I thought you were sleeping," Delroy said.

"No, sir, I was catnapping," Walter said, frowning. "Never make a mistake about that. I don't sleep. I catnap. Keeps me sharp and ever vigilant."

"I'll remember that."

"Anyway, I was listening to Clarice and you talking about what the next seven years will probably be like. During the Tribulation." Walter made another turn, driving past the Domino Parlor.

Delroy recognized George standing beside the pickup truck, the man who'd driven him to the cemetery. The old man waved at him and smiled. Delroy waved back.

"All that talk about the Antichrist and this being maybe the last chance to get right with God," Walter said, "I got to thinking." He looked at Delroy. "You know what I got to thinking?"

"No."

"That's okay because I'll tell you. I got to thinking that if Satan wanted to win himself some souls that'd be cheap for the taking, why this would be one of the places to come directly." Walter shrugged. "Ain't nobody here gonna stand up to Satan and tell him no in this neighborhood. And he'd probably be offering most folks here a better deal than they've ever got in their lives."

An old woman crossed the street in front of the cruiser. She carried a small paper bag of groceries, and her back was bent from age and from the weight of the bag. A floral patterned scarf wrapped around her head was faded from years of use.

"I come down here now and again," Walter said. "Mostly I bust up domestic fights and take reports from people who've been beaten, robbed, and burglarized, and all of us knowing there ain't nothing I'm gonna be able to do to get their stuff back, and ain't no way I can keep it from happening again. Even if I catch the people who did it the first time, somebody else'll take their places."

"You paint a pretty bleak picture, Deputy."

"Yes, sir. I suppose I do. Only it ain't no picture. It's a photograph. That's what's going on here."

Delroy rubbed his face. He'd shaved this morning, using the toiletries from his duffel, and his skin was soft to the touch. He'd also put on his dress whites because he'd felt compelled to. He wanted a piece of himself back, and those dress whites after all those years in the navy were like pulling on armor. Shaving and dressing had helped him get his sense of self back, but he knew it was all outward appearance. He felt just as confused and lost on the inside as he had that night at Terrence's grave.

"Have you got a point to this?" Delroy asked.

"Why sure I do," Walter said. "What? You think I just talk to hear my head rattle?"

Delroy politely refrained from comment. Silence and Walter Purcell wouldn't have recognized each other.

Walter kept driving and sipped from the Styrofoam cup. "My point is this: Where you gonna go from here?"

"Back to my ship. Like I told you last night."

"Yes, sir, that you did. And your ship's part of that war going on between Turkey and Syria."

"Aye."

"And the Middle East was a powder keg with fuses lit at both ends after Rosenzweig invented his fertilizer even before Syria decided to up and invade Turkey." Walter stopped at an intersection and got his bearings, then accelerated again. "I have to ask you what you think you're gonna do when you get back to that ship of yours."

Delroy tried to answer but couldn't.

"You figure on stepping back aboard her and taking up where you left off?" Walter asked.

"Aye."

"Do you really think you can do that, Chaplain?" Walter stopped the car and looked at Delroy. "Do you think you should? By your own admission, you were mostly a waste of air these past five years. I listened to you telling Clarice that last night."

Delroy didn't answer.

"How much good do you think you can do them boys that you're gonna be talking to?" Walter shook his head. "No, sir. I look at you this morning in the clear light and I see you ain't much better than you was the other night when I picked you up out of that graveyard."

The accusation stung Delroy as if he'd been slapped. He got mad, but he only got mad at himself because he knew Walter was correct in his assessment.

"Oh, you cleaned up pretty good," Walter said. "And you look good in that uniform." He reached over and tapped Delroy on the heart. "But what do you have ticking inside there, Chaplain? You got any heart left? What do you have that you can give them boys that could be going off to die? What are you going to tell them when they ask you if God's gonna be watching over them? They deserve better than some man givin' lip service to God 'cause he ain't got nothing better to do with hisself and is too afraid to figure out—or maybe just remember—what he's all about."

"You're a hard man, Deputy Walter Purcell," Delroy said in a cold voice. "I suppose I'll tell you thank you for your hospitality and find my own way from here." He reached for the door release.

"Yes, sir, I suppose that I am a hard man. Been called a lot worse from time to time. Sometimes even had friends call me those things. If I'd told my wife what I planned to do today, she'd have flat give me what for. But I just can't help myself and I knew better'n to tell that woman I was gonna be so harsh with a preacher. No, sir, she wouldn't have stood for it." Walter sipped his coffee. "But I'm gonna tell you something else, Chaplain. If you take a step outside that door before I tell you that you can, I'm gonna arrest you and lock you up."

"For what?"

"General stupidity. And don't think I won't do it. You may be big, Chaplain, but I've fought hard and long all my life. And when I figure I'm fighting for something I believe in, I won't quit. You'd have to kill me to make me quit. Giving up on something has never been in me. That's why it hurts me so much to see quitting in you. Me and you, I don't figure we're cut too much apart from the same cloth. But some-where along the way, you lost something real important to you."

My father. My son. My wife. My God. Delroy thought all those things, but he didn't say anything.

Walter let the tense silence drag on for a while; then he broke it. "I'm going to show you one other thing, Chaplain. Then I'm gonna get you to that car lot and leave you there if that's where you want to go."

"Do it," Delroy said flatly. "The sooner the better."

Without a word, Walter took his foot from the brake and left the quiet neighborhood filled with bleak houses and fearful faces.

In less than a minute, Delroy knew where Walter was taking them. He looked at the deputy and felt panic growing in him. "Don't do this."

❁ ❁ ❁

United States of America
Fort Benning, Georgia
Local Time 0937 Hours

Talking to teenagers about the Tribulation wasn't as easy as Megan had hoped. Too many of them lacked even the basic grasp of the book of Revelation, and the ones who seemed most familiar with the concept of Armageddon appeared to have learned details from horror movies. Most of these kids had been to Sunday school and church socials, but even these selected leaders lacked any real understanding of what would happen after the Rapture.

Megan stood in front of the group of twenty-nine kids she had handpicked. They sat at desks in the schoolroom where geography and political science were normally taught. World maps hung on the walls. A shelf to the right held dozens of books on countries around the world.

Eight of the teens had come from Camp Gander, which made them more or less a captive audience because Megan had awakened them, fed them breakfast, and loaded them into Goose's pickup to get them here. The other twenty-one had come because their friends had come, or because they'd wanted a chance to see and talk to the counselor who'd nearly convinced Leslie Hollister to kill herself. There were even rumors that Megan put "death messages" in her counseling sessions. Those lies had hurt Megan the most, but she had tried to ignore the bulk of the gossip.

Megan knew that the teens—and the post—still talked about that night. She continued to get looks while she was in the commissary. That night seemed like a lifetime ago now, but Leslie was still in the hospital. She was doing fine, according to the reports Megan was given, and responding well to treatment. There was even some talk of letting her out of the hospital in the next couple of days if an adult could be found to take custody of her until Sergeant Benjamin Hollister returned from service in Turkey.

Trembling a little, afraid of the course of action she had set for herself, Megan resisted the impulse to cross her arms. Body language like that would have distanced her from the kids.

Devon Snodgrass frowned. She was a redhead who had a rebellious streak and had been a constant source of trouble for her mom, an army helicopter pilot currently assigned to the post. Megan had chosen Devon because, if she came around to Megan's point of view, the young girl could be a firebrand, a natural leader.

"The world is going to end in seven years. That's what you're telling us?" Devon sounded completely skeptical about the information.

And that, Megan knew, was the problem in dealing with teenagers who didn't want to hear what was being said. They painted everything in black and white, in yes and no, and in doing so, they stepped away from any kind of receptive mode.

"Yes."

"How is the world going to end?"

"Jesus Christ will return and take all the believers and set up a kingdom that will last a thousand years," Megan said. Even as she started answering the first of the questions, she hated how fantastical those answers sounded. But she was trapped by the very concepts of heaven and immortality. If heaven were a lot like the world around them, how was it any different? If a person could live forever, why didn't he or she just do that now?

"Jesus," Devon repeated with a note of sarcasm. "I have to ask you, Mrs. Gander, what is Jesus going to do with all those people whose religion doesn't talk about Him or the Rapture or the Second Coming?"

Megan sincerely wished she had a chaplain here. Seconds after the class had begun, she'd trekked out into uncertain territory. What she knew about the Tribulation wasn't enough. The knowledge and the concept were still so new to her that she knew she wasn't a good representative to talk to the kids.

But you're all they have, she reminded herself. *This has to start somewhere.* She just hoped she didn't bungle things so badly that no one would listen. *God, You may really regret not giving me some help with this.*

"During these seven years," Megan said as confidently as she could, "the people who have been left behind are going to see miracles come to pass. As these things happen, I feel that more and more people will turn to their Bibles to seek answers for what they're supposed to do. They're going to see for themselves, and they're going to discover the same answers I'm bringing to you today. But only if other people point the way."

"And that's what you're doing?" Devon asked. "Pointing the way? So you're like what? A pathfinder to Jesus?"

Megan kept from reacting to the young girl's challenging tone through sheer effort. She kept her voice normal. "That's what I'm trying to do, Devon."

"Who pointed the way for you?" Juan Rodriguez asked from the back corner. He was tall and athletic, a senior in high school and a crush for most of the girls on post. He leaned forward as if interested. "I mean, did you like get a vision or something?" His accent was faint, more put on than natural.

"No," Megan answered, turning to face him, "I didn't get a vision."

"God talk to you through a burning bush or something?"

"No."

"Maybe He talked to you through the Internet. A Web page or something."

A few of the kids laughed.

"No," Megan said. She struggled to think of how to bring the discussion back to the subject in the correct manner. The last thing she wanted to do was step into the disciplinarian role. She suddenly realized she was dealing with her emotions for a change. Her insecurities, her lack of knowledge, and her fears were on display now instead of those of the teens. She felt incredibly vulnerable and uncertain standing in front of them.

But she had come too far, said too much even in five minutes to back away now.

Juan shook his head. "I thought all of God's prophets talked to Him in some special way."

"God hasn't talked to me," Megan said.

"Then how are you so sure that the world is going to end in seven years?" Geri Krauser demanded. Like Devon, Geri was pretty and popular, but she tended more toward the geeks and the freaks than the preppies. She wore her hair in a punky spike and had piercings through her nose and eyebrows. She also maintained a 4.0 average and had scholarship offers from seven colleges at last count.

"Because I read the book I've handed some of you today," Megan answered. She'd gone to the PX and found twelve copies of the book she and Jenny had read and liked so much.

Juan peered over the shoulder of the young blonde in front of him. Kristi Coker looked a little perturbed at Juan's actions, but she let him take the book. Kristi had been a close call for Megan, and she'd added the girl to the class at the last minute. She was bright and articulate, but not much of a people pusher, which was what Megan felt she needed to have to get the word out.

"And this book says the world's going to end in seven years?" Juan asked, flipping through the pages. "So, what? It's got a date in here somewhere?"

Megan got a stranglehold on her anger just in time. She was beginning to feel that she was back in Major Trimble's office. "The book
doesn't give a date," Megan replied.

"Then how do you know it's seven years?"

"Because the book shows that the Bible says the world will end
seven years after the Rapture."

Juan shook his head. "I'm Catholic, Mrs. Gander. My church
doesn't believe in the Rapture." With obvious disdain, he dropped
the book back on Kristi's desk and leaned back in his seat. "*I* don't believe in the Rapture."

Megan took two steps toward Juan although she never moved her
presence from the front of the room. It was all body language again,
an effort on her part to narrow the room down and focus it all on Juan
and her. For the moment it was a contest of wills. All she had to do
was pull the belief and support in the room in her direction.

"What do you think happened to all the people who disappeared?" Megan asked.

"I don't know," Juan said. "I know I don't believe that God just
scooped them up and took them off to heaven in the twinkling of an
eye."

"So which is it then?" Megan pressed. "Aliens or some secret
superweapon?"

Juan shrugged.

"And if it's either of those," Megan went on, "why haven't we
heard from the aliens again? Why hasn't the superweapon been discovered or used again?"

Holding a hand up to fend Megan off, Juan said, "You know, I got
out of bed to come here because I thought you might have something
I wanted to hear. But now you're talking about the Rapture, the Second Coming, and all this mumbo jumbo that I'm not going to buy. I
don't mean to be disrespectful, Mrs. G, but I don't see how listening
to you is going to help me."

Several other teens agreed.

"Actually, there's a new theory going around," Shawn Henderson
said. He was a gamer and a computer junkie, brilliant but barely making passing grades because he refused to apply himself to school-
work. He often knew more than the teachers who taught computer
science and mathematics.

Everyone in the room turned to look at him.

"I was watching the news," Shawn said. "Anybody seen the new
Romanian president who's got everybody talking?"

"Carpathia," Kyle Lonigan said. Like Shawn, Kyle was a gamer, but he was also a jock. Tall and good-looking, with a weight lifter's physique, he sat in the back with one of the books open on the desk before him.

"Right," Shawn said. "Carpathia and Chaim Rosenzweig—that's the guy who invented the chemical fertilizer that made Israel rich, for those of you who don't keep up with current events—have postulated that the earth's natural electromagnetic fields combined with some mysterious or so-far-unexplained atomic ionization left over from atomic-weapons tests in the past and nuclear power plants in the present."

"Electromagnetism?" Devon scoffed.

Shawn nodded. "Electromagnetism is one of the most prevalent kinds of energy in the world. To a degree, your body is a walking electromagnetic production plant that stays in tune with nature around it. Gives you a constant cause-and-effect relationship with the world."

A chorus of jibes followed Shawn's statement and completely embarrassed him.

Pushing his glasses up his nose and looking away from Devon as his cheeks colored, Shawn continued. "Rosenzweig and Carpathia think that only those people with low electromagnetic levels got zapped. Their fields couldn't stand the sudden discharge of electromagnetism the rest of us never even noticed."

"Can't believe you made the cut, Henderson," Kyle quipped.

"They say young kids and babies have low electromagnetic levels," Shawn said. "That's why they vanished."

"Vanished how?" Tobin Zachary asked. He was quiet and easygoing, a long-distance runner and a writer for the school paper. He wanted to be a journalist or a novelist.

Shawn shrugged. "They really didn't go into that. I guess those people's polarities just kind of . . . came *undone*. Their atoms got released back into the world and they were . . . erased."

The statement took a lot of the levity out of the room. Most of the kids in attendance had lost loved ones. For her part, Megan couldn't bear the thought of Chris just . . . evaporating. Like he'd never been. Nausea twisted through her stomach.

He's not right, Megan told herself. *That's not what happened. Chris is fine. He's just not here.*

"Sorry," Shawn said quietly into the silence that followed. "Got foot-in-mouth disease."

Megan looked around the room, knowing that she had lost the

kids. She wasn't at all certain that she knew how to get them back. Their losses were still too real to them, too fresh and too hurtful, and she was not here in an authority capacity. They'd already sensed that.

Juan threw his hands up and stood. "Sorry, Mrs. G, but I've had about all the grins and giggles I can stand for the morning. This is all too depressing to me. You don't have any real answers, and the day outside is just right for some volleyball in the park. Since this morning seminar is voluntary, I think I'm going to just chuck it and say thanks, but no thanks." He started for the door.

Before he reached it, most of the other teens got up from their chairs and started to follow him.

"No!" Susan January, one of the quietest girls at the post, shoved herself up from her seat. She turned on the other kids like a wounded tiger. "Don't you see how stupid all of you are being?"

Shocked by Susan's outburst, the group stopped. Susan was never one to yell at anybody

Tears ran down Susan's face. Although she was seventeen, she looked twelve years old. She was lanky and cute, and didn't look as though she would hurt a fly.

"I saw my mother disappear," Susan said in a ragged voice that was only a step above a whisper. "It was a school night, and we were up late watching a movie. We'd rented a DVD and had intended to watch the movie earlier, but we got tied up doing things around the house." She stopped, choked by emotion.

Megan hadn't heard the story. All she knew was that Susan had been present when her mother had disappeared. Susan was one of the few people—and the only one that Megan personally knew—who had actually seen someone vanish. In counseling sessions, private and group, Megan had tried to get the girl to talk about what had happened that night. Susan never had.

"She was sitting there," Susan said in a tight voice and waving her arm to her side, "sitting there right beside me. We were laughing at the movie, laughing and not even knowing we weren't going to see each other again."

The kids stood inside the room. Most of them were uncomfortable because of the raw emotion Susan exuded, but all of them were mesmerized by her story. They'd seen accounts of the phenomenon dozens of times on television, but they'd never heard one in person.

"There was no warning," Susan whispered hoarsely. "No sound before, during, or after my mom disappeared." She paused, struggling to go on. "Mom was just . . . just *there*. Then she was . . . *gone*. We were laughing together; then I heard only myself and saw her empty clothes on the couch where she'd been sitting beside me."

Some of the girls started to cry. As tough as she presented herself to be, Geri Krauser was the first to reach Susan's side and throw an arm around the girl's shoulders.

"It was like I blinked," Susan went on, her voice dry and harsh. "Mom was there; then I blinked and she wasn't. It happened that fast."

"Man, that's harsh," Shawn said.

"It *was* harsh," Susan said. "Since that time, I've been looking for an answer, trying to figure out what happened. Mrs. Gander came here today with an answer that I'd already started thinking about. I go to church. Mom made sure I went to church every Sunday. She read me Bible stories when I was little, and she talked to me about God." She choked back a sob. "More than that, my mom *believed* in God. That's something I couldn't do. I just doubted. I mean, the whole God thing—" she shook her head—"it's just too big, you know. Somebody up there watching over you. It was just more than I could handle."

No one said anything.

"I didn't believe in God when the Rapture happened," Susan said. "But I'm working on believing now. And do you know why?"

The group remained cowed and quiet.

"Because," Susan said, her voice, breaking, "because I plan to be with my mom again. In heaven. We're going to finish watching that movie, finish eating that bag of popcorn, and I'm going to tell her I love her again. I will."

Juan shook his head. "Susan—" he shrugged—"that whole Rapture thing. How can something that big only be known by part of the world? Are you going to tell me something as big as that isn't going to be in every major religion?"

"Juan, do you know the biggest thing wrong with you?" Susan wiped the tears from her face. "You always have to be right. You always have to think you've got all the answers wired. You always have to be the guy in the know." She took a ragged breath. "Well, you aren't. If you did, you'd know that what Mrs. Gander is trying to tell you about is the truth. The Rapture did happen. The world will come to an end in seven years. A lot of people are going to die between now and then."

"The electromagnetic theory—"

"The electromagnetic theory," Susan shouted, "means that all of those people are *gone*, Juan! *Forever* gone. Is that what you want to be-

lieve about your little sister? Do you want to believe that you will
never see Luisa again?"

"Maybe there's a way to reverse it," Juan said. Pain racked his face
and Megan knew he was hurting. "Maybe whoever figures this thing
out can bring the people back by dialing in their electromagnetic sig-
natures or something."

"Juan, this isn't *Star Trek*. Engineering isn't going to give you the
latest bit of technobabble fluff and a device to save the day. Mrs. Gander is trying to help you to understand what happened. More than
that, she's trying to give you enough information so you can take responsibility for your own life and save yourself." Susan took a deep
breath. "Weren't you listening? This is the end of the world. *Nobody*
gets out alive."

Megan held her breath. For a moment no one moved.

"You know what?" Juan said finally. "This is crazy. I'm not going
to be part of this. The last thing I want to do is step away from the
things I know."

"You already did that," Susan said. "That night when everyone
disappeared."

"No," Juan said. "My world's still here. Just changed a little. I'm going to be all right. But I'm not getting into this weirdness. Somebody'll
figure out what we're supposed to do. And I guarantee you it'll be more
along the lines of how to take care of the world we got left than it will
be to try to get to the next world." He lifted a hand and waved. "Check
you later. I'm outta here." He turned and walked out the door.

Slowly, other teens joined Juan, following him down the hallway.
Megan's heart turned cold with pain as each one left the room.

But Susan's words had reached some of them. When the exodus
ended, twelve teens remained.

Megan looked at them. Twelve leaders for the twelve books she
was able to purchase. *And Jesus had twelve apostles. There were twelve
tribes.*

Shawn Henderson, Kyle Lonigan, and Geri Krauser stood beside
Susan January. The other eight were just as strong.

"Okay," Megan said, feeling the tightness in her voice. "If you're
ready to begin a deeper study of what lies ahead of us, let's get
started." She was surprised at how much her legs trembled. "Before
we do, I have to admit that this is new to me. I was raised in the
church and taught about the Rapture, but I didn't know anything was
going to be expected of me. I really didn't think I was going to have to
deal with anything like this."

"That's okay, Mrs. G," Shawn said, walking forward and taking a seat at the front of the class. "I bet if we all work on it together we'll come up with something."

Megan nodded. "You're right. That's why I picked the group that was here this morning."

The other teens all chose seats near the front of the class.

"Don't you think that's weird?" Geri asked, flipping through her book and looking around. "We started out with twenty-nine people and ended up with just enough to each get a book."

"No," Megan said. "Somehow it just seems right. Maybe the matching numbers is a sign that we're doing the right thing. That we're not supposed to set our expectations too high."

Shawn leafed through the book. "Judging from the response this morning, getting people to believe what's going on is going to be nearly impossible."

"That's all right," Megan said. "Every journey begins with a single step. We'll start here today, and every day we'll try to build."

"So where do we start?" Kyle asked. "Looks like a lot of material here."

"With a prayer," Susan said. "We ask God to bless our efforts, and we ask for His guidance as we try to understand what He's given us." She took a deep breath. "That's where we begin."

"I think that's a good idea," Megan said. "Who would like to lead us in prayer?"

"I will," Kyle Lonigan said. He looked surprised to find that he had spoken. "I pray a lot in football for the team. Make sure nobody gets hurt. That kind of thing." He hesitated. "I think that's what we're looking for here."

"Thank you, Kyle," Megan said.

"Okay," Kyle said, glancing around self-consciously. "A little nervous now. I usually do my praying by myself when nobody's looking. Let's stand and join hands."

Quietly, the group did as he suggested. They formed a circle at the front of the room, heads bowed, and hands clasped.

"God," Kyle said in a soft voice, "we come to You today to ask your blessing for this undertaking. Help us to see and learn what You would have us see and learn." He paused. "And help us stay strong, God, because it looks like the way is going to be hard."

As she listened to Kyle's prayer, Megan felt a little stronger, a little closer to God. Some of her uncertainty about what she was doing seemed to pass, but there were still so many things she was unsure of.

❀ ❀ ❀

Shackleton Heights
Marbury, Alabama
Local Time 0940 Hours

"You've got no right to do this," Delroy told Deputy Walter Purcell. In the passenger seat of the car, the navy chaplain watched as the streets became more and more disturbingly familiar.

Less and less of this area had changed, but those changes had definitely been for the worse. What had once been streets lined with well-kept houses were now potholed thoroughfares punching a thin layer of civilization between decrepit dwellings. Screens still covered a few of the verandas and front porches, but rust clung to the mesh like cancer. Litter lined the cracked and peeling white picket fences that leaned first one direction then the other like drunks too far gone to make it home. Several of the homes were obviously abandoned, marked with broken windows, broken doors, and graffiti.

God, Delroy wondered, drawn into the hypnotic spell of the once-familiar territory so far removed from everything he had known, *how bad can this be?*

Walter didn't look at the chaplain, just kept driving. "I don't know what else to do, Delroy. Honest to God, I don't. Now I was never much of a praying man before all this happened. I guess maybe I kind of got away from that when that drunk driver killed my boy. And truth to tell, I didn't really think that much about praying even after all them people disappeared. But when I found you the night before last lying at your boy's grave and next to your daddy's, why I prayed that you'd be okay. Surprised the tarnation out of me, I have to tell you. Didn't even know who you were then, and there I was praying for you. Didn't even think about it. Just up and did it. Me, who ain't been big on praying for a lotta years. I thought that was strange. Yes, sir, I truly did."

Delroy sat back and tried to relax. A thousand memories spun through his mind, and he tried to avoid every one of them. "What you're doing isn't fair, Deputy."

Walter sighed heavily. "No, sir, I suppose not. But when I got up this morning after listening to you and Clarice all night, this was the only thing on my mind. Tell you the truth, I thought it was plumb stupid, too. Knew it was unfair. But I figured that was the only way I could get your attention." He paused. "More'n that, I'm halfway convinced this ain't even my idea. As crass and forward as I am, I generally don't take such liberties with another man and his problems. I figure it's well enough to give that man room to sort 'em out by himself. Only I seen you working at yours, and I know you're stuck. That decision you've made about getting back to your ship? That's a good call. But I listen to you, and I know you're doing it for the wrong reasons."

Less than two minutes later, Walter pulled the cruiser to a stop in front of the old church. Seventy years ago, it had been built on an acreage at the end of a dead-end street. The bell tower stood high with an iron cross atop it that had sometimes drawn down lightning but had never caught the roof on fire even before lightning rods were put in. Two parking areas had been cut out of the trees on either side of the church. Both had cracked asphalt and weeds that had somehow made it through the winter, and enough old cars to make them look like car lots.

Seeing the abandoned church sitting there as it was now—peeling paint and broken windows, missing shingles, and empty bell tower— almost broke Delroy's heart. Multicolored, spray-paint graffiti marred the walls, much of it ugly and profane. The white picket fence that ran around the main building and the two outer buildings where Sunday school had been taught was missing planks, had broken planks, and needed paint.

The flower beds his father had put in and his mother had tended with love and tenderness lay choked with weeds. Tall weeds and lightning-blasted trees grew in back of the church where Josiah had always kept a truck garden to help keep food on the Harte table and give away to the needy in the congregation. They'd kept chickens and a milk cow back there as well.

A faded sign hung by one chain in front of the picket fence. Time and neglect had faded the letters but Delroy knew what they said: Church of the Word. A Gathering Place of God's Faithful.

Despite the fact that he truly believed all he wanted to do was leave, Delroy reached for the door release and stepped out of the cruiser. "What happened? There was a minister who took over after my father was killed."

"Reverend Stamp," Walter agreed, getting out of the car. "He was the one who lasted the longest, though he never even came close to how long your daddy stayed. There were nineteen preachers that followed him. None of them stayed like your daddy did. None of them made this place a home. I asked around yesterday while you were

sleeping. Don't know what made me do it. I just did. I already knew
the church was closed down."

"When?" Drawn to the unbelievable sight before him, Delroy
walked toward the church. *Daddy, can you see what's become of our
church? Can you see what's happened to it? How could anyone let this happen after everything you did for it?*

"Four years ago," Walter answered, hitching up his gun belt and
following. "The last preacher got beat up by a group of gangbanger
wannabes. Put the minister in the hospital for a few days with a
cracked skull. He was young, and they scared him good. When he refused to go back to the church, the community—what few of them
cared because financially the church wasn't even making ends meet—
couldn't find another pastor. So they put chains on the doors and
closed the church down. Vandals have had at it ever since. Now and
again I chase teenagers outta there that's moved in with a few beers
and an eye toward romance."

"Glenda never said anything about this in her letters." Delroy
reached for the gate and tried to swing it outward, only to have the
hinges tear loose with a screech and the gate come away in his hand.
He set the gate aside and entered the church grounds.

"When I saw the surprise and hurt on your face," Walter said, "I
knew she hadn't. I apologize for that. I thought you did know. I just
felt I had to bring you here. Where your daddy was so strong for so
long. Don't ask me why. Just had a strong feeling to get you here this
morning. I expect I owe you an apology. This is probably the last
thing you needed to see."

In stunned disbelief, Delroy walked up the short flight of stairs
he'd helped his father build. Delroy had been ten when they'd put the
new steps in, and he could still remember the pride he'd had when
he'd helped pour the concrete to set the support poles, framed the
structure, put the steps on, and watched the congregation come up
the new stairs the next Sunday. The support poles still stood, weathered and faded, but solid as ever.

"You can go on up," Walter said. "That porch is a fine piece of
work."

"I know," Delroy said. "My daddy and I built it. He was always
one to build something to last. Always said that a building, especially
a church, knew when a man put his heart into it." He walked up the
steps, listening to his footsteps thump against the wood. "I didn't
come here much after my daddy was killed. Too many memories. I
should have, but I didn't. Just didn't have the heart for it. But I

brought my boy—I brought Terrence—here a few times. I wanted him to see where his granddaddy preached." He stepped onto the porch and looked at all the destruction. "I was married here. Did you know that?"

"No, sir, I didn't." Walter took his hat off and held it in his hands. He waited at the foot of the steps.

"I was," Delroy said, remembering how he and Glenda had stood in front of the pulpit and said their vows that Saturday morning. "I told Glenda I wanted to be married here the night I asked her to be my wife. My daddy was killed a few months later. Before he could marry us. Before he even knew we were getting married. He never got the chance to give his approval."

"I expect he knew," Walter said. "Daddies know things like that a lot of times. And if he hadn't approved of your wife, I'm sure you'd have knowed that too."

Delroy ran a hand along the double doors. "I wasn't going to have the wedding here afterwards, but Glenda talked me into doing it. I was glad she did. Reverend Stamp married us." He shook his head as the memory swelled within him. "I swear, Walter—" emotion choked his voice for a moment—"I swear that on the day I married Glenda I felt my daddy standing next to me inside this church."

Walter spoke softly and earnestly. "He probably was, Delroy. I heard your daddy put a lot of himself into this place. Man leaves a mark like that, I don't figure God will prevent him from coming back now and again to check on things."

Delroy pulled at the chain securing the doors. "I've never seen this place locked up. My daddy always kept these doors open. He always said that people who needed to pray needed a place to do it in."

Walter came up beside Delroy with a key ring. He went through five keys before he found the right one. Then the lock snapped open and he took the chains away.

"If that was your daddy's policy," the deputy said, "I don't see no reason why we should go changing things now." He pushed the double doors open. "Go on in. Have a look around. I just want you to know: what you see in there is probably gonna break your heart." Walter pushed the doors open wide.

United States of America
Fort Benning, Georgia
Local Time 0958 Hours

"I think one of the key points we need to work on is identifying the Antichrist."

Megan looked up from the book about the end times and focused on Shawn Henderson. "Why?"

"So we don't fall into his traps."

Shaking her head, Megan said, "I don't know if I agree with that."

"Mrs. G," Shawn said patiently, pushing his glasses back up his nose, "knowing the enemy is like one of the most important things you do when you're at war. Correct me if I'm wrong, but this whole section dealing with the Tribulation seems to center on the war that will be fought between heaven and hell for those who have been left behind."

"It's not our fight," Megan said. "We just need to survive."

"And work on our faith," Susan January added. "That's what kept us here when everyone else left."

"Before we do that," Kyle Lonigan said, "I really think we're going to have to define what faith is. We need to know what it is we're looking for."

Everyone in the room looked at him.

"How do you define faith?" Megan asked.

Kyle looked uncomfortable. Over the years that she had known him, Megan had always found Kyle to be insightful, something that he usually tried to hide around the other jocks he hung with.

She hadn't often seen Kyle in counseling sessions, but he had lost

his father a few years ago to a heart attack. His mother was a drill sergeant on base, a dedicated Ranger, and one of the few to have served
in active duty in Iraq during both wars as well as other hot spots
around the globe that had captured American military attention.

His father had died while his mother had been overseas. Kyle had
been staying with another family on base at the time and had experienced a lot of trouble coping with the loss of his father. His mother
had struggled with her husband's death a long time before finding
peace within herself. Kyle had actually come to terms with the loss before his mother had because she'd been carrying the double whammy
of survivor's guilt as well as having been away while her husband had
lingered for nearly two days in ICU before finally succumbing. Even
Red Cross assistance with the air connections hadn't gotten her home
in time to see him alive. Kyle had continued family counseling sessions for a while, more to keep his mom together than for any personal needs.

"Okay," Kyle said, then took a deep breath, "my definition of
faith. And this is just a baseline, a starting place to give us something
to look at. Evidently going to church every Sunday and giving thanks
for every meal isn't exactly what faith is all about. We've got people in
this room who do that now." He nodded toward Susan. "But that
wasn't enough."

Susan looked miserable and her lower lip trembled.

"Yeah," Geri Krauser said. "But when you think about all the kids
our age and the adults who vanished, those are the people who are
missing."

Kyle spread his hands. "So more often than not, those people we
perceived as good Christians are gone. We can only make one as-
sumption from that: those people's faith was true."

"But those aren't the only people missing," Marcus Raintree said.
He was a full-blooded Seminole Indian and new to the post. He was
fifteen and totally into music, having put together two bands that reflected his interest in rock and roll and jazz. "Private Jurgens, one of
the new privates who's been playing in my rock band, is gone. He
didn't go to church every Sunday. I know because a lot of Sundays we
jammed when he wasn't at post."

"How old was he?" Shawn asked.

"Twenty."

"More important," Kyle said, "what kind of person was he?"

"He was a good guy," Marcus said. Unconsciously, his hands
drummed an almost silent beat on the desktop. "He was a great bass

guitarist. Had an ear, you know? He liked comic books and fantasy novels. We traded a lot of stuff back and forth. If you needed help with something, Private Jurgens was one of the guys you went to first."

"Did he talk about his faith much?"

"No." Marcus hesitated. "I knew he was a Christian from the books he had on his shelves, but he never pushed anything at me. But we were talking one time when he was getting ready to ship out to Iraq for a peacekeeping tour. I asked him if he ever got afraid while he was out there, knowing he might get shot at any time. He told me he didn't, that he'd made his peace with God a long time ago and knew that he was going to heaven."

"And he's gone?" Geri asked.

Marcus nodded. "After all this craziness went down, I went over to his base apartment. Had to break in, but I had to know because he was my friend. He came to our house last Christmas 'cause he doesn't have any family of his own. My mom and dad liked him a lot." His dark eyes teared up and he couldn't go on for a moment. "I found Marcus's clothes on the couch where he must have been watching television when he . . . when he left."

Megan let the quiet stay in the room for a time before continuing. "So you don't have to go to Sunday school or pray before every meal or witness to others."

"Faith is an internal thing," Kyle said. "It's not based on outward behavior. My dad used to tell me that all the time. Even when he was in ICU fighting for his life. He told me he wasn't afraid of dying, but he didn't want to leave me behind." His voice hung just for a moment but he quickly mastered the emotion that tugged at him. "He told me God loved everyone and wanted a personal relationship with us. Sometimes God expects more from some people than He does from others."

"Because they've got more to give," Geri said.

The other teens looked at her in surprise.

"My aunt," Geri said. "She told me that the Bible says, 'To whom much is given, from him much will be required.'" She shrugged. "Aunt Lil was an EMT. I asked her one day how she could stand to look at everything she saw every day and not go crazy. You know— dead people, hurt people, decapitated people. Some of the stories her friends would tell totally creeped me out. I told her I couldn't have done her job. She said that God had given her a gift and that she was meant to help others. So He made her strong enough to do that."

"The stats I looked at involving the disappearances," Shawn said, "show that a bigger percentage of EMTs, hospital workers, and firefighters disappeared than other professions."

"People whose careers are to help others," Megan said, thinking of Helen Cordell and how she had disappeared from the post hospital that night. "Have you talked with your aunt lately?"

Geri shook her head and tears glinted in her eyes. Stubbornly, holding true to her independent nature, she crossed her arms and shook her head. "She disappeared. I talked to my uncle Bob. He's pretty upset." She paused. "I think I'll call him after we get out of here and let him know what we're finding out." She nodded toward the book in front of her. "Maybe he can get a copy of this book. Maybe it'll hurt."

"What about your aunt?" Kyle asked. "Did she advertise her Christianity?"

"No. She didn't pressure you into faith either. But she was open to talk about it. She . . . she was just one of the coolest people I ever knew. Always there, you know?"

Megan remembered the aunt from her counseling sessions with Geri. There were a lot of issues Geri had with how things went in the Krauser household. Mrs. Krauser was a closet drinker and Lieutenant Krauser hadn't been faithful to the marriage. Geri had brought those things up, but neither parent had been in to talk about it or even deal with it in the relationship. Aunt Lil had been Geri's major confidante.

"A personal relationship with God is what my mom always talked about," Susan said. "She said she enjoyed church and talking with people about God, and never forgot to thank Him for the blessings He'd given her. But she said the most important thing anyone could ever have was that personal relationship."

"How do you get a personal relationship with God?" John Reynard asked. He was always quiet, always intense. He was gawky and socially inept to a degree, springing partly from the fact that his father was an artillery specialist and trained at several different posts, moving his family each time. He'd been overseas a number of times. John dressed and acted goth, with painted fingernails and dyed hair that drove his military father crazy and gave his mother more ammunition to argue with his father over. He had his arms crossed over his chest and peered from under a sheep dog's forelock of dusty blue hair.

"You ask for it," Geri said. "That's what Aunt Lil always told me when I asked."

"Not like you can dial up 1-800-GOD," John said.

"You pray," Susan said. "That's what my mom told me too."

"You pray and what? God answers?"

"Yes," Susan said.

John looked troubled and shook his head. "You ever heard Him speak to you?"

"It's not like that," Susan said. "My mom said she'd pray about something that she couldn't handle or needed guidance with; then she'd leave whatever it was with God. Kind of the way Kyle guided us in prayer a few minutes ago." She shrugged. "You just don't get an immediate answer."

"Why not?" John asked.

"Because then it wouldn't be faith," Kyle replied. He took a deep breath. "When my dad was in ICU and the doctors told me he might not recover, I knew Dad was in a lot of pain. I could see it in his eyes when he was conscious those few times. I . . . I got the feeling that he was hanging on for me. That he wouldn't go because he was trying to stay with me till Mom got there."

Megan felt Kyle's pain resonating within her. She hadn't known that any of the kids she had assembled had ever had to be so strong.

Kyle took another deep breath and tears ran down his cheeks. "The second morning after he had his attack, I prayed to God to give me the strength to let my dad go. A few hours later, when my dad was conscious again, I felt okay about everything. Even though Mom wasn't there. I'm talking about a real sense of peace, guys, and I haven't felt anything like that since that morning. I told my dad that I had talked to God and that if he needed to go, it would be all right because I knew God would be with me." Kyle gulped air. "Less than an hour later, my dad died. Peacefully. Like it was no problem at all." He wiped his tears away. "It was hard to do it, but I thanked God for His mercy."

"I couldn't have done that," Susan whispered.

Still teary-eyed, Kyle smiled gently at her. He whispered in a hoarse voice, "That's the whole secret, though. Dad always said that you never knew what you could do until you asked God to help you."

"Then why are you still here if you believe in God so much?" Marcus asked.

"That's just it," Kyle said. "I didn't believe. Not really. Not even after that morning. I asked God for a favor and He gave it to me. Kind of like asking a stranger for help. Sometimes you get help from that stranger, but sometimes you get ignored. Even if the stranger helps you, you still don't know him." He looked around at the group. "I think if you're going to truly become a Christian, you have to go to

God in prayer, ask Him what you can do, and then listen to what He has to say."

"I thought we just agreed that God doesn't talk to you."

"Not directly," Geri said. "Aunt Lil said sometimes He puts things on your heart. Like me with this seminar. When Juan got up and left, I had every intention of leaving too. Only I couldn't after Susan said what she did about her mom. It reminded me too much of Aunt Lil. In that instant, things just seemed to get clearer. I'd prayed about that this morning. Which is why I came here in the first place." She frowned a little as if struggling to make the others understand. "I think that if you listen, you'll understand what you're supposed to do."

"But first," Susan said, "you have to ask. Like Kyle did at the prayer we had at the beginning of this meeting." She pursed her lips. "I think it's made a difference. I know I feel better about everything."

The others quickly agreed.

"We can't forget about the Antichrist," Shawn said. "I think we should keep our eyes open for him." He flipped through the pages of the book on the desk. "I mean, look at this. War. Famine. Plagues. An earthquake. And that's just the beginning. One simple fact of the situation is that the farther we are from the Antichrist, the safer we are."

"The Antichrist!" The voice ripped through the schoolroom, jerking everyone's attention to the doorway. A Ranger captain stood there, dressed in a crisp uniform and staring at Megan with a narrow-eyed and hostile gaze. He was fit and tan, with a mustache that colored his narrow upper lip beneath his hooked nose. "Mrs. Gander, just what do you think you're teaching these kids?"

Taken aback, not believing she hadn't heard the approach of the captain or of the six MPs that flanked him, Megan didn't know what to say.

※　※　※

Church of the Word
Marbury, Alabama
Local Time 1001 Hours

Delroy stared in helpless confusion and rage at the damage that had been done to the church where he had spent so much of his young life.

Dust filled the cavernous vault of the church's main worship area. Sunlight streamed in through broken windows. Only a handful of pews were left, and most of those were broken or in a state of disrepair.

More graffiti, all of it lewd and vicious, colored the church's walls. Beer cans and bottles littered the floor. The vandals hadn't had any regard for the craftsmanship Josiah Harte had put into his church.

Taking his hat off and tucking it under his arm, numb from the shock and overwhelmed by the memories coursing through his mind, Delroy strode into the sanctuary. His steps sounded hollow and loud against the scarred hardwood floor and the silence that filled the church.

Four years. It looks like an eternity has passed.

Walter's walkie-talkie buzzed for attention. He tried to reply but the signal wasn't clear. Excusing himself, he walked back to the cruiser.

Bitterly Delroy looked around the church. He remembered running through the building as a child, squealing in delight as his daddy chased him while he took a break from whatever work he'd been doing. Hundreds of summer days and winter evenings had been spent inside this church with other kids, all of them playing checkers and Monopoly, trading baseball cards and dreaming of being on baseball cards.

But on Sunday mornings their faces were scrubbed and they had on their best clothes to listen to Josiah Harte tell them of God's love and God's punishment of the wicked. They'd learned of heaven and they'd learned of hell, and Delroy had never been prouder of his daddy than when he'd seen him in front of the congregation stoking the fires of righteous indignation and preaching the fear of God.

Dazed and bewildered, Delroy walked slowly through the church. Strains of the songs sung by the choir, his momma's voice pealing among them, seemed to come to his ear. One particular Sunday morning, Josiah had invited Glenda to church shortly after she and Delroy had started dating. When he closed his eyes, Delroy could still hear her sing:

> *"On a hill far away stood an old rugged cross,*
> *The emblem of suffering and shame;*
> *And I love that old cross where the dearest and best*
> *For a world of lost sinners was slain."*

Delroy remembered how Glenda had looked that morning, so full of life and love and hope. She'd worn a pale peach dress that emphasized her dark skin. Her voice had filled the church, mesmerizing all those in attendance, drawing tears from some of them because she sang so beautifully.

People had talked about her singing for weeks. When she and Delroy walked down the street together people would come up and congratulate her, telling her how much it had meant to them. Glenda had been so embarrassed by all the attention.

Even you, Daddy, even you were surprised by her voice and her conviction to the Lord. A lump formed in Delroy's throat as he looked at the defaced picture of Jesus Christ behind the water tank where baptisms were done. *God, why did we have to have all that innocence taken away from us? Why couldn't we just have remained simple and loving in Your eyes? We would have served You forever.*

Shadows moved in the church as the wind blew the branches outside.

"Do you know why men and women are tested?" Josiah Harte's voice rose up from Delroy's memory and filled the church around him. "I ask y'all, brothers and sisters, do y'all know why the Lord God Almighty allows Satan to tempt y'all with earthly things like money and big fine cars like y'all see some folks driving?"

The deacons in the church had answered, "No, Reverend."

In his mind's eye, Delroy saw the church as it had been then: the wood floor polished, the pews set in exact rows with Bibles and hymnals stacked neatly. His father had paced in front of the choir as he always did. Josiah Harte had never been a man to stand still.

"Y'all know what a lot of people think, don't y'all?" Josiah had demanded. "They think God wants us tested because He wants to know what's in our hearts. Let me ask y'all that. How many think that's why God allows that old devil to tempt so many of us? So that God will know what's in your hearts?"

Several of the parishioners had raised their hands. Delroy had raised his right along with them.

"Oh and look at y'all!" Josiah had exclaimed. "Ain't none of y'all been listenin' to what I been preachin' all these years." He smacked his Bible in his hands and looked skyward as he spread his arms to his sides. "Lord God, I ask that You show mercy on these people because they've come a long way, but it's evident they got a ways to go. But be patient with them, because I think You and me can get 'em there before we're done."

A great embarrassed silence had fallen over the church the way it always did when the congregation knew they'd been found wanting by their fiery pastor.

"God Almighty, I ask that You give me patience too, because I know that You know I ain't a patient man when it comes to muleheadedness. I lead them to Your Word, Lord, but I cain't make 'em drink. No, sir, I cain't make 'em drink not one drop."

At nine years old, Delroy had sat silent and chastised on the front row where the minister's family always sat. He wished he'd never lifted his hand, but he'd felt certain that he'd been answering correctly. Satan was at the root of all evil; that Delroy had known for certain.

"Y'all listen," Josiah had roared. He'd pointed people out and called them by name. "I know y'all got a heaviness on your hearts. Some have told me about your troubles, and some I've seen in trouble even though y'all ain't admittin' it even to yourownselves. Y'all got troubles, and want to blame God for gettin' y'all in the pickle y'all's in. Y'all want to blame the devil 'cause all evil in the world is his. But do y'all know why God in all His infinite wisdom allows y'all to be tempted, brothers and sisters?"

The silence that had followed was uncomfortable.

"I'll tell y'all why we're allowed to be tempted," Josiah had yelled, slamming his fist on the pulpit so hard that Delroy had thought the top would split. "It's so y'all can know for yourownselves how strong y'all are in the ways of the Lord. So y'all can all triumph over Satan and his evil ways."

"Amen," the deacons said.

"An' here y'all sit, choosin' to be afraid of God an' what He might do to y'all when the worst thing that can be done is what y'all's doin' to yourownselves."

Quiet had rung out over the congregation.

"It ain't temptation that y'all gotta worry about the most, though," Josiah had roared. "Ol' Satan thinks he's almighty sly about that, but that's not his real trick. Y'all know what his real trick is?"

No one had dared to answer.

"Satan's real trick is gettin' y'all to believe y'all got something to fear from the Lord. If the devil can get y'all afraid of God, why then he's got y'all in the worst trap possible. Turn from God an' y'all are lost."

"Amen," the deacons said.

"But y'all ain't gotta be afraid of God. Satan don't want y'all to remember that, though. Satan don't want y'all to ever learn that in the first place." Josiah had marched across the front of the church, then down the main aisle looking at his congregation with the fiery-eyed determination of a battlefield general. "God already knows where y'all are strong and where y'all are weak. Don't y'all know that God already knows all our secrets? If y'all do, y'all only got fools for company, brothers and sisters." He hurled the word out among them. "Fools!"

The congregation hung their heads, not daring meet their pastor's gaze.

"All the things y'all want to hide from ever'body God knows. He even knows the things y'all hide from yourownselves." Then Josiah had paused long enough till the last echo of his voice had died away. When he continued, it had been in a softer voice. "But know what, brothers and sisters? Know what the biggest surprise of all is? I'll tell y'all: Satan knows how strong y'all are, too."

That thought had scared Delroy as a child. Just thinking that Satan was on such familiar terms with him was almost too much. That Sunday morning, Delroy had almost been able to feel the devil sitting at his shoulder.

"Satan knows how strong y'all are," Josiah repeated. "He knows how strong y'all are, an' he knows how weak y'all are. But it's y'all's strength that Satan fears. Do y'all know what Satan's hopin' as he sets there temptin' y'all with pride an' jealousy an' greed?"

"No, Reverend," the deacons had answered.

"Satan's hopin' that y'all don't know how strong y'all are in your faith an' devotion to the Lord God Almighty. 'Cause if y'all ever learn how strong y'all can be through God's Holy Word, if y'all ever believe in the strength God gives when y'all cain't fend for yourownselves 'cause y'all got a period of weakness comin' on an' have to call on Him for succor, why there ain't nothing Satan can do. Let Satan tempt away. Y'all will be invincible warriors in the service of God Almighty! Can I get an amen?"

"Amen!" the deacons had shouted, and the body of the church had joined them till Delroy had thought the rafters were going to blow straight through the roof.

When the furor died away, Josiah had continued. "We grow stronger with each temptation we turn away from. Satan cain't help that. There that ol' serpent is, a-tryin' to lead us down the wrong path to ever'thin' that's unholy, a-tryin' to lead us away from the Lord an' His love for us, an' Satan cain't help but make us stronger ever' time he fails. An' he cain't stop hisself from tryin' an' temptin' neither. I tell you, brothers and sisters, the devil's gotta be the most frustrated creature in this here world because his job's so hard."

The congregation had laughed a little at that, sensing that their pastor was once more proud of them.

"Ain't none of y'all perfect, brothers and sisters. Ain't a perfect person out there."

"Amen," the deacons had said.

"An' I'm here to tell y'all just in case y'all's wonderin'," Josiah continued, "there ain't no perfect man standin' up here today either. I got my own strengths an' weaknesses. An' I been tempted. My hand on a stack of Bibles, I've been tempted. We've all been tempted. An' some have fallen today, some yesterday, an' some the day before that. Y'all know when y'all give in to the devil's temptations an' answer the callin' of evil what's in this world. That's between y'all an' God. But don't be foolin' yourownselves that God don't know."

The congregation had grown quiet again.

"Ain't a sparrow what falls from the loneliest tree in the forest that His eye ain't on it to mark its passin'."

"Amen," the deacons said.

"But y'all know what?" Josiah had paused. "God loves us all. An' no matter what Satan does or says, he cain't take that away from us. Satan cain't take God's love. What y'all gotta do is remember that. Don't be afraid. No matter what happens, no matter what goes on in y'all's lives, trust in the Lord God Almighty. An' if y'all slip an' stumble from the path, ain't gonna take but one step to head back in the right direction. Just that one step, brothers and sisters, an' God makes for certain that y'all don't gotta take that step alone. 'Cause he steps with y'all."

"One step," Delroy remembered, coming back from the memory and looking around at the church with new eyes. He felt strengthened a little. He had forgotten his daddy's sermon on temptation and Satan's place in the world.

"One step," a mocking voice asked. "Do you really think that's all it takes, Preacher? One step? One step out of a mile leaves another five thousand, two hundred and seventy-something feet to go. I wouldn't feel like one step accomplishes all that."

Whirling, recognizing the voice at once, Delroy faced the back of the church and saw the creature standing in the open doorway.

❊ ❊ ❊

United States of America
Fort Benning, Georgia
Local Time 1005 Hours

While Megan stood speechless, the captain strode into the room and stopped near the podium beside her. He picked up the book about the end times she and the teens had been studying and dropped it back down.

"Religion, Mrs. Gander?" the captain sneered. "As a counselor for this post, that's not exactly your purview, is it?"

"Captain—" Megan glanced at his name tag—"Stashower, as counselor, I speak on a number of issues concerning the youth of the base. Religion is definitely one of them." But she knew she was stretching her actual responsibilities. She could talk about religion if those issues came up but not initiate them. And she was supposed to refer serious problems regarding faith and questions of faith to the chaplain's office.

"Mrs. Gander," Stashower said, "I've been sent here to shut down your little dog-and-pony show before it becomes an embarrassment to this post."

Anger overrode some of Megan's insecurity at being confronted by a Ranger captain and a squad of armed MPs. "An embarrassment, Captain? I resent that remark."

"Resent it all you want to," Stashower advised. "As of 0800 hours, in an attempt to lessen public-relations problems with the city of Columbus, the gates to this post were opened to admit outside personnel. Those personnel include media people."

Megan remembered that. There had been a memo in her morning e-mails. "I fail to see what that has to do with what I'm doing in this classroom, Captain Stashower."

Stashower glared at her. "General Braddock has given me orders to send you packing. Now, I can either send you home or I can remand you to the provost marshal's office till the matter gets settled through Joint Services. You're going to cease and desist."

Disbelief swept through Megan, but anger was hot on its heels. "Captain, I'm trying to help these kids understand what is happening to them and what they are going to go through during the next seven years."

"By telling them that Jesus Christ Himself is going to return and lead them to heaven?" The captain looked apoplectic. "No, ma'am. Not on my watch. These kids have been through enough without you traumatizing them further."

"Captain—"

Stashower wheeled on Megan, shoving his face into her space and causing her to back up involuntarily.

"No, ma'am," Stashower said in a loud voice. "Another thing, Mrs. Gander, if it had been me on shift the other night when you talked the Hollister girl into shooting herself—"

"I didn't talk her into—"

"I'd have had you locked down," Stashower finished, raising his voice to talk over her. "You're a menace to these kids. You've got no business talking to them. And that's going to be in my report."

The teens stood and tried to defend Megan.

"Corporal," Stashower growled without turning from Megan.

"Yes, sir."

"If those young men and women cause a problem, I want them arrested and charged." Stashower glared at Megan. "Ma'am, if you have any control over these kids, I suggest you use it now."

Without breaking eye contact with the captain, Megan called for the teens' attention. "Do what Captain Stashower says. I don't want anyone getting into trouble this morning. That's not what we're here for."

"They can't just make us leave like this," Geri protested. She jerked her arm away from one of the MPs.

"I can and I am," Stashower declared. "And that's happening right now."

"Go," Megan said in a firm voice. "If any of you get into trouble, we might not be able to do this again."

Silently, the teens allowed the MPs to herd them out into the halls. As Shawn passed by Megan, he mouthed the words, *See? War.*

The suggestion jolted Megan. Was that what was happening here? Had some malevolent force somehow sensed they were gathering, that people were going to be educated to the truth? to God's truth? Even as she thought that, she disregarded it. That was impossible. There had to be another reason, another way Stashower had known they were here.

Watching the kids file out into the hallway, Megan spotted Juan Rodriguez standing against the wall. His dark, hooded eyes met hers for just a moment. There was no sign of guilt, no sign of remorse. Then he shook his head as if in disgusted disbelief, turned, and walked out of sight.

The captain lifted the book from the podium again and sneered at it. "*The end times*, Mrs. Gander?" He shook his head. "That's what this is going to be for you when General Braddock finishes with you."

"Can I quote you on that, Captain Stashower? That was a very strong and somewhat witty statement using the book's title like that. Especially when coming from a United States Army captain heading up a six-man security unit of brawny military police officers and directed at a single young woman who serves the troubled youth of Fort Benning."

A woman's heavily accented Southern voice surprised Megan and pulled her attention to the second doorway at the end of the room. A camcorder operator stood at the woman's side. As Megan watched, the cameraman moved his machine back and forth.

"Who are you?" Stashower demanded.

The woman was in her early- to midforties. She had platinum blonde hair cut short, blue eyes, and a pale complexion. Tall and slender, she looked elegant in the light brown business suit.

"Ms. Penny Gillespie," the woman said in her syrupy Southern drawl. "This is my colleague, Herman."

Herman the cameraman waved nonchalantly, but never took his eye from the camcorder's viewer or his finger off the Record button.

"You're not supposed to be here," Stashower growled.

"I understand that the timing appears to be quite awkward for you, Captain Anthony Jerome Stashower," Penny Gillespie assured him.

"This place is off-limits."

"That's not," the woman stated, "what I was told at the front gate." She crossed the room with a stroll that was somehow both business and pure class. "I was told, and I have it on the best authority—a Major Frederick Donleavy, who, if memory serves me correctly, holds the position of Fort Benning's chief public-information officer—that members of the media are allowed to roam the post freely as of this morning. As a gesture of goodwill toward the city that hosts this fort, in light of the post's last few days of marshal law and general selfishness regarding the problems of others. We can roam freely, except for the restricted areas, of course. Those, I've been instructed, are clearly marked and guarded." She looked around the room with wide eyes. "I found no such warnings or guards on this building or in this very room, Captain Stashower."

"You're a member of the media?" Stashower demanded.

"Indeed," Penny answered. "I am a member in very good standing. I represent Dove TV, a local Christian television station. I have a small show. Perhaps you've heard of it. *Penny for Your Prayers.* The title is somewhat self-aggrandizing, but I assure you I had no choice in the matter. My father can be a very obstinate man when he chooses. I specialize in human interest stories about people who can use the prayers and kindness of others. People who have, in the past, given generously of themselves."

Megan had heard of the program. Dove TV, with the white dove the station used for its logo, was a local network out of Atlanta and had a considerable fan base among Christian viewers. *Penny for Your Prayers* was one of the top programs. Looking at the woman now, Megan recognized her as the host.

"We're very small in comparison to the major networks also represented here today," Penny said, "but I assure you that we get picked up quite regularly in syndication. Many viewers are interested in receiving a Christian viewpoint on national domestic events that capture headlines. That is quite true these past few days. Especially in light of this singularly unique set of circumstances regarding the disappearances, which Mrs. Gander was attempting to explain to those students when you so rudely burst in and interrupted."

Megan stood in shock. Stashower's unannounced arrival was staggering, but coupled with the sudden appearance of a Christian television reporter, events were almost going too fast for her to comprehend.

"I did not burst in," Stashower objected.

"My dear captain," Penny said in a crisp and cool voice, "I do remember a time not so very long ago when a man—especially a man wearing the uniform of this country's military and standing as a symbol of courage and honor and everything that is decent about a man—did not call a lady a liar."

"I did not—" Stashower caught himself. He ground his teeth. "Perhaps we have a difference of opinion."

"And I," Penny told him, stopping in front of him with her cameraman just behind and to the side of her so he could film the confrontation, "I have a very interesting digital recording, Captain. Perhaps I could show this recording to my viewers and have them vote on it. About bursting in or being invited in? Many of my viewers are very big on manners." She smiled, flashing white teeth that were somehow as threatening as a shark's. "I could let you know the results in just a short time, I am sure. You and your commanding officer . . . General Braddock, I believe?"

"Maybe the general will have a word with your station owner," Stashower said.

Penny gave a mock gasp, put a hand over her heart, and let her jaw drop in astonishment. "Why, I declare. I do think I have been chastised. Or would you say *threatened*, Herman?"

"Oh, I'd say threatened," Herman said. "You've been threatened before, Penny, and this sounds like one of those times."

"It must be so hard to come up with original threats," Penny said. "But I understand your need to do so, Captain."

A muscle along Stashower's jaw quivered.

Giving a disapproving shrug and a wave of dismissal, Penny said, "Well then, Captain, certainly threaten away if you feel you must. And you have my blessing to contact my station owner regarding my story if you wish. My father—the station owner—why he keeps an open-door policy. I'm sure you'll have no problems setting up such a meeting. My father would probably feel up to entertaining your General Braddock as well."

Despite her anxiety about everything going on and her lack of control over these events, Megan had a hard time not bursting out laughing at Stashower's inept attempts to extricate himself from the confrontation.

"But I feel I must warn you," Penny said. "My father, Beauregard P. Gillespie—*the* Beauregard P. Gillespie of the Atlanta, Georgia, Gillespies—does not always suffer threats in the spirit of good sport in which I am sure your own threat was offered. He may very well insist on a pound of flesh over such an occasion, and he keeps a quite competent legal staff that dotes on him zealously, even when they know he's being overly sensitive. They would love to see the digital footage Herman has shot of your conversation with me, I do believe."

Stashower closed his mouth.

"Now," Penny said, "if you're through threatening Mrs. Gander, Captain Stashower, I should like very much to ask her for a moment of her time." She shifted her attention to Megan without awaiting the captain's reaction. "Mrs. Gander, I must say, it is quite a privilege to meet you. I'd been looking forward to it since I talked with one of the snarly-mouthed young people outside this building who said military police officers were on their way to break up your little 'Jesus Saves Party,' as they so crudely called it." She extended her hand.

Mesmerized by the woman's audacious confidence, Megan took her hand. Penny Gillespie's handshake was warm and strong.

"Thank you," Megan said. "I've seen your show." She wished the comment hadn't sounded so inane, but that was the first response that popped into her head.

Penny smiled. "You *are* a dear." She offered a final squeeze and took her hand back. "Am I to assume, then, that you are free for the moment, Mrs. Gander?"

"Yes," Megan said.

"Good. This will work out perfectly, because—after hearing about this very interesting class and seeing the attention and retribution offered by General Braddock and his staff—I would actually like more than a moment of your time. I have a proposition that you might find at least entertaining, and hopefully more than a little interesting."

Penny took Megan by the elbow. "Captain Stashower, may I assume that since Mrs. Gander has been unequivocally threatened by you and had her 'Jesus Saves Party' properly routed—as ordered by General Braddock—that she is now free to go?"

Stashower remained tight-lipped for a moment.

Megan suddenly realized that the phrasing of Penny's question, if answered affirmatively, not only let her go but also admitted for public—and camcorder—record that Stashower had threatened her at the general's orders. On her show, Penny was always quick-witted and often punished anyone who tried to lie to her or had willingly caused strife in the lives of others.

"No," Stashower replied.

Megan knew that the captain was trying to deny the accusations couched in Penny's question, but he had stepped into another part of the trap that Penny had laid for him with dismaying ease.

"Oh my," Penny said in a worried tone. "Do you mean that you have to threaten Mrs. Gander further, Captain Stashower? If I had been Mrs. Gander, I'm afraid I might have been petrified to even breathe. I may have to put a discretionary warning on this segment of my show when it airs."

Herman the cameraman kept recording.

"No," Stashower said. "No threats."

"Well, that's good," Penny said with enthusiastic relief. "It was very hard going through those first few. I'm sure our viewers will be a little more relaxed knowing that Mrs. Gander is not going to be further persecuted for having the personal strength and conviction to show her Christian faith to young people of this post who need guidance in these troubling times." She smiled. "Do you require anything more of Mrs. Gander, Captain Stashower?"

"No," Stashower gritted out.

"Then we'll take our leave, Captain, and wish you a good day." Penny gently pulled at Megan's elbow.

Reluctantly at first, knowing all kinds of repercussions from the military lay ahead of her, Megan followed Penny Gillespie out of the room.

Church of the Word
Marbury, Alabama
Local Time 1011 Hours

The creature wore the visage of a young man. He was black this time, wearing black motorcycle leathers and wraparound sunglasses. A pencil-thin mustache and a goatee framed his mouth. Rastafarian dredlocks covered his head. Gold hoop earrings dangled from his ears and two gold teeth gleamed in his mouth. When the dappled sunlight fell on him, reptilian scales showed shadowy images.

Beyond the creature, Walter stood outside the cruiser talking on his handset. He gave no indication he saw the creature.

The creature smirked as it examined the front of the church. "Well, this place has certainly seen better days. Guess nobody around here even believes in paint." He peeled a long strip of paint from the doorframe. "So how you feelin' today, Preacher? All rested up?" Even its accent was changed, but it was the same creature.

Delroy didn't speak.

"So, you gonna buy into Deputy Dog's little pep talk? Take a walk down memory lane and get your religion back? Is that what this is all about?" The creature shook its head. "You're still looking for that quick fix, Preacher. Still looking but not finding."

The mocking words ate at Delroy's confidence. How was he supposed to know what to do if God kept allowing this creature to dog his steps and undermine every advance he made toward getting himself back together?

The creature shook its head again. "I have to tell you, Terrence is plenty upset with you. He's still lying in that coffin when you could have at least freed him."

Delroy turned away, closed his eyes, and told himself he would ignore whatever it said.

"Don't turn away from me, Preacher," the thing ordered. "If you don't listen to me, maybe I'll walk out to that deputy and slit his throat ear to ear while he's talking on the walkie-talkie. He don't see me now; I can promise you he won't see me then."

Trembling with rage and fear, all but exhausted even after the sleep he'd gotten the day before, Delroy faced the creature, fully expecting it to walk into the church and start closing in on him.

Instead, the creature remained at the door. "What is it with you, Preacher? Are you just too dumb to give up? or too prideful? Neither one of those qualities is exactly something God treasures now, is it?"

Delroy peered past the creature, wondering how Walter Purcell hadn't noticed it standing there. Instead, the deputy stayed on the radio, gazing around the neighborhood as if nothing was going on.

"He can't see me," the thing said. "I'm here just for you."

Delroy felt broken and humbled, but he remembered his daddy's words. "Are you here to tempt me?"

"With what?" the creature asked, smiling. "What have I offered you?"

"Doubt," Delroy said. "And fear."

The creature grinned. "You're fooling yourself, Preacher. You've already loaded your own cupboard with those things. And you're not as important in the grand scheme of things as you seem to believe you are. You're just an amusement." It stepped forward, hesitant for the barest moment till its foot touched down on the other side of the threshold. As it moved down the aisle, the creature glanced around. "I've never been in a church before." It kicked at an empty beer bottle and sent the brown glass rolling across the room. "Of course, most churches I've seen have been cleaner. This place is a pigsty. God hasn't even been able to keep this place clean much less filled with believers."

Delroy stared at the creature, paralyzed by the effrontery and the anger it evoked.

"What?" The creature looked at him with a big grin. "You thought I wouldn't be able to step into this hovel because it's supposed to be some sacred place? I'm not a vampire, Preacher. I'm something much, much worse. I'm the dark side of you that never learned to be afraid of God or of living your own existence." It clenched a fist and started for Delroy. "Now, since you are so stupid, I'm going to finish that beating I started in the cemetery two nights ago."

Delroy raised his hands. He was still sore and bruised all over from the struggle in the graveyard. He knew he wouldn't last long against the creature, but he couldn't run. There was nowhere to go.

Even as the creature drew its right hand back to swing, Delroy felt a *force* pass over him, under him, and around him. Some of it even flowed through him, jostling him a little and turning him cold for an instant.

But the force hammered the creature like a nuclear weapon. It staggered back three steps, then exploded into a swirl of flaming bones and burning, tattered clothing that blew through the double doors like a comet.

"Get out!" yelled a voice Delroy immediately recognized.

The voice belonged to Josiah Harte.

"This is the house I served my heavenly Father in," the voice continued. "You will not taint this place with your foul filth, you unholy thing. Nor will you harm my son in this place. This place is sacred, an' it is protected."

The spinning, blazing tumble of bones and cloth blew out into the middle of the church courtyard, then rolled into one of the weed-choked flower beds. A heartbeat later, the flames extinguished and left behind charred bones and cloth.

"Daddy," Delroy whispered, staring into the dust storm that had risen around him. Nothing moved. There was no answer, and he was already wondering if he'd only imagined the voice. Stunned, he walked outside and stared at the smoldering heap of bones in the front yard.

The bones shook and shivered as a skeleton pushed itself up from the ground. By the time the creature was standing, it wore flesh and clothes again and looked none the worse for wear. It turned its dark-lensed gaze heavenward and threw up its arms in disgust.

"You can't protect him," the creature yelled. "He's weak. He can't make it on his own. He can't be what You want him to be. He's afraid, and he's filled with doubts. He's going to be *mine*." The creature lowered its gaze and pointed at Delroy. "You're *mine*, Preacher. You'll slip and fall, and when you do, I'll be waiting."

"Delroy?"

Turning toward the voice, Delroy saw Walter holding up the handset of his walkie-talkie. He wanted to tell the deputy what was going on but somehow knew that Walter wouldn't see the thing even after he was told about it.

"Got some business to do," Walter called from the cruiser. "Shouldn't take more'n fifteen or twenty minutes. You gonna be all right here while I'm gone?"

Delroy struggled to find his voice. No matter what else happened, he knew that at the moment he didn't want to leave the church. For the moment the building offered security against the creature; he knew that because it didn't even try to come back up the steps. And Delroy wanted to know if it had really been his father's voice he'd heard inside the church. "Aye," Delroy croaked as fear continued to tighten his throat. "I'll be fine."

Walter waved and climbed into the cruiser.

When he glanced back at where the creature had been standing, Delroy was surprised to see only the weed-choked garden.

The creature was gone.

Slowly, Delroy turned and walked back inside the church. He stared at the walls, picturing how the church had looked before the vandals had struck and sprayed graffiti everywhere.

Surprise filled him as he realized he was looking for his father. "Daddy?" Delroy stumbled through the debris on shaking legs. It *had* been his father's voice he'd heard. And something had blown the creature out of the church. He raised his voice. "Daddy?"

No one answered.

God, I'm not going crazy. I know that was my daddy I heard. He's the only man I ever knew that had a tone of voice like that.

Overcome with doubt, frustration, and fear, Delroy walked to the small raised dais where the pulpit used to stand in front of the small section that held the choir. Both of the pulpit's wooden arm railings were shattered.

He knelt in the dust. "Daddy, I know it was you I heard. I know you chased that thing from God's house. And from me. But I need answers, Daddy. I swear I need answers in the worst way. I need to know what I'm supposed to do. I can't keep going like this without direction. I need a rudder, Daddy, Lord. I need a rudder, or I fear I'm going to be lost forever."

Resolutely, making himself do something that once had been so easy, Delroy took his hat off and shoved it under his left arm, then clasped his hands in front of him and started to pray. He could not believe how badly his hands shook. He kept the prayer simple.

"'Our Father in heaven, hallowed be Your name. Your kingdom

come. Your will be done on earth as it is in heaven.'" Delroy felt more calm as he repeated the prayer that had been taken from Matthew and Luke and spoken by Christians for centuries. "'Give us this day our daily bread. And forgive us our debts, as we forgive our debtors. And do not lead us into temptatation, but deliver us from the evil one, for Yours is the kingdom and the power and the glory forever. Amen.'"

"Amen," a woman's voice said behind Delroy.

❋   ❋   ❋

United States of America
Fort Benning, Georgia
Local Time 1019 Hours

Once outside the schoolroom in the bright morning sunlight, Penny Gillespie led Megan to a gray Lincoln Continental parked beside a van bearing the logo of a white dove on a field of blue—the registered trademark belonging to Dove TV.

Using the remote clicker, Penny unlocked the doors. "Please seat yourself inside, Mrs. Gander. I truly would like to talk to you."

Megan was torn. As they'd walked outside, she noticed that a crowd numbering five or six dozen—men women, and young people—was beginning to gather around the elementary school. She stood outside the car and gazed in bewilderment.

On the other side of the car, Penny paused. "Mrs. Gander."

"What are they doing here?" Megan asked.

"They heard about your class this morning," Penny said. "Probably the same way I heard about it. Evidently some of the young people who walked out on you this morning talked to other young people. They, in turn, talked to their parents and other adults. I assure you, had not Captain Stashower interrupted your class, it might have turned out to be quite the event. I think more than a few people were very interested in listening to what you have to say."

Megan couldn't believe it.

"Mrs. Gander, I know a little restaurant in Columbus, Rosemary's Bushel Basket. Maybe you've heard of it? I found the restaurant yesterday when my team and I arrived. I believe you might find the atmosphere and the menu to your liking. If I may, I'd like very much to treat you. You'll probably get more peace there than you will at home or work right now. And you look like you could use a breather."

In a daze, Megan opened the car door and got in.

Penny slid behind the wheel, started the engine, and smoothly backed out of the parking area.

Megan was startled when someone knocked on her window.

A heavyset man in a sports coat loped alongside the car. "Mrs. Gander, I'm Chuck Deighton. With CNN News. I need to speak with you."

Thumbing the electric window button down to lower the passenger window a few inches, Penny said succinctly, "Mr. Deighton, I'm afraid Mrs. Gander has pressing business and is otherwise engaged at the moment, as I'm sure you can see perfectly fine for yourself. Now, unless you'd like to become a hood ornament on this vehicle, I do advise you to step away."

The man grimaced and stopped running, letting the car slide away.

"I don't understand," Megan said.

Penny put the car in drive and drove toward the nearest street. "Mrs. Gander, over the last few days you have become something of a celebrity. Many people outside Fort Benning have heard of you and the things you have been involved with here."

Megan digested that, not believing it.

"You are one of the reasons I drove over to Columbus," Penny went on. "The other being that Fort Benning is the largest military infantry installation around. I'm afraid I do multitasking. In this day and age, you can hardly get away from it, though it does not bode well for social niceties. My father and I are convinced that in light of all the tragedies and problems around the globe, the military will be relentlessly called upon to handle civilian unrest, effect rescues, and set up supply stations and possibly an infrastructure to keep transportation moving throughout the country to make certain food and other things we take for granted continue to get where they are needed."

"I'm no celebrity," Megan protested.

"Meaning no disrespect, Mrs. Gander, but I'm afraid I'm going to have to disagree with that naïve vision of your present circumstances. I do beg your indulgence—or your forgiveness, as the case may be—as I try to explain my thinking." Penny drove with amazing efficiency. "You have lost a son to this mysterious occurrence—which, by the way, I also believe was the Rapture—have a husband currently fighting for his life in that mess in Turkey, are being tried for dereliction of duty by the United States Army during a time of martial law, have a civil suit pending against you that could have far-reaching consequences, tried to save a child from what I gather are abusive parents—"

"An abusive father," Megan corrected. "Gerry's mother is just . . . self-involved."

"—during a dramatic suicide attempt," Penny went on.

"Gerry didn't jump. He fell."

"We're splitting hairs here, Mrs. Gander. The boy did indeed climb up on that rooftop with the possible intention of throwing himself off." Penny looked at her.

"Yes," Megan answered.

"You have decided to fight the military in the dereliction of duty case instead of knuckling under to the military's demands and risk so much of your personal freedom. Only two days ago, you were in the bedroom of another young person who tried to take her own life, and now you stand accused of convincing her that suicide was a viable option to living, though I have been told you were only trying to get that poor girl to lie down and relax. Very probably, you will be brought up on charges regarding that matter as well."

As the litany of problems rolled from the other woman's mouth, Megan started to feel overwhelmed.

"Instead of staying close to ground as many other people would have done, you undertook a personal crusade against the ranking base chaplain to get his office to start teaching the youths you have taken responsibility for about the coming Tribulation. Then, when Major Augustus Trimble would not aid you, you took it upon yourself to start teaching that information as best you could." Penny looked at Megan. "Did I leave anything out?"

"I don't think so."

"Good." Penny smiled. "I do pride myself—in moderation, of course, for I don't ever want to become offensive in that self-indulgent practice—in being most thorough when I undertake a project."

Amazed, Megan asked, "Where did you find all of this out?"

"Oh, here and there." Penny waved nonchalantly, as if the feat were nothing. "People love to talk. A good journalist loves to listen. You get those two together, why, you can produce the darndest things. It's a kind of professional gossip skill, I suppose. And I am a world-class player in that sport, though I don't indulge in petty or vindictive chatter. Hopefully, if you have seen my show, you already know that about me so my assurances are merely redundant."

"Why did you come to see me?"

"Because I believe you are a most fascinating woman, Mrs. Gander. Truly, I do."

"Call me Megan."

"Thank you for that kindness. And you must call me Penny."

"Penny," Megan said.

"You should know there will be a lot of reporters interested in you, Mrs. Gander, as more of your story goes public. But I feel as though I must warn you: Many of those reporters might not have your best interests at heart when they do their stories. Many will exploit you till something better comes along or treat you as an oddity—like a two-headed calf—then move on to the next oddity. They won't see that you are truly trying to make a difference in the lives of those children."

Megan looked at the woman.

"You're wondering why you should trust me," Penny said.

"Yes."

"You're direct and honest, Megan. I do like that about a person. Though, as I have so often found, there are a great number of people who do not look upon those two traits as endearing qualities."

"Especially in a woman."

Penny glanced at her and smiled. "Too true, my dear. That is a sad thing in this world."

A Hummer loaded with MPs drove by the Lincoln Continental in the other direction.

"As to the issue of whether or not you can trust me, Megan, you'll have to make up your own mind about that. I can only offer what you choose to see of the person I am before you. But I am in your corner. Truly, I am. You see, my father and I want to get the same message out that you do."

"I don't have a message."

"Then why did you feel compelled to educate those children about the coming Tribulation?"

"Because someone needed to."

"Yes, but that's not where your message actually started. First, you told them that the Tribulation was here, that they are living in it now. That is your primary message." Penny paused and turned the corner. "My father and I—since we have figured out that very thing too— believe that it is our bound duty to tell people as well. To warn them of what pitfalls and snares lie ahead. And we chose to start that message by helping you with yours."

Megan took a deep breath and let it out. "Look, I appreciate your support, but if what you're talking about is my being on your television program—"

"It is."

"—then I can't do that."

"Why not?"

"My attorney—"

"Lieutenant Douglas Raymond Benbow."

Megan was surprised. She hadn't known Benbow's middle name.

"By all accounts, Lieutenant Benbow is a good man. An exemplary man. But new to the legal practice." Penny glanced at her. "As I have said, Megan, I am very thorough."

"Have you talked to him?"

"Oh, heavens no. I am quite certain Lieutenant Benbow wouldn't want me—or any other media person—within a country mile of you."

"No," Megan agreed, "he probably wouldn't."

"I'm sure the lieutenant told you that you should keep from making waves—"

"He called it keeping a low profile."

Penny beamed. "Very lawyerly of him as well as suiting the military nomenclature. Very good advice once upon a time. Keeping a low profile might have worked for you at the beginning of this thing, Megan. But the incident involving young Miss Hollister, the confrontation with Major Trimble, and now this Tribulation class that has drawn the wrath of General Braddock himself . . . not to mention the fact that I showed up there today too." She shook her head. "I'm afraid the days of your maintaining or possessing a low profile are forever over. The time comes when you must sometimes take strength in your weakness."

Megan's stomach rolled. She suddenly felt panicked and trapped. "I should be back with the kids."

"And I think you should be with me."

Megan studied the other woman.

"Megan, may I speak frankly?"

"Of course."

"Quite truthfully, I hardly know any other way to speak. I don't think you've gotten a true grasp of where you're standing. You've been tossed from one emotional situation to another since this thing began, and you've hardly had time to draw a breath."

That's true, Megan thought.

"You're standing in the path of a storm," Penny said. "A very large, very nasty storm that seems hell-bent on bringing you to ruination. Personally, I believe you have been there purposefully, but I do not believe it was some vindictive measure. Now you can try to run from this storm, which I can assure you from looking everything over in the charges and motivations against you that you won't be able to do, or you can attempt to ride it out, which I honestly think will wash over you and break you down should you chose that course of action."

"You don't sound very hopeful."

"No, I am very hopeful. I believe in you and in what you're trying to do. That's why I came here yesterday after I found out the post would be opening up this morning. I want to help you. And I truly believe I can." Penny was quiet for a moment. "If I sound too presumptuous I do apologize in advance—for that is in no way my intention, but I also believe that God put you on my heart and in my thoughts so that I can at least make the attempt to aid you."

"How?"

"There is a third way to handle this storm coming at you so fiercely, Megan," Penny said. "A very scary way, I must admit. But the only way I see that you can save yourself and do the work my father and I believe the Lord Himself has put before you."

"I don't understand."

Penny checked the intersection ahead of them and drove through. "You must step inside the storm, Megan. You must draw the storm to you like a lightning rod draws lightning, and you must become the very eye of the storm. You must dare to tell the world the truth and put God's work ahead of everything else."

Megan thought about that. "Even if I believed that was true, I don't know if I could do that."

"Pray to God to help you."

A lump formed in Megan's throat. "I have been praying. I pray all the time. But I don't think He's listening. Or maybe He just doesn't care about me. Every time I think things are going to get better, something else happens that puts me even deeper into this mess. It's like I don't even have a choice about what I'm doing anymore. My life just continues to get worse. I don't think I even know what I'm supposed to do anymore."

"The Bible says that God never gives you more than you can handle." Penny reached across and patted Megan's arm. "Some people, my dear, can just naturally handle more than others, so God gives them more to do."

"If that's true, it's not fair."

"No. No, I suppose it's not. It's just what is."

Tears came to Megan's eyes. She wiped them away. "I'm scared, Penny. Really scared. And I feel so alone."

"I know. I know how you must feel. But you are *not* alone. I saw those young people with you, and I've talked to a few of your friends this morning. Only briefly, true, but it was enough. You're not alone. You have their hearts and their prayers." Penny passed out of the front gates. "Let's you and me go have something to eat. We'll talk about what we can and can't do, about what we should and shouldn't do, and we'll figure out what we will do."

"You make it sound easy."

"Planning's a deceptive process," Penny said. "You're often deceived because you have the audacity to even consider taking the bull by the horns. Things always look easier on paper. When that trial starts in the morning, I'm sure things will be plenty hard then."

✿   ✿   ✿

Church of the Word
Marbury, Alabama
Local Time 1003 Hours

Slowly and warily, Delroy turned toward the voices he heard behind him and got to his feet. His body screamed in protest from all the abuse it had suffered recently. Automatically, he brushed the dust from the knees of his dress whites.

A black woman hunkered on her knees just inside the doorway of the church. She was thin and worn, wearing a shabby coat that had long ago seen its better days. She had on purple hospital scrubs and wore a name tag over one breast. She was at least in her midthirties but she looked older. Her curly black hair was cut short, framing a triangular face that had worn hard over the years. She had her arms spread across the backs of three teenagers. Two girls in jeans and jackets knelt on her right, and a boy who was almost a man knelt on her left.

"Reverend," the woman said in a hesitant voice as she gazed at Delroy hopefully. "You are a reverend, right?"

Delroy looked at her. "I'm a United States Navy chaplain, ma'am."

"That's the same thing, ain't it? You're a preacher?" The hope in her voice was thick and fragile. "A man of God?"

Oh, Lord, Delroy prayed, *help me here, because I don't know quite how to answer that. You know my faith hasn't been what it should.*

"I struggle to be, ma'am," Delroy answered.

"When I first saw you in here, dressed all in them whites, and me tired as I am from working a double shift at the hospital last night, I swear I thought you was an angel. Thought all that white was for sure angel wings."

Delroy felt embarrassed. He should have known better than to wear the dress whites. No matter where he went, he was sure to attract attention. "No, ma'am."

"Then when I saw you praying in this abandoned church, I thought it must be some kind of miracle." Tears sprang from the woman's eyes. "Don't know how much you know about this place, but we ain't had no preacher here in four years."

"Aye, ma'am. I'd heard that."

"I didn't mean to intrude if you was wanting to be by yourself," the woman said. "I . . . I . . . ." She looked helplessly at her children. "I just need some help. With my chir'ren."

Delroy nodded. "I've got some money I can spare." He started to reach for his wallet.

"No, sir," the woman said, holding her head up with a touch of hot pride. "I don't mean money, Reverend."

"Chaplain," Delroy said automatically.

"Chaplain." The woman wiped the tears from her face. The girls were crying with her now, and it was plain to Delroy that they were all scared. "I ain't needin' money. I'm needin' answers."

"I'm afraid I don't know many answers," Delroy admitted. "I've got a lot of questions myself."

"You're a man of God," the woman accused. "You read the Bible. You trained for this sort of thing."

"What sort of thing?"

"All these people disappearing, Reverend." The woman's hand shook as she continued to wipe at her face.

Delroy reached into his pocket and took out one of the mono-grammed handkerchiefs Glenda had ordered for him and kept in regular supply. He crossed the room and handed the handkerchief to the woman, then helped her to her feet. She seemed so fragile and light, and she trembled terribly.

"One of my chir'ren disappeared when all them people disappeared," the woman said. "His name was Rashad. I came home that morning, fount my other three chir'ren, but I didn't find Rashad. I

was so scairt. I thought somebody done went an' stole my baby."
Overcome by exhaustion and grief, the woman almost collapsed but
Delroy caught her by the arm and kept her on her feet.

Guiding the woman by the arm, pulling her against him so he
could support her, Delroy reached down and rocked one of the pews
back upright. The pew wobbled but stayed level. He sat her there. Uncomfortable with how he towered over her, he dropped into a squatting position.

"How old was Rashad?" Delroy asked in a gentle voice.

The woman tried to speak and couldn't.

"Rashad weren't but seven," the boy said.

"What's your name?" Delroy asked.

"Dominic."

"And your momma's?"

Dominic hesitated.

"It's okay, Dominic," Delroy said. "I just want to try to help."

"Phyllis," Dominic answered.

Delroy nodded. "Phyllis."

The woman looked up at him.

"*All* the children disappeared that night," Delroy said. "You know
that, right?"

"That's what I been tole. But I was so scairt. I just knew someone
had done stole Rashad. I just knew once the DHS office fount out I
done lost one of my chir'ren, they'd be along soon enough to take the
rest of 'em." Phyllis wept, mouth working as she tried to continue
talking. "Reverend, my babies is all I got outside of a hard job an' bills
what don't stop an' a life when I ain't carin' for my chir'ren." She
shook her head helplessly. "I didn't want the DHS to come an' take
my babies. I didn't do nothin' wrong."

"You didn't do anything wrong," Delroy agreed. "All the children
twelve and younger disappeared that night. There was nothing you
could have done to stop that."

"We heard aliens got 'em," one of the girls said.

"That ain't what happened, Nisha," Phyllis said. "I done tole you
God took up them chir'ren."

"But you ain't ever said why, Momma," the other girl said.

"I know, Taryn. That's 'cause Momma don't know yet." Phyllis
looked from her daughters back to Delroy. "I been watchin' TV,
Chaplain. Been readin' my Bible. But I got no head for what I'm
seein'. I just cain't understand ever'thin' what's happened. I talked to
my friends, an' I talked to all them people I could at the hospital. Ain't

nobody got no answers that I can give my chir'ren about what's happened to their baby brother." Her voice broke for a moment. "An' I cain't even guarantee them that they ain't gonna be next."

"No more children will disappear," Delroy said.

Phyllis searched his face. "Do you know what's happenin'?"

Delroy hesitated for a moment, knowing he was hovering dangerously close to the edge of something that could swallow him up. He didn't want to get involved with the woman or her children or their pain. All of them were more than he could handle, and he knew that. A man always had to know his limitations. Delroy did. He was already way in over his head. He just wanted to go back to the safety of USS *Wasp*.

And even as he thought that, he knew that if his daddy could know his heart and mind in this church right now, Josiah Harte would be ashamed.

"Aye, ma'am," Delroy said. "I know what's happening."

"Then I need to know," Phyllis pleaded. "I gots to tell my chir'ren so they understand. I don't want them afraid no mo'. I didn't work this hard tryin' to bring them up to be God-fearin' young men an' women to have them lost."

Delroy shook his head. "Ma'am, I really don't think I'm the one to answer your questions. Don't you have another pastor?"

"Pastor Leonard was one of them what disappeared," Dominic said. "He taught a Bible study group at the Salvation Army an' coached some roundball."

"There's women I talk to in my prayer group," Phyllis said. "They's tellin' me that despite ever'thin' we done seen, we ain't seen bad yet. But it's comin'."

Delroy took in a deep breath and let it out. "Ma'am, I'm weak. I should be at my post on my ship right now. I should be helping young men prepare for battle. I'm not. I let my own self-interest take me away from them." He shook his head regretfully. "I'm just not the man to do what you're asking."

Phyllis's face turned cold. "Mister, all I'm askin' you to do is help me explain to my chir'ren what we needs to do. Them ladies in my prayer group, they says the end of the world is upon us, that we missed bein' called up to be with Jesus because we ain't where we ought to be in our hearts, an' that the devil hisself is set loose right in the middle of us like a fox in a henhouse. I ain't askin' for you to do it for me. I'm just askin' for some guidance. That's all. Just help me understand things I cain't understand on my own."

The woman's words stung Delroy like a whip.

"You ain't gotta dirty your hands or even break a sweat," Phyllis said. "I just needs to know what's comin' so I can see my chir'ren get off to heaven like they deserve." She stood with her head held high and tears sparkling on her ebony face. "But if you ain't man enough to help us out, I best not waste any more time on you." She took her girls' hands as she stood and started toward the door.

Delroy watched her. He remembered when he was five years old and he asked his daddy what it was like to be a preacher.

"Well, now, little man," Josiah had said, reaching down to take his son into his arms, "bein' a preachin' man is mighty hard work. You gotta believe so hard that you not only believe enough for yourownself, but you also believe enough for them folks what cain't believe enough for themselves for a time."

"How do you do that, Daddy?"

"Well, Son, sometimes you scare the devil right out of 'em."

"Like when you tell 'em what hell is like an' how their family's going to miss 'em in heaven?"

"Yes, sir, that's one way."

"You're real good at that, Daddy. Sometimes you scare me."

"Well, I'm sorry for that. I truly am."

"That's okay, Daddy. I don't ever have nightmares like them movies make me have. Sometimes I like it when you scare me about God and stuff."

"Well, now, Son, I think sometimes we all do. Reminds us that makin' that choice to live for God is a mighty important thing. Important enough that even that ol' devil has to sit up an' take notice of us. But do you know what I mostly do?"

"What, Daddy?"

"I look at them people an' I realize how scared they are about what's comin'. Then I take 'em by the hand an' I lead 'em in the path of the Lord."

"Ain't that hard, Daddy?"

"Only when they's bein' muleheaded an' ain't listenin' any too good. But when you got a man or a woman—or a youngster like yourownself—what's wantin' to know what the Lord has said about somethin', why all I have to do is open the Bible an' give 'em God's Word. Sometimes I get surprised at how strong an' rested all that hard work makes me."

The woman had almost reached the door when Delroy called out to her. "Phyllis."

She went stiff-backed for a moment; she halted but didn't turn around.

"Phyllis, I'm sorry." Delroy stayed where he was, knowing he couldn't go after her. The decision to come back had to be hers. "My daddy was Josiah Harte. I don't know if you've ever heard of him, but he used to preach right here at this church. He preached long and hard to the folks that lived around here. I never saw him a day in his life when he didn't know how to handle his relationship with God."

The boy and the two girls turned to look at Delroy, but their mother held her ground.

"My daddy was a good man," Delroy said. "A great preacher. He had a way with words that could ignite a congregation, scare them, and bring them home to Jesus in droves." He paused. "But I'm not my daddy. I never have been. But if I let you walk out of this church—my daddy's church—without at least trying to help you, I know I don't deserve to be my daddy's son. And, ma'am, that's something that I just can't do."

Dominic pulled on his mother's arm. "Momma, come on. Let's listen to what he has to say."

"I apologize, ma'am," Delroy said. "I truly do. I've been lost myself for a long time. I'm still trying to find my way back to a lot of things I guess I took for granted."

Slowly, Phyllis turned around. "It's rare to meet an honest man, Chaplain. An' rarer still to meet one what admits his failin's. But I'll tell you somethin': all of us that got left behind, I figure we're all just a little lost. Maybe it'll take all of us together to find our way."

A smile was on Delroy's lips before he knew it, and lightness dawned in his heart. "Aye, ma'am. I expect you're right."

"I got to warn you, Chaplain, I got a powerful lot of questions." Phyllis brought her children back up to the front of the church.

"Aye, ma'am." Delroy straightened the pew she'd sat in, then got a chair for himself. He started to talk then, to outline the overall seven-year period that followed the Rapture. As he talked and discussed God's Word and God's plan, he discovered that talking about those things seemed the most natural thing in the world to do.

As he spoke, another young couple appeared outside the church door. They held hands and looked frightened.

Delroy stopped. "Is there something I can do for you?"

"We was just wonderin'," the young woman said, "if the church was open. We know it's only Thursday, an' ain't no notice been hung, but if the church was open, we wondered if we might come in an' talk." She shook her head. "We've spent days worryin' an' wonderin' about what's gonna happen to us. We just want to know what to do."

Delroy hesitated, uncertain how much responsibility he wanted to take on.

"You come right on ahead, chile," Phyllis said. "Church is open today."

United States 75th Army Rangers Temporary Post
Sanliurfa, Turkey
Local Time 2056 Hours

"—the name of the Father, of the Son, and of the Holy Ghost," Corporal Joseph Baker said as he reached for the young soldier's face, then pinched his nose and covered his mouth. They were standing in the water tank Baker used to perform baptisms.

Goose stood at the back of the makeshift church. He leaned a hip against the line of sandbags that had partially converted the church area into a bunker against artillery attacks and tried to find a position that provided relief for his aching knee.

Rain continued to pound the street and the ground. Rivulets of water threaded through the metal chairs and crates and wooden boxes that had been set up to seat the attendees. The generator and the lights had been scavenged from bombed-out buildings in the city.

The church never shut down. Services were held all day and all night, twenty-four hours around the clock. When Baker couldn't be there because of posting or sleep, other men took his place. Some of them were chaplains, but not all of them. Many had been deacons and youth ministers and Sunday school teachers back home. Some still were. Others had never had much to do with church at all until the last few days. Somehow all those men had been called into service at Baker's church.

The church had begun small. Now it took up nearly six times the room it originally had. Somehow, though, the church continued to find the room and the means to grow.

One of the nearby buildings had been a restaurant. When the

SCUDs fell, the owners had left. Soldiers had come forward and told Baker they wanted to help, and they'd seen to the refurbishing of the restaurant kitchens. Soup and sandwiches were served constantly. No one came to Baker's church and went away hungry. Not physically and not spiritually.

And that was what everyone had taken to calling the worship place under the pieced-together, salvaged tent material: Baker's Church.

Goose had mixed feelings about the church. When he was there, he somehow felt closer to Chris, more connected. It felt as if his son were no more than a baseball throw away, ready for Goose to catch up to him at any moment. But he also felt uneasy because being there created friction between Remington and himself. The captain despised the church and Baker, thinking that they created weakness or a zealot's belief in the men he commanded and relied upon. As a compromise, Goose attended the church, but he let his postings and other responsibilities keep him away probably more than they should have.

The congregation gathered here came from U.S. Army Rangers and the Marine Corps, from the general populace of the city, from the U.N. Peacekeeping teams, and even—surprisingly—from the Turkish army, many of whom were not Christians. At least, they hadn't been Christians before the war had broken out.

Every time Baker delivered a sermon, he led people to Jesus. Goose had witnessed that call and those who answered at least a half-dozen times. It was always the same. It had been that way tonight after they had finished their postings. Besides the man currently in the water tank, seventeen more stood waiting their turn.

The soldier in the tank held his arms crossed over his chest while Baker talked quietly to him for a moment. The soldier nodded. He wore his BDUs, which were already soaked from the rain that had lasted more than twelve straight hours. His boots and socks stood in front of the tank.

A six-piece band that played mostly in tune stood nearby on empty ammo crates with their instruments in their hands. When Baker finished the latest round of baptisms, they were going back to music to end the evening service.

With deceptive ease, Baker lowered the soldier into the water. The lights shining on the stage area reflected from the water. Two camcorders from media people played over the scene. Apparently their news directors never tired of the footage.

After a brief moment, Baker brought the soldier back up. Goose saw the smile spread across the soldier's face as tears mixed with the water that ran from his hair down his features. He turned to Baker and hugged him fiercely.

Baker hugged the soldier back, talked to him briefly again, and helped him from the water tank as he would help a child.

The congregation clapped and called out thanks and praise to God and Jesus Christ.

"That's a moving ceremony," a feminine voice said at Goose's side.

Glancing over his shoulder, Goose spotted Danielle Vinchenzo standing halfway in the evening's shadows. She looked tired and her hair drooped from the moisture in the air.

"Miss Vinchenzo," Goose greeted.

"You're a hard man to catch, First Sergeant."

"I didn't know you were looking, ma'am." During the last few hours, Goose had checked through the Rangers to find out what kind of shape his men were in. Knowing Remington would want to put a mission together soon kept Goose active.

Danielle crossed her arms and watched the baptisms as Baker prayed for each individual. "Does he ever sleep?"

"Five hours out of every twenty-four," Goose replied. "Captain Remington's orders. But he doesn't always sleep all five in one shot."

"How does he do it? I'm dead on my feet and I'm getting seven or eight, with a few catnaps crammed in there for good measure when I can make it happen."

Goose shook his head. "You'd have to ask Corporal Baker."

Danielle frowned. "I did. He told me that God was giving him strength."

"Then I suppose that's what it must be."

After a moment watching the baptisms, Danielle said, "You were there when the retreat from the Turkish-Syrian border took place."

Goose thought about ignoring the statement but couldn't because it was too impolite. He did feel uncomfortable discussing those events. People who had not been there had trouble understanding what had happened.

"Yes, ma'am."

"During our discussions, we've never talked about that." Danielle looked at Goose. "Did it happen the way I've heard?"

"I don't know how you heard it, ma'am."

"I was told that a delayed explosion from an earlier SCUD launch brought that mountain down that night," she said. "And I was told that a demolitions team of Rangers or marines sped up into that mountain and planted explosives so the mountain would come down on the pursuing Syrian troops and block their advance." She took a breath, her violet eyes searching his. "I also heard that Corporal Baker started reciting the Twenty-third Psalm and God knocked that mountain down on top of the Syrians."

"Yes, ma'am," Goose said. "I've heard all those stories, too."

"Which one was it, First Sergeant?"

Goose deliberated, knowing he was stepping into uncertain territory.

"First Sergeant?"

"There was no demolitions team in the mountains," Goose replied. "There wasn't time. We were running flat-out when the way got jammed up and we got stuck."

"So was it a SCUD or was it a psalm?"

"Are you putting this in a story, ma'am?"

Danielle was silent for a moment. "At this point, no. I'm trying to stick with things that I can prove or disprove. And I'm keeping focused on the ongoing war effort. I'm also trying to stay with stories that I understand." She nodded toward Baker. "That's why I've kept away from stories involving this church."

"You don't understand the church?"

"I understand church," Danielle said. "I just don't understand this one. I've been on battlefields before, but I've never seen anything like this."

"Neither have I," Goose replied. "But then, we've never been involved in military action where a third of the world's population disappeared overnight either."

Now that the last person was baptized, the band struck up a modern Christian rock song that soon had everyone clapping and singing along. The sound was spiritually uplifting. If the debris of the city hadn't started right outside the pool of light given off by the tent church, Goose would have sworn the gathering was more like the tent revivals he'd attended back in Waycross, Georgia.

"You didn't answer my question, Goose," Danielle said.

The use of his nickname came across a little too familiarly to Goose. He felt uncomfortable because of the questions and because of the attention the woman gave him.

"Was it a SCUD or a psalm?" Danielle repeated.

"Ma'am," Goose said, "I never heard an explosion up in that mountain that night. I heard the voices of those men trapped up there, all of them probably certain they were going to die. And in the next moment, that mountain fell."

"Like the walls of Jericho." Danielle smiled.

"I wasn't at Jericho. I couldn't say."

"Why is the CIA so interested in you?"

Goose looked at her, knowing instinctively from the confident tone in her voice that she knew something. "I don't know."

"You're not going to deny that they are interested in you?"

"Do you want me to, ma'am?"

A surprised grin fitted itself to Danielle's face. "I wouldn't believe you."

Goose didn't say anything.

"Did you know that even now as we speak one of CIA Section Chief Cody's agents is watching you from across the street?" Danielle's smile turned superior and mocking.

Looking at her, Goose said, "Are you referring to the agent on the second floor of the building directly across from us? Or are you talking about the agent on top of the building to the northeast? And unless I'm mistaken, a third agent comes by in a Toyota four-wheel-drive pickup every half hour or so. I'm sure he's the transport part of the surveillance team."

Danielle's eyebrows rose. "Okay, I'm impressed. I spotted the one guy because I recognized him from earlier."

"From where?"

"The burning building that came under terrorist attack." Danielle gazed at him coolly, the hanging lights from the church reflecting in her eyes. "The one where you carried the man out and placed him in a jeep while all the other survivors were taken to the hospital or released."

Goose didn't say anything. He shifted uncomfortably, realizing his knee felt like it was about to explode. "As I recall, you didn't know the man's name when we talked earlier."

"Which man?" Danielle asked. "The one you carried out of that building and disappeared with?"

Goose avoided that topic for the moment. "The CIA agent you were talking about that morning."

Danielle gazed at him as if taking his measure. "Things have changed since I talked with you yesterday."

Goose waited, curious now at how much she knew. If she had managed to somehow identify Icarus, she could be a danger to herself as well as to the double agent.

"I didn't get any joy from you," Danielle said, "so I sent Cody's picture to a friend of mine at OneWorld NewsNet."

"You had a camera?"

"Of course. I never go anywhere without one."

"I'll remember that in the future."

Danielle nodded. "I hope that in the future we're working on the same side."

Goose didn't say anything.

"My friend at OneWorld NewsNet was young," Danielle said.

"You're young," Goose stated.

"Lizuca was younger than me," Danielle said. "She was bright and intelligent and one of the friendliest people I've ever met."

Was. For the first time Goose realized that Danielle was talking about her friend in the past tense. He attributed the miss on his part to fatigue and his aching knee. A knot of apprehension stirred in his guts.

"She helped support her mother and her sister financially," Danielle said. "The economy in Romania is still problematic. I'd been giving her some overtime, which she loved because that gave her a little extra money to spend on herself, and she learned more about the news business. She was hoping to get the chance to move to America."

The band played another lively rock song that seemed at odds with the story Danielle was telling. "Yesterday my coordinator at OneWorld NewsNet ordered Lizuca off the assignment I'd given her."

"That person knew what she was doing?" Goose asked.

"Stolojan only knew that I had asked her to find out the name of the man in the picture I'd sent her."

"Had Lizuca identified Cody then?"

"Lizuca—" Danielle's voice broke—"Lizuca never identified Cody as far as I know. A couple hours after I sent her Cody's picture, she was dead. Someone tracked her to the cybercafé, where she worked when she was away from OneWorld, and brutally murdered her. Shot her down in front of several people."

Goose drew in a deep breath and exhaled. Suddenly the idea of Cody's three agents stalking him wasn't as insignificant as he'd first thought. But he still didn't think they meant him any harm. Otherwise they would have already tried. There had been opportunities before now. He believed they were watching him in hopes of catching Icarus, using him as bait. Taking three men out of Cody's troops had improved Icarus's chances of getting away or remaining hidden, whichever the man had intended.

"Was the gunman identified?" Goose asked.

"No."

Goose rubbed his jaw, thinking the problem over and evaluating the parameters of it. "I don't think Cody keeps an agent in Romania."

"I don't either. He could have hired someone, though."

"And cut a deal that quick?" Goose shook his head.

"But who would let Cody know Lizuca was searching for him?"

"She was searching OneWorld NewsNet's archives when she was killed," Danielle said. "For the murderer to show up there, they had to be tracking her from the link to OneWorld NewsNet."

Considering that, Goose knew that only one conclusion could be drawn. He was certain that Danielle had already made the same one.

"Someone at OneWorld NewsNet tipped off the killer," Goose said. "How did you identify Cody?"

"I went through another source."

"Who?"

Danielle shook her head. "I don't even know. The person I contacted remains hidden."

"But you can trust this person?"

Her eyes flashed. "I got Cody's name, didn't I? And you haven't bothered to deny it, so I know I've got that name right. If that's right, then the rest of what I learned must be right."

"How did that person get the name?"

After a brief hesitation, she replied, "The initial information came from OneWorld NewsNet. The CIA files after that."

"No one noticed?"

"There was an incident. Someone tracked my information specialist back to a false address in Australia that was being used. A man showed up at that address within minutes. But by then the person searching for Cody's name had already broken into OneWorld's hidden files and gotten the information we were looking for. *Some* of the information."

"Can your information specialist be tracked any further?"

"I was told no."

"Whoever tipped the killer about Lizuca knows that you put her up to that search. They're going to figure you're at least involved in the second one. Going after that information again so soon could have been a mistake."

Danielle's tone grew short. "Don't you think I thought about that?"

"Yes, ma'am," Goose answered. "I just wondered if you thought about it before or after the *incident*."

Some of her anger dissipated.

"The information specialist you were using for the second attempt should have known that too," Goose stated. "I don't know how professional that person is—"

"Good enough to get into OneWorld's computers as well as the CIA's."

"Yes, ma'am. I understand that. But he was also good enough to call the dogs down on you. If they sent a man after him, intending to do what was done to your friend, they may well come after you."

Danielle nodded. "I know." She hesitated. "I'm scared."

"Do you believe you're in danger?"

"Of course I'm in danger," Danielle snapped irritably. Then she took a moment to get herself under control. "I sent Lizuca the picture. I think the only thing that's saved me this far is that no one knows I know as much as I do."

"What do you know?" Goose lowered his voice. He was confident that the noise of the church and the pounding rain would defeat any electronic eavesdropping the CIA surveillance team might attempt, but he still felt exposed and vulnerable standing there.

"What I *need* to know," Danielle said, "is whether I can trust you." Her eyes searched his.

Goose didn't answer. The trust couldn't come from his end; she had to choose to trust him. And in that moment, he understood more about the faith issues Baker had talked about. Faith was a matter of trust as well, and it had to come from the person who wanted it, not be worked out by actions and demands put upon God.

She wanted him to say something or do something that would let her know she could trust him, but he knew if he said or did anything to persuade her, that trust would be false. She would base her trust on his persuasion rather than on his actions and what she knew of him, not how she really felt.

A memory unlocked in his mind. Chris had been three when Goose had built the fort in their backyard. Though only four feet off the ground, the fort had at first been scary to Chris. The bridge between the two main units had rails, but Chris had been afraid. Still, he'd wanted to cross it. Goose had hunkered down at the other end and held his arms out to his son.

Goose had talked to Chris, cajoled him, and tried to build his confidence. In the end, as he'd sometimes done when working with soldiers trying to improve their performance on the obstacle course, Goose had simply sat and waited, becoming a rock and letting them know by his stationary position that he would not move. After a time, Chris had released his hold on the other end of the bridge and run across. That had been trust—the innocent trust of a child, which can so quickly evaporate. The Bible distinguished between the trust of a child and the trust of a man as well.

"Okay," Danielle said after a short, intense silence, "if I hadn't thought I could trust you, I wouldn't have come looking for you, and I wouldn't have told you everything I've told you so far." She smiled, but there was little humor in the effort. Fear lingered in her gaze. "The problem is, once I tell you what I know, there's no taking it back. If anyone finds out I've talked to you about this, your life will be in danger too."

Goose thought about Icarus and the secrets he was already holding on to, about the way he had betrayed Remington's confidence in him. "My life is already in danger, ma'am. And that's in addition to being out here on this battlefield."

Danielle shook her head. "It's just hard to know how much you know."

"Enough to get me killed," Goose assured her.

She was silent for a moment, and she looked sad. "Do you trust me?"

Goose had to think about. A lot of things were at stake, and secrets seemed to be tumbling out of the woodwork.

"If you don't trust me," Danielle warned, "if I unload what I know and you try to hold back on me when you know I've put my neck on the chopping block to come this far, I'm gone. I swear to God on that, Goose." Unshed tears glimmered in her eyes and her voice grew hoarse. "Lizuca lost her life because of me and because of these people. What I have to tell you is big. If we don't handle this carefully, we could both end up dead. The people we're after don't hesitate to kill. And they've got too much at stake to just go away quietly."

"I trust you," Goose said, knowing he was going to step across the line in one fell swoop. "But there's something you should know. About your boss."

"I already know," Danielle said, letting out a tense breath. "CIA Section Chief Alexander Cody works for Nicolae Carpathia. And it was probably Carpathia who ordered Lizuca's death."

Goose looked at her for a moment, then nodded. Maybe she hadn't put everything together, but she'd put together enough. And she'd put together the fact that CIA Section Chief Alexander Cody worked for Nicolae Carpathia, who was quite possibly the Antichrist warned of in the book of Revelation.

Standing there in front of Danielle, Goose felt the eyes of the CIA agents who were keeping him under surveillance, and he had to wonder if they were peering through sniper scopes.

Crossroads Shopping Center
Columbus, Georgia
Local Time 2213 Hours

Joey Holder sat in the back of the six-year-old Cadillac Zero had hot-wired and stolen from the house where they had spent last night. The Cadillac belonged to the doctor who owned the house in one of the more affluent gated communities on Columbus's north side. Normally the security would have kept thieves—and them, Joey admitted; he couldn't quite cross the line and think of himself as a thief—out of the area.

But many of the power outages remained in effect throughout the city's suburban areas. Several of the houses around the doctor's home had been lighted by generators. Knowing that the "borrowed" home they'd spent the night in had so many neighbors had worried Joey. He knew that if he hadn't been drunk when they got there just before dawn and too tired to go any farther, he might even have argued with Zero about staying.

Well, maybe not argued, Joey admitted to himself as he stared at the darkened strip mall in the shadowed parking area that Zero steered the big car through. *But I would have pointed out that we could have gotten caught.*

They hadn't gotten caught, though. This morning they had stuffed themselves with food, played pool, and looted the house. The cream and gold Cadillac was only the iceberg tip of the things they had taken.

Stolen, Joey reminded himself. The others continued to refer to the thefts as borrowing, but he couldn't do that anymore. During the last couple days, the guys had gone completely out of control. Zero had led the way.

Joey hadn't taken anything except the food and drink he'd needed to survive. *And the liquor and beer,* he thought, belching and still tasting the latter. He'd played pool in the game room and looked through the assortment of video games in the home-entertainment center, but without power, the game systems remained inert. He couldn't help noticing that several of the games were ones Chris and he had seen advertised on television but had never been able to afford.

Zero had slept most of the afternoon and early evening. But as soon as full dark came, he'd roused and grown irritable, wanting to go out. RayRay and Bones had griped, already half wasted because they'd gotten up before Zero, and said that they should stay in, pointing out that they had plenty of food.

Reports were starting to hit the radio news about people who were getting busted by police and the Georgia National Guard for squatting in houses where the owners had either vanished or were away. Twice, homeowners had returned to find their homes invaded by vagrants and squatters and had shot them dead. One of the squatters had been a thirteen-year-old boy. It wasn't just the thieves getting whacked, though. Seven homeowners had been killed so far, and dozens of others had been injured.

After listening to the others in the group, Zero had pointed out that everything they'd said was true. Then he'd added that if they only had a generator to power the stove, microwave, water heater, and hot tub, they could probably stay for days. So he'd hot-wired the Caddie and they'd come to town looking for a generator.

Joey had felt certain the generator thing was just an excuse. The longer they'd gone without finding the aliens Zero said took all the people, the more Zero had gotten upset.

Zero pulled the Caddie through the parking lot in front the darkened strip mall he'd selected as their target. That was what he'd called it, Joey remembered. Their *target.* Like he was some kind of general in one of the video games they'd played at the arcade center.

The strip mall had only a couple dozen shops. This part of Columbus had fallen on hard times. The little center's clientele had been lured away by newer and larger malls, and the businesses here lingered rather than thrived.

Across the street, the blue-and-purple neon glare of a strip club flared against the night. The sign announcing the Peeping Tom Club showed flashing neon outlines of a naked woman dancing. The banner that read LIVE! NUDE GIRLS! ran along the bottom.

The basso throb of the multiple generators that kept the power surging through the club filled the night and laid down a heavy bass line for the screaming heavy metal rock music that ripped over the neighborhood. Cars, pickup trucks, and motorcycles filled the gravel parking lot to overflowing.

"Hey, man," RayRay said, his eyes gleaming and filled with the reflected neon lights. "We get done here, maybe we can go check out the action over there."

Joey wasn't interested in that at all. During the past few days, he'd been thinking of Jenny and had—unbelievably—started getting homesick. He wanted to see Jenny. Even more, he wanted to see his mom. He knew she had to be worried. Columbus was slowly being restored to law and order. Joey knew the excesses of his little gang soon had to come to a stop or they'd be locked up, but there was still a lot of craziness out there.

"Kind of amazing," Derrick said. "I mean with the way those people will make sure a place like that stays open and even go there when so much of the city is still a wreck."

"They don't care," Joey said. He knew that because part of him still wished he didn't care. Not caring—if a person could do it—seemed the best way to go right now. But he was having more and more trouble doing that. He went to sleep at night thinking about his mom and Chris and Goose, and they were always the first things on his mind when he woke in the morning. The alcohol he was drinking no longer blocked those thoughts.

He'd even started praying for them, though not for himself, because he didn't think he deserved it after everything he had done. He prayed for his family because he had messed up things so badly even before he hadn't gotten back to the post in time to get Chris. Or been there, like he should have, when his mom had gotten called in to work.

Prayer had been a habit when he'd been a little kid. His mom had taught him. Then, when Chris had started doing his prayers, he'd insisted that Joey do them with him. It was surprising how easy it had been to kneel down beside the bed with Chris and pray.

"Now I lay me down to sleep. . . ."

The words rolled through Joey's mind as Zero parked the Cadillac in the alley at one end of the strip mall. His throat tightened. His prayers, he was sure, were a wasted effort. He felt certain that God wouldn't listen to him.

"Hey, man," Zero said in his deep voice.

Joey suddenly grew aware that Zero was peering back at him over the front seat.

"Something wrong with you?" Zero asked. "You look like you're crying."

"Allergies," Joey mumbled. He brushed at his eyes and felt his fingers come away wet.

Bones, seated in the front passenger seat with RayRay sandwiched between, snorted and said, "More like he's suffering a hangover." He looked at Joey. "I told you, man, if you want to shake a hangover quick, you gotta drink a little again when you first get up. Just enough to put a buzz back in your brain."

"Can't," Joey said. "Makes me sick." That was no lie. He'd tried, and it had.

"Whatever," Zero said. "Keep up or get left behind if we have to move fast." He popped the door release and pushed himself out. None of the car's interior lights flared to life because he'd removed them all.

Dropper was seated next to one of the rear doors. When he got out, Joey followed.

Standing outside in the cool night air, Joey felt a little better. It helped to be up and moving. He didn't have time to dwell on things that way.

Zero opened the Caddie's trunk and took out all the crowbars and screwdrivers they'd been collecting to make their scavenging easier. He passed the tools out, handing Joey a pry bar. Then he took out the gleaming .357 Magnum he'd found a few days ago. Joey hadn't known what kind of gun it was. But Zero identified it and occasionally talked about the kind of damage it could do.

They'd taken other weapons since that night. Everyone carried a handgun. Even Joey carried a 9mm that Zero had insisted he keep with him while they were on "missions" to hook up with the alien invaders Zero was certain were out there. Joey never took the weapon off of safety, and had returned it to Zero at the end of every mission.

"Okay," Zero said as they walked to the mall's receiving door behind the building, "we got two dozen shops in here. All small places. I checked the phone book." He grinned. "Works just like a catalogue because it lists all the places inside. They even got the answering service working now, but the power's not back on in this grid. Which is why the strip club with the generators is the only place open."

Joey fell in behind the other boys. He felt ill at ease. His stomach rolled and he kept hearing Chris' singsong voice inside his head: *"I pray the Lord my soul to keep."*

"Phone book doesn't come with a map, though." Zero shoved the end of his crowbar into the jamb between the receiving door and frame. "So we go in, split up, and cover each other's backs." He pushed, and the sound of screeching metal filled the dark alleyway for a split second. Then it was over and the door hung open crookedly.

Joey watched both ends of the alley. No police cars or National Guard jeeps suddenly swooped into view. He relaxed, but only a little. They were still on someone else's premises and in the wrong.

"Somewhere inside this mall is a sporting goods shop," Zero said. "The place is called In The Wild. The ad I saw for it said they have generators. We want as many as we can fit into the back of the Caddie." He banged the crowbar against the receiving door. "With this door still being locked, I've got hopes nobody has ripped this place off yet."

"Until tonight." Bones grinned and pushed his glasses back up.

"Let's go shopping," Zero said.

Joey let the others go first, noticing that Derrick hung back with him. Then he went through the door.

Down the long hallway that ran through the heart of the mall, Zero and the others flicked on their flashlights and played them over the shops. The beams shone at the tops of the shops, picking up the names.

"You know," Derrick said as he turned his own flashlight on, "Zero is really starting to creep me out."

"I know," Joey said. He started forward, walking through the mall. Ahead of them, Zero and the others cut left, following the bend in the hallway, and were instantly out of sight. The pool of light they dragged around after them took a little longer to disappear.

"Do you have any idea what he's going to do when he finally realizes there are no aliens waiting out there to make him an ambassador or a prince?"

"Yeah," Joey said. And the thought filled him with dread.

"I'm telling you, man, he's going to totally freak." Derrick shone his flashlight from side to side.

"I know," Joey said.

"He could end up hurting himself," Derrick said. "He could end up hurting *us*."

"I know. I've been thinking about that. He may act tough, but I don't think Zero's dealing with the disappearances too good."

"I don't think he lost anybody." Derrick snickered nervously. "Everybody Zero knows is too mean to have disappeared."

The way Chris did. The painful thought ripped through Joey's heart.

"Now I lay me down to sleep. . . . Say it, Joey. You're 'posed to say it with me."

"Okay, little guy. Now I lay me down to sleep. . . ."

"We could go back to the post," Joey said.

Derrick turned his flashlight on him.

Joey raised his hand to block the bright beam. "Hey."

"Sorry," Derrick apologized. "Is that what you've been thinking of the last couple of days?"

Joey shrugged. "Maybe."

Derrick shook his head. "Not me."

"Why?"

"Nothing back there for me."

"What about your dad?"

"No way. At least my mom was nice to me, but I didn't really need her that much either. She was always working at the hospital, going in on her days off. Stuff like that. As long as I stayed out of trouble, she let me do what I wanted to do."

Joey knew that wasn't exactly how things had happened. Derrick's mom had doted on him and had cared about him deeply. Everyone could see that, but Derrick had taken that relationship for granted and never given his mom anything back.

Realizing that he could see that in his friend's relationship with his mother made Joey feel guilty. While he hadn't treated his own mom as badly, Joey knew he hadn't treated her well either. His guilt continued to swell within him, dragging him down. He hadn't been a good son.

"Now I lay me down to sleep. I pray the Lord my soul to keep. . . . C'mon, Joey, say it."

He hadn't been a good brother either.

"Hey," Derrick said, pointing his light at the shop to their left. "I thought I saw a light in there."

Adrenaline buzzed through Joey's body as he looked at the shop. "Turn the flashlight off." He turned off his own.

When Derrick switched off his flashlight, it became immediately apparent there was a light inside at the back of the shop. The soft blue glow was incredibly out of place.

The shop was called Eastern Treasures. Shelves filled with knickknacks covered most of the available floor space. Dolls, paper fans, and bowls of beads shared space with Japanese swords and knives and fake jade dragons and other mythological creatures. Decorative calendar scrolls on rice paper hung on the walls with tapestries depicting epic battles between warriors and demonic creatures. Headbands with rising suns, Japanese kanji, and Chinese characters covered the checkout counter. Packages of Japanese and Chinese candies filled bowls.

"You know what that looks like?" Derrick asked, whispering now.

"No." Joey instinctively whispered back.

"A television, man. I swear it looks like a television screen."

"Can't be. There's no power."

"It's a small set. Maybe a battery-powered portable. Gotta be something. Let's take a look."

Joey's natural curiosity pushed at him to take a look too, but he shook his head. "Let's leave it."

"No way. If that set's in there and is on, maybe there's somebody in this mall with us."

"That's just another reason to leave right now." Paranoid and starting to get really creeped out, Joey glanced around. His imagination immediately rewarded him with imaginary creatures that seemed to lunge out of the shadows at him.

"Without telling Zero?" Derrick shook his head. "No way. If he gets surprised by a security guard and finds out we didn't take a look, he'll probably kill us." He sipped in a quick breath. "I say we take a look and find out what's what. Then find Zero and beat feet."

Joey wanted to argue, but before he could say anything more Derrick was dropping and slithering under the steel chain-link security wall that had dropped down to shut the shop off from the rest of the mall. The wall was a couple feet off the ground, offering proof again that someone might be in the shop.

Unwilling to leave Derrick alone and not knowing what else to do, Joey slithered under as well.

Derrick wasted no time getting to the back of the shop. He stood poised at the door with his crowbar in both hands as he gazed at the television screen.

Joey looked around the small office. The television sat on a desk built into the wall. Papers, neatly stacked, occupied the wall space above the desk. A coffee cup and ashtray sat beside the inert computer. A man's gray sweater hung from the back of the office chair in front of the desk.

"C'mon," Joey whispered. "We need to get out of here."

"Hey, man," Derrick said, "look. Your mom's on TV."

The statement, so inane and unbelievable, especially under the frightening circumstances he was now part of, almost paralyzed Joey's brain. Then he stared at the screen and saw that his mom *was* on television.

Megan Gander's picture was inset into the upper two-thirds of the screen. The main feed showed a platinum-haired lady reporter standing in front of Fort Benning's main gates. The slug line under the picture read PENNY GILLESPIE. FORT BENNING, GEORGIA. LIVE.

Oh, God, please, Joey prayed, *please don't let anything have happened to my mother.* He moved into the room and found the volume control on the TV. He turned the sound up.

"—Mrs. Megan Gander's military trial begins in the morning, friends and viewers," Penny Gillespie said. "Mrs. Gander stands accused of dereliction of duty, a serious offense under any circumstances when dealing with a military body, and possibly even more serious in light of everything that has happened since the disappearances."

Joey couldn't believe it. His mom, derelict? She was the most duty-driven person breathing. But at least she wasn't, like, dead, or anything. *Thank You, God,* he thought when he realized that his mother wasn't some kind of casualty.

"Mrs. Gander was taking care of a young boy in her charge the night of the disappearances," the reporter went on. "That boy fled from the hospital and from his father. The father, Private Boyd Fletcher, arrived in what I have confirmed through the testimony of witnesses was a totally inebriated state, and attacked two military police officers in the hospital hallway."

"Hey, man," Derrick said, "sounds like your mom is in some serious—"

"Shhhh," Joey ordered, turning the TV volume up again.

"The young boy, Gerry Fletcher," the reporter went on, "climbed to the top of an adjacent building."

The picture behind the reporter changed from Megan Gander to a blocklike building that Joey immediately recognized as one of the base's residence complexes.

"Witnesses from that night," the reporter said, "told me that young Gerry Fletcher was poised to hurl himself to his death over the side of that building. Only Mrs. Gander's efforts—first through counseling, then through striving physically to hang on to the boy after he fell over the side—prevented him from plummeting four stories to his certain death."

Joey stood amazed. He hadn't heard anything about that. He'd known his mom was in trouble over Gerry Fletcher's disappearance, which he thought was stupid given that all of the other kids in the world had disappeared, but he hadn't known she'd done stuff like that. Joey felt ashamed at the way he'd left the house the next morning, not even talking to his mom about anything, just upset that so many of the post's kids had come knocking on her door for help. He'd resented them, and he'd resented her. All he'd thought about was how he felt. Now he realized that maybe his mom had felt pretty ragged too.

"There is a difference of opinion about Gerry Fletcher's disappearance," Penny Gillespie went on. "The boy's father contends that Mrs. Gander hid the boy and made it look like he'd hurled himself from the building's rooftop by pitching his clothes over the side. Mrs. Gander's defense claims that God reached down in that moment and took Gerry to heaven when He raptured all the others who are now missing."

The scene behind the reporter switched to the base provost marshal's office. Joey fully expected to see his mom there in chains, escorted by MPs. Thankfully, that didn't happen.

"The dereliction of duty charges brought against Mrs. Gander by the military seem to be triggered by the grievance Private Boyd Fletcher has filed in civil court against Mrs. Gander regarding her failure to notify him or his wife that his son was in the hospital. The legal advisors I have interviewed all believe that Mrs. Gander's case should have been dropped, especially in light of the disappearances of all the children in the world at the moment Gerry Fletcher dropped from that building. And, given that Private Fletcher was heavily inebriated during the time that he's complaining about not getting to see his son, they feel that Fletcher's charges are driven by something other than parental feeling."

A picture of a hard-faced man smoking a cigarette while handcuffed and standing between two MPs took the place of the provost marshal's office.

"Private Fletcher," Penny said, "has hired a well-known attorney in this matter. Once the military court has finished with their case against Mrs. Gander, she will face Fletcher in the civil courts. Mr. Arthur Flynn of the Atlanta, Georgia–based law firm Flynn, Flynn, and Elliot has filed suit against Mrs. Gander for the loss of the time Private Fletcher would have gotten to spend with young Gerry."

The television view changed to a well-dressed man speaking in court before a jury.

"Mr. Flynn is an accomplished attorney," Ms. Gillespie said, "and is highly regarded in the field of civil litigation. He's been successful in getting millions of dollars in judgments for previous clients. Experts I talked to in the legal profession say that it is Mr. Flynn's expectation to secure a judgment against Mrs. Gander, and then leapfrog from that to judgment against the United States Army, and quite possibly the United States government itself."

Joey tried to digest that, but it was too big, too strange. His mom had never been in any kind of trouble his whole life.

"Mrs. Gander ran afoul of the military again this morning," Penny said, "by teaching a class on the Tribulation."

The inset image this time showed footage of Megan Gander in a confrontation with a U.S. Army captain. Joey got mad instantly. He was protective of his mom. Joey knew that the man, captain or no captain, wouldn't have stepped into his mom's space like that if Goose had been around.

"During my interviews with Mrs. Gander," Penny stated, "I have found her belief in God to be very strong, though she admits that her faith failed her as she dealt with Gerry Fletcher. However, she points out that we all have had quite an eye-opener recently regarding what God can do."

Joey heard Chris's voice in the back of his mind: *"Now I lay me down to sleep. . . ."*

"Mrs. Gander tells me that she believes those among us who disappeared were taken in God's rapture of His church," Penny said. "She also said that she went to the head chaplain here at Fort Benning yesterday and discussed the possibility of teaching special classes about the Tribulation—about the biblically foretold seven hard and dangerous years that will pass before Jesus Christ returns to this world at the Second Coming—to the young people she is responsible for as a counselor for the post. She feels that these young people will need this knowledge to find the Lord so they may hope to be delivered into heaven when their time comes."

The blonde woman's image was replaced by footage of a heavyset officer waving off cameras as he walked to a military Hummer. MPs stepped forward and kept the cameras back.

The reporter's voice-over continued, and her image reappeared in a corner of the TV screen. "Major Augustus Trimble is in charge of those post chaplains. According to Mrs. Gander, he not only declined the suggestion but went so far as to tell her that he did not believe the Rapture occurred." The reporter shook her head. "Unfortunately, Major Trimble would not agree to an interview with me, nor did he agree to respond to this report by phone." She looked at the camera. "Friends in faith, I do believe that Mrs. Megan Gander has been pushed into a position to stand for us all in this regard. Scared and alone, she has gone forth with her message: that the Rapture has occurred and that we are now beginning the tumultuous times of the Tribulation. Many of us, as the Bible bears witness, will not survive these troubled times ahead. Now I come to you, as I so often have since this show began airing, in the service of the Lord our God, and ask that you make time in your hectic and troubled days to pray for Mrs. Megan Gander."

The news channel cut to commercial, an advertisement for a book and audio book on the end times.

For a moment, Joey couldn't breathe. How had his mom gotten into so much trouble? What could the army do to her? He got hold of himself, blowing out a breath and taking another one in. He had to get home. He couldn't stay away with something like this going on.

Chris's singsong voice whispered in the back of his head: *"Now I lay me down to sleep. . . . C'mon, Joey, say it with me. Now I lay me down to sleep. I pray the Lord my soul to keep."*

"What are you doing here?" a man's voice demanded.

Startled, Joey turned around, swinging so fast that the pry bar he carried slammed into the desk.

A slender Asian man stood in the doorway. He held a pistol in both hands, pointing it first at Derrick then at Joey and back again. The barrel looked huge.

In the back of Joey's mind, Chris's voice whispered, *"If I should die before I wake . . ."*

Over the past few days, Danielle Vinchenzo had seen a lot of Sergeant Samuel Adams "Goose" Gander. She had seen him in command, confident and fighting fit, and she had seen him in his downtime when he didn't realize she was watching, when his haggard face had shown her how much the death and destruction taking place around him had taken from him physically, emotionally, and—yes, even though it wasn't something Danielle thought about much—spiritually.

One thing she was convinced about First Sergeant Goose Gander—there was a lot going on spiritually within him. She was sure of it. It wasn't just the times she'd seen him at church or in the company of Corporal Baker. The spirituality she'd . . . *felt* surrounding him resonated within him. He was a natural-born leader, a man other men looked up to. But there was something more to him than that. Something that seemed to be growing. It had to be growing, she knew, because she hadn't *felt* it about him as much when she had first met him during the rescue in Glitter City. And it wasn't that she'd missed it, because she knew she would never have missed something like that.

Mostly she remembered the stark images of the first sergeant, the way he had looked when he'd swooped in and taken charge of Glitter City after the initial SCUD attack, announced himself and his unit, and told everyone there that the U.S. Rangers were there to save them. And she remembered the image of him when he'd carried that wounded marine from the fallen helicopter, the image that OneWorld NewsNet had turned into an icon for the Turkish-Syrian conflict news footage.

And wouldn't that be a kick in the pants, she thought as she stood there in the darkness of the alley less than an hour before dawn, if OneWorld found out their chosen hero-guy is the one working to bring their little empire of assassins to the ground?

Just as quickly as that thought occurred to her, Danielle dismissed it. If OneWorld NewsNet discovered what she and the first sergeant knew, if Nicolae Carpathia had any inkling that they were trying to put their hands on materials that could possible damage his bid for international attention—and maybe the office of secretary-general of the United Nations, if the scuttlebutt Danielle had heard was true—she and Goose would be killed.

It's not like all the Rangers are in on this, Danielle told herself. *There's no safety in numbers.* So far, the resistance movement consisted of an unknown computer hacker, herself, and First Sergeant Goose Gander.

Despite all the ways she had seen him—on the battlefield and off, winning and losing—Danielle had never seen Goose like this. She hid in the shadows across the street from the two-story building Goose had identified as one of the hidden headquarters of Alexander Cody's CIA team and watched him, barely able to make him out in the darkness and through the rain that continued to assault the city. The storms to the south hadn't stopped either, nor did they show any signs of slackening.

Goose was dressed in all black, a drenched shadow out in the night. The black suit he wore was standard night wear for these kinds of operations. His pants fit into high-topped combat boots. A matte-finish combat knife rode in a black sheath at his right ankle. He still carried an LCE, but instead of the M-4A1 he normally carried, he'd switched to an MP5 SD3. The small machine pistol was fitted with a suppressor to prevent any gunfire from being heard very far over the falling rain. He carried his M9 on his hip, but it had been outfitted with a suppressor as well.

Danielle had noted the change in weapons but hadn't asked him about them. She knew why the first sergeant carried them. Alexander Cody and his men were killers. Goose didn't intend for them to kill him.

Without warning, Goose vanished on the other side of the street.

Anxiety ripped through Danielle. Goose had taken charge of their escape from the three-agent CIA surveillance team two hours ago. They'd managed a two-hour nap in one of the public areas in the downtown sector after leaving Baker's church, then lost themselves in the maze of alleys and side streets Sanliurfa was full of.

Goose's knowledge of the city's layout was staggering. They'd gone on foot, making better time and passing relatively unnoticed. When she'd asked him how he knew so much about the city, he'd told her it wasn't a city; it was a battlefield. A sergeant's job was to know a battlefield, every natural feature that could be turned to an advantage, every structure that offered a brief staging position, and everything that moved through that zone.

He'd had to learn the strengths and the weaknesses of the city, and know the strengths and weaknesses of his men. Then he had to be able to convert those things on a sliding scale on the fly as ground was lost or gained, as men were moved forward or brought back.

Goose was the one who had thought of the way to get Mystic's information through a satellite burst transmission. Looking back on it now, Danielle guessed that the first sergeant had known how he was going to do it—how *they* were going to do it, Danielle corrected herself—the instant she had told him of the information packet.

Getting the packet through OneWorld NewsNet's satellites was suicide. Getting it through another news service's satellite link wasn't secure and probably not very likely, given the troubles they were still having. Danielle had hoped Goose would tell her that he could get access to the army's computers, but he'd shot that down when she'd finally asked him about the possibility.

The option she hadn't thought of, the possibility that had brought them here now, was the existence of the CIA's computers. If Alexander Cody was running a covert operation within the CIA, he had to have satellite access. As it turned out, Goose had known he was being spied on, and he'd tracked the CIA back to their hiding holes in the city. He'd admitted he might not know where they all were, but he knew where three of them were, and this one had a communications link to a satellite.

Goose hadn't wanted to bring Danielle here tonight. But she hadn't given him a choice. She knew the Web address where Mystic could be reached. She had refused to give it to him when he'd pointed out calmly how dangerous it was for her to come, or when he'd gotten irritated and told her that her presence was going to be a danger to him as well.

That had almost gotten her. Knowing that she might be responsible for his death had almost been too much. But she wouldn't have the story she needed if she wasn't there to get it firsthand.

And if push came to shove, no one would know how First Sergeant Goose Gander had truly died in the back alleys of a doomed city.

She breathed through her mouth, trying to be as quiet as she could. She stared through the darkness so hard that her eyes hurt. With the distance and the rain, she barely saw the satellite dish mounted on the building.

On the second floor a door opened, and light from inside the room spilled out over the covered patio area. Some of the light touched the first few steps of the stairs that led up to the patio from the ground. Beyond the small roof, the light turned gray in the rain and created a misty bubble, vanishing before it reached another surface.

The man was tall and medium built, dressed in khaki pants and a dark golf shirt. He wore a pistol in a shoulder holster under his left arm.

Danielle drew back a little farther into the night. *Looks like Goose's information was correct.* Then she caught herself. *Intel. Military guys call it intel.*

The man cupped his hands in front of his face and lit a cigarette. The lighter's flame illuminated his hard features and blond hair, but it also brought out the fact that Goose stood behind the man with his back against the wall. The first sergeant's face was tiger striped in green and black combat cosmetics. Then the lighter snapped off and darkness covered the patio area.

The man's cigarette glowed like a red ember. A moment later, the cigarette dropped to the patio floor and exploded in a small flurry of orange sparks before extinguishing.

Danielle could barely make out the two struggling shadows on the patio. Panic set in, urging her into flight, but she was too afraid to move, too afraid that someone would see her.

Then Goose was in motion, stepping into the light from the doorway and going through it.

❖   ❖   ❖

United States of America
Fort Benning, Georgia
Local Time 2222 Hours

Megan watched the end of her interview with Penny Gillespie, feeling less hopeful this time than she did the time before.

"Now I come to you," Penny said on the screen, "as I so often have since this show began airing, in the service of the Lord our God, and ask that you make time in your hectic and troubled days to pray for Mrs. Megan Gander."

Megan sat in an almost comfortable office chair at the small metal desk in Lieutenant Benbow's office. The television set had a nine-inch screen but the picture was clear and in color. She'd been an hour late to the meeting to review for the start of the trial tomorrow, but the young lieutenant hadn't been surprised.

Benbow sat on the other side of the desk with his elbows propped on his chair arms and his chin resting on his thumbs while his forefingers tapped lightly against his nose. His uniform was crisp, looking like he'd gone home and changed just before their meeting.

The story had aired more or less constantly on one channel or another since it had first broken on *Penny for Your Prayers* on the Dove TV channel. Since that time, several other local channels had aired sound bites of the broadcast. Too many of them seemed like they were taken out of context.

"Well?" Megan said.

Benbow looked at her, but there was a bit of reluctance in that look. "I don't know what to say." He picked up a pencil from the desk, turned to face her, and drummed the pencil against the legal pad in front of him. Notes covered the lined yellow page.

"Do you think I shouldn't have agreed to the interview?"

"I wish you had talked with me first."

"Would it have changed anything?"

"Would I have been able to change your mind?"

Megan considered the question. Talking with Penny Gillespie about everything she understood about the world had seemed right. She'd guessed that Benbow would disapprove of the interview before, during, and after she'd done it.

"No," she answered. "You wouldn't have been able to change my mind."

Benbow hesitated for a moment, then exhaled and shook his head. "Then no, talking to me first wouldn't have done any good."

"Would you have told me not to do it?"

Benbow leaned back in his chair. "I don't know. I have to admit, Ms. Gillespie is quite a persuasive woman. The piece was really good. But this much exposure at this time in the case—" he shook his head—"I don't know if it's going to help us."

"I don't think Penny's program hurt us."

"Hers didn't," Benbow agreed. He flicked the remote control and the television changed channels. "Dove TV is repeating the program every hour on the hour, and they're going to do so until the trial finishes."

"I didn't know they were doing that." Megan had gotten home and sat through the original airing. However, with all the noise in the Gander household, she'd missed the fact that there were going to be repeated airings.

"They are. And I like that, Megan, I really do. It means they're standing behind what you're trying to do. Not just grabbing a handful of headlines like a lot of these other stations are trying to do. Some of the major news networks are taking the opportunity to blast you. Have you seen OneWorld NewsNet?"

Megan shook her head. "I didn't know OneWorld NewsNet was covering the story."

"Oh, I don't think they're covering it, but they are featuring a few sound bites from it. None of it is favorable."

"Why would they take an interest?"

"Because Nicolae Carpathia owns a majority stock interest in OneWorld NewsNet," Benbow replied, "and because your statement that God raptured the world and took all the missing people flies directly in the face of his theory—and Dr. Chaim Rosenzweig's theory, I might add—that a random surge of electromagnetism is what caused the disappearances."

Tired and insecure as she was, the idea was enough to inspire Megan to anger. "That," she stated flatly, "has got to be the stupidest thing I have ever heard."

Benbow shrugged. "In a way, the theory makes sense."

Megan sighed. "How, Doug? Because Carpathia and Rosenzweig mentioned nuclear energy and electromagnetism? Because it sounded like technology? Do you know what their theory does?"

Looking a little put off, Benbow said, "I get the impression that you're going to tell me."

"Carpathia and Rosenzweig are taking away our humanity," Megan said. "They're putting us on equal footing with an image on one of those children's sketchpads." She remembered how Chris used to draw on the cheap little pads for long periods of time, telling her stories about every image he had drawn. Most of them were superheroes. Megan could always tell because Chris drew them wearing capes. "Those pads that kids can draw on, then lift the carbon paper in the middle and the image disappears?"

"I know what you're talking about. I have little brothers."

That surprised Megan. She hadn't even thought about the possibility that Benbow had a family. *All of the children disappeared.*

"How . . . how old are they?" Megan asked.

Benbow pursed his lips. "Neither of them disappeared, Megan. They're twenty-two and seventeen."

"Did you lose any family in this?" Megan didn't know why she hadn't already thought to ask.

"My mother." Benbow took a deep breath and let it out. "My dad was up late watching a Lakers game when some of the players disappeared off the court. He went in to tell my mother, but she was gone."

"I'm sorry."

Benbow inclined his head. "Me too."

"Have you been back home?"

"No."

Megan gazed at him. "I don't even know where you're from."

"Kansas. Coffeeville, Kansas."

"You shouldn't be here. You should go home. Your family needs you. You need to deal with everything that's happened."

"I am dealing with it," Benbow said. "I talk to my dad nearly every day. My two younger brothers are with him. I know he's all right. Just hurting." He swallowed. "We're all hurting."

"You should be there."

"You need me here."

"There are other legal counsels."

Benbow looked at her with a half smile. "Would you prefer another legal counsel?"

"No," Megan said. "I was just pointing out that there are others who could take your place while you took care of your family."

"My dad and my brothers are quite capable of taking care of themselves."

"But you need some closure too, Doug. You need to go home and see that your mother isn't there."

"I will, Megan." Benbow pursed his lips. "I will soon enough." His voice caught. "But you're wrong about there being other legal counsels for you."

Megan looked at him.

"Nobody wanted this assignment when I got it," Benbow said. "I was the new guy, and it was going to be my first turn in the barrel. My commanding officer thought it would be a good idea for me to work this case, get a taste of losing so I'd know what that felt like and develop a taste for winning."

"He thought you would lose?"

Benbow nodded. "Yes. Most of the counsels—" he stopped himself and smiled wryly—"*all* of the counsels still think I'll lose. That *we'll* lose."

Cold and scared suddenly, Megan wrapped her arms around herself. "And what do you think?"

"I think I've met a wonderful woman—a counselor, a mother, and a wife—who is just going through a truly staggering run of bad luck," Benbow said.

Megan looked at him. "I'm not making things up, Doug. I'm not imagining things. Your mother did not come undone like some Etch a Sketch figure. My son did not come undone like some Etch a Sketch figure. I will never accept that."

Benbow regarded her. "No, ma'am. I can see that you won't."

"There's a reason for all of this," Megan said.

Benbow looked uncomfortable. "Unfortunately, Megan, I can't put God on the stand and have Him testify that Gerry Fletcher is missing because He chose to rapture that boy a few days ago. God is not on trial. *You* are."

Megan was silent, and the fear that filled her chewed in a little more deeply. "We don't have much of a defense, do we?"

Releasing a heavy sigh, Benbow shook his head. "No. Most of the stuff we could combat the provost marshal's office with is going to work against you as well as for you. A lot of it we won't even be able to introduce into the court. The bottom line is that you were derelict in your duty. You were, by law, supposed to notify the parents that their son was in the hospital."

Megan nodded, feeling the hope inside her dwindle.

"The only thing I hope to be able to use is the fact that Private Boyd Fletcher, while inebriated, fought with two MPs in the hospital so fiercely that both men had to receive hospital treatment. If I handle it right, I might be able to color the jury with the opinion that his condition, at that time of night, was about the usual."

"How are you going to prove that?"

Reaching down beside the desk, Benbow lifted up an expandable portfolio. "I've got over four dozen statements from soldiers who were at the bars Private Fletcher liked to frequent. There was hardly a bar that Private Fletcher did *not* frequent."

Megan was amazed at the thick sheaf of papers inside the folder. "I didn't know that."

Benbow held up a hand. "No. That is not what I want to hear you say up on that witness stand. Did you know that Private Fletcher had a drinking problem?"

"Yes. His drinking and his ability to handle it are noted in some of my files."

"Along with anger-management issues he had?"

"Yes."

Benbow referred to his notes. "Those anger-management problems generally took place at night?"

"Yes."

"Would it surprise you to know, Mrs. Gander, that the army has records of Private Fletcher's instances of out-of-control drinking as well as his anger-management issues?"

"No."

"In fact," Benbow said in a professional voice, "I believe as counselor for young Gerry Fletcher, you had access to those files."

"Some of them." Megan smiled a little as she watched the young officer work. He seemed to grow more confident as he went.

"The ones that reported the incidents of Private Fletcher's reprimands for being drunk and disorderly in military bars as well as civilian bars? The same reports that were no doubt used in Private Fletcher's court martials that busted him down in rank twice."

"Yes."

"Did you notice the times recorded in those reports for those problems Private Fletcher had?"

"No," Megan said, thinking back.

Benbow flipped to a new sheet of paper in the legal pad. "All right. We definitely have a problem with that question. But that's okay. I can work around it." He finished a quick notation. "Mrs. Gander, could you look at these reports and tell me if the incidents of public drunkenness and fighting took place in the morning or evening?" He smiled. "At this point, you will tell me that they took place in the evening. I know because I looked through every record."

Megan looked at the folder. "That's a lot of work."

Giving her a tired smile, Benbow said, "I told you I believe in you, Megan. When I haven't been with you or been on the phone with you, I've spent every minute on this case. We're still going to have a tough time getting the willful dereliction-of-duty charge past a military jury, but Boyd Fletcher is his own worst enemy, and I intend to show that. He's not going to get a free ride through that trial."

"That's still not going to erase the fact that I was derelict," Megan pointed out.

"No, but maybe I can build you in some sympathy. If I can get you off with a light reprimand at this point, I'll be happy. And I trust that you will too."

Megan didn't like the idea, but she nodded so she wouldn't take anything away from Benbow's efforts.

"I've been digging into Tonya Fletcher's history too," Benbow said. "Did you know she had a habit of turning the phone off at night?"

"No."

"You never called her at night?"

"No. I always contacted Private Fletcher through his cell phone." Megan thought for a moment. "I called her that night, though."

Frowning, Benbow asked, "What night?"

"The night Gerry disappeared."

"You're sure?"

Megan nodded. "I called her twice."

"And she answered?"

"Yes."

Benbow made another notation. "That's too bad. I would have loved to show that Tonya Fletcher never answered her phone at night so you couldn't have reached her even if you'd tried." He finished writing and looked up. "Why did you always contact Private Fletcher regarding Gerry?"

"Gerry's file requested that the father be called first. Tonya signed the agreement."

"Is that unusual?"

"It's not unheard of."

"So you knew that if you called you'd definitely get Private Fletcher?"

"As long as he answered his phone."

"Good. That will work for us. Knowing that you'd be talking to Private Fletcher and that he was probably drinking at that time of night, I think the jury will understand your hesitation—and the hospital's hesitation—about making that call. We're going to go into that courtroom looking pretty good. If we could somehow negate the question of dereliction of duty, maneuver things so I put your record up against Private Fletcher's, I think I could probably get you a Purple Heart for dealing with that jerk." Benbow sighed. "But we're not going to be able to do that. All I can do is hope to soften the edges a little." He glanced at the television he'd muted and saw the interview with Penny Gillespie again. "With as much airtime as this is getting, maybe it will help pull in some more public support. You've got a lot of Christians in the military."

"*Had* them," Megan said, thinking of Bill Townsend and how he was gone.

Benbow looked at her. "There are still a lot of us, Megan. Those of us left, we just didn't pass muster the first time. But we will the next time."

Despite her fears, Megan smiled. "Maybe you weren't as disbelieving as you acted."

Smiling, Benbow shook his head. "No. My mother was a good woman, Megan. If anybody went to heaven when all those disappearances took place, she did. Now I've just got to work on getting right with God myself, believing and trusting so I get to see her. If I don't, she'll never let me hear the end of it."

Megan laughed a little, and the release of emotion brought tears to her eyes. She was beginning to feel like everything was going to be all right.

The desk phone rang. Benbow picked the handset up and spoke his name. Then he listened for a while. All the levity left his features. He said thanks to whoever was on the other end of the line and hung up.

"There's been a change in plans," Benbow stated grimly.

"What?"

"Major Trimble has taken it upon himself, at General Braddock's insistence I'd bet, to take the position of opposing counsel during the trial." Benbow looked at his notes.

"Is that going to be a problem?"

Benbow paused a moment before speaking. "Major Trimble is a ranking officer. He's got a lot of history here at this fort and probably with the men and women who will make up the jury. They're going to weigh everything he says in his favor. In addition to that, he's the head chaplain, which creates some tension with the interview you just did with Penny Gillespie and her religious program." He sighed and locked his hands behind his head as he looked down at his notes with regret. "Yeah. I'd say this is going to be a problem."

❀ ❀ ❀

United States of America
Fort Benning, Georgia
Local Time 2223 Hours

"Jenny! Phone!"

Roused from fitful slumber, Jenny woke in one of the living-room chairs and glanced at the time on the cable box on the television across the room. When she saw the time, she remembered Megan was in a meeting with Lieutenant Benbow.

"Phone," Casey Schmidt called again. She hovered near the phone and seemed to have an almost psychic ability about when it was going to ring.

Jenny walked to the kitchen and took the cordless handset from the girl. Jenny covered the mouthpiece. "Who is it?"

The girl shrugged and continued dealing cards. "I didn't ask. He didn't say." She wrinkled her nose. "Whoever it is, he sounds like he really has a problem."

Reluctantly, Jenny pulled the phone to her ear. Since Megan's interview on Dove TV had aired, the Gander phone line had blazed with activity.

"Hello," Jenny said.

"Hey, girlie," Jackson McGrath greeted in his whiskey-roughened voice.

"Dad." Jenny's heart plummeted. "You're drunk." The words were out of her mouth before she even knew she'd thought them. She instantly felt guilty. The last few days of stress and helping out were really taking their toll on her. Now, with Megan's trial starting in the morning and all the attention from the media people regarding Penny Gillespie's interview, the stress levels had cranked up.

"Well, now," her dad blustered, "ain't that a fine how-do-you-do? Here I am, callin' to apologize, and you up and blast me with something like that." He snorted. "And I'm not drunk. I admit I've been drinkin' some, but it's Thursday night and they say the end of the world is right around the corner so I figure I'm entitled."

Jenny walked through the kitchen and out onto the patio. She stood alone in the darkness, staring at the long rectangle of light that spilled out from the kitchen window.

"I'm sorry," she said. "I'm just tired."

"What from?"

"I'm helping a friend."

"Hope the pay is good," Jackson McGrath said. "Them people at the Kettle O' Fish called and said you ain't got no job no more. Can't believe you done let yourself go and get fired."

"I didn't get fired," Jenny said, feeling the guilt at once. "The restaurant is closed for right now. Sounds like maybe they're not going to reopen it."

"And now whose fault is that?" McGrath belched in her ear.

"There are a lot of businesses that are closing down, Dad," Jenny said. "Haven't you been watching television?"

"Naw. Too depressin'. But I been out lookin' for work."

Jenny knew the statement was a lie from the tone in his voice. "Find anything?" she asked hopefully. If he found something to do that he enjoyed he usually stayed sober at least for a while.

"Naw. And I talked to the apartment managers, see if they was gonna work us some slack what with all this stuff goin' on. They said they wasn't. We're already a week late on this month's rent."

"I paid this month's rent," Jenny said. "I saw the receipt."

Her dad lit a cigarette at the other end of the phone connection. "Actually, girlie, you paid last month's rent three weeks late."

Jenny remembered the receipt then, remembered how February had been scratched out and March had been written in. Her dad had said they'd made a mistake on the receipt, written down the wrong month and hadn't wanted to write a new receipt.

"*You* changed the month," she said.

He paused. "Yeah. Yeah, I guess I did."

"You were supposed to pay February's rent."

"Well, now, I would have. I surely would have. But I had that mechanic work done on the truck."

Jenny fought back tears. "I saw the bill for the mechanic. It was less than half the cost of the rent."

"I know, I know, girlie. But the problem was, I didn't have *all* the rent money, now did I?"

"You spent it."

"Yeah, yeah I did. An' I gotta admit, it was gone before I knew it. I figured we'd just make it up next time. Me an' you pay double rent. Only the apartment folks was pressurin' me."

"Why didn't they call me?" They always had in the past.

"I told 'em not to. I told 'em it was mine to take care of 'cause you were just a kid."

And we haven't lived in this place long enough for them to know you can't be trusted.

"I tried to work a deal with the managers," Jackson McGrath said. "I told 'em the world might end tomorrow way it was goin'. Told 'em would be better knowin' they was gonna get their rent money a week late as to not get it at all. They said if we don't pony it up by Monday next week, they're gonna slap a lock on the door."

We, Jenny thought and felt tears of helplessness fill her eyes. *You don't mean we, Dad. You mean me.*

"Now," McGrath said, "it won't bother me none to live outta the truck again for a while, till things gets better, but I know how you hate it."

"Dad," Jenny said, fighting to stay calm, "I've got more than half the rent money put back. I didn't tell you, but I've been keeping money—"

"No, you don't," her dad said in a softer voice. "Not anymore you don't."

He'd found her money. Jenny leaned back against the house and quaked from anger and frustration and pain. Hiding money in the McGrath household was a game, a brutal and vicious game. She couldn't keep money in her purse because her dad went through her things. She couldn't keep money in her room because she had to go to work and he stayed home. At different times, she'd hidden the money she'd been able to save in different places in whatever residence they'd been living in at the time.

"Gotta admit, though," her dad said with a little pride in his voice, "hidin' the money in the truck like you did was dang smart. I'da never looked there if the police officer hadn't pulled me over and asked to see my insurance verification. Didn't have no insurance, though, but I had to give him a show. While I was goin' through the glove box, I found that money."

"Dad—" Jenny sucked in her breath and struggled for control—"I work for tips."

"Girlie, I know that."

She made herself speak. "The check I get, if I even get it, is nothing. That won't even begin to pay the rent."

Jackson McGrath was silent for a time. "Well, now, I guess we'll just have to do the best we can. That's all anyone can expect." He puffed on his cigarette. "Anyways, I was calling to let you know that we'll probably be out on the street come Monday. And to apologize."

"Apologize?" Jenny wiped tears from her eyes. "For taking the money I'd saved back?"

"Well, that, too. But I was talkin' about not comin' and gettin' you yesterday mornin' like I said I would. I just got caught up in a few things."

Was dead drunk to the world, Jenny thought. She'd even forgotten that her father was supposed to come get her. Things at Camp Gander had been hectic as always.

"But I'm sorry about takin' the money too," McGrath said. "Sure didn't mean to do that, girlie. But it was just settin' there an' I got to feelin' sorry for myself after the police officer took my driver's license an' told me I was lucky he didn't have time to impound my truck. Man had a real attitude on him, I'm tellin' you."

"How much trouble are you in?"

"Some. Got me drivin' under a suspended license an' a couple of back bench warrants. Told me if he had room for me in his jail, he'd probably have loaded me up under it. I'm gonna have to pay some heavy fines. Maybe even rack up some jail time, which I ain't gonna do. Could be we're gonna have to move out of Columbus for a while. But that's okay. I never much liked this place anyway. Too big and noisy."

Jenny's stomach churned. Leaving Columbus meant leaving the opportunities the city offered. Her father would, as he had done so many times in the past, drag her into another small town in a rural area of the state and settle into whatever menial ranch labor or construction or concrete job he could find.

Jackson McGrath sighed again. "I tell you, girlie, I ain't had nothin' but bad luck in a month of Sundays. I know I told you before, an' I'll tell you again. You are the best thing that's ever happened to this ol' cowboy."

A woman's voice murmured in the background, but the words were too indistinct and slurred for Jenny to make them out.

"Look, I gotta go," her dad said. "I'm over at a friend's house an' she's gettin' a mite irritated at me tyin' up the phone." He lowered his voice into a whisper. "An' I think she's kinda sweet on your ol' man."

So he'd gotten drunk and found someone to share it with, Jenny realized. He was also probably paying for the booze as long as that held out.

"I just wanted you to know that I'd be by in a couple days. I see they opened up the base there—"

"Post, Dad," Jenny corrected automatically. "They call it a post."

He laughed. "Well, listen to you. You gone all army on me now, girlie?"

Jenny refused to answer.

"Well, I just want you to know that I think that's kind of cute."

"Dad—"

The woman's voice sounded in the background again, more demanding now.

"Look, girlie, I really gotta go before she gets ticked. I just wanted you to know that I'd be by there in a day or two and we can figure out—"

"No," Jenny said. Everything suddenly felt surreal, as if she were a step outside herself.

"What?" The black anger that sometimes filled Jackson McGrath sounded in his voice.

"I said no, Dad." Jenny drew in a long breath. *Help me, God. I've never stood up to him before, and I just can't do this anymore. I don't know what else You have planned for me, but this can't be what You want for me.*

"What you tellin' me no about, girlie?" Some of the drunkenness disappeared from Jackson McGrath's voice.

"No, I'm not going with you. I've been carrying you for years now. Taking care of you. Paying the bills. Listening to every excuse you ever shoved my way. Well, I'm done. This world has changed. *I've* changed. I probably changed before all of this happened, but I know I've changed now. I'm not going to do this anymore."

"Now you look here, Miss Jenny Raye McGrath!"

"No. You do what you want to, Dad. Whatever you want to do. But you give me the same privilege." Jenny broke the connection, afraid that if she gave him the chance to start speaking again she would weaken.

She checked the number in caller ID, saw that it was the one her dad had called from, then punched in call-blocker to block any further phone calls from that number. Then she stood quietly in the darkness, cried, and prayed to God that she had made the right decision.

❖   ❖   ❖

United States 75th Army Rangers Temporary Post
Sanliurfa, Turkey
Local Time 0524 Hours

Still in motion, knowing from the conversation he'd heard earlier that there was at least one other CIA agent in the apartment, Goose hurried through the door. His injured knee quivered threateningly for just an instant but held up under him.

The other agent sat at the sophisticated array of computer hardware filling one wall of the living quarters. The computer screen showed a war game in progress, the view through a sniper scope sweeping over a jungle area as the agent moved the mouse.

"Hey, Craig," the agent said. "You gotta see what Donovan is trying now. Guy thinks he can get me with that old bait-and-switch tactic by offering me one of his grunts to expose my sniper. Can you believe that?"

He leaned forward and typed an obscene message on the screen. Whoever was playing at the other end wrote back in kind immediately. The CIA agent laughed and reached for the package of peanut M&M's by the keyboard.

Goose covered the distance across the hardwood floor in long strides, pushing the MP5 SD3 ahead of him. The suppressor at the end of the barrel made the weapon look like an artillery piece.

"Craig?" The agent looked up. His eyes went wide as he saw Goose closing on him.

Goose pointed the machine pistol at the center of the man's chest. He didn't speak. The message was clear enough.

Instead of being frightened, though, the man reached for the pistol snugged in a shoulder holster under his arm as he stood.

If the op had been a sweep-and-secure mission against a known hostile force, Goose would have shot the man, stepped over his body, and kept going. But fatalities were out of the question. The CIA agent was either too young or too stupid to give up, or he'd seen too many action films.

Without breaking stride, Goose closed and chopped the CIA agent's wrist as he freed the pistol from the shoulder holster. The pistol fell to the floor at their feet with a thud. Goose was thankful it didn't go off.

Sweeping the MP5 up, Goose drove the abbreviated buttstock into the agent's forehead and popped his head back, hoping to disorient him. The agent reached forward blindly, opening his mouth to scream.

Goose resisted the immediate impulse to slam the machine pistol into the guy's mouth and stop the scream. The man would have lost a lot of teeth that way. Instead, Goose reached forward with his left hand, chopped the edge of his hand along the CIA agent's Adam's apple hard enough to choke him down but not break the larynx, then grabbed his shirt collar and lifted his left foot into the man's crotch.

All the fight left the man in a rush. He bent over, gagging and throwing up. Goose helped him on his way, putting a hand in the back of his head and shoving him facedown on the floor. He let the MP5 hang from the whip-it sling around his shoulder, put a foot in the agent's back, and applied a sleeper hold that shut off blood flow from the carotid arteries in the neck.

After a handful of seconds, the CIA agent slumped.

Satisfied the man was out, Goose took up the machine pistol and quickly went through the three-room apartment. He already knew the general schematics from other apartments in the area: living room/kitchen, bedroom, bath were set up in a straight shot.

No one else was there.

He returned to the front door, intending to wave Danielle into the building. He almost ran into her as she ran up the steps to the second-floor patio. The rain dogged her footsteps. She wore dark clothes and a black watch cap he'd found for her.

"You were supposed to stay put," Goose growled.

"I got worried."

"If I hadn't secured the room, you might have got dead." Goose bent down and grabbed the first man by the ankles.

"Did you kill him?" Danielle asked.

"No. I choked him down and knocked him out. I didn't come here to kill anyone." Goose dragged the man from the patio into the apartment and closed the door. He nodded toward the computer. "Go. We don't have much time."

Danielle hesitated, then seated herself in the chair at the computer. She looked at the screen. "What is this?"

"Computer game."

"I see that, but these players are linked."

"So?" Goose laid the first man by the second and dug a roll of ordnance tape from his chest pack.

"What if the guy on the other end can shut down this computer from where he is?"

Goose tore off a strip of tape and started binding the first man's hands behind his back. "I don't know."

Danielle stared at the screen. "Whoever it is wants to know if I'm still here."

Goose moved to the computer and looked at the screen, scanning the type at the bottom of the screen.

>YOU THERE?

>YOU THERE?

>HASKELL, YOU THERE?

Leaning forward, Goose typed:>BRB.

"Be Right Back?" Danielle asked.

"Gamespeak," Goose said. "They use it on Net Chat too."

"And you learned this how?" Danielle asked.

"Joey. My teenager. He games a lot. I've watched him play. Gamers get used to starting and stopping play. I'm hoping these guys aren't any different."

>OK. GOTTA TAKE CARE OF SOME STUFF AT THIS END FOR A MINUTE. LEMME KNOW WHEN YOU WANNA GET YOUR TAIL KICKED SOME MORE.

Goose nodded at the computer. "Okay, let's get it done."

Danielle opened the Internet window and started typing. With the satellite connection, the Internet stayed on.

Goose finished binding, blindfolding, and gagging the two CIA agents. Then he took the removable hard drive from his LCE and hooked it into the computer system. A pull-down menu floated to the top of the screen and revealed that the computer had found the new hardware.

"You have to love the new plug-and-play stuff," Danielle said.

Goose didn't say anything as he watched her work.

Muckraker:>R U THERE?

The reply came almost immediately.

Mystic:>HERE. I'D ALMOST GIVEN UP ON YOU. THOUGHT MAYBE THE GREMLINS GOT YOU.

Muckraker:>WORKING OUT OF THE GREMLINS' DUNGEON, SO WE HAVE TO WORK FAST.

Mystic:>NO JOKE?

Muckraker:>SERIOUSLY. I'LL TELL YOU MORE LATER. IF I GET OUT OF HERE. I NEED THE FILE.

Mystic:>I'M GETTING A STRONG PING ON YOU. ONLY TAKE A FEW MINUTES. I'M SENDING.

Another pull-down window appeared on the screen, asking where the file was to be delivered. Danielle pointed to the icon for the removable hard drive. Then a blue line popped up and showed the progress of the download.

Goose breathed shallowly, keeping the mind-numbing fear at the back of his skull. He was exposed and vulnerable, and he knew it. Even if he got Danielle and himself out of the CIA safe house alive, which he had every intention of doing, Remington would know he had been there and want to know why. Danielle could step away from those questions, but Goose couldn't. And he wasn't prepared to answer those questions yet.

The blue bar finally crept across the screen and read 100 percent.

Mystic:>YOU'RE DONE.

Muckraker:>THANKS.

Mystic:>IF YOU LIVE, LET ME KNOW HOW IT TURNS OUT. OR MAYBE I'LL READ ABOUT IT ON THE NET.

Goose let out a tense breath as he disconnected the portable hard drive and put it back in his LCE, making sure the protective foam was in place. He took Danielle's elbow. "Let's go."

Danielle worked the trackball, opening file folders all across the screen. "Wait. Maybe Cody and his team have more information in here. It'll only take a second—"

"We're done," Goose said. He released her elbow and picked up the computer tower. The screen went blank as the connections pulled free.

"Taking the computer?" Danielle asked.

"No." Goose didn't want any trace evidence left on the computer's hard drive of who had been there and what they had done. He stepped out onto the patio, leaned over the side, and dropped the computer into the half-filled Dumpster below.

Hurrying down the steps, favoring his bad knee, Goose took an AN-M14 TH3 grenade from his LCE, pulled the ring, then popped the spoon. He tossed the grenade into the Dumpster, then turned, caught Danielle's arm, and shoved her toward the other end of the alley.

"Run," he growled.

"Was that a bomb?"

"Grenade," Goose replied, and the liquid *whoosh* of the explosion filled the alley. A wave of heat washed over him and he ducked instinctively. When he glanced back, light belled out over the Dumpster and the metal sides were already turning to molten slag. There was no way anything of the computer would remain that could be used to find out what they had done.

"That wasn't a grenade," Danielle said, peering back at the fiercely bright destruction. The rain hissed as it touched the cherry red Dumpster.

"Yeah. It was. Thermite grenade," Goose said. "Burns up to five thousand degrees and capable of destroying any equipment it's placed on. That's what they were designed for. Pretty amazing. You can pop those things underwater and they'll burn for forty seconds." He looked at Danielle. "We need to go. Even in this rain, this will draw someone's attention."

Danielle nodded, then turned and followed him back into the shadows. "What do we do now?" she asked.

"We look over the material," Goose said. "See what we have. Then we make a plan."

She trotted, catching up to him to walk at his side. She hunkered her shoulders against the rain and thrust her hands into her jacket pockets. "We're still talking about the CIA here."

"Cody's group," Goose said, wanting to cut down the odds they stood against as much as he could.

"And Nicolae Carpathia and his organization, which seems to be spread around the world."

Goose hesitated. "There's more going on than what you think, Danielle. There's more at stake than you realize."

Danielle glanced at him. "So now you're going to go all mysterious on me?"

Goose shook his head. "I'm just not the guy to explain it to you."

"Then who is?"

"Corporal Baker."

A look of surprise filled her face. "Corporal Baker as in Baker's Church Corporal Baker?"

"Yes." Goose let out a breath. "He needs to be in on this with us."

"This is my story."

"Baker isn't a reporter, ma'am. And I think, after you talk with Baker, that you're going to see that you've got a bigger story than you thought you had."

"Bigger than Nicolae Carpathia's not being the golden boy everybody thinks he is?"

Goose looked at her. "Ma'am, you have no idea how bad Nicolae Carpathia can be." His headset beeped for attention. He stepped into an alleyway as a jeep filled with Rangers on patrol rumbled down the street. The headlights flashed across the street and narrowly missed him as he pulled Danielle out of sight. "Phoenix Leader."

"Phoenix Leader, this is Dispatch."

"Go, Dispatch."

"You've been instructed to return to base, Phoenix Leader."

The announcement sent a cold chill through Goose. He had to wonder if Remington had already somehow found out about the assault on the CIA safe house.

"Affirmative, Dispatch. Phoenix Leader is en route." Goose took the portable hard drive from his LCE, still wrapped in its protective sleeve, and handed it to Danielle. "Take this and find out what's on it. Get with Baker and tell him I told you to bring it to him. Tell him I want him to tell you everything we figured out."

Danielle took the drive. "What have you guys figured out?"

Goose shook his head and looked back down the street where the jeep had pulled in at the flaming Dumpster.

"There's no time, ma'am. I've got to go. If the captain's not wanting to see me because of this, then it's something else I've got to move on." Goose was already thinking that Remington was ready to spring whatever plans he'd been forming since the rain had hit. "I can't say when I'll be back." He looked at her. "Trust me, ma'am. The story you're really after is the biggest thing anyone has ever seen."

She wanted to ask more questions. Goose saw that in her face.

"Baker," he reminded her. Then he was gone, double-timing through the night to find out what Remington wanted, hoping that his secrets were still hidden from the Ranger captain. Goose knew that Remington couldn't deal with everything Goose already knew and was beginning to suspect.

❂   ❂   ❂

Crossroads Shopping Center
Columbus, Georgia
Local Time 2225 Hours

Joey stood frozen like a deer in headlights.

"What you two boys doing in my store?" the Asian man demanded again. He looked at the pry bar Joey held and shook his head. "You boys no good boys. You thieves. That why I sleep in back of shop. I know thieves come here, try to steal. But I have gun."

Nausea swirled through Joey's stomach and he thought he was going to throw up.

"You boys keep hands where I can see them," the man ordered.

From the corner of his eye, Joey saw that Derrick had his pistol up and was pointing it at the shop owner. "Don't, man!"

"I've got a gun," Derrick said. "Just put your gun down and nobody will get hurt." His hands trembled violently.

Joey wondered if Derrick had even thought to take the safety off, but he knew for a fact that Derrick was going to get both of them killed.

"No!" the old man shouted, swiveling his gun on Derrick. "You put gun down or I shoot you!"

"Don't," Joey pleaded in the calmest voice he could. It wasn't very calm, he knew, because his words sounded scratchy and thin even to his ears. "He won't shoot you, mister. The gun's probably not even ready."

"You put gun down!" the old man yelled. "You put gun down right now!"

Over the old man's shoulder—the movement slowed down as

time dragged because Joey's senses were spinning so rapidly—Joey saw Zero step out of the darkness. Zero's face caught part of the bluish cast thrown off by the TV that was once again showing a story about Megan Gander. He looked like a swimmer surfacing out of the shadows, like something evil that had stepped into view.

"I kill you!" the old man shouted. "You put gun—"

The cannonlike reports of Zero's .357 Magnum blew away the old man's voice. All of the shots struck the man. Joey saw his frail body jerk with each impact.

The gun fell from the old man's hands. Then he stumbled forward, crossing the short distance to Joey. Blood dribbled from his mouth and coated his chin as the television glow caught his face. In two more staggering steps, the man grabbed Joey's shoulders and held on tight. Then his knees buckled and he fell. His grip remained tight and he almost pulled Joey down with him. Joey bent, barely remaining on his feet as the man hooked his fingers into his jacket.

The old man stared at Joey, and his eyes looked sad and scared, like he couldn't believe what had been done to him.

Zero stepped forward and kicked the man's arms, knocking his hands from Joey's shirt. Roughly, Zero grabbed Joey's neck and pulled him into motion. "Get moving," Zero ordered. He cursed and shoved at Joey until Joey headed out of the shop at a dead run. Derrick ran at his heels.

Dropper, Maxim, RayRay, and Bones fell in with them, all of them racing for the receiving door that led out into the alley. They didn't stop until they reached the Cadillac.

Joey slammed into the Cadillac and nearly fell over. Then the nausea swirled up inside him and he stayed bent over, throwing up so hard that he got light-headed. Spots spun in his vision.

Bones cursed, breathing hard from running. "What happened?" he demanded.

Zero stood there with the .357 Magnum in his fist. "I killed a guy in there. Had to. He was going to blow these two jerks away."

"You killed somebody?" RayRay asked in disbelief. "The police are going to be looking for all of us. We've got to get out of here."

"You didn't have to kill him," Joey said, somehow finding the strength and conviction to stand and face Zero. "He didn't shoot Derrick or me." Joey was angry and scared, and he couldn't keep his mouth shut. Everything that had happened was so unfair. "I don't think he was going to shoot us."

Zero stepped up into Joey's face. "I say you're wrong. I say I saved your life." He cursed and called Joey names. Without warning, he slapped the pistol across Joey's face hard enough to knock him to the ground.

Blinded by the pain, almost knocked out, Joey pushed himself up to his hands and knees. He sucked in a breath and tried to block the agony. Before he could recover, Zero kicked him in the ribs and knocked the breath out of him, then reached down and took the 9mm from Joey's jacket pocket.

"You're stupid, Joey," Zero said, holding up the gun for display. "You didn't even try to use this on me. You don't have what it takes to survive. You had a gun when that man 'fronted you in the store, too. You should have blown that guy away, not waited on me to come save you. When the aliens get here, they're not going to want a weakling like you as their ambassador." He stomped Joey mercilessly.

Joey felt two of his fingers break as he tried to protect his head during the vicious beating. He rolled onto his side and pulled into a fetal position.

Finally, exhausted or maybe realizing the police might arrive at any second, Zero stopped. He breathed loudly, cursed some more, then ordered Dropper and Bones to put Joey into the Cadillac's trunk.

Joey tried to fight back, but Zero pointed the .357 at him.

"You're going in the trunk for now," Zero said. "Maybe later I'll let you beg for your life. Or maybe you can figure out how you're going to convince me you won't rat us out." He spoke louder, for the benefit of all the others. "If anyone finds out that we were here tonight and that I shot that guy in the mall, we'll all be tried for murder."

The others didn't say anything. Not even Derrick.

"So we all stay together," Zero said. "When we get back to the house, we'll figure out what to do with Joey."

Dropper and Bones threw Joey into the trunk and closed it.

Hurting and out of breath, Joey lay still for a while and tried to recover. He knew once they returned to the house where they were currently crashing, he was dead. He'd seen that in Zero's eyes. The others wouldn't stop Zero from killing him because they were afraid of Zero and they were afraid of getting charged with murder.

Desperate, Joey pushed aside the pain and took out his flashlight. He knew several luxury edition cars had trunk releases built into them. Shining the light around, he located the release on the left, waited till the car slowed. Then he popped the release, shoved the trunk lid up, and rolled out.

He fell, tripped up by the car's forward momentum. But he

pushed himself back to his feet and started to run toward an alley to his right. Brake lights flared ruby red behind him.

Pistol shots rang out. Bullets ricocheted from the street near his feet, then from the alley wall as he ran inside. Sparks jerked into motion, then flared out and died.

Joey ran, ignoring the tearing pain in his side, knowing if he stopped even for a second they would catch him and kill him. His friends weren't his friends, and he was in more trouble than he'd ever imagined in his life. All he wanted was for everything to be normal again.

But it seemed like the whole world was against him.

Rubber shrieked behind him, letting him know someone had turned the car around or they'd taken off. Joey didn't know which. He didn't look. He just ran.

GAP International Airport
Sanliurfa, Turkey
Local Time 0606 Hours

They didn't call it a suicide mission. None of them talked about the fact that many of them—maybe all of them, if the op really turned sour—wouldn't come back. They were Rangers of the twenty-first century, some of the best fighting men the United States of America had ever turned out.

More than that, they were the team of professional soldiers First Sergeant Samuel Adams Gander had chosen for the op behind enemy lines. Sixty men strong, they'd been bloodied in wars and conflicts long before the current action that ran from the Turkish-Syrian border to Sanliurfa.

As he stood watching them load into two CH-47D Chinook helicopters, Goose felt proud and scared. He'd handpicked the men for the mission, disagreeing with Captain Remington's calls for the team only occasionally because he had more information regarding the men's current physical health than Remington did. And Goose had had that edge only because the captain hadn't yet called for or received his morning report.

After Goose reached the command center thirty minutes ago, Remington had ordered him to the airfield with the briefing to follow later. By the time Goose reached the airfield, thirty of the men he and Remington had agreed on were already there.

Remington's investment in this mission was considerable. The 75th had originally fielded roughly six hundred men for the peace-keeping mission that had turned into a war. Those men had been divided along the front line and fallback positions before the border skirmish had escalated into war. Two hundred and eight of those men had vanished across the board just days ago, leaving behind their empty uniforms and dropped weapons. Another hundred and seventeen were casualties, either dead or too wounded to stand a post. The unit had a lot of walking wounded, too. The Rangers had been taking hits ever since the initial battle along the border, and they'd had major damage from the last attack two days ago. Remington had assigned sixty of the healthiest men to Goose's mission.

The Rangers stood in the rain, their ponchos covering them and the seventy-pound packs they carried. All of them had stripped their gear down to water, light rations, ammo, and medkits. If the op went as planned, they'd be away from the city for fourteen hours. Of course, they all knew that ops never went as planned.

More Rangers arrived by jeep, RSOV, and cargo truck as Goose clambered out of the Hummer he'd been assigned. He walked to the back of the vehicle and took out his own pack. He secured the heavy weight across his back and shoulders and fastened it to his LCE, then checked the headset communications.

The op was set up through Remington's new access to whatever satellite array he was currently using. Goose knew the array wasn't the standard mil-sat set they were assigned to use. Having to depend on an outside source for communications unnerved Goose, especially when he remembered the way Nicolae Carpathia had so quickly and callously rescinded the satellite access he'd given Remington during the confusion immediately following the Rapture.

The Rapture, not "the vanishings" or "the disappearances." Goose realized that was now how he thought of the event. The Rapture. *You have come a long way in your thinking,* he told himself.

But maybe not in his beliefs, he knew. Goose still had doubts there, about whether God really knew him or God cared. About whether a weary soldier could ever figure out how he was supposed to get closer to God. He wasn't sure if he even showed up on God's radar, or if God's radar—like Remington's—so often seemed to be focused more on the big picture than on one worn-out, noncom on the front line of a shooting war.

He wondered how Danielle Vinchenzo was getting on with Corporal Baker. During his last brief headset communication with his men, he'd made sure that Baker was standing down at the moment and could meet with her, though he hadn't mentioned her by name.

Baker had known Goose was spending time with her, and Baker knew whom he was referring to. It was hard keeping secrets from his unit.

And it was harder still keeping secrets from Remington. The whole time they'd handled the prelim brief, Goose felt that Remington knew something was up. But if he did have an inkling of what was going on, the captain had never asked. When it came to a mission—especially a mission the captain had put together—Remington was all about the mission.

But Goose knew that Remington was hiding secrets of his own. He'd seen the weight of them bearing down on his friend. Some of it, Goose had known, was from sending his troops into battle against superior Syrian forces.

That's not all of it, though, Goose told himself. After years of serving together, they knew each other pretty well. The parts they didn't know were the parts they had tacitly agreed were off-limits.

Limping only slightly, feeling the rain in his face, Goose approached the group, immediately spotting the soldier he was looking for. "Lieutenant Keller," Goose called, raising his voice to speak over the noisy throb of the rotors.

Lieutenant Charlie Keller turned instantly. He was trim and fit, and he had enough experience under his belt to be useful in a tight spot. "Yes, First Sergeant," Keller responded.

"First Sergeant Gander reporting, sir," Goose said, firing off a quick salute. He hitched his thumb in his rifle sling to make it more comfortable against his shoulder. "I'm designated to Alpha Detail. Your detail, Lieutenant."

"Glad to have you, Sergeant." Keller looked out over the two teams still loading into the helicopters. "You checked the troop manifests?"

"Yes, sir."

"I'm glad to know that." Keller glanced at Goose. "No offense to the captain intended, Sergeant. The captain is good at what he does, but I'm glad to know you had a chance to eyeball the personnel. Never hurts to double-check."

"Yes, sir." Goose knew that statement was meant neither as a put-down to Captain Remington or as praise for him. As first sergeant, Goose served as Remington's ranking NCO. He was the man who made sure that everything the captain wanted or needed was where it was supposed to be when it was supposed to be there.

"Nasty bit of business ahead of us, Goose," Keller commented.

"Yes, sir."

"Did the captain give this op a name?"

"Alpha's part of the op is called Run Dry."

Keller smiled a little. "Not exactly the weather for an op called Run Dry, is it?"

"No, sir." Goose stared through the drizzle falling from the brim of Keller's helmet.

"Who's Bravo's lieutenant?"

"Lieutenant Matt York, sir."

Keller gave a satisfied nod. "York's a good man."

"Yes, sir," Goose said. "When the time comes and we need him, he'll stand tall."

"We're going to need him."

"Yes, sir."

"Who's our radio operator?"

"Corporal Tommy Brass, Lieutenant."

"Get him up and running, First Sergeant. I want to make sure we're operational."

"Yes, sir."

"We've got thirty men to our unit, First Sergeant. You're heading up Alpha One and will be designated Alpha Leader. Who are our other sergeants?"

"Sergeants Crosby and Foley, sir."

"Crosby is Alpha Two. Foley will be Alpha Three. I will be Alpha Prime. Make it so."

"Yes, sir." Goose saluted again. Turning away, he trotted toward the first helicopter that Alpha Detail would use and opened the headset channel. "Corporal Tommy Brass."

"First Sergeant," the young man quickly replied.

Goose kept moving across the airfield toward the waiting helicopters. "Corporal Brass, your first orders are to find me."

"Yes, First Sergeant. On my way, First Sergeant."

Goose kept moving, feeling the eyes of the men around him. All of them were tense and nervous, but they were ready too. Each one of the men he'd selected for this mission knew he'd trained for what they were about to do.

The two Chinooks stood waiting, their engines idling and their rotors turning in the darkness maintained over the airfield. First developed in 1961 by Boeing after that company bought out the design and Vertol, a helicopter manufacturer in Philadelphia, the Chinook remained one of the best troop and cargo helos in the business of war.

Many soldiers referred to the helicopter design as banana-shaped because of the way the two propellers were placed in tandem, one at either end of the fifty-one-foot-long aircraft. The rear of the helos had cargo hatches that stood open now, receiving troops and equipment.

The closer Goose got to the Chinook, the more the rotorwash slapped the rain from the airport pavement across him. He was drenched in seconds. The Rangers around him wearing ponchos didn't fare much better, and several of them had ripe comments to offer about the weather conditions.

Corporal Tommy Brass met Goose at the helo's rear hatch. He was young and earnest, a tech head who'd originally intended to use his army experience to land a job in the new Silicon Valley shaping up in Seattle, Washington, his hometown. Instead, he'd gotten caught up in the Ranger lifestyle and had stuck around. In addition to being a tech head, he was also an extreme-sports enthusiast, everything from motorcycles to rock climbing, and he had the scars to prove it.

Goose outlined the call signs, then let the other sergeants handle their own squads while he tended to his.

Seven minutes after his arrival at the airfield, Goose was on the first Chinook with his team and Lieutenant Keller. The seating in the CH-47D ran along both sides so the troops sat facing each other. Talking was hard over the constant throb of the engines, so as soon as the helo lifted everyone stopped talking.

Seated by one of the few windows, Goose watched as the darkened ground dropped away beneath them. Gaping holes where Syrian artillery shells had landed pockmarked the airfield. One of the opposing army's first plans of action had been to destroy the airfield so large supply and troop planes couldn't land. For the most part, the Syrian's efforts had been successful. Few lights gleamed in the darkness, and even those quickly dimmed so enemy aircraft couldn't use them to find their target.

Goose leaned his head back and got as comfortable as he could in the foldout seat despite the helo's constant vibration and noise. He tipped his helmet down to shade his eyes, even though the dim light inside the cargo area would have made a firefly's tail look like a comet by comparison.

He thought about Megan and Joey. The phones in Sanliurfa still hadn't come back online so he hadn't been able to contact his wife to find out how they were doing. He prayed that they were doing well. And he thought about Chris as well. The ache in his chest wasn't all about the coming battle. His loss was still there, a constant agony that he could ignore only when duty or sleep took all his attention. So it wasn't surprising that, when he finally nodded off to sleep for a few minutes, he met his son in his dreams.

❋   ❋   ❋

**United States 75th Army Rangers TemporaryPost
Sanliurfa, Turkey
Local Time 0623 Hours**

Captain Cal Remington stood in the command center and stared at the big wall screen that showed the flight paths of the two Chinook helicopters streaking toward the west. A readout in the upper left corner gave their altitude as 1,232 feet, well below the helo's practical ceiling of 14,000 feet. Running nap-of-the-earth as they were, they looked like they were trying to avoid possible antiaircraft weapons. Still, they were on a straight route to Diyarbakir City with no sign of trouble so far. The readout also noted that they were moving at 223 kilometers per hour, near the copter's max of 259 kph.

"They don't look particularly threatening or suspicious, do they?"

Turning, Remington gazed at Felix Magureanu.

Despite the early hour, Felix looked well rested and bright eyed. He had on a dark silver suit that looked like it had just been pressed. The creases in his pants legs stood out sharp as razor blades. The burgundy turtleneck he wore beneath the unbuttoned jacket looked as dark as fresh blood but captured red highlights. He stroked his copper-colored goatee in self-satisfaction. The gesture made him look a bit like a cat. The wraparound sunglasses he wore, despite the low light in the command center, hid his eyes.

"No," Remington answered, "they don't look suspicious. They're not supposed to."

"If I were the Syrian army commander," Felix said, "I'd believe you were trying to transport wounded to Diyarbakir City."

"Good. That's just what I want the Syrians to think." Remington had put that particular rumor into circulation right after he'd given Goose and the two lieutenants their orders. Goose had been the only one he'd called to the command center for the briefing. Goose was also the one Remington most trusted to see the mission through to the bitter end. The others would give their lives if they had to, but Goose had always been able to come up with a little bit more than any normal soldier—or even any extraordinary sergeant, for that matter.

That was one of the reasons Remington had decided to take the OCS route, to break his constant competition with Goose that the other sergeant never even seemed to notice. To Goose, they were equals, brothers in arms. And Goose's lack of recognition of the competition between them had been just as insulting in its own right as the fact that Remington often came up short. Goose was winning without even knowing he was in a race.

But once Remington had made officer, there was no more competition. Remington had won, had proven himself the better man by stepping into the ranks of the military's power structure. Then he'd gotten attracted to the power of command, the attention officers got from each other as well as the media and the politicians.

Goose, though, remained an excellent sergeant, one of the best weapons in Remington's arsenal.

"Still," Felix went on, "as bloodthirsty as the Syrian army is apparently getting to be, what with dropping the bodies of your own dead among you, I'd think that two helicopters flying all alone and so close to the earth would be tempting targets."

"Maybe, if it wasn't raining." For the first time, Remington noted that Felix's suit was perfectly dry, even the trouser cuffs. How could he have gotten to the command center without getting soaked like the rest of them? But even as he noticed that, he decided that the detail didn't matter. Only the fact that Felix was helping him mattered. His help was essential, in fact. They couldn't do the job without it. And that was why Remington had granted the man the freedom to roam through the command center.

"I don't know," Felix said with a grin. "I think I'd still make a try for them."

"I'm glad you're not the Syrian commander then," Remington said. "I'm hoping he's paying no attention whatsoever. Is there anything I can do for you, Mr. Magureanu?" Remington remained polite. After all, the man had patched him into a network of satellites that essentially used much of Nicolae Carpathia's system—though with deniability, in case it came to that. From the looks of things, Remington could tell that Carpathia was well on his way to sliding into the U.N. secretary-general's seat. If other members of the world's nations found out that Carpathia was shading the war between Syria and Turkey, the fact would cause him to stumble and possibly wreck his momentum.

"No, Captain Remington," Felix said, "I don't require anything. I just thought I'd come down to watch the festivities."

"The real festivities won't start for another fourteen hours,"

Remington said. "That's when Alpha and Bravo hit ground zero at the Syrian encampment."

Felix checked his watch. "It will be dark again by then."

"Yes."

"Will you be able to see?"

That puzzled Remington. Obviously Felix didn't understand everything about the satellite system's capabilities. How had the man gotten access to them, when he didn't even know what they could do? Unless he really was just an emissary for Nicolae Carpathia and not an equal at all.

"The satellites have thermographic and low-light capabilities," Remington said.

"You'll be able to see in the dark."

"Yes."

"Wonderful." Felix walked away then, scanning the other screens the computer intelligence teams kept watch over. Many of the screens were keyed in on the Syrian encampment on the Turkish side of the border. Very little movement showed there.

Still other screens displayed world news, especially from the stations reporting on Sanliurfa's plight. The city and her defenders hadn't exactly captured the eye of the world. The big news story was still the global disappearances and all the confusion that had ensued. But it seemed that a number of channels out there followed the war stories.

Remington glanced at his watch. Alpha and Bravo were due to deploy in two more minutes. He swept the nearby monitors and spotted a story currently being carried on the BBC. The news report bore the outline of the Turkish nation as well as the red flag with its crescent moon and single star.

The reporter's name was Sid Wright. Remington recognized the man at once as one of the media personnel inside the city. He'd seen him a few times at press conferences and briefings.

Crossing the room, Remington picked up the headset that connected him to the audio portion of the broadcast. He glanced down at the private manning the computer. "Are you taping this?" Remington asked.

The private nodded. "Yes, sir. Anything coming out of Sanliurfa we download and burn to VCD for you."

Remington sometimes reviewed the media stories in his private quarters, though he hadn't been able to do that much lately.

"—claim that their brother, Abu Alam, was abducted at gunpoint by a group of American soldiers," Sid Wright said.

The screen changed to the interior of a building that had evidently suffered bomb damage. Cracks splintered all the Sheetrock walls, and the windows were broken out.

"They came and got Abu," the young man dressed in Bedouin robes said. Only his dark eyes showed on the screen. "Those men— those *Americans*—" he added something in his own language that could only be extremely derogatory—"they came to get my cousin. They killed three of my family. Then they took Abu." He faced the camera. "When we find these men, Allah grant us the satisfaction, we will kill them like dogs."

For a moment, the memory of Abu Alam in the basement pleading for his life haunted Remington. Nausea swirled in his stomach. Then he pushed that weakness away, telling himself he had to concentrate on the mission at hand. *That's done,* he told himself grimly. *Blow it off and get on with the show. The guy was scum and deserved to die. And if he hadn't died, your Rangers would never have had the chance they do out there now. You did the right thing.*

But he couldn't help thinking that if Felix had reached him a little earlier with the satellite information, then Abu Alam wouldn't have had to die. The black-market chief had been captured, but he'd had no idea why, until Remington had shown him the map and started asking questions.

Fate, Remington thought. *It was just meant to be, and it's better it was Abu's bad luck than ours. We're trying to do something right in this world.*

The on-screen scene shifted back to Sid Wright standing in front of one of the bombed-out buildings near Sanliurfa's downtown.

"How much truth is there to this accusation, Sid?" the off-screen anchor asked.

"At this point, I don't know. It's a rather interesting story, and there appear to be many witnesses to back up these people's claims. I'm going to follow up on it and will let you know."

Remington made a mental note to talk to Hardin and find out what he'd done with Abu Alam's body. Reporters sniffing around after the man changed things. The situation had changed from don't-want-to-know to need-to-know.

He put the earpiece down and checked his watch. Less than a minute remained. He glanced at the wall screen, aware that Felix was roving around the command center and chatting with people manning the equipment. It seemed like the man had gotten to know everyone in just minutes.

The headset beeped for Remington's attention.

"This had better be important," Remington warned.

"Sir, I think it is, sir," Corporal Donleavy of the security detail outside the command center announced. "I've got a man here, sir, who claims to be with the CIA. He says his name is Alexander Cody, sir."

"I know Agent Cody," Remington said. "What does he want?"

"To talk to you, sir."

"Inform Agent Cody that at this juncture talking with me is impossible."

"Yes, sir."

In the background, Cody raised his voice and said, "You tell Captain Remington that if he doesn't talk to me, he's going to be talking to his superior officers. No one manhandles my agents. You tell him that I'll have his—"

"Corporal," Remington interrupted, shocked. He'd taken no action against the CIA agents since returning Agent Winters to them the day before. Harsh words had been exchanged then, but Cody hadn't seemed as agitated as he was now.

"—roasting on a fire three feet high, and I'll take a knife to his—"

"Yes, sir," Donleavy answered.

"—and pull it out through—"

"Send Agent Cody in," Remington said. "With adequate supervision."

"Yes, sir."

Remington closed the headset frequency. He glanced at the wall screen again, counting down in his mind and knowing Goose would have his troops going by the numbers.

Ten, nine, eight, seven, six—

❊   ❊   ❊

47 Klicks East of Sanliurfa, Turkey
Local Time 0627 Hours

"—five," Goose counted out, standing beside the CH-47D's rear jump gate, "four, three, two, one! Go! Go!" He slapped the first Ranger standing in the jump line on the helmet.

The Ranger took a running start, arms wrapped around his chest pouch, and hurled himself through the jump gate. He fell through the air toward the ground that was, according to the helo pilot, 1122 feet below. The static line attached to the big hook over the gate reached the end and yanked his parachute open. The black mushroom belled at once.

LALOs—low-altitude, low-opening—parachute drops were dangerous even under the best conditions. Jumping now, with the rain and in the purple-and-gold twilight right before dawn, could be an invitation to disaster. But it was the fastest and safest deployment for the two units assigned to the op.

"Go!" Goose bellowed over the rotorwash to the next man in line. He slapped him on the helmet, starting him on his way.

In seconds, the twenty-nine other Rangers had evacuated the Chinook and were hurtling toward the earth suspended under black parachutes in a fairly straight line.

"Sir," Goose said to the lieutenant, reaching up to verify that the man's static line was clipped in place to the hook.

Keller nodded and gave Goose a thumbs-up. "See you on the ground, First Sergeant."

"Yes, sir." Goose slapped Keller on the helmet.

The lieutenant stepped through the jump gate and fell, plummeting till the static line snapped taut and popped the parachute free.

Still counting in his mind, Goose snapped his own D-ring into place, then ran forward, wrapping his arms around his chest pack. He experienced a moment of disorientation as he ran out of ramp and stepped off into the sky.

For a moment everything was still, till gravity reached up for him with greedy claws. Then he was falling like a rock. The *zzziiinnnngggg* of the static line paying out echoed inside his helmet. A second after that, the pop of the parachute releasing sounded a heartbeat before the crack of silk overhead and the immediate jerk of the harness as his fall was slowed almost as soon as it started.

Goose released the chest pack after checking to make certain it was still attached properly. Losing gear and having to backtrack for it and hope that it survived the impact wasn't the ideal way to start a battle. Getting battered by it during the descent because it had pulled loose also wasn't ideal.

He reached up for the cords and held on. With the older, round-parachute design, he had only a little control over his flight. The near-darkness stretched across the landscape and the blinding rain made visual sighting of a landing area even harder.

He counted the parachutes out of habit, noting with relieved satisfaction that they had all opened. That didn't always happen.

Glancing down, he saw the ground coming up rapidly. Covered

with one hundred fifty pounds of gear including the parachute equipment, Goose knew that breaking an ankle or a leg on the slippery turf was too easy. The main thing he had to avoid was landing on another Ranger. He made a small adjustment, then aimed himself at a clear spot below.

Goose set himself, hit, and immediately rolled, sliding and slipping through the muddy turf. He came up tangled in parachute shrouds and caked in mud. Standing quickly, he pulled at the lines and gathered the parachute in.

"Gather 'em up," he yelled to the men. "Gather 'em up before they fill with rain and make it even harder." He popped his trenching tool free of his LCE and started digging a hole to shove the parachute into.

For now, no one used the headset radios. They wouldn't be used until the op was in play at the Syrian base. For the moment, Operation Run Dry was all alone in the world.

Goose hurried through the other Rangers, helping men, encouraging men, and getting them all headed back west, trying to stay ahead of the sun. Getting dropped off by the Chinooks was only the first stage of the op. If Syrian military forces had become interested in the helos, there could have been problems from the get-go. In that case, Remington would have warned them and ordered an exfiltration.

But for the moment, they were forty-seven klicks east of Sanliurfa, more or less behind enemy lines. No one would come to their aid once the helos got out of range, and that state of affairs was only minutes away.

"Let's go," Goose said as he hurried through the soldiers. "Let's go. You're burning daylight."

The men responded, pulling their gear and themselves together and falling into their respective squads under their sergeants.

The Syrian fuel depot that Remington had somehow uncovered and mapped out for the op lay fifty-three klicks to the west. They had fourteen hours to get into position, and no way to get there except on foot.

Goose felt twinges from his bad knee but so far the pain showed no signs of increasing. While jump preparations were being made, he'd had one of the med corpsmen inject him with cortisone. The painkiller would help keep the pain at bay, but it wouldn't prevent further damage to the knee. And if the knee gave out on him, prevented him from taking part in the mission, the other Rangers would have no choice but to leave him behind.

Please, God, Goose prayed as he pushed himself into that distance-eating lope he'd first learned in basic and spent all his adult life working with, *please see me through this. My men need me.*

The Rangers fell in behind him, letting him take the lead until three men sped forward and took up point and wing positions. They stayed with the terrain, avoiding the spots with running water and treacherous mud, finding the high ground at a glance and keeping up the pace.

Goose took his M-4A1 in both hands, holding the assault rifle across his chest as he pushed himself up to speed. His injured knee felt stiff and distant, causing him some momentary panic; then it started to warm and loosen, giving in to the familiar motion.

Just help me get through this one, Lord, Goose prayed. *I'll try and see if I can't get through the next one on my own.*

Church of the Word
Marbury, Alabama
Local Time 0819 Hours

"You don't look like a man who got much sleep last night, Chaplain,"
Deputy Walter Purcell commented.

"It wasn't your bed's fault," Delroy said, stifling a yawn.

"Well," Walter said, nodding his head, "you put in a hard day yesterday, I'll have to say that for you. Probably a lot more than you
should have."

"I shouldn't have left when I did," Delroy said, remembering how
chaotic yesterday had been.

After Phyllis and her children had arrived at the church, followed
by the young couple who had been just as troubled and needing answers, more and more people had come from the neighborhood.
Delroy had not done a head count, but he guessed that three or four
hundred had come in for counseling.

He felt bad that he didn't have a proper place to welcome them, or
even enough chairs to sit them in. After the new arrivals started coming, he'd tried to get the church in order, surprised at how he could
hear his mother's voice in the back of his head telling him that she
didn't want people in the church if it wasn't fit to keep hogs in.

The church back in those days had always looked homey and neat
as a pin. But yesterday Delroy hadn't had much of a chance to clean.
There had been too many people with questions about what had happened, about what was going to happen next.

After the discussions they had divided up among themselves and
started cleaning the church. Of course, the ladies had initiated most

of that effort, but the men had quickly fallen into line. They'd collected brooms and mops and trash bags at first, then chairs for people to sit in. By evening, men had come with tools and glass and paint, and they'd quietly set to work repairing and restoring the church.

At first as Delroy had talked to the neighborhood folk, he'd taken strength from their presence. It was surprising how much it seemed they had to give. Finally, though, when even he had been forced to admit his voice was giving out, he'd allowed Walter to take him back to the Purcell home, eaten the meal Clarice had prepared, and had fallen into bed. When he got up this morning, he'd discovered Clarice had washed and ironed his dress whites.

"You couldn't have went on, Chaplain," Walter said, waving the excuse away. "Why, if you had'a, you wouldn't have been able to go back today."

Delroy accepted that. "I know."

Walter pointed. "We're gonna stop up here at Mitchell's Donut Shop. Gonna rent us a five-gallon coffeemaker and buy plenty of grounds. I figure it's gonna be another long day."

After they'd parked in front of the small building, Delroy followed Walter inside the shop. The smell of donuts greeted him but didn't tempt him. In addition to doing his laundry, Clarice Purcell had prepared a breakfast that even a sailing man had to respect. And Delroy had eaten his fill.

Delroy insisted on paying for the rental and the coffee, and Walter finally agreed to go halves. While Walter picked up the equipment from the back, Delroy's attention was drawn to the television hanging in one corner of the shop's small dining room.

"... trial begins today here at Fort Benning, Georgia," a woman reporter was saying as she stood in front of a building marked Office of the Provost Marshal. "Colonel Henry Erickson is sitting at the bench of this military court."

The scene changed to show a woman with dark hair and dark eyes.

"As you may recall from my interview with Mrs. Megan Gander on last night's show," the woman reporter said, "Mrs. Gander is on trial for dereliction of duty here at Fort Benning."

The news caught Delroy's attention even more. It seemed like he remembered the name. People at the church yesterday had been talking about Megan Gander, but he couldn't quite remember what they'd said.

"Mrs. Gander tried to save a young boy from jumping to his death on the night of the disappearances," the reporter went on. "According to her story and the stories of a few others I have talked to, the boy did indeed fall from that building. But he disappeared, just like all the other children."

The story clicked into place in Delroy's head. He'd wanted to see the story, but there had been no television at the church. By the time he'd arrived at the Purcell home, he'd forgotten all about it.

"Many people don't believe those disappearances followed a pattern," the woman reported. "There are many doubters out there who subscribe to the theory advanced by Chaim Rosenzweig and Romanian President Nicolae Carpathia that some bizarre chain of events involving built-up nuclear energy and electromagnetism caused the disappearances of so many people around the world. But Mrs. Gander contends that the Rapture occurred that night, that the hand of God came down and took all the believers from the world, leaving behind those who had missed out on the opportunity to have a personal relationship to Him through Jesus Christ, our Savior."

"Quite a story, isn't it?" Walter asked as he returned to the front counter with the coffeepot. "I got a chance to watch the interview last night."

"What did you think?" Delroy asked.

"Well, I'll tell you," Walter said, "I don't think I'd have believed as much of it as I did if I hadn't heard you talking about the same thing all day yesterday." He nodded toward the television. "That Mrs. Gander there, she appears to be a fine woman. A stand-up woman. But she's going up against the United States Army, and that's no easy thing. I think she believes what she's saying, but she doesn't know as much about the Tribulation as you do."

"We'll all learn about it," Delroy said. "Those of us who have been left behind. We'll see it firsthand."

"Yes, sir, I believe you when you say that." Walter glanced back at the television. "But that lady there, she's gonna need to pull a rabbit out of her hat to convince them military folks. I listened to an interview with Major Augustus Trimble last night, too, and you can see he's all ready to lock up Mrs. Gander there as a nut job. If I wasn't comin' around to seein' things the way you're talkin' about 'em, I'd be inclined to agree with him."

"I know," the counterman said. "News was talking about the Gander woman this morning, telling about how she hypnotized some girl she was counseling to get her to shoot herself."

"Why would she do a thing like that?" Delroy asked.

The counterman shrugged and rang up Walter's charges. "Don't know. Guy on the news was kinda suggesting that the Gander woman had convinced the kid she'd get to heaven faster that way."

Delroy shook his head and glanced back at the screen.

"We're asking anyone with information that might help Mrs. Gander today in court to come forward," the reporter said. "I'm going go be here all day for anyone that wants to stop by and talk. I'm Penny Gillespie for Dove TV."

"Hey," the counterman said, snapping his fingers, "aren't you that new preacher everybody is talking about? The one that's preaching at the old black church over in Shackleton?"

"I'm not a new preacher," Delroy said. "I'm a navy chaplain. My name is Delroy Harte."

The counterman thought for a moment. "There used to be a preacher here named Josiah Harte."

"My daddy," Delroy said.

"My father used to go there when Josiah preached." The counterman smiled at the memory. "As I recall, there wasn't a lot of white faces in that church."

"They were always welcome," Delroy said, remembering there had been a few white people in the congregation, and wondering which one of them might have been the counterman's daddy.

"I know. I remember my father taking me there. He always said that that church was one of the best when it came to singing the gospel. And he loved to listen to your father pound that pulpit. He always said he'd never met a preacher that could bring a man to meet Jesus faster or more sure than Josiah."

Delroy smiled and felt tightness in his chest. "I appreciate your kindness." He held his hand out and shook the counterman's.

"Not a problem."

Delroy turned to go. The counterman called to him before he stepped through the door. "Preacher . . . uh . . . Chaplain," the counterman said, looking a little nervous.

"Aye," Delroy said.

"People I've seen in here this morning, some of them say you're going to be at the church today."

"I am."

The counterman shrugged. "I was thinking, I get off here about eleven, and I was wondering if it would be okay if I came by. Thought maybe I'd bring my wife and a couple of my teenagers." He rubbed his chin. "Things that are going on around here, not much of them are making any sense. People I talked to, they said you had some good words to say."

Delroy smiled in wonderment.

"You see, Son," Josiah had told him so many times, "it ain't so much that a preacher has to go out an' find him a congregation, or even work on buildin' hisself one. God, well, He just knows when people's right for one another. You only gotta listen to Him. You take it upon yourself to serve the Lord as a shepherd, Son, why God will give you the sheep."

"What's your name?" Delroy asked.

"Eddie," the counterman replied. "Eddie Fikes."

"Well, Eddie Fikes," Delroy said, "when you get time, you come on down to the Church of the Word. Bring your family. You'll be welcome."

Eddie smiled. "I'll do that, Chaplain. I know some other people that might like to drop by, too."

"Well, then, bring them on." But a small part of Delroy was wondering if he wasn't biting off more than he could chew. The ride to the church was mostly silent as Delroy continued to wonder what he was going to do, what he was going to say.

"You want my opinion?" Walter said when they were within blocks of the church.

"Is there any force in this world that's going to keep you from giving it to me?"

Walter appeared to consider the question for a moment; then he shook his head. "Nope."

"Well, as my daddy would say, I guess you'd best let that dog run."

"Well, sir, you're overthinkin' things. You just need to relax. Go with the flow." Walter looked over at him. "Your daddy an' God have prepared you for this place an' this time, Delroy." He shook his head. "What I saw yesterday in that church, well . . . it's just meant to be, Delroy. That's all I gotta say. It's just flat meant to be. You just listen to your heart an' to your faith. You'll do just fine."

"There's a danger in being too prideful," Delroy said.

"An' if you get there," Walter said, "I'll thump a knot on your skull myself."

In spite of the tension he felt, Delroy laughed. "You probably would."

Walter laughed with him.

Only minutes later, they pulled up to the church. The sight took Delroy's breath away.

At least two hundred people—men, women, and children—stood in the churchyard. Many of them were painting the church's exterior, some standing on the ground, some up on scaffolds and ladders. The early morning sunlight glinted off the church's new windowpanes. The sign in front of the old place had been rehung and repainted.

Church of The Word

A Gathering Place of God's Faithful

Stunned, Delroy stepped from Walter's truck. The church wasn't as pristine it had been all those years ago, but it was a monumental change for the better from yesterday.

Phyllis, looking more chipper and less worried than she had yesterday, came forward. "Good morning, Chaplain."

"The church," Delroy said, unable to say anything further for the moment.

"I know," Phyllis said. "Nobody wanted to leave after what you got started yesterday, so we up an' divided our ownselves into shifts. Some gettin' materials, an' them what was handy usin' 'em." She shrugged. "'Course, they ain't nobody in this neighborhood what don't fit a paintbrush to they hand. So we got paint." She smiled brightly. "We even got pews."

"Pews?" Delroy repeated.

"One of the men knew where some was. Locked up in a storage business what he works at. He cut a deal with the owner, got them pews for a song, and trucked them over here in the dead of night. Come on in an' see for yourself."

Dazed, knowing that he was looking on the work of the Lord, Delroy followed the woman into the church.

The walls all sported a new coat of paint. The floors had been shined. They still showed several scars and rough places, but all the litter and dirt were gone. A pulpit stood at the front of the church. A scarred piano stood to the left of the pulpit.

And in the center of what had appeared as a cavernous empty room only yesterday, pews covered the floor. Bibles and hymnals filled the slots. They didn't match and they weren't new, but they were there.

Overcome, Delroy knelt and clasped his hands. There were some things that had to be said that way. "Thank You, God, for this place and these people. Work Your best through me that I might give them what they need and what You want them to have. You know their needs, Lord. You know their needs are strong. Let them lean on You for a little while, so that others may lean on them and bring them to know more of You. In Jesus' sweet name, I pray."

When he opened his eyes, he was astounded to see that all of the people—inside the church as well as outside—had knelt to pray with him.

He stood, and the church stood with him.

❋   ❋   ❋

**United States of America
Fort Benning, Georgia
Local Time 1047 Hours**

"State your name for the record," Major Augustus Trimble said from the opposing counsel's table.

Seated in the witness chair, Megan Gander looked out at the faces gathered in the military courtroom. A knot of congealed, greasy fear rolled in her stomach. Out of all those faces, most of them in army uniforms, she was surprised at how few of them she knew. Working in Joint Services, she'd met a number of people here on the base, but almost none of them were in the courtroom today.

She did have her few supporters. Jenny McGrath sat in the back in the audience seats. Lieutenant Doug Benbow sat at the defense table with his notes and portfolio in front of him.

Boyd and Tonya Fletcher sat just behind the opposing counsel's table. Boyd looked stern and angry, like some prophet from the Old Testament come down from the mountain to deliver a message of God's wrath about to be visited upon someone. In this case, Megan knew who Boyd Fletcher's wrath would be visited on if he had his way.

A well-dressed man wearing an impatient look sat beside the Fletchers. From time to time, he spoke on a cell phone, always in a whisper that never reached Colonel Henry Erickson's ears where he sat as judge. However, the constant calls had drawn the colonel's attention all the same. Megan supposed the man was Arthur Flynn, Boyd Fletcher's civil attorney.

She swallowed hard and leaned forward to speak into the microphone. "My name is Megan Gander." Her voice boomed over the court, followed by feedback from the equipment, embarrassing her.

"Mrs. Gander," Trimble said, covering one ear with one hand, "you don't have to lean into the microphone like that. The audio pickup is quite good enough to do the job."

"I'm sorry," Megan whispered.

"Now, Mrs. Gander, you will have to speak up louder than that. That is not spy equipment." Trimble paced in front of his table.

Lieutenant Benbow stood. "Colonel, Major Trimble is badgering the witness."

Erickson held up a hand. He was a grimly efficient man approaching fifty. He was dark haired but with silver at the temples. "Lieutenant, I'll be the judge of whether or not someone is being badgered in this courtroom."

"Yes, sir," Benbow said. He sat back down.

"Major Trimble," Erickson said, "you'll please refrain from continuing your comments about the court equipment."

"Yes, sir." Trimble appeared untouched by the judge's caution. He came forward and stood in front of Megan, his hands clasped behind his back. "Now, Mrs. Gander, you've heard testimony from several other people in the courtroom this morning about how you treated Gerry Fletcher. That testimony proves that you failed to notify either of his parents of his whereabouts."

Megan didn't respond. He wasn't asking a question.

"Mrs. Gander, you did hear that testimony, didn't you?" Trimble asked.

Benbow stood again. "Colonel, I don't believe the major's attempt to test Mrs. Gander's memory or her hearing is what we're here for."

Trimble spoke quickly and smoothly. "I beg to differ, Lieutenant. It seems to me that Mrs. Gander's memory of the time in question is very important."

"Colonel," Benbow pleaded.

"Lieutenant," Erickson said. "Sit down."

Benbow sat.

Megan felt naked and vulnerable in the witness chair. So far this morning, she'd sat at the defense table and listened to her behavior being pummeled by witness after witness. Trimble had had officers reading from the codebook regarding dereliction of duty, emphasizing that civilians fell under the military court system during times of martial law, just as it had been declared at the fort since the disappearances. He'd had nurses who had been on duty that night, who'd checked Gerry Fletcher into the ER. He'd built up an ironclad case that she'd not called the Fletchers to let them know where Gerry was.

The case had started out against her from the beginning, and Trimble had taken little time in getting to her and boxing her in.

"Major," Erickson said, "get to the questions you have relevant to the proceedings."

"Yes, sir." Trimble stared at Megan as if he could break her.

Megan remembered how angry he had gotten when she'd been in his office, how vindictive and petty, and how . . . afraid. Now that she thought back, she could clearly remember his fear that she was right. She took a deep breath.

"Mrs. Gander," Trimble said, "do you have any history of psychological impairment?"

"If I did," Megan said as plainly as she could without getting emotional, "I'm sure you would have dug it up and trotted it out for the court."

Angry red fire lit up Trimble's face. He burst into motion, turning toward the judge's bench. "Colonel, I must object to this kind of treatment. It's egregious."

"It also," Megan snapped, "happens to be the truth. If you could have found something like that against me, you would have had a witness up here testifying to that."

"Mrs. Gander," Erickson said, "I will have order in the courtroom."

"Yes, sir," she said but stared at Trimble.

"Major, continue your questioning."

Trimble pulled at the bottom of his uniform jacket and gathered himself. "Mrs. Gander, do you have a history of psychological impairment?"

"No."

"Have you ever had a coworker, another counselor, mention that you were under a lot of stress?"

Megan thought about that one for a moment, then realized that any interview with any of her coworkers who knew her would have turned up only one answer. "Yes," she said.

"Has that been mentioned on more than one occasion?"

"Yes."

"By more than one coworker?"

"Yes."

Trimble nodded as if he were completely satisfied. He turned and faced the jury of twelve army personnel—officers and enlisted men and women. "Have you ever been treated for stress?"

"No."

"Oh really?" Trimble turned on her. "Have you never taken part of the day off after a particularly unsavory encounter with a teen in your charge?"

Megan knew she had no choice. "Yes."

"At another counselor's recommendation?"

"Yes."

"By different counselors at different times?"

"Yes."

"By different counselors concerning the same day?"

Like when Jill Thompson tried to commit suicide? Megan thought. "Yes."

"Did you take those days off?"

"Sometimes."

"But not always?"

"No."

"Why not?"

"Because I didn't feel like I had to."

Trimble pinned her with his gaze. "Was that your professional opinion?"

Megan squelched her anger. "Yes."

"Mrs. Gander, have you ever heard the advice that a physician treating himself or herself has a fool for a patient?"

"Yes."

"Would you say the same thing about counselors?"

Megan took a breath in and let it out. "Yes."

"Yet, did you not refuse the advice of professionals in seeking some relief for your own emotional stress?"

"I did. And I managed on those days just fine."

"Did you?"

"Yes."

Trimble retreated to his desk and glanced at notes.

Megan felt the silence in the courtroom grow unbearable.

Trimble spoke without turning around. "Were you stressed the night you went into Leslie Hollister's home?"

Megan's gut clenched. She felt immediately vulnerable. The MPs' testimonies about that night had been unshakable. Leslie had even signed a statement that she felt Megan was to blame for her shooting herself. Megan understood the girl's motivation, though. She was a teen and having something like that be her fault was too much.

"Not any more than anyone else has been these past few days," Megan answered.

Trimble turned around. "Mrs. Gander, where is your husband?"

"In Turkey."

"Fighting against the Syrians in what is very likely to be a losing proposition?"

"That's what the news says. I believe in my husband."

"Your husband is not an army, Mrs. Gander."

"No," she said, "but First Sergeant Sam Gander is one of the finest soldiers the U.S. Army has ever turned out, and I know he'll do his best to do his duty and come home."

A few of the soldiers in the audience nodded and smiled.

"I'm sure he'll do his best, Mrs. Gander. But are you convinced that he will come home?"

Megan searched her heart for the truth but was scared of what she'd come up with. She knew God existed, that God had raptured the church, but she wasn't sure God cared. If God cared, would He have let her be put on trial to possibly lose her freedom and her family's financial stability?

"Mrs. Gander," Trimble prompted.

Still she didn't answer.

"I'm not asking for a percentage figure, Mrs. Gander. Just an acknowledgment that you have been and are concerned about your husband's well-being."

"Yes," she whispered.

"So that was on your mind that night?"

"Probably."

"Yes or no, Mrs. Gander. 'Probably' isn't much of an answer."

"Yes," Megan said.

"That was on your mind that night?"

"Yes."

Trimble stepped back in front of her. "Didn't you also lose a son to this phenomenon?"

Megan's eyes teared as she tried to hold back her anger. "Don't you use my baby against me," she whispered. "Don't you dare do that."

"Colonel," Trimble said, his eyes never leaving Megan's, "please instruct the witness to answer the question."

"What kind of man are you?" Megan demanded.

"I'm a man trying to get at the truth of that night," Trimble said in a quiet voice. "Colonel."

"It's no surprise to me that you were left behind," Megan said. "There you stand in your uniform, wrapped in all the pomposity of your office, and you don't stand with God."

Trimble's face went livid. "How dare you!"

The colonel banged his gavel. "Mrs. Gander, that's enough."

Megan barely restrained herself. She forced herself to breathe out. "Yes, Colonel."

"I want no more outbursts like that," Erickson said. "And you will answer the major's questions."

Megan nodded.

Trimble straightened his uniform blouse again. "Did you lose a son to the phenomenon?"

"Yes." Megan made herself grow cold and distant inside. *God, how can You allow this?* She barely held back her tears, restraining them only because she knew Trimble would react to them like a shark would to blood in the water.

"Was the stress of your son's loss on your mind the night you dealt with Leslie Hollister?"

"Yes."

"Do you have another son, named Joey?"

"Yes."

"Do you know where Joey is?"

Megan cursed Trimble, knowing that the man knew more than she had expected.

Benbow stood. "Colonel, I fail to see the relevance of Mrs. Gander's other son in these proceedings."

"Colonel, these events all help demonstrate the frame of mind Mrs. Gander has been in for several weeks." Trimble never took his eyes from Megan. "In addition to her oldest son's present status as a runaway, the boy has been of some trouble to Mrs. Gander for some time. These things all add up, Colonel. I want to show that Mrs. Gander was unfit for her role as counselor at the time she worked with Leslie Hollister and Gerry Fletcher."

"I'll allow it," the colonel said. "Lieutenant, sit down."

Benbow looked unhappy, but he sat.

"Do you know where Joey is?" Trimble asked again.

"No."

"So he was on your mind that night as well?"

"Yes."

"Was Joey late for his curfew the night you were dealing with Gerry Fletcher?"

"Yes."

"Did you know where he was?"

"No."

Trimble put his hands behind his back, once more in complete control of himself. "The night you saw Gerry Fletcher, you were worried about your husband and your son, correct?"

"Yes."

"Do you think your judgment was impaired?"

"No."

"But didn't you choose not to notify the Fletchers that their son was in the post ER?"

"Yes."

"And you knew that was against the rules and regulations of this post?"

"Yes."

Trimble leaned forward and put his hands on the witness-box railing. "Do you consider yourself above the rules and regulations of this post, Mrs. Gander?"

"No."

"How can you say that after admitting that you willingly broke those rules and regulations?"

"I *bent* those rules and regulations in order to help Gerry Fletcher."

"Didn't the boy tell you he fell off his house?"

"Yes, but that wasn't the truth."

"And what was the truth?"

"Gerry said his mother and father got into an argument that night," Megan said. She tried to make her voice strong and controlled. "Private Fletcher struck his wife. More than once." She turned to the jury as Benbow had instructed her to.

"Mrs. Gander," Trimble called, trying to step into her line of vision.

Megan hurried on. "Private Fletcher struck his wife more than once. Gerry tried to intervene. Private Fletcher then struck his own son, injuring him to the point that he needed emergency-room attention."

"Mrs. Gander," Trimble said. "Would you look at me?"

Megan did.

"Do you believe that was the truth?"

"Yes," Megan said, "I do."

Trimble returned to his table and came back with a piece of paper. "I have the doctor's report from that night. It states that Gerry Fletcher fell off his roof."

"Objection," Benbow said. "The major is making a statement, not asking a question."

"Sustained," Erickson said. "Major, please address the witness with a question."

Trimble nodded and asked, "Mrs. Gander, have you seen Gerry Fletcher's hospital report from that night?"

"No."

Trimble passed the paper over. "Please have a look at it now. Look at the reason for treatment."

Megan looked.

"Please read it for the court," Trimble directed.

"'Patient said he fell from his rooftop while stargazing.'"

Trimble took the paper back. "I used to do a lot of stargazing in my youth. But I never did it from my rooftop. Do you know why?"

"Objection," Benbow said. "The major is leading the witness. Unless she grew up with or had prior knowledge of Major Trimble while he lived at home she could not possibly have the answer to that question. Given the age difference between the two of them, I don't think that's possible."

The comment drew a withering stare from Trimble, but Benbow withstood the effort with ease.

"Sustained," the colonel responded. "Major, a less personal question, if you please."

"I will be happy to oblige, Colonel." Trimble smiled, showing everyone there he was in control. "Did you ever stargaze, Mrs. Gander?"

"Yes."

"Ever from the rooftop of your own home?"

"No."

"Why not?"

Megan hesitated, knowing there was no way around the answer she had to give. "Because my parents wouldn't allow it."

"Why wouldn't your parents allow something as innocent as stargazing from the rooftop?"

"They felt it was too dangerous."

"Why was it dangerous?"

"Because I might have fallen."

Trimble turned and walked away. "Did you ever go up on the rooftop, Mrs. Gander? In spite of your parents' orders?"

"No. I did not."

"You obeyed them?"

"Yes."

"Did you know that Private Fletcher told his son not to go up on that rooftop?"

Megan halted for a moment. "No. I didn't know that." But she felt certain Fletcher was lying.

"Did Gerry mention that his father told him not to go up on the rooftop?"

"No."

"Would it surprise you to learn that boys sometimes don't obey their parents?"

Megan knew that the insinuation was there for the jury and everyone else that Joey hadn't been obeying either. "No," she said, "it would not."

"Has your son ever come home and told you a fib to get out of trouble?"

Benbow said, "Colonel, I fail to see the relevance of that question, and I find it insulting."

"Colonel," Trimble said in a calm tone, "the question lends itself to both Mrs. Gander's professional capacity as a counselor and to her personal experience as a mother. Children lie to their parents to keep out of trouble. It's a fact of life."

"Not all children," Megan said. Chris had never told a lie a single day in his life.

"I'll allow the question," the colonel said.

Obviously disgusted, Benbow shook his head and sat.

"Did your son Joey ever lie to you, Mrs. Gander?" Trimble asked.

"Yes," Megan answered, and her heart ached.

"On more than one occasion?"

"Yes."

"So you are no stranger to the fact that children tell lies?"

"No."

"In fact, haven't young people and children that you've worked with in your counseling job also lied not only to their parents but to you as well?"

"Yes."

"And they did it, many times, to keep out of trouble?"

"Yes."

Trimble leaned on the witness-box railing again, only a few feet from her. "Did Gerry Fletcher lie to you that night when he said his father beat him?"

"No."

Trimble drew back for a moment. "Did you see Private Fletcher beat his son, Mrs. Gander?"

Megan forced her breath out. "Of course not. I would have had Private Fletcher up on charges so fast it would have made his head swim."

"Then how do you know Gerry Fletcher was telling the truth?"

"Because I believed him."

"Did the people at the front desk believe him when he said he fell from his house?"

Megan had heard their testimonies. "Yes. But Helen Cordell and Dr. Craig Carson didn't believe the story about falling off the house. That's why they called me."

"Because you are—*were*—Gerry's counselor?"

"Yes." Trimble's hesitation over word selection brought it home to Megan that Gerry was gone, that Chris was gone.

"Did they think you could figure out which truth was the true truth?" Trimble asked.

"They already knew the truth," Megan said. "They were hoping I could get Gerry to open up and tell about the beatings he'd been getting from his father."

"Beatings?"

"Yes." Megan gazed fiercely at Boyd Fletcher, who returned her gaze impassively. "On more than one occasion."

"Gerry told you about those beatings?"

"No."

"Then how did you know?"

Megan felt trapped and frustrated. "Because you get a feel for these things. I've been a counselor for years."

"A feel?"

"Yes."

"Isn't that a rather unscientific term?"

"I suppose."

"So you *felt* that Gerry had been getting beaten at home?"

"Yes."

"Why didn't you do anything about that?"

"I tried. Without Gerry coming forward, I didn't have a case."

"Do you have a case now?"

"No." Megan looked at Boyd Fletcher. "But I wish I did."

"Do you feel animosity toward Private Fletcher?"

"I don't like men who beat their kids."

"Can you offer any proof that Private Fletcher beat his child?"

Megan breathed out. "No."

"Would Dr. Carson's and Helen Cordell's testimonies have helped your accusation against Private Fletcher?"

"Yes."

"Isn't it a shame that they're no longer with us?"

Megan didn't answer the question.

"Objection," Benbow said. "That question is too personal and too inflammatory."

"Fine," Trimble said. "I'll withdraw the question."

Frustrated, Benbow sat back down. Megan knew Trimble had done all the damage he needed to by presenting the question. The jury had been reminded that she was the only one who maintained the story.

"Do you have a personal vendetta against Private Fletcher?" Trimble asked.

"No."

"Any personal prejudices?"

"I don't like the kind of father he was to Gerry."

"Don't you have an ex-husband, Mrs. Gander?"

Megan hesitated. "Yes."

"Do you like the way he fathers your oldest son?"

"No."

"Yet he is your son's father?"

"Yes."

"Would you be willing to say there are a number of different fathers—of parenting *styles*, I believe they're called—in the world?"

"Yes."

"Is it possible that you objected to Private Fletcher's role as a father to Gerry because it didn't fit your ideal?"

"I don't like men who beat their children."

"Again, Mrs. Gander, I have to ask you if you have any proof that these beatings took place?"

"No."

Trimble walked away, pacing for just a moment as if gathering his thoughts. "A moment ago you said something very interesting to me. You said something about me being 'left behind.' Could you explain that reference to me?"

Megan glanced at Benbow, knowing then that they were in trouble.

Benbow stood. "Objection. Colonel, again I fail to see the relevance to this line of questioning."

"This line of questioning deals directly with Mrs. Gander's ability to perceive the world around us," Trimble said. "As we've seen in the news, a great number of people are struggling to accept all the disappearances. I want to show that Mrs. Gander's present problems have only grown worse since the disappearances, and that there were any number of problems before that time."

Colonel Erickson was silent for a moment, then said, "I'll allow it. For a short time, Major, but I want this kept on track."

"Of course, Colonel," Trimble said, "of course." He cleared his throat. "Please explain to the court what you meant by 'left behind.'"

Megan took a deep breath. "Those people disappeared because God raptured His church. That's why all those people disappeared."

"What do you mean by the word *raptured*?"

"I mean that God reached down and took the believers from the world," Megan said.

"The believers, Mrs. Gander?"

"Yes."

"So all the people 'left behind,' as you term it, are nonbelievers?"

Megan hesitated over the question.

"Let me withdraw that question," Trimble offered, "and ask you another. Do you believe in God, Mrs. Gander?"

"Yes."

"Then how is it, if God took all the believers, that you are still here? left behind with us?"

Then Megan saw what Trimble was doing. He was forcing her to alienate everyone else in the courtroom, pointing out that by her own logic none of them were good people.

"I did believe in God," Megan said.

"Did?"

"Still do."

"Then how is it you're not gone with all those missing people?"

"I don't know," Megan answered. "I'm still trying to work that out for myself."

"Do you feel like the time for that reevaluation of self is growing short, Mrs. Gander?"

Trimble wasn't going to back off. Megan saw that now. "Yes."

"How much time do you think we have left?"

"Seven years," Megan said. Then, realizing she had no reason to hold back, she plowed ahead. "You can read about what's going to happen in the book of Revelation. We're going to experience war, famine, plague, pestilence, and dozens of other things."

"And an Antichrist?" Trimble asked. "I am somewhat familiar with the Bible myself, and I do remember the mention of an Antichrist."

"Yes," Megan answered. "The Antichrist will rise to power."

Trimble turned and looked at the jury. "Do you wonder why it is that not many other people are coming forward with this idea, Mrs. Gander?"

"No. It took me a long time to recognize what was going on myself."

"A long time?"

"Yes."

"So you've been planning this for some time?"

The question caught Megan totally by surprise.

"Did you not hatch this little scheme of yours days, weeks, or possibly even months ago?" Trimble asked, turning back to her.

"No."

Benbow started to rise, but the colonel waved him back to his seat. "Major," the colonel called, "where are you going with this?"

"I think Mrs. Gander already had a plan in place the night Gerry Fletcher climbed up on that building. I think Mrs. Gander may be the victim of overwork and worry. It's possible her mind has been working on this end-of-the-world architecture for some time. If she was not mentally stable the night she climbed up on that building after Gerry Fletcher, I think perhaps we can see that. I want to explore that."

The colonel thought for a moment, then nodded. "I'll allow it."

Trimble turned immediately back to Megan. He leaned forward like a predator. "Did you talk Gerry Fletcher into going up on that building that night?"

"No. His father arrived at the hospital. Private Fletcher was obviously drunk and out of control. He scared Gerry and Gerry ran."

"Gerry climbed to the top of that building through his own decision?"

"Yes."

"Did you follow him up there?"

"Yes."

"Why?"

"I wanted to get him down from there. When I got up there, he threatened to jump."

"Did he jump?"

"No. He fell."

"And disappeared in midfall?"

"Yes."

"Do you really expect this court to believe that?"

"That's what happened."

Trimble turned and walked away from her, then wheeled and pointed a finger at her. "Did the phenomenon that occurred and took every child from this world—including your own son Christopher—happen while you were on that rooftop?"

Megan put a hand to her mouth, remembering how everything had been, remembering how Gerry had fallen and she'd held on to him, remembering how his hand had started sliding through hers, remembering how she had kissed Chris good-bye for the last time and hadn't known it and had been in such a rush— "*I'm just going to sleep for a little while, Mommy, so you can come and get me soon*"—that she'd left Chris there all alone in a strange place.

"Yes," she answered. The tears came then, and she couldn't stop them.

"When that happened," Trimble said, "when Gerry vanished in front of your eyes, did you immediately think the Rapture had occurred?"

"No. I had no idea."

"But the idea didn't take too long to come to you, did it, Mrs. Gander?"

Megan had no clue what Trimble was talking about.

"Did only a few seconds pass before you figured out what you were going to do?"

"I don't understand," Megan said.

"MPs were on their way up to the rooftop, correct?"

"Yes. I was holding on to Gerry. He'd fallen over the side of the building. He was too heavy. I couldn't pull him back up to safety. I felt his hand sliding through mine. I was so afraid they weren't going to get there in time."

"Or were you afraid that they would get there too soon?"

Megan stared at him.

"When did the idea to pick up Gerry Fletcher's clothing after he had vanished come to you, Mrs. Gander? When did you think to set yourself up as a failed rescuer by dangling those empty clothes over the side of the building? Did you intend to set yourself up as some new messiah in that instant, to go forth with your message that the world is ending?"

"Gerry Fletcher fell from that building," Megan said, stunned by the accusation. "People saw him fall."

"Did you know, Mrs. Gander," Trimble asked in a calm and patient voice, "that I have talked to more witnesses who say it might have only been the boy's clothing they saw hanging from your hand rather than a boy? Do you remember how dark that night was? Or were you counting on that so no one could see what you were truly doing?"

"No," Megan said. "That isn't right. You're making all of that up."

"Didn't you come to my office just a couple days ago, asking me to set up classes on the Tribulation for the teens you're counseling?" Trimble asked.

"Yes, but—"

"Was it your plan, Mrs. Gander, to talk all of those kids into committing suicide the way you tried to convince Leslie Hollister that she was in a dream so that if she shot herself she wouldn't really be hurt?"

"No!" Overcome by emotion, hurting and frustrated, Megan surged from the seat and turned to the courtroom. "Trimble is lying! He's afraid that I *am* telling the truth!" She sucked in a ragged breath, knowing she was out of control but was unable to stop herself. "This isn't about me! This is about what's coming! It's called the Tribulation! It's in the Bible! Everything that's going to happen in the next seven years is in the Bible!"

The people in the courtroom only stared at her as if she were a madwoman. *Oh, God,* she thought, *help me. Help me to make them see.*

"This is about all of us," Megan said. "We were left behind. For whatever reason, we are still here, and we have to figure out why and what we have to do to get right with God. This is not about Gerry Fletcher or me. This is about *us.*" She shook as she ran out of gas and looked around the courtroom. "You don't believe me. You can't see what's really taking place all around you. That's part of the reason you're still here. You have to get past that. You have to before it's too late."

Silence reigned in the court for a moment.

Exhausted, Megan sat back down.

"Well," Trimble said into the silence that followed, "I'm finished here, Colonel."

Looking at the disappointment on Benbow's face as well as the astonishment on the faces of the jury and the audience, Megan felt she was finished also.

Where are You, God? Why aren't You here? This is Your fight. I can't do this on my own. Please, You have got to help me.

Delroy stood as the anchor at the end of the long rope the congregation used to hoist the church bell off the ground. He dug his feet in and pulled as the other men holding the rope joined him and pulled. Walter was there, adding his considerable strength, and so was Eddie Fikes, the counterman from the donut shop.

"Pull!" Delroy roared, heaving again as he gained another step. The other people around them took up the cry, echoing Delroy's command.

The heavy church bell rose another foot into the air. Men on scaffolds at the side of the church guided the bell and kept it from slamming into the side of the church.

"Heave!" Delroy yelled again, and the men surged after him, gaining another foot.

Four years ago Reynard Culpepper had found and bought the original bell that had been housed in the church steeple at the Church of the Word sixty years ago, back when the area hadn't been quite so developed and some of the surrounding land had still been farmland. Culpepper was a trader, a man who made his living selling and buying, trading and bartering. He had developed an online business by teaching himself the computer and then the Internet, which was surprising for a man of eighty-three. If someone wanted something for a fair price or wanted to swap out, Culpepper could get it. Plus commission. He'd always intended to sell the bell or drag it across the public scales for the money he could get. But he never had been able to.

Culpepper had told Delroy only this morning that he had known Josiah, and there had been times during his wild and wicked days that he felt certain Josiah had rung that church bell just to get him out of bed with the devil and into the Lord's house come a Sunday morning. Some of those sermons Josiah had preached had taken, Culpepper had acknowledged during his brief conversation when he'd driven up with the bell in the back of his battered pickup.

"But not all of the Lord's Word," Culpepper had said shamelessly with a grin that showed all of his dentures. "Elseways I wouldn't still be here with ya'll."

He'd given the bell to Delroy for free. Even thrown in a shining.

"Heave!" Delroy yelled again, feeling the sweat pop out. The exertion was hard and his body complained of all the bruises he still carried from fighting the creature at Terrence's grave. But he put his heart and his soul into it.

And in there he found a song. He pulled again and sang:

> "Swing low, sweet chariot,
> Comin' for to carry me home."

Delroy matched the driving pull of his back, arms, and legs into the rhythm of the song, using the cadence to draw fresh air into his lungs and strive again.

> "Swing low, sweet chariot,
> Comin' for to carry me home."

He leaned instinctively into the rhythm of the song, the way field hands and cotton pickers had done when he was a child and sometimes worked with them alongside his daddy, who was harvesting their immortal souls while they pulled someone else's crop to put food on their own tables.

Four hundred and more people had gathered at the church now. All of them knew the song. The words burst out over the neighborhood, swelling as the bell rose high into the air, coming from the throats of every man, woman, and child there.

> "I looked over Jordan, and what did I see,
> Comin' for to carry me home,
> A band of angels comin' after me,
> Comin' for to carry me home."

The bell continued to rise, and Delroy found more strength in himself than he ever had. The pulling and straining of the other men holding the rope evened out and became more of a concerted effort. They sang with him, putting their voices to his:

> "Swing low, sweet chariot,
> Comin' for to carry me home,
> Swing low, sweet chariot,
> Comin' for to carry me home."

Hands clapped, keeping time to the song. The applause rolled over the neighborhood, gathering strength and rhythm, missed beats leveling till they came as one.

> "If you get there before I do,
> Comin' for to carry me home,
> Tell all my friends I'm comin' too,
> Comin' for to carry me home."

The song kept on, growing higher and stronger as the bell rose alongside the steeple. Men scrambled on top of the roof and guided the bell over the roof's edge. Then the bell was in the steeple once more.

"Hold what you got," Dion Dupree called down. He was in his fifties and still spry as a child. He called himself an inventor, but his wife, LaQuinta Mae, said he "wasn't nothin' but a tinkerer on his best day, an' he ain't had but a few of them days."

Still, the love between the two of them was unmistakable.

"Hold what you got," Dion called again as he scrambled inside the bell tower.

Delroy held on, feeling the rope bite into his hands. But the pain felt good, let him know he was doing something worth doing.

Long minutes later, Dion yelled down, "Okay, you can let go now. It's up there. Ain't goin' no place else."

Slowly, with more than a little trepidation, the rope was eased back. The bell hung solid and a cheer went up. In another couple minutes, the clapper was released and everyone called for Delroy to come up and ring the bell.

He went, feeling as excited as a child, the way he had when he was four years old and his daddy had let him ring the bell on a bright

Sunday morning. He pulled the rope hard, listening to the clangor ring all across the neighborhood.

The bell sounded clear and strong, a sound that would drive away evil and darkness.

They'll come, Delroy knew. *They'll come, and they'll want to know what's going on.* He looked into the blue sky past the bell tower as he descended. *Look, Daddy. People are coming to our church again, coming to visit with God and learn His ways.*

Now that the bell was in place, the picnic that had been brewing all morning suddenly let loose. Folding tables and picnic tables loaded with food and guarded by the women were suddenly declared open and fair game.

"Come on, Chaplain," Walter said. "Grab a plate an' let's dig in."

"You hold those people up," Reynard Culpepper yelled. "Ain't one o' ya'll touching that food till the chaplain's done asked a blessin' for it." Skinny and tall and bald, Culpepper started toward another old man who had considerable girth and a round face under a straw hat. "An' you, Elvin Smith, I know you done poked somethin' in your mouf after I tole you not to do that. You keep that up an' I'll whup you an' take them store-bought teeth away."

When the churchyard grew quiet, Delroy stepped near the tables. He bowed his head and asked a blessing for the food, thanked God for the companionship and the church, and for keeping them all safe while they'd been foolish enough to pull the bell up into the church steeple themselves instead of waiting for the proper equipment. He finished the prayer, and a multitude of voices joined his in saying, "Amen."

When he looked up, he saw Glenda standing out by the fence.

The last few years had been kind to his wife. She still had her figure and her looks, but there was a little more gray hair in the coal black than he remembered. She was a natural beauty, standing there in matching dark green blouse and pants.

Mesmerized by the sight of her, full of joy for all that had happened at the church, Delroy went to her. He stood on the opposite side of the fence.

"Glenda," he whispered, looking down at her. After that, he couldn't speak. There were too many things that he wanted to tell her: That he was sorry. That he was glad to see her. That he still hurt over Terrence and his daddy. That he was so confused about what he was supposed to do.

Her gaze was hot and hurt, her eyes wet with unshed tears. "All this time you've been in town, Delroy, and you haven't even been considerate enough to stop in to check on me. Not even to see if I was still here." She shook her head. "Ain't that something? Even as bad as everything got, I really didn't think it would ever come to this."

"Glenda—"

She held up a hand. "Don't you talk to me. I don't want to even hear any of it now, Delroy. You just go on about your business, and you leave me out of it like you left me out of everything else these past five years." Without another word, she turned and walked away.

Delroy threw a leg over the fence and started after her.

"Chaplain."

Caught astride the fence, Delroy looked back at Phyllis.

"You want some advice?" Phyllis asked, looking at him with a raised eyebrow and her hands on her hips like a woman who'd better be listened to.

"You and Walter," Delroy grumbled.

"Well, Walter ain't here right now, so I figure I best go ahead an' handle this. Probably more my area of expertise anyways." Phyllis nodded toward Glenda. "You go after that woman right now, my guess is you're gonna get your head ripped right off. That woman's been done wrong. Got her heart all fulla pain an' regrets. Don't know what-all you done to her, but you best be sorrowful an' apologizin' all over yourownself next time you see her. But for now, be best if you just give her some room."

Delroy watched Glenda walk away. "If I don't go after her, I may never see her again."

Phyllis sighed in exasperation and rolled her eyes big and white. "You menfolk. I swear I don't know why the Lord made y'all so stupid about love, but He done did an' there it is. I suppose He had a reason, an' they's probably a joke in there too. 'Course, a few of you He done went an' give some looks to. You ain't no Denzel yourownself, but you're a right good-lookin' man when the light catches you just right." She smiled. "Now you get on over here an' fill you a plate an' let that woman take care of herself the way she wants to for right now."

Delroy stared after Glenda, watching her disappear around the corner.

"Don't you go frettin' none over her, Chaplain," Phyllis said. "She be back."

"You think so, do you?"

"I know so. Bet you a twenty-dollar bill against it, an' you can give me a five if you win. Which you won't."

"The Lord frowns on gambling," Delroy said.

"Shoot, Chaplain—" Phyllis smiled sweetly at him—"ain't no gamble to it. I know I be gettin' that five bucks just as sure as we hung that bell." She shook her head. "That woman loves you. That's writ on her face just as certain as the hand of God writ on Moses' tablets."

✻   ✻   ✻

Operation Run Dry
26 Klicks South-Southwest of Sanliurfa, Turkey
Local Time 1813 Hours

Full dark hadn't yet descended over the Syrian fuel depot when the sixty Rangers arrived at the area after their fifty-three-klick run.

Goose waved them to ground among the low hills overlooking the war zone, well out of sight of the Syrian guards posted at the perimeter. They maintained radio silence, communicating through hand signals and messengers the way Rangers had since the Revolutionary War.

Lieutenant Keller lay in the same shadow-covered ditch that Goose used for shelter. Both of them were already soaked from the incessant rain and buried deep in the mud that sucked at them. Thankfully, though, the rain and the mud were warm, not cold as they had been in many places Goose had been before.

Goose took his 10x50 binoculars from his chest pack, switched them over to light-amplifier mode, and scanned the Syrian hard site. To his west, to the right from his current northerly position, a small airfield stood covered with camo-colored tarp. Three Syrian cargo helos, Russian Mi-8s that reminded Goose of the army Hueys, sat under the tarp. Eight men, two to a side, guarded the airfield. They stood under the tarp, though, and smoked cigarettes, indicating that they didn't feel threatened.

To the east, Goose's left and forward, the ruins of an ancient city stuck out of the mud. Archeological maps Remington had shown them indicated the existence of huge rooms beneath the ground. Remington said that the Syrian army had stockpiled barrels of fuel in those rooms, laying in a supply for their next advance.

Alpha Detail's mission was to take out the fuel stockpile—the reason the mission was called Run Dry, because their efforts were supposed to cause the Syrians to "run dry" on fuel—and to execute some of the higher-ranked Syrian army commanders. Bravo was supposed to destroy the armored cav foundering in the mud, secure the airbase, and take the Mi-8s hostage to use for escape. Failing that, Bravo was supposed to destroy the helos along with the armored cav. Any escape at that point would be on foot.

Goose took in the Syrian armored cav units, counting four T-55 main battle tanks and two of the newer and heavier T-72s. The T-55s carried a 100mm cannon, a 12.7mm machine gun, and a 7.62mm machine gun. The T-72s were armed with a 125mm cannon and 12.7mm and 7.62mm machine guns.

Five BMP-1 APCs sat next to the tanks. The armored personnel carriers held crews of three and could transport up to eight more soldiers. They were armed with a 73mm cannon, a 7.62mm machine gun, and a Sagger antitank missile. Three BRT-60 APCs kept them company. Their armament was lighter, consisting only of a 14.5mm machine gun and a 7.62mm machine gun. However, they could carry fourteen troops.

A handful of warehouses that had once been homes for desert traders still existed, all of them tucked up against the ridgeline.

When it came to raw manpower, the Rangers were outnumbered three to one. The Syrians had bivouacked two hundred men in the area. Twenty-two of them were tank crews. Another 103 were APC crew and transport troops for quick strikes. That left seventy-five men for security detail, pit crew, and on-site mechanical repairs and replacement.

And, Goose told himself, *somewhere in there are four high-ranking Syrian military officials.*

Keller tapped him on the arm.

Goose looked at the lieutenant, read the signs for pulling back, and nodded. Together, slowly, they pulled back through the mud and rain. Over the ridge, out of line of sight, and too far away to be heard, Goose hunkered down with the lieutenant.

"Well?" Keller prompted.

Goose nodded. "It'll be tough, sir."

"There are a lot of guys there, a lot of armor."

"Yes, sir," Goose agreed. "But if we stick to the plan, if Bravo goes in and secures the cav—takes out the security there and booby-traps the units—then we go in and take out our four assigned targets, we should have confusion going everywhere. Bravo will scoot for the airfield, and we'll take out the fuel supplies."

"Those rooms are supposed to be big."

"Yes, sir," Goose agreed. "They'd have to be big, sir, to hold all the fuel the captain says they have there. That's what makes this a primary target."

"And it gives us a chance for a little payback," Keller said.

"Yes, sir. Captain Remington believes that the Syrians have never seen how Rangers work behind enemy lines. He figures if we introduce them to our work, they'll dodge shadows for a while and not be so hasty in their advances."

Keller looked up and squinted against the rain. "Right now we've got them vulnerable."

"Yes, sir."

Keller scraped his boot through the mud. "But this mud isn't exactly friendly."

"No, sir," Goose replied. "This is where we apply that old saying 'The enemy of my enemy is my friend.'"

"I didn't know that applied to mud and rain."

Goose grinned. "Tonight, sir, tonight it does."

"Okay," Keller said, "pass the word. We hold back until 2100; then we move Bravo into position and start leapfrogging through this."

"Yes, sir," Goose said, sliding away to go find Corporal Tommy Brass. His knee quivered and ached after fifty-three klicks and a full pack. He was surprised it had held together the whole distance. But he'd prayed the whole way, and he knew his team needed him.

Goose moved silently through the night, just another shadow drifting through the rain. But the Ranger first sergeant was one of the most lethal shadows on the move.

✴ ✴ ✴

United States of America
Fort Benning, Georgia
Local Time 1108 Hours

"Okay," Lieutenant Benbow said in the small room the provost marshal's office had given them for privacy, "I've got to admit to you, Trimble managed to do some real damage in there."

Sitting beside Megan, Jenny McGrath felt like that was one of the biggest understatements of the century. She was afraid for her friend and didn't know what she could do to help.

More than anything, Jenny wanted to know what would happen to Megan if the jury found her guilty today. In the beginning of the trial, Major Trimble had promised all concerned that it would be speedy.

"I know I didn't help in there," Megan said. Her voice was a shadow of its former self, as if she was all washed out and didn't have anything more to give.

"Under the circumstances, I think you did the best you could," Benbow said.

Jenny put her hand on top of Megan's in a gesture of support. She was surprised at how cold her friend's hand was.

"What do we do now?" Megan asked.

Benbow shifted in his chair. "I'm going to work on the cross. Since Trimble called you to the stand and introduced a lot of these other elements, I've got some latitude to bring in more of the information we have about Boyd Fletcher."

Jenny didn't understand much of the legal work. She did know that in a civilian trial Megan would never have had to take the witness stand unless she'd wanted to. In a military court, she'd had no choice. And Trimble had been able to call her to testify, which was also something that wouldn't normally have been allowed.

"I'm going to do a hatchet job on Boyd Fletcher," Benbow said. "Maybe I can earn us some sympathy from the jury there."

"They think I threw Gerry's clothes over the side of the building," Megan said in a dull voice. "Trimble has made me out to be some kind of . . . of . . . conniving crackpot."

Benbow sighed. "I have to admit, I didn't see this coming." He looked at his notes. "I don't know, Megan; maybe I can talk them into a deal. Trimble has laid the groundwork for a possible mental-health defense."

"And he did that as well," Megan said.

"I think so. He was just putting a golden parachute into place for you." Benbow smiled a little. "I was watching Arthur Flynn while this was going down. He's not a happy guy. Trimble, jerk that he is, is so set on getting you and breaking down your testimony that he's killing the civil suit."

"So if I'm crazy I could get off," Megan said.

Benbow nodded.

"Do you think I'm crazy?"

"No, Megan. I don't think that."

"Do you think I threw Gerry's clothing over the side of the building?"

"No, I don't believe that either."

Megan took a breath. "Then do you believe me when I say the Rapture occurred that night?"

Benbow pushed out his breath in a long sigh. "When it comes to that, I just don't know. I mean, it could have been an incredible stroke of good luck that an electromagnetic event like the one Rosenzweig and Carpathia are suggesting happened when it did and zapped Gerry Fletcher before he fell to his death."

"No," Megan said. "I refuse to believe that was luck. I gave up my final hour with my son for a reason, Doug. It has to be a good reason. I was up on that rooftop to save Gerry Fletcher for as long as I could or—or—" Her voice broke.

A knock sounded on the door.

Benbow glanced up and waved the person inside. "What is it, Corporal?"

"Sir," the corporal said, "I'm looking for a Miss Jenny McGrath. I was told she was in here with you."

Jenny turned around and looked at the young corporal. "I'm Jenny McGrath."

"Yes, miss," the corporal said. "I'm sorry to inform you, miss, but there's been an accident."

"An accident?" Jenny's heart jumped inside her chest.

"Yes, miss. It's your father. He's in the hospital in Columbus." The corporal hesitated, looking unsure. "It's pretty bad. They said you should hurry."

✿   ✿   ✿

Church of the Word
Marbury, Alabama
Local Time 1409 Hours

Seated at the desk someone had brought into the cramped office space at the back of the church, Delroy stared down at his daddy's Bible. Over the years, reading that book, remembering how his daddy had read to him from it and elaborated on all the stories of the Old and New Testaments, had brought Delroy a lot of contentment and peace.

That had all seemed to end when Terrence had been killed. Almost the same day that he had learned the news of his son's death, Delroy had laid that Bible down, packed it away, and not looked at it. He'd used other Bibles in the intervening five years, but his daddy's Bible had been a grim reminder of God's seemingly hollow promise to Delroy Harte, the young boy.

Delroy put his forefinger in the Bible to mark his place, then rubbed at the leather exterior where his daddy's blood had soaked in all those years ago. No one knew why his daddy had been killed. Josiah had been at the church by himself that night, and circumstantial evidence—the description of the car, the gun being owned by Clarence Floyd's dad and being a unique German pistol from World War II, and the fact that Josiah had given young Clarence a dressing-down in public over his use of harsh language around women—wasn't enough to hold him for questioning, according to the district attorney. There'd been no chance of convicting Clarence Floyd for murder.

When the congregation had met Delroy this morning and shown him the office, he'd taken his pictures from his duffel and put them on the desk. Pictures of his daddy and momma, Terrence, and Glenda now shared space atop the empty desk.

He glanced at the legal pad in front of him, not surprised to find that he hadn't taken a single note. There hadn't been any notes the last time he'd looked either.

Daddy, Delroy thought, *I got a lot of people out there waiting on me, expecting me to have something powerful to tell them. I look inside myself and I find I don't have one thing to say. Was that why I was brought here? To say nothing?*

He looked at Glenda's picture. She hadn't been back. It looked like Phyllis was going to be proven wrong about that. He should have bet her. At least he'd have had twenty bucks to show for his trouble.

Daddy, you and God are going to have to help me out here, but I definitely feel like I'm in over my head.

After a brief prayer, he went back to searching through the Bible, trying to find something right, something that he could give the people who had shown up. Hundreds of sermons lay at his fingertips. Over the years he had delivered them all, getting so they came with practiced ease.

But what do you give folks looking straight down both barrels of the Tribulation?

Looking up, he glanced at the small TV set on the corner of the desk. The news station showed a brief piece about Nicolae Carpathia and the United Nations; then it shifted over to Penny Gillespie at Fort Benning, Georgia. Curious, Delroy reached over and turned up the volume.

"—no excuse for this morning's brutal attack on a fine woman like Mrs. Megan Gander," the news reporter was saying. "Unfortunately, no one in the courtroom seems predisposed to keep Major Trimble from badgering her."

Delroy continued listening for a few moments, thinking how bad it must be to face the kind of prosecution and persecution Megan Gander must be going through. He said a quick prayer for her, then reached up to turn the television off.

At that moment, a young man in uniform pushed through the crowd in front of the provost marshal's office. He waved a rectangular box at Penny Gillespie. "Ms. Gillespie. *Ms. Gillespie.*"

The reporter finally noticed the young man and brought him up to her.

"Ms. Gillespie, my name is Private Lonnie Smith. I'm stationed here at Fort Benning." He took a deep breath and looked out at the crowd surrounding him, as if noticing for the first time he had their complete attention. Nervously, he turned his attention back to Penny Gillespie. "I was there that night. When that boy, Gerry Fletcher, fell from the rooftop."

"You saw that happen?"

Delroy was intrigued. Maybe Mrs. Gander was getting a break, and it sure sounded like she was in need of one.

"More than that," Private Smith said. "I filmed the whole thing on my video camera." He pushed the rectangle at her. "This is it."

Penny took the tape. "I don't understand. Why haven't you come forward before now?"

"Ms. Gillespie, I didn't think they'd actually try her for anything. That boy vanished. She didn't have anything to do with that. It was God who did that."

"I know, Private Smith. But that's not what Mrs. Gander is on trial for."

"I understand that now. I was just—I just got caught up in what I was going through myself." The young man hesitated. "I didn't believe what I saw at first, but as I watched that tape—over and over—I saw it again and again. It changed my life. I swear it did." He took a deep breath. "Wednesday night, I was saved. I went forward when the preacher called, and I was baptized." He looked at the reporter. "I've never believed in God a day in my life until that day. I thought my life didn't matter."

Penny Gillespie smiled. "Private, if this tape really has on it what you say it has, I'd say your life matters a whole lot. Come on inside here with me."

Delroy watched the reporter and the young private enter the provost marshal's office. A boy getting raptured by God's own hand. That would be a sight to see.

And in that moment, the sermon he knew he had to deliver started to fall together in his mind.

A knock sounded on the door. When Delroy turned to look, he saw George, the old man who had given him a ride to the cemetery, standing there.

"'Member me?" George asked.

Delroy stood and took the old man's hand. "Aye. Of course I do. What brings you here?"

George grinned. "That bell. What else? Been a lotta years since I heard that bell ring. Never figured on hearin' it again in my lifetime; I'll guarantee you that." He wiped his mouth with a calloused hand. "When your daddy shepherded this church, I never come in here. But I figured if you was gonna be here today, I was gonna come." He jerked a thumb over his shoulder. "I brung some company too."

Delroy poked his head out the door and glanced down the hallway. Six other old men stood there, each of them clutching an instrument case.

"Gentlemen," Delroy greeted.

"Pastor," they greeted.

"*Chaplain,*" George said. "I done told y'all he's a chaplain. A navy man." He looked back at Delroy. "This here's one of the finest blues bands in the state."

"Blues," Delroy repeated.

"Yes, sir," George said. "But don't worry. They play gospel just fine. Gospel ain't nothin' but blues what's got more hope. Same problems, just a little light at the end of the tunnel. I brung 'em here 'cause I figured you cain't have a revival without some good ol' gospel music."

"A revival?"

"That's what we done been tole."

"A revival." Delroy said it again, and the idea started to feel right. He looked at George, then at the men. "You want to play? Here?"

"Yes, sir. If'n y'all'll have us."

Delroy grinned and shook his head. "I'll have you."

"Thank you, Chaplain. You won't regret it. We'll do you proud."

"I'm sure you will."

"You gonna be along soon?"

"Aye."

"Well, we'll go an' warm 'em up for you." George turned and walked back down the hallway. His hand drifted up to his bib overalls for his cigarette pouch.

"George."

Turning, George said, "Yes, Chaplain."

"There's no smoking in this church," Delroy said. "There was no smoking allowed back in my daddy's day, and there won't be any today."

"Yes, sir. Been meanin' to give 'em up anyway." George waved and went on his way, the band falling in behind him.

Delroy grinned, feeling better about everything. The thing that still bothered him was Glenda's absence. He wished with all his might that she were here. He went back to the small office and knelt on the floor the way he had seen his daddy do so many times before. He held his daddy's Bible in both hands, closed his eyes, and prayed.

"God, I'm going to need You with me now. Please make me strong enough to make a difference. And, Daddy, keep an eye on me and help me to make you proud. Amen." Then Delroy pushed himself up and went to face his congregation, hoping he had the message they needed to hear. Hoping it was one *he* needed to hear.

Operation Run Dry
26 Klicks South-Southwest of Sanliurfa, Turkey
Local Time 2116 Hours

Dressed in black, his head covered by a watch cap and his face striped in black-and-green camo, Goose waited patiently atop the ridgeline over the line of warehouse-like structures across from the open pit where the Syrians had stored their forward fuel reserves. His night-vision goggles lifted the darkness from the surrounding area and turned the Syrian guards green.

Forty or fifty years ago, the buildings had housed archeological teams that had come to the nameless city and poked around in its remains for some forgotten prize that relic hunters and scavengers hadn't already made off with. They'd left the buildings behind. If the archeologists had found anything, Remington hadn't mentioned it in his brief. Goose reflected that it was interesting archeologists could leave things behind that would eventually be studied by other archeologists.

On the computer map, the target site where the fuel was kept was designated *Ruins* and the buildings were designated *Buildings*. The armored cav area was labeled *Armored Cav*. The Ranger captain liked keeping things simple. Complicating them for no reason tended to make missions run ragged in timing and in effective use of manpower.

Goose preferred his hit-and-git missions the same way. Down and dirty, quick in and quick out. That was why he and Remington had performed so well together as sergeants and now as captain and first sergeant. They knew each other, and they knew how to be the very best Rangers. When the time came, they could both be vicious and merciless against their enemies.

Back in the Revolutionary War, when Major Robert Rogers had first put together the rules that became his Standing Orders, Rogers had made it clear that the enemy should be taken advantage of. They weren't to be fought fairly. They were to be encountered and put down as quickly as possible, with as little loss to a Ranger as possible.

"Let the enemy come 'til he's almost close enough to touch. Then let him have it and jump out and finish him with your hatchet." Those SOs were grim and ruthless, but the men who had learned to fight with them against the British in those days had beaten the best land army around. And they'd done it by breaking the rules that had been in existence at the time.

Goose had made his peace with himself over the men he was going to kill tonight. He'd said his prayers and focused on the atrocities his enemies had done, judging them fit for no mercy if they chose to fight. The Syrian army had launched SCUDs into metropolitan areas, killing hundreds of men, women, and children. And they had attacked San-liurfa on different occasions, killing civilians as well as brother Rangers.

Payback was coming, and it was dressed in Ranger black and wearing the bruised shadows of the night on its face.

Goose felt the wind blowing in from the east, mixed with the spitting rain that collected and slid down his features to soak the turtleneck he wore. He carried his M-4A1 slung over his shoulder, his M9 on his hip, and took up an MP5-SD3 machine pistol with suppressor as his lead weapon for the moment. His LCE was loaded with grenades and extra ammo for his weapons.

A shadow flitted along the ridgeline to Goose's right. He picked it up instantly in his peripheral vision. He shifted the MP5 across his knees a little, getting his body ready to move and bring the deadly machine pistol up if he needed to.

Goose stayed hunkered down, putting most of his weight on his good knee so he could save the injured one. The bad knee had swelled tremendously, filling his pant leg and promising days of agony to come.

But he was with his men in the field and that was where he belonged. Megan could never understand that about him. Not the warrior spirit, not the avenger inside him that lived to break the hold evil men had on others. For some people, being a soldier was a profession, but Goose had always felt it was a calling, something in his nature that he could never deny. He'd fought and would fight to protect those who could not protect themselves, and he would make the sacrifices necessary to see that done.

Tonight men would die because of his willingness to do that.

And the more he thought about all the terror and oppression that were coming in the next seven years, the stronger that spirit in him felt. The action against the Syrian army was a delaying tactic, a maneuver that would buy the armies occupying Sanliurfa a little more time. A chance at life or a slower death.

But what was he going to do after that? The question had hung heavy in his mind during the fifty-three-klick run through the rain-sodden land. Even when the action was over in Turkey—and God grant that it would be—there would be new wars to fight. The Four Horsemen were coming. Nicolae Carpathia might be the Antichrist.

Goose wondered if he would recognize the evil in the man if he saw it, or if he would be pulled into it. And what if Icarus had it wrong? What if Carpathia wasn't Antichrist? What if the Antichrist hadn't shown up yet?

The possibilities made Goose's mind dizzy. His father had always told him that sometimes a man could simply know too much. Wes Gander had always advised Goose to take each day as it came, to make a battle plan, then find out what mistakes were made the day before and correct those.

But that wasn't possible now. No one knew what mistakes were being made.

"First Sergeant." Corporal Tommy Brass hesitated in the brush ten yards away. The Rangers knew better than to creep up on each other unannounced.

"Here, Corporal," Goose replied in a soft voice that didn't carry far.

"Bravo Detail is in position. Lieutenant Keller says we're go on your go."

Keller was holding two Alpha squads back for the moment. Goose's primary mission was the takedown of the four targets designated by Captain Remington for termination—all four were ranking officers in the Syrian army. Goose had seen the files on all of them. They were butchers, men who used the power of the military to further their own bloodlusts and desires.

The deaths of those four men were going to be a message. So far, the Syrian army thought of the Rangers only as peacekeepers. But when the Syrians had used the dead bodies of the men who had fallen during the border skirmish, they had crossed the line. Tonight, the Syrian army was going to learn a little about retribution.

"Gonna be readin' 'em from the Old Testament," Wes Gander used to say when he talked about people he'd had confrontations with.

And that was what it was, Goose knew—an Old Testament reckoning right here in the holy lands where so much of that bloody history had played out.

"Affirmative, Corporal," Goose said. "Stand by to go live on the sat-link when I call for it. When we hit the house, those four targets we're after are going to scatter."

When they left Sanliurfa, Remington had tagged all four men through the spy-sat recon. Once the sat-link kicked in, Remington's specialty teams would guide Goose and his men to the targets.

And once that ball was in play, Keller would take the other two squads into the fuel dump site and destroy those supplies. Bravo Detail would explode booby traps they had on the armored cav, then proceed to the airfield and attempt to secure it. If everything went well, the marine wing from Sanliurfa could make a surprise strike and take out the remaining Syrian army.

"Yes, First Sergeant."

Goose took a final deep breath, then took up the rope secured to a stake shoved deep into the mud. The drop over the ridgeline was steep, made even more treacherous by the mud clinging to the side. The roofs of the buildings were thirty feet below.

He held the MP5 in his right hand and used his left to rappel the steep descent Australian style, which put him face forward and ready to use the machine pistol. He kept his hops short and low, staying close to ground to absorb more of the cover provided by the irregular surface and brush that grew along the way.

Kicked free by the steel-toed boots he wore, muddy clods of dirt skidded downhill. For a moment Goose was afraid the dirt would crash across the top of the building below and alert everyone inside, but it tumbled into the space between the building's back wall and the hill.

A moment later, Goose put his foot down on the roof of one of the buildings and took up a position in the shadows. Most of the Syrian guards around the building were more interested in staying out of the rain than in security.

"Go," he called up.

Instantly, nine rappelling lines snaked down the hillside, followed immediately by nine Rangers dressed the same as Goose. Like him, they also carried suppressed MP5s as their lead weapon.

Goose gave hand signals, breaking the squad into the two predesignated five-man teams, taking charge of one himself. He stayed along the edge of the building where the support was strongest so there would be less chance of making any noise.

Movement caught his attention as he neared the edge of the rooftop. He threw out a hand, signaled, and brought the four men behind him to a stop, spread out on their stomachs on the roof.

Slithering forward on his belly, sliding easily due to the rain, Goose peered down at the Syrian soldier walking patrol below him. Taking shelter against the side of the building, the man reached under his raincoat and took out a pack of cigarettes.

From twenty-five feet over the man's head, Goose saw that the lighter the Syrian soldier used was a Zippo and knew that it had probably come from one of the dead American or European soldiers who had been left at the border. He stilled the immediate surge of anger, going cold and placid inside.

He also knew the second half of his team was moving into position and expecting his team to do the same. Glancing back at the Ranger behind him, Goose signaled again, then shrugged out of his M-4A1 and MP5. He took off the NVGs. The other Ranger took Goose's assault rifle, machine pistol, and the goggles.

Slipping his Ka-Bar fighting knife from his calf sheath, Goose held it point down along his right forearm, then slithered over the side of the building. He hung by his left arm, made certain the Syrian soldier still faced away from him, and dropped to the ground behind him.

※　※　※

United States of America
Fort Benning, Georgia
Local Time 1419 Hours

After lunch, when the trial reconvened, Major Trimble declared that the opposing counsel's case was finished. Benbow had asked to reserve the right to bring Megan back on cross-examination, and Colonel Erickson had granted that.

For the last hour and ten minutes, Benbow had called people forth from his meager witness list. They were soldiers who had served with Private Boyd Fletcher, men who had seen his excessive drinking binges as well as his temper.

But none of them had ever seen him mistreat Gerry.

Megan sat beside Benbow, keeping quiet and hoping she looked sane, not like the raving, plotting, egomaniacal lunatic Trimble had tried to make her out to be. She didn't think that was working. Several members of the jury kept looking at her as if they expected an alien to jump out of her skin or something.

The idea was so much like something Chris would have suggested that she wanted to laugh and cry at the same time. Neither one of those things, she knew, would be especially good, and both of them together might well have been the kiss of death.

She was also apprehensive about Jenny and her father. The corporal hadn't had any more information than he'd given them. Only that her father had been involved in some type of traffic accident. Jenny had left immediately, saying she would call as soon as she knew something. More than enough time had passed for her to find something out.

Halfway through yet another repetitive testimony of a soldier who had served with Boyd Fletcher, one of the MPs working security in the courtroom walked up and gave Colonel Erickson a piece of paper.

The colonel read the paper, then motioned to Benbow.

Benbow approached the bench and talked briefly. The judge declared a five-minute recess, and Benbow walked by the table where Megan sat. "Stay here," the young lieutenant said. "Maybe we caught a break. I'll be right back."

Megan waited, fidgeting under the gaze of the jury and the audience.

Just shy of five minutes later, Benbow returned to the courtroom pushing a media cart.

"Lieutenant Benbow?" the colonel asked. "What's the meaning of this?"

"It's part of a testimony," Benbow said. "I've got a VHS tape here that I want Mrs. Gander to verify the authenticity of."

"This is irregular," the colonel declared.

"Yes, sir," Benbow said. "Major Trimble seems to have pushed us very deeply into irregular. I'm going to try to bring us back on track. If you'll permit me."

"Permit what?" Trimble demanded.

"To show you what happened on that building rooftop the night of March first," Benbow said.

Trimble turned toward Colonel Erickson. "Sir, this is preposterous."

"Major, with all due respect," Benbow said, "you're the one who accused Mrs. Gander of taking advantage of Gerry Fletcher's disappearance and setting herself up to play messiah. You opened this line of inquiry during your direct of Mrs. Gander. I'm just following up on it on cross."

Erickson looked at both men, then leaned back in his chair. "I'll allow it."

"Colonel," Trimble protested.

"Sit down, Major," Erickson said. "I allowed you your leeway when you pursued your investigation. Lieutenant Benbow is only following in the path you prepared. I'll allow it."

Trimble looked fit to be tied.

"And I'll not expect one more word of protest, Major."

Trimble sat, but he looked as petulant as a child who hadn't gotten his way.

Megan felt curious and threatened at the same time.

"Corporal Kirk," Benbow said. "You're dismissed."

The corporal who had been testifying nodded and stepped from the witness box.

"At this time," Benbow said, handing the media-player cords to the MP standing at the colonel's side, "I'd like to call Mrs. Gander back to the stand."

The colonel looked at Megan and nodded.

Megan stood on shaky legs and made her way to the witness box. She wished she knew what Benbow was doing, but she reminded herself that she trusted him. As she sat down, she spotted Penny Gillespie taking a seat at the back of the courtroom.

Penny had been conspicuously absent till now, although she had made her presence known on Dove TV. Snippets from her interview with Megan regarding the Tribulation kept showing up all over television, starting to actually compete with the pieces on Nicolae Carpathia. Megan had no doubt that the Romanian president would find some new way to seize the media spotlight again, though. He seemed to be a magnet for that kind of attention.

Catching Megan's eye, Penny offered a smile and pressed her palms together in prayer.

Megan took a deep breath, remembering how she had looked when Trimble had her on the stand.

"Mrs. Gander," Benbow said, "I promise not to have you on the stand for a long time. I know you've had a rough morning."

Megan nodded. No verbal response was necessary.

Benbow glanced at the MP. "If I could have the television screens dropped into place, please."

Television screens slid down from the ceiling and locked into place all around the room. Evidently military trials often depended on video presentation or the room was sometimes used as a training resource. The screens came on with a burst of white light that hurt Megan's eyes.

"Sorry," Benbow apologized to everyone in the room. He pressed another button on the wireless remote control. "What you're looking at is a VHS tape of the night Gerry Fletcher climbed on top of that building and Mrs. Gander went after him to rescue him. Unfortunately, we didn't get footage of the whole event, but I think we have enough."

"Where did you get this tape, Lieutenant?" Trimble demanded.

"From Ms. Penny Gillespie," Benbow answered, his attention riveted on the screen. "She, in turn, got this from Private Lonnie Smith, who lives in an apartment in that building."

"If this tape is important, why didn't Smith come forward with it before now?"

"Because he didn't know Mrs. Gander was actually going to be put on trial. He felt certain that she would be exonerated of any wrongdoing." Benbow paused. "Private Smith also found what he saw that night—and what he later found to be on the tape—uncomfortable."

"Why uncomfortable?" Trimble challenged.

"Because Private Smith is—" Benbow stopped himself and smiled slightly, the expression evident to everyone in the courtroom because light from the screen in front of him lit his features—"because Private Smith *was* a confirmed atheist."

That statement caused a rumble of conversation through the courtroom, which Colonel Erickson quieted with his gavel.

"What does that have to do with this?" Trimble asked.

"Because Private Lonnie Smith was baptized two days ago, Wednesday night, and could no longer deny what he had seen on this tape. He said it changed his life 'irrevocably,' according to Ms. Gillespie."

Conversation and murmurings ran through the courtroom. The colonel banged his gavel again, having more difficulty controlling it.

"Are we going to see this mysterious tape?" Trimble demanded, "or are you going to persist in this flummery and mumbo jumbo?"

"Mumbo jumbo," Benbow said, smiling even more broadly. "Major, I'm going to remember that you said that. In fact, I wouldn't be surprised to find you quoted in newspapers and on television news quite often after today."

"Lieutenant, is that some kind of threat?"

"No, sir. Just a statement of fact."

"Lieutenant," Colonel Erickson said, "are we about ready?"

"Yes, Colonel." Benbow pressed another button.

The screen opened up on a dramatic scene. Megan saw herself at the rooftop's edge desperately holding on to Gerry Fletcher. It was immediately apparent that the boy was slipping away from her.

"Oh, Gerry," Tonya Fletcher wailed. All through the court proceedings she'd said nothing.

Benbow paused the tape. Megan knew he'd done it at that spot on purpose, just a heartbeat before Gerry fell. She could still feel his fingers sliding through hers.

"Mrs. Gander, is this you in the film?" Benbow asked.

"Yes."

"These are the events that happened the night of March first of this year?"

"Yes." Megan felt a little better. At least in the videotape it was plain that she had been hanging on to Gerry Fletcher, not throwing his clothing over the side as Trimble had suggested.

"Who is the boy?" Benbow asked.

"Gerry Fletcher."

Benbow walked to the defense table and picked up a folder. "I've got pictures of the boy here." He handed them to the MP and asked him to distribute them to the judge and the jury. Turning to the Fletchers, Benbow asked, "Mrs. Fletcher, can you identify your son from this videotape?"

Tonya gasped in pain. "Yes. That's him. That's Gerry." She covered her mouth with her hand. Boyd Fletcher reached for her, and Megan had the distinct impression that he sank his strong fingers into his wife's leg to shut her up, because she yelped.

"We're fortunate that the equipment here has slow-motion capabilities," Benbow addressed the court. "Otherwise you might miss what I'm about to show you. You see, it happened very quickly. In the twinkling of an eye, some might want to say." He pressed another button.

In sheer wonderment, Megan watched as the videotape advanced at a snail's pace. Gerry's hand slipped from hers. Then he fell, plummeting toward the street. The video camera operator, Private Lonnie Smith, lost Gerry for just an instant, then caught up with him again.

Gerry fell, arms and legs moving in slow motion as he tried to stop himself. Fear etched the boy's face. Benbow pressed another button and the picture zoomed in, filling the screens with Gerry's face.

Megan's heart rate shot up as she remembered all the terror and helplessness and anger that had fueled those moments of that night.

Then, incredibly, the fear on Gerry's face went away. His eyes widened in surprise, and a kind of joy that only children knew filled his features. He reached up with his right hand, a move so instinctive that it made Megan's heart ache as she remembered Joey and Chris when they were babies learning they could reach out and interact with the world around them.

Gerry reached up the way a child would, his hand clutching for the fingers of an adult's hands, a hesitant grasping, then a firm squeeze. And as soon as he took hold of whatever he'd reached for, just that quick he was gone. A shimmer of light, so faint it might have been imagined, passed through his body; then his empty clothes dropped to the concrete below.

Benbow stopped the tape, reversed it so that Gerry reappeared in his clothing, then disappeared again. And again. And again.

The sound of men and women praying filled the courtroom.

As she gazed around, Megan saw men and women on their knees, some of them crying openly, others so terrified they could hardly control themselves. Only a few appeared to be unmoved at all.

"Mrs. Gander," Benbow asked in a quiet, powerful voice, "is this what you saw that night?" He turned to face her and his eyes held a bright sheen.

"Yes," Megan said. "I didn't see it that clearly, but yes, that's what I saw. I saw Gerry disappear."

Even Colonel Erickson forgot to use his gavel to quiet the courtroom.

Benbow spoke over the crowd noise. "Colonel, the defense rests." He looked at Trimble, who was on his knees retching and quaking in fear. "Major, we're all through with the mumbo jumbo now."

❊   ❊   ❊

Operation Run Dry
26 Klicks South-Southwest of Sanliurfa, Turkey
Local Time 2122 Hours

The splats Goose's boots made as they hit the muddy earth didn't travel far, but they alerted the Syrian soldier. The man turned with a cigarette in his mouth, the tip glowing orange in the darkness and illuminating his features under his helmet.

Goose's knee almost went out on him when he landed. The pain blinded him for a moment. Then he pushed up, lunging, covering the six feet of space separating him from the enemy soldier. The Syrian clawed for the AK-47 that hung from his shoulder, but he never got the assault rifle pulled around before Goose was on him.

The first sergeant's weight and rush took them both to the ground. Goose landed on top of his opponent, finding the AK-47 in the mad tangle of arms and legs and shoving it deep into the mud. He surged up and swung his combat knife forward, raking the blade across the Syrian's throat.

Blood splashed over Goose's face, but he had closed his eyes right before the knife made contact. When he opened them, his vision remained clear but he felt the hot rush of blood spreading over his features.

The Syrian bucked and shuddered beneath Goose for just a moment. Then he grew still as life left him. Goose gazed into the man's eyes, seeing the thousand-yard stare settle into them as they remained unblinking in the spitting rain.

Goose was a hunter. In the country outside his hometown of Waycross, Georgia, he'd hunted deer and turkey, squirrel and dove, under his father's tutelage. Goose had never hunted for pleasure, only to put meat on the table. A hunter ate what he killed, or he gave it to provide for those who needed it.

Hunting men was different than hunting game. Men were more dangerous, more unpredictable. But a hunter couldn't have a conversation with a deer or a turkey. There was no opportunity for common understanding.

Goose's father, Wes Gander, had served in Korea after the war there. North Korean snipers had taken out one of Wes's best friends, and Wes had killed some of them in retaliation. When talking to some of the North Korean soldiers after the war, Wes had discovered that they were men pretty much like himself.

That, Wes Gander had said, had ended a lot of his youthful innocence. When he'd worn the marine uniform, he'd been a hero and the North Koreans had been the enemy, not men at all. Not long after that, Wes had ended his military career and moved back to Waycross.

Goose understood why his father had felt that way. He'd seen other men go through the same decision after being in heavy combat and meeting their enemies face-to-face instead of firing at distant targets.

It was harder mentally and emotionally to kill a man up close and personal while taking advantage of that man's moment of weakness or indecision or inexperience. But the physical part of the killing was much simpler, less dangerous, and often saved other lives.

Goose had done it only when he'd known there was no other way. There'd been no other way with the Syrian. Trying to take him alive could have compromised the mission and jeopardized the lives of every man in the unit.

Breathing out, getting past the emotional impact of taking the man's life, Goose wiped his knife on the man's uniform and slid it back into the sheath. He glanced up at the soldier who was holding his weapons. Then he caught first his M-4A1 and then the MP5, quickly sliding the assault rifle over his shoulder. He pulled the NVGs back on.

He held up two fingers and pointed to the front of the building.

Parker and Huddleston slid forward on their stomachs and took up support sniper positions. Two more snipers were posted at the other end. Lieutenant York should have posted four himself to maintain a kill zone over the armored cav. The teams should have overlapping fields of fire.

In the lead again, Goose stayed close to the building's wall and went forward. Berger, the last Ranger in line on the ground with him, caught hold of the dead Syrian and slid the corpse behind the building.

At the corner of the building, Goose scanned the nearby terrain, spotting Corporal Cliff Conner at the other end of the building. Conner spotted him as well and signaled that everything was secure.

Goose signaled again, letting Conner know that he was moving ahead. He tapped Private Darren Fieldstone behind him, and they went in tandem, swapping positions as they kept moving forward.

The front of the building was blank and squared off. The archeological crew that had constructed the warehouse hadn't designed it with anything but function in mind. There were no frills, no extras. A single door with a few office windows occupied the north end where Goose was, and a garage bay was on the south end. Tools and vehicles had been stored there.

Dim lights showed in the heavily curtained windows on the first and second floors. Generators in the basement supplied the power. Buried deep in the earth as they were, little noise reached the outside world. The light was carefully blocked so it would not draw attention from aerial attack. In addition to that, if Remington hadn't somehow tumbled onto the fact that the site was there and operational, Goose doubted they would have found it unless they had recovered the lost ground.

A small satellite dish also assured that the Syrian outpost had a communications array. That was going to be a problem. Remington hadn't mentioned that the site had a sat-relay. That capability changed the dynamics of the op drastically. As soon as the Syrians knew they were under attack they could radio for help if the dish was not taken out.

The main body of the Syrian army lay within ten minutes by helo. Goose had no doubt that once the distress call went out the Syrians would scramble to their attack helos.

The time frame on this mission was drastically cut. Even taking the satellite off-line could trigger an alarm and achieve the same result.

Goose and Fieldstone reached the main door. Trying it, Goose found it locked. The fact wasn't surprising, but in the middle of occupied territory it was possible that it wouldn't have been locked. He pointed toward the door.

Fieldstone slung the machine pistol over his shoulder, knelt, and took out a picklock kit. Not all Rangers were trained in those skills, but with urban assault becoming more and more a part of the war effort, new skills were being taught.

Glancing at the other end of the building, Goose got Conner's attention, then pointed to the dish. Conner signaled back; he'd already seen the dish. Goose signaled again, letting Conner and his team know he and Fieldstone were going to search for the communications center.

Fieldstone tapped on Goose's elbow and stood with his weapon once more in his hand.

Goose nodded and pulled open the Velcro strap on his left wrist, revealing the pictures of the four targets they'd been sent to take out. All four men wore Syrian uniforms of their rank and faced forward. With the ident-kits open and ready, Goose reached for the knob, turned it easily, then pushed the door and went inside.

According to the blueprints Remington had gotten from somewhere and included in the mission briefing, the interior of the warehouse had been remodeled. When it had been built, it had provided sleeping quarters for forty people, a huge kitchen and dining room, a common room with a fireplace, and lab space that occupied an area even larger than the common room. The second floor housed labs and more sleeping quarters, and Goose was guessing that was where they would find the com center.

During the interim, according to information Remington said he'd gleaned from the nomadic traders who wandered among the southern cities of Turkey and even down into Syria, different people had owned the warehouse. Or laid claim to it with gun and knife.

The building had been used for all kinds of business, including the manufacture of drugs, which it had supposedly done during its last incarnation before the Syrians had invaded and discovered the ruins and the possibilities the caves offered. According to the intel Remington had gotten, the Syrian officials the Rangers had been assigned to take out had made arrangements with the drug suppliers to remain in operation while they were there. The intel suggested that the Syrians had cut themselves in for a percentage.

The door opened onto the common room. A low light in the center of the room shone over a pool table where three men stood chatting. Opulent ofas and chairs surrounded them.

Seeing movement, two of the three men reached for assault rifles while the third pulled at a holstered pistol.

Goose threw himself forward, going low and pushing the MP5 ahead, touching off three-round bursts. The initial burst caught the first man from right hip to left shoulder, throwing him back. The second tri-burst caught the next man in the face. Goose thought one of the rounds might have missed, but the other two more than did the job.

He missed the third man entirely, and the 9mm rounds chopped into the wall over the man's head. Sliding across the wooden floor on his stomach, Goose turned and pulled the MP5 down, firing under the pool table as the man dove the opposite way for cover. One of the rounds ripped splinters from the pool-table leg, but the other two caught the man in the legs and knocked him down.

Fieldstone plunged into the room, following Goose's play like he'd trained to do it all his life. He fired directly into the surviving man's head before the guy could give voice to a warning or a cry of pain.

"Clear," Fieldstone said, moving toward the door on the left.

Pushing himself to his feet, ignoring the biting pain in his knee, Goose lifted his weapon, changed to a fresh magazine, rotating the partially spent one to the rear of his bandolier. He used the doorframe for cover, aware that Conner and his people had entered the front door. Nothing moved in the dining room.

"Clear," Goose called. "Conner, set the door."

Conner quickly shoved an M18A1 Claymore mine's three prongs into the wall next to the door at chest height. Loaded with steel bearings embedded in plastic explosive, the Claymore detonated like a shotgun round containing buckshot. The front had a little sticker that said THIS SIDE TOWARD ENEMY. A red light flashed on its side, then turned green, letting Goose know it was ready to receive electronic signals to detonate.

"We're live," Conner said, stepping back. "We own the front door."

"Okay," Goose said, knowing that for the moment they were still running silent, "move out. Conner, this is your door."

"Affirmative, First Sergeant." Conner stepped into position as Goose moved away to flank Fieldstone. "Always wanted to know what was behind Door Number Two."

"Let's move," Goose told Fieldstone.

The private went forward, stepping quickly and smoothly. At the juncture of the next hallway, they swapped positions, offering overlapping fields of fire as Goose took the lead, still shoulder to shoulder, moving as much by feel as by sight.

At the end of the hallway, they went up the stairs. Fieldstone covered their back trail as Goose kept his MP5 pointed at the switchback stairs. Goose wished they had the headsets up and operational, but he knew the signals could have been detected and set off warnings for the Syrians. Going room to room without satellite thermographic recon was nerve-racking.

The stairwell opened on another long hallway that ran north and south the length of the building. The hallway was dark but the NVGs lit the area.

Nothing moved.

A door filled the wall ahead of them, probably leading to what had been one of the upstairs labs.

Fieldstone tried the doorknob. "Locked."

"Unlock it," Goose said in a low voice. He took the younger soldier's MP5 and stood with a machine pistol pointed down to the end of the hallway.

"Unlocked," Fieldstone said.

Goose handed the private his weapon, then opened the door. He pushed the MP5 slightly ahead of him, keeping it safely tucked into the frame of his body so it couldn't be easily taken away from him.

He'd expected a large, empty room. Instead, he found three women shackled to a single eyebolt in the floor. *Two women*, Goose amended. One of them couldn't have been over fifteen, and she looked enough like one of the older women to be her daughter.

They cringed away from him, cringed away from the weapon he carried.

God help us, Goose thought. *We've got civilians loose inside the target zone.*

"First Sergeant," Fieldstone said in surprise from behind Goose's back.

And that was when the wheels finally came off and the play went bust.

Goose turned to Fieldstone just as the young private's head disappeared. Fieldstone never heard the shots that killed him, and by that time he was deadweight falling forward on Goose as the staccato rattle of a fully automatic weapon opened up in the hallway.

❊ ❊ ❊

United States 75th Army Rangers Temporary Post
Sanliurfa, Turkey
Local Time 2128 Hours

The sat-link relay to Operation Run Dry came alive at once with a harsh squawk; then First Sergeant Goose Gander's voice filled the command center.

"Base," Goose said in a hoarse voice. Gunfire sounded in the background, followed immediately by the terrified screams of women. "Base. Base. Do you read? This is Alpha Leader. We've got a busted play. I say again, we have a busted play. I need sat-link now."

Remington strode across the room and stopped behind the op tech that watched over Alpha and Bravo Details. "Put me into the channel," the captain ordered, pulling his headset up from his neck and fitting it into place.

"Base," Goose called again.

More gunfire sounded, cutting into the screams of the women.

"That sounds like women, sir," the private manning the station said.

"Very astute, Private. Now patch me into that channel." Remington peered at the satellite picture of the terrain.

The warehouse where Goose was with his Alpha squad showed up plainly.

"You're in, Captain," the private said.

"Alpha Leader," Remington said smoothly, "this is Base."

"Base." Goose grunted and growled, like he was shifting deadweight. "The play's busted, Base."

"You have your orders, Alpha Leader."

"We have civilians on-site. I've got three women—two women and one girl—here with me. There may be more."

"Affirmative, Alpha Leader. Get done what you can get done. If you can get those people out of there, do so." Remington clicked out of the link. He knew that if Goose found civilians on-site he wouldn't leave until he had them clear or there was no chance. "Bring that screen up in thermographic. I want those people inside that warehouse tagged and followed. I've got targets up and running, and I want to know where they are."

"Yes, sir."

Back in the radio link, Remington said, "Alpha Prime, do you read?"

"Alpha Prime reads, Base." Keller sounded calm.

"You have your objective, Prime."

"Affirmative, Base. We're about finished here."

Remington watched as the screen shifted hues, changing to thermographic display.

Felix stepped up beside him, almost seeming to appear out of nowhere. Remington didn't know where the man had been earlier.

"Innocents are in the way of harm, are they, Captain Remington?" Felix smiled as he watched the frantic activity of the yellow and red figures on the screen. Dozens were in motion now. "Strange that with all this equipment and the information you got from Abu Alam, you didn't know there were women there."

Remington glanced at the man, feeling the need to show Felix that he was more in control of the situation than it looked. "I knew they were there."

Felix lifted his eyebrows higher than his sunglasses. "But you didn't tell your teams."

"No."

"Why not?"

"They didn't need to know."

"It appears that they do now."

Remington nodded. "So now they know."

Felix smiled. "You didn't want them searching for the women."

"No," Remington said, "I didn't want my guys holding back when they went into that building."

"And if an innocent had died under friendly fire that wasn't?"

"Sometimes," Remington said, "losing an innocent can't be helped. I accept that possibility."

"I see." Felix smiled again. "You are an interesting man, Captain Remington. I shall enjoy seeing more of how your mind works as our friendship continues."

"Trust me," Remington said. "You've only just started to watch my mind work."

The buzz of conversations between Alpha and Bravo Details continued, rapid-fire exchanges that were interspersed with gunfire and explosions.

Looking back at the screen, Remington saw that explosions had started deep within the underground storage area where the fuel was. The explosions—roiling blue and orange on the screen—grew exponentially as the fuel reserves blew and gathered force. A lot of the fuel in the underground caverns was high-grade air gas for the planes and helos.

More explosions took place out in the Syrian armored cav. Remington was impressed. The raid was going much better and had gone much further than he would have thought.

"Alpha Prime, Bravo Prime," Remington barked.

Both lieutenants radioed back that they had heard him.

On-screen, red and yellow thermographic figures that had to be Lieutenant Matthew York's Bravo Detail scrambled for the Syrian airfield, where the Mi-8 helos sat under a canopy.

"Your missions are accomplished," Remington said. "Get your teams out of there."

"Alpha Leader is still in the building, Base," Keller responded. "We can't leave him."

"Negative, Alpha Prime. Leader will make it out under his own steam."

"Base, he's got women with him."

"I understand and appreciate that, Alpha Prime, but I have sixty Rangers in a hostile twenty that's about to go critical." Remington moved down the line of screens, looking at another screen that showed the main Syrian army encampment. On the screen, green icons that resembled helicopters were lifting off and flying west toward the reserve fuel depot.

"Alpha and Bravo Prime, be advised that a major contingent of Syrian gunships are now en route to your twenty," Remington said. "Bottom line, gentlemen: I want my Rangers out of there this instant."

"Affirmative, Base."

"Fascinating," Felix said. "You're leaving your friend trapped in that building against hostile guns?"

"He knew the risks when he took this assignment," Remington said.

"You gave him that assignment. You knew what he would do." Felix took a deep breath. "You knew those women were there."

Remington nodded. "Abu Alam had a side business. White slavery. He'd kidnapped at least a dozen women out of Sanliurfa after the SCUD attack and the vanishings. He traded some of them to the Syrians, who in turn were going to sell them to warlords in their country and this country in exchange for treaties."

"They're annexing criminal tribes in this area to use against the Turkish people?"

"Yes." Remington glanced at the screen. "If I could get that done, buy extra soldiers, supply routes, or just negotiate neutral treaties to allow passage of men and equipment through potentially hostile territory, I'd do it too. The Syrians are here to grab as much land as they can. The more they have before a cease-fire is worked out, the more they get to keep."

"I'm really beginning to understand what Nicolae sees in you," Felix said.

Remington listened to the headset for a moment, understanding at once that Alpha and Bravo were leaving the area.

"So why do you set your friend up to die?" Felix asked.

Remington kept his heart cold as stone. Goose had to go. That had become plain after talking with CIA Section Chief Alexander Cody and finding out about the attack on the CIA communications base.

Goose had betrayed him. Although the two CIA men hadn't been able to identify Goose, Remington was convinced it couldn't have been anyone else. Furthermore, Corporal Baker's tent church continued to be a threat to his command, building a tension in his troops to potentially choose between him and God. And Cal Remington didn't intend to take second place. Not even to God.

Goose's betrayal cut deeply into Remington. Some of it had started when Goose had chosen to marry Megan Holder, to put his family before their friendship. That was why Remington hadn't stood in as best man and why he'd kept his distance from Goose's family. Goose choosing Bill Townsend, a corporal and a God chaser, had been another slap in the face.

Remington wasn't about to have his command split because Goose could no longer toe the line and stay with the program. Having a first sergeant who could work independently was a good thing, but having an independent-minded one could also seriously jeopardize chain of command.

"I didn't set Goose up to die," Remington said. "He set himself up. I just helped him negotiate the time and place."

Felix chuckled. "You sold your friend out."

"I did," Remington said, "but I didn't sell him out cheap." He walked to another set of screens. He pointed at a cluster of airplane icons. "Do you know what that is?"

"No."

"That's most of the aircraft that I control. They took off ten minutes ago. Do you know where they're going to be in five minutes?"

"Tell me."

"Bombing the main Syrian line," Remington said. "If you'd watched the screen, you'd have seen that the Syrians scrambled most of their available air units to cover the attack at their hidden fuel depot. By the time they get there, it's going to be too late to save anything. The only thing the depot had going for it was secrecy."

"Which Abu Alam betrayed?"

Remington nodded.

"But the Syrians want their pound of flesh?"

"Yeah," Remington said. "Their mistake. And I'm going to capitalize on it in—" he glanced at his watch—"three minutes, when my air division lights up their whole world."

"You used your friend and those Rangers as bait."

"Expensive bait," Remington said. "There was no guarantee the Syrians would go for it."

"But they did. And now you have lost your friend."

Remington looked at Goose's thermographic image locked in battle on the screen. "I lost my friend a long time ago. He's just been a memory walking around taking up time and space. It's time he was put to rest." He paused. "And he should thank me. He's not just a casualty. After all the media attention he's been getting, he's going to be a martyr."

"Yes," Felix said. "I'm sure if he had the opportunity, he'd thank you."

More than a thousand had crowded into the church by the time Delroy stepped to the pulpit. The little church had never held more than eight hundred in the past, and the building was hard-pressed to hold them all now. In fact, dozens stood outside the open windows, sitting in lawn chairs or on the grass, waiting to hear the chaplain speak.

Delroy placed his Bible on the pulpit and stared out at them. He was surprised at how intimidated he felt.

It wasn't the number of them that was intimidating. While on board the USS *Wasp*, he'd often spoken in front of more than two thousand men at a time during different functions. The intimidating thing was that Delroy was conscious of preaching at his daddy's church. He looked out over the congregation and felt his mouth go dry.

"Daddy, do you think I'll ever get to preach from your pulpit?"

"Why, little man, if you want to preach so much an' you feel God's hand on your heart, why I'll put you up at that pulpit this Sunday."

"I don't know about that, Daddy."

"Why not?"

"Because I don't know if I'm ready."

"Well, if I know one thing about preachin' God's Word, it's this."

"What?"

"If the Lord wants ya'll to speak His Words, why I swear you ain't got no choice. You might try to close your mouth an' swallow them words right up, but God, He's gonna find a way to squeeze on you till you pop like a balloon an' just tell ever'body you know what it is God wants you to say."

"You think so, Daddy?"

"I know so. You know somethin' else?"

"What, Daddy?"

"God wants ya'll to say what's in your heart so much that you're just naturally gonna have to tell ever'body. 'Cause that's who God's Word is for. Ever'body. Ever' man, woman, an' chile. Now if ya'll pass up a chance to talk to people in a group, why, it's gonna take you a long time to go from do' to do' with them words."

"Brothers and sisters," Delroy began in the deepest and strongest voice he could manage, and his words seemed to echo right into the wood so that he heard his daddy's words, "I bid you welcome to this church. God's house."

"Amen," several men said.

"We all come together in God's house because we want to know what the Lord wants us to do," Delroy said. "But I have to admit something to you." He paused and listened to the silence that followed his words. "I have to admit to you that I've been lost."

Some of the women shook their heads.

"Five years ago, my son was taken from me," Delroy said. "He died in a war a long way from home." His voice nearly cracked from the pain that came with the memory. "I wasn't there to hold my son. I wasn't there to comfort him. I wasn't there to make sure he wasn't alone." He left the pulpit, walked out in front of it so it didn't stand between him and the people waiting to hear God's words. "I forgot something that I shouldn't have. Forgot something I spent my whole life learning." He looked out at them, barely controlling his voice. "I forgot that my son loved God."

"Amen," several of the men said.

"But more important than that," Delroy said, "I forgot that God loved my son."

"Amen."

"I forgot because I tried to take on the responsibility for everything that happened," Delroy said. "I felt guilty because I didn't talk my son out of making a career in the military. I felt guilty because I didn't know my son was going to get killed." He paused. "Coming here, seeing this church the way it was only yesterday, hurt me, brothers and sisters. Hurt me all the way to my soul. The things that had been done to this church were horrible."

"Amen."

"Coming back here after everything that's happened in the world," Delroy continued, "reminded me that I didn't just step away from God; I stepped away from my daddy's teaching too. It embarrasses me to have to admit that." He waited a moment. "But I am. And do you know why I admit that, brothers and sisters?"

They waited expectantly.

"Because when it's all said and done, I am my daddy's son." Delroy looked at them. "I am my earthly daddy's son, and I am a child of God."

"Amen."

"My son died in a war," Delroy said. "He was also a child of God. So when I was away on my ship, do you know who held him as he died?"

"God," the congregation answered in unison.

Delroy turned and slapped the pulpit the way his father used to. The sound cracked through the church. "Brothers and sisters, I *know* you can surely do better than that."

"God!" came the answer, loud enough to ring through the church.

"Do you know who comforted my son when he died?" Delroy demanded.

"*God!*" the congregation cried.

"And do you know who made sure my son was not alone when he died?"

"GOD!"

"That's right, brothers and sisters. It was God." Delroy felt the fire and passion stir in him that he hadn't felt in years, the fire and passion that he'd never truly unleashed in his capacity as chaplain in the navy. "Now there are a lot of bad things that have happened in the world over these past few days—things that many of you are only now beginning to understand."

"Amen."

"I came among you," Delroy said, "a forgotten son who was almost a stranger. A stranger even to myself. Do you know who welcomed me into this church?"

"God!"

"That's right, brothers and sisters. Because no matter what you do, no matter where you go, all you have to remember is that you have a loving Daddy in heaven who will always welcome you back home again."

"Amen."

"But I'll tell you another thing a good daddy does," Delroy said. "A good daddy tells you when you've fallen short of the mark."

A quiet descended over the congregation.

"I have to tell you that *we've* all fallen short of that mark. Take a look around and you'll see that you're not alone. Maybe you even think you're in good company." Delroy paused. "The thing is, you might even be in good company. But you know what?"

The congregation waited expectantly.

"God already took His faithful," Delroy said. "And He took His children. So I expect a lot of you are sitting around feeling mighty sorry for yourselves." He looked around at the congregation. "It's mighty scary sitting here knowing that the book of Revelation tells us that awful things are going to happen to all of us who have been left behind."

"Amen," a few people said.

"Some of you might even be thinking that God has thrown you away, that He just flat doesn't care anymore. You know the problems you have. You know the mistakes you've made in your life. But you know what?"

No one spoke.

"God knows too. He knows all about them. But I'll tell you something else." Delroy paused. "God loves you."

No one said anything.

Delroy struck the pulpit again. "Are you awake, brothers and sisters? I just told you that God loves you and there you sit like a bunch of knots on a log!" He felt the anger of his daddy upon him then. So much was now so clear to him. How could it not be clear to the people sitting out there? "Do you know who provided this church?"

"God did," someone said in a timid voice.

"Yes, God did," Delroy said. "But did you see how God put this church here? Through you." He pointed at various people. "You and you and you and you, and all of you. None of this would have happened if you hadn't pulled together and done what God wanted you to do."

"Amen."

"God brought us all together here in fellowship," Delroy said. "And He brought us together so we would learn. So learn!"

"Amen."

"God took all of His faithful from this world and moved them right on up into the next. Do you know what you're supposed to do now?"

They all looked at him.

"I don't want you to think of this place as a world anymore," Delroy said. "In seven years, this place won't even be here anymore. Not in the shape it's in. It's going to be something better. Something beautiful. And it's going to be that way for a thousand years. Can I get an amen on that?"

"Amen!"

Delroy walked through the church the way his daddy had, making some of the congregation cringe in their pews. "I want you to think of this place by another name." He turned his back and started back up to the front of the church. "Somebody ask me, 'What name, Chaplain Delroy?'"

"What name, Chaplain Delroy?" Reynard Culpepper asked as he sat on the front pew.

Delroy turned and faced them again. He saw Glenda standing in the doorway. She wore her Sunday best and looked like a dream. His heart ached and he almost faltered.

But she smiled at him, and there was some of the old promise in that smile that touched him deeply.

"I want you to think of this place as Halfway," Delroy said, growing stronger. He kept his eyes on Glenda, wondering if she was going to stay or leave. "Can you say that with me? Halfway."

"Halfway," the congregation responded.

"You know something about Halfway?" Delroy asked. "It's a whole lot better than No Way. Can I get an amen?"

"Amen."

Before he could stop himself, Delroy began to walk the length of the center aisle, and—God help him—it seemed longer than the *Wasp's* flight deck. And as he walked, Glenda did too. He met her halfway, took her by the hand, and looked into her eyes.

"Chaplain Delroy?"

Turning, Delroy saw Phyllis on the front row next to Walter and Clarice Purcell. "You bring your missus right on up here where she belongs," Phyllis said as she scooted one of her boys out of the pew and had him sit on the floor in front of her.

Holding Glenda's hand, Delroy gently guided her to the front row. She sat by Phyllis, who patted her on the arm.

"And why do we call this place Halfway?" Delroy asked.

No one answered.

"Because God has met you halfway," Delroy answered. "He has given us a second chance at redemption. For all of you who were doubters, you've now got proof that there is a God and He is alive and working in this place."

"Amen."

"All you have to do is look at the wonders God has wrought." Delroy looked around, aware of Glenda sitting so close. "But Halfway means something else too, brothers and sisters. You have to take stock and figure where you're halfway *to*."

"Amen," Reynard Culpepper bawled.

"You're on a trip now, brothers and sisters," Delroy said in a quieter, more intense voice. "You're on a trip and you're halfway. But my question to you is this: Are you halfway to heaven? Or are you halfway to hell?"

"Amen."

"That's the message God has put on my heart today, brothers and sisters," Delroy said. "Are you halfway to heaven or are you halfway to hell? And if you're halfway to hell, do you know that you can turn around and get back on the path to righteousness? Do you know what it takes, brothers and sisters? Do you know what it takes to get right with God?"

"Your daddy knew the answer to that one, Chaplain," Reynard Culpepper called out. "He done taught it to me all them years ago. You want to get right with the Lord, why you just up an' take one step. Just one step in the right direction."

Delroy smiled broadly. "That's right, Brother Reynard. You take just one step in God's direction. Not only will He help you with all the rest of the steps, He'll help you with that first one."

"Amen!" Reynard yelled, throwing his hands high into the air.

A shadow darkened the church's doorway, causing a silence to fall over the congregation.

The man standing there was old and white haired. His back was bowed from years of hard living. Scars mixed with the hard lines on his face and the map of alcohol veins. He wore jeans, a pearl-snap cowboy shirt, and cowboy boots. He carried a Stetson in his gnarled hands.

"Is that right, Preacher?" the old man asked in a dry voice brittle with age. "All it takes is one step to get back close to God?"

Walter Purcell had already stood and made his way back the side aisle to intercept the old man.

Delroy knew the old man in an instant. He tried not to let his hurt, anger, and confusion spill over. "That's right," Delroy answered.

The old man rubbed his face. "Do you know who I am?"

Delroy nodded. "I know you."

"Name me," the old man challenged.

"Clarence Floyd," Delroy said in a hoarse whisper.

Whispers rose in the congregation. Evidently several people knew who Clarence Floyd was.

The old man nodded. "A lot of people say I killed your daddy all them years ago."

"What do you say?" Delroy asked.

Floyd hesitated. "He was sassin' me. Talkin' down to me like I didn't know nothin'. Makin' me out like I was stupid. Some kind of moron. Him black as the ace of spades talkin' like that to a white man in front of other white men."

Indignation ran through the church. Several men stood up, ready to fight.

Delroy raised his hands and froze them in their places. "I don't want any slurs in this church."

"Weren't no slur," Floyd said. "Didn't intend no slur. Just tellin' you how it was. It was awful hard comin' here today, Preacher." He looked around. "I heard about the church, though, an' somethin' told me I just had to come. I wasn't hearin' voices. Been through some of that in my life too, but this weren't nothin' like that." He worked his jaw. "Just knew I had to be here."

"Why?" Delroy asked.

Floyd sucked air through his teeth. "Because I hear the world's comin' to an end. An' I believe it." He took a deep breath. "When I was a child, I used to believe in Jesus an' God. But I got away from it. Fell in with some bad men an' some evil women, an' got me a taste for whiskey." He shrugged. "Women are harder to come by these days, but I can still afford the whiskey. Doc said it's gonna kill me one day, but it ain't yet."

"Why did you come here today?" Delroy asked.

"Couldn't stay away," Floyd said. "Been thinkin' about what's goin' on in the world. To me, even the first day, it was plain as the nose on your face. Had to be the hand of God what took them people up." He grinned, but there was no mirth there, only anger and sadness. "An' in all that gatherin', He done up an' missed me. Can you believe it?"

"You're interrupting my service," Delroy said.

"I reckon I am." Floyd made no move to walk away, just stood there looking like death in a Renaissance painting.

Delroy walked back toward him, watching Walter tense up. "Why are you here?"

"I had to come see you," Floyd said. "Heard it was you. Heard you were Pastor Harte's get."

"I am."

Floyd wiped his face with a hand. Tears watered in his pale blue eyes. "I killed your daddy, Preacher. Shot him stone-cold dead all them years ago. Watched him die right out there on the porch of this church."

Startled exclamations ran through the congregation.

Anger burned through Delroy, violent and hot.

"I had to come here an' tell you that," Floyd said.

"Why?" Delroy's voice was so tight it turned the word into a dry whisper.

"Because you're the onliest man I can meet face-to-face that could possibly hate me as much as God must after ever'thin' I done," Floyd announced. "So I figured I'd come to you, tell you what I done, an' let you tell me to go straight to hell or kill me where I stand because I just don't care no more." He wiped at his face and tears ran into the scars and wrinkles. "I know God hates me. But He don't answer an' I knew you would. An' if you, a man of God, cain't forgive me, I know God ain't goin' to."

Delroy stared at the man who had taken his father away, who had brought so much pain into his life. He didn't know what to say.

After a long, tense moment, Clarence Floyd turned, clapped his hat back on his head, and walked out the door.

"Clarence Floyd," Delroy called, stepping out onto the porch where his father had been shot down.

Floyd froze, then slowly turned around.

"I can't promise that I'll ever forgive you," Delroy said. "I'm just a man. A struggling man. But I'll tell you one thing I know for sure."

Tears continued to run down Floyd's seamed face. He looked so out of place, a withered scarecrow cowboy at a nearly all-black church.

"If you believe Jesus Christ died for your sins," Delroy said, "and you ask God to forgive you of your sins, you will be saved."

Floyd nodded. Then he licked his lips. When he spoke, his voice was dry and hoarse, but it was with the pain of a child. "I cain't pray. I've tried. I've tried for years. I don't remember how."

Delroy hesitated. Then he left the porch, approached the old man, and held out his hands.

Floyd didn't know what to do for a moment; then he offered his hands to Delroy.

"Kneel with me," Delroy said. "I'll pray with you. Just repeat after me."

They knelt there in the churchyard, where faith had started to grow again, a murderer and a broken chaplain who'd lost his faith and found it in a church that had once come to the end of its days. Delroy Harte, despite holding on to his own prejudice and hate and hurt, delivered one more soul to God.

❋ ❋ ❋

United States of America
Fort Benning, Georgia
Local Time 1439 Hours

As they waited on the verdict, Megan stood behind the defendant's table and stretched, aware that everyone in the courtroom was still watching her.

After the videotape presentation, Colonel Erickson had ordered a fifteen-minute recess. Penny Gillespie had disappeared, presumably to tape a live segment of what had just happened. Benbow had taken Megan back to the small conference room and waited. Neither of them had talked much. Megan supposed both of them were more than a little overcome by what the tape had revealed and by how strong the reactions of the jury and crowd were.

"I never should have doubted you," Benbow had said at one point. "I knew you were innocent of the dereliction-of-duty charges—"

"I was derelict," Megan pointed out.

"For good reason," Benbow said. "We just can't prove it. What I'm talking about is the Rapture. My mother and my grandmother raised me in the church. I guess I just didn't listen close enough. Like I didn't listen to you close enough. I'm going to have to work on that."

"We all are," Megan had said.

By the time they had returned to the courtroom, the story of the tape had spread. Media people crammed the foyers and waiting rooms. Several of them called out to Megan to get interviews. However, no one new was allowed into the courtroom.

Megan ignored them all. She still didn't know if she was going to be free when the court case was resolved. Quite frankly, Benbow was irritated that Colonel Erickson didn't throw the whole case out, but the problem was that Arthur Flynn waited in the wings, ready to pick over the bones of whatever was thrown his way.

Upon their return, Penny had slipped back into the courtroom, and Trimble offered a mediocre closing argument. Benbow had stated that the evidence, and Mrs. Gander, had spoken plainly enough and anything he added to that would only dilute it.

Then the colonel had given the jury their final orders and sent them on their way.

"Relax," Benbow said.

"I'm trying," Megan replied in a low voice. "I feel like I've been left hanging here. I don't know how Goose is. I don't know where Joey is. I don't know if Jenny's all right."

Benbow was silent for a short time. "Megan, all those things will come. Just give it time. What you've been given here today—" he shook his head—"I think it's just the beginning of a wonderful gift."

"No," Megan said. "Do you even know what the next seven years are going to be like? All the lies and deceits and treacheries that are going to take place?" She took a deep breath as images of all those things—of wars and famines and plagues—swept through her mind. "What we've seen so far—those people disappearing, the suicides and murders—they're nothing compared to what's coming."

"This has made a difference, Megan. I swear to you, I really think it has."

Megan glanced at Trimble and caught him looking at her. He quickly turned away.

"I hope so," she said. "So many people are going to be lost if they don't start listening."

"Try to sit down and relax. I'll bet we don't hear from the jury again today and they cut us loose at four-thirty."

At that moment, the door near the judge's bench opened and Colonel Erickson's MP entered. "All rise," the big man said.

"What's going on?" Megan said.

Benbow looked totally surprised. "If the colonel's coming back, that can only mean that the jury's on its way back." He glanced at his watch. "Seven minutes. I've never heard of a return that fast."

"What does it mean?"

"They made up their minds really quick," Benbow said. "Could be either good or bad, but it definitely means there's no hung jury on this one."

Colonel Erickson took his seat. "Be seated," he said.

Another MP opened the jury door and let them file back into the room. They took their seats to Megan's immediate right.

Staring at the impassive faces of the men and women of the jury,

Megan couldn't tell which way the vote had gone. Her stomach rolled sickeningly. *God? God, are You with me?*

There was no answer.

Megan forced herself to remain calm.

Benbow reached over to her and squeezed her hand reassuringly. "We're going to be okay," he said.

"Captain Seaver," Colonel Erickson said, "has the jury reached a verdict?"

"Yes, sir," Seaver replied. He was compact and tanned, an easygoing man with an air of command.

"What is your vote?"

"Sir," Seaver said, "we decided that we all feel so strongly about this that we want our individual votes counted."

The colonel looked surprised. "You do have a unanimous decision?"

"We do, Colonel. But we want our votes and our statements made part of the court record, part of the public record of this trial and of our findings."

Erickson hesitated. "All right."

"Is that normal?" Megan asked.

"Not normal," Benbow whispered. "But it happens. 'Rare as hen's teeth' as my grandmother used to say." His own interest was evident.

"Will the defendant please rise and face the jury?" Erickson said.

Megan stood and faced the jury. Benbow stood at her side.

"All right, Captain Seaver," Erickson said, "you may begin."

"Captain Merle Seaver." The man saluted Megan. "In the matter of dereliction of duty, I find the defendant, Mrs. Megan Gander . . . not guilty. I believe she was following a moral code higher than the one in the military handbook for which she was held accountable, with no disrespect intended to the service that I love and honor and will give my life for should that need ever arise. We are Rangers, and we serve God and country, and I believe there is a reason for that rank designation." He took a deep breath. "I also want the record to reflect that I believe there is a God, and He is alive and doing well, Colonel Erickson. I believe He chose wisely when he pulled this woman to Him to work as she did for Gerry Fletcher."

Megan felt like the floor had opened up beneath her. Her legs trembled and she almost fell, but Benbow was there to shore her up. He held her as, one after the other, the remaining eleven members of the jury all echoed the captain's statement, changing only their rank and name.

There is a God, and He is alive and doing well. The message grew
stronger and gathered momentum as each juror recited the verdict,
and the audience picked up on those words till it became a litany each
time, a prayer shared with the other members of the trial. *There is a
God, and He is alive and doing well.*

* * *

Operation Run Dry
26 Klicks South-Southwest of Sanliurfa, Turkey
Local Time 2122 Hours

Trapped by Private Fieldstone's corpse, Goose struggled to bring the
MP5 up as the Syrian soldier stepped into the doorway with an AK-
47. Goose fired from the point, trusting his instincts. A line of 9mm
rounds zipped up the man from crotch to sternum, jerking him backward.

Goose talked quickly, relaying to Remington what was going on,
how the play was busted and there were civilians in the fire zones. The
women screamed in terror behind him, causing everything to be just
a little more confusing.

At first, with blood all over him, Goose wasn't sure that he hadn't
been shot as well. But when he moved to shove the dead private off of
him, everything seemed to be in working order.

He stood with effort, feeling his bad knee shaking beneath him.
Scooping up Fieldstone's MP5, favoring the machine pistols for the
inside work he was going to have to do to get them all free, he said a
quick prayer to God, asking Him to watch over the young private.
Then he turned his attention to the hallway.

Bracing his back against the doorframe, he peered out into the
hall over both machine pistols, crossing his wrists so he had overlapping fields of fire.

Down the hall, a Syrian soldier peered around the door. Goose
tracked a short burst across the wall and into the man's head, knocking the corpse out into the hallway.

"Alpha Leader, this is Prime," Lieutenant Keller radioed.

"Leader reads you, Prime." Goose watched the hallway carefully.

"Base has ordered us out of the area."

"I heard." Goose still didn't know why Remington gave the other
team orders not to help him. Rangers didn't leave a man behind
when they could help it. Especially not a living soldier.

"Conner got out of the building. Are you and Fieldstone going to be able to get clear?"

"Fieldstone's dead, Prime." Goose turned back to the three women.

They jerked back from him, hitting the ends of the chains attached to the collars around their necks.

"Take it easy," Goose said, "I'm a United States Army Ranger. I am First Sergeant Gander."

All of the women looked worse for the wear.

Goose didn't know what they'd been through, didn't even want to guess at the moment. During his stay in Turkey, he'd heard that some of the drug warlords and terrorist organizations trafficked in white slavery, taking victims from American, European, and Russian women.

"I'm Hannah," the oldest woman said. She was the blonde who looked like she could be the mother of the young girl.

"Ma'am," Goose said. He knelt gingerly, turned so he could keep an eye on the doorway. His mind raced, listening to the rapid-fire blasts of explosions outside the building.

All three chains connected to a single eyebolt in the center of the floor.

"All of you get down," Goose ordered. He stood and shifted, moving around so he was between the women and the eyebolt. He aimed one of the machine pistols at the eyebolt and squeezed the trigger. The 9mm rounds struck sparks from the heavy ring and made it jerk.

Please, God, Goose prayed, *I can't leave these women behind, and the later we get started, the harder it's going to be to get away.*

He fired again. This time the rounds chewed through the ring. At the same time, a shadow crept around the doorway. Lifting the machine pistol at once, Goose squeezed the trigger and held it, driving the Syrian soldier back with the 9mm rounds.

Goose switched out magazines, taking fresh loads from Fieldstone's bandolier. He looked back at the women. "Hannah. Ma'am."

She looked at him.

"You're going to have to pick up your chains and carry them," Goose said. "I can't do anything about taking them off yet."

The chains were heavy and thick, probably weighing a good five or ten pounds. Enough weight to throw someone off while running if he or she wasn't used to it.

On top of that, Goose thought, *these women are scared to death.* He glanced back at Fieldstone's body, then noticed the medkit the young private had carried. Laying one of the machine pistols down, Goose reached into the medkit and took out a roll of heavy surgical tape. He tossed the roll to Hannah.

"Hannah," Goose said, "use the tape to secure the chains in coils. Just loop it around and around. If the chains are in coils, they'll be easier to carry. And if you drop one, it shouldn't hang low enough to trip you."

"All right." Hannah tore off the strips of tape with expert ease.

"Nurse?" Goose asked.

She looked up at him, startled. "How did you know?"

"A lucky guess, ma'am. That's all."

"I was part of the U.N. Peacekeeping force," Hannah said as she went to work on the young girl's chain. "Just over for a week. Brought my girl, Julie. Nothing like this was supposed to happen. We've been praying that someone would come for us. That slave trader Abu Alam brought us here yesterday."

"Yes, ma'am."

"I'm sorry about your friend."

"Yes, ma'am. I am too. Private Fieldstone was a good soldier."

Hannah finished binding the third chain. "Don't you have other men in the area, Sergeant?"

Goose guessed she must have overheard Fieldstone address him as sergeant. He wore no rank insignia. "There are, ma'am, but they're under orders to evac and scoot."

Hannah looked like she couldn't believe it. "They're just going to leave us here?"

"No, ma'am," Goose said. "I'm here with you. I'm going to get you out of here." He stood, favoring his bad knee. "Are you ready to go? We don't have much time. They'll leave us sure enough if we're not there."

"Not exactly heroic, is it, Sergeant?"

"Ma'am," Goose said, "soldiers aren't heroes. They're men doing hard, dangerous jobs. They're also men who take orders. Men who get unlucky and sometimes die." He spoke across Fieldstone's corpse, but neither of them looked at the dead man. "We're running short on soldiers in Sanliurfa as it is. I can get you out of here, but you're going to have to listen to me."

"All right. What do we do?"

"There's a garage below."

"I saw it."

Goose admired the way the woman adapted. Hannah had gone from victim to survivor in seconds. Some people spent their whole lives and couldn't make that jump.

"Our SIGNIT intel indicates that there are vehicles inside that garage," Goose went on. "We're going to take one and attempt to rendezvous with the rest of my squad."

More explosions pealed outside. Some of them were close enough now that concussive waves vibrated through the building.

"All right, Sergeant," Hannah said.

"Do you know how to use a weapon, ma'am?"

"No. All I ever volunteered for was nursing."

Goose nodded. "Keep these two with you. Keep them moving." He scanned the hallway. "I'm going to secure the hallway. Don't leave this room until I tell you we're clear."

"All right." Hannah wrapped her arms around her daughter, who held her and cried.

Goose stood and moved out into the hallway with both MP5s at the ready. Having a two-man team would have been better. He felt like he needed to grow eyes in the back of his head. His bad knee felt stiff and uncomfortable, but it functioned.

Movement in the stairwell alerted him, letting him jerk his head back just as a Syrian soldier fired. The bullet cut through the corner of the stairwell and spun through the space where Goose's head had just been.

Dropping his right-hand MP5 so the machine pistol hung from the whip-it sling around his right shoulder, Goose took an M67 frag grenade from his LCE, pulled the pin, slipped the spoon, and counted off two seconds of the four-second fuse. He pitched the grenade underhanded, rolling it just above floor level so that it hopped into the stairwell.

A startled exclamation triggered a flurry of frantic footsteps; then the grenade detonation made Goose temporarily deaf.

"Sergeant!" Hannah yelled.

"Yes, ma'am," Goose responded. "Hold up just a minute more." He checked the stairwell and spotted the Syrian soldier lying facedown on the second flight of steps.

Goose moved down the hallway, found two other dead Syrian guards he and Fieldstone had accounted for, as well as the com center. It was too late to stop any communications.

"Base," Goose said, hustling back to the stairwell. "This is Alpha Leader. Base, do you read?"

"Base reads you, Alpha Leader," a man's voice answered.

"Can I get an assist?" Goose asked.

"What do you need? The other teams are already working their own exfiltration."

"Do you have thermographic access to the building for a scan?" Goose asked.

"Affirmative."

"I'm on the second floor. You've probably got me tagged."

"Affirmative, Alpha Leader."

"I got three civilians with me. They're on the same floor."

"Affirmative."

"Tag them for me in case we get separated during the evac."

"Done, Alpha Leader." The op tech hesitated. "You need to get moving."

"Got retaliation coming in from the main camp?"

"Affirmative. You'll probably have a bit of a dust-up; then they'll pull back."

That caught Goose's immediate attention. "Why?"

"Base has an air strike headed their way that should reach out and touch them in less than two minutes."

Goose let out a long, angry breath. Remington hadn't mentioned anything about an air strike against the main campsite. Alpha and Bravo Details had been bait. The hit-and-git they'd managed here had resulted in the loss of thousands of gallons of fuel and some armored cav units as well as at least one of the four officers they'd been after.

"Sweep the bottom floor for me," Goose said.

"I've got two unfriendlies. One near the front door and the other in the kitchen."

"Hannah," Goose called, "time to go." He started down the stairs and picked up the electronic detonator to the Claymore Conner had put on the front door. Picturing the building's layout in his mind, he triggered the detonator and stepped around the corner near the stairwell.

The explosion drowned out all other sounds for a moment; then a man screamed in agony.

The Syrian soldier in the kitchen was caught by surprise. He'd gone to the door near the common room to check on his partner. Too late, he saw or sensed Goose's approach. He brought his AK-47 up, already firing.

Rounds stitched the wall beside Goose as he walked into the gunfire. One of the rounds caught his Kevlar vest with a glancing sledgehammer blow. Goose put a three-round burst through the Syrian soldier's head, blowing him backwards.

Remaining cautious, Goose peered around the corner and spotted the wounded Syrian guard who had screamed lying by the front door with his assault rifle snugged up against his arm. Goose shot the man just as the soldier spotted him and tried to bring his weapon up.

"Hannah," Goose called, swapping magazines and moving toward the garage access door on the other side of the kitchen area.

"We're here."

"Base," Goose called.

"Here."

"Sweep the garage. Vehicles and troops."

"Three vehicles. Four men. One of the men is in the vehicle nearest the garage door. Two are in the corner directly opposite you. The last man is to your left, next to the wall six feet from your present twenty."

"Affirmative." Goose selected another M67 grenade, pulled the ring, then opened the garage door and tossed the grenade into the opposite side. The light from the explosion filled the garage for a moment, and the sound of painful screams rolled over Goose.

Looking up the wall by the door, realizing the materials were cheap and not bullet-resistant, Goose burned a full clip tracking down the wall.

"Two down," the op tech said. "One still in the car and one still in the corner opposite your present twenty."

Goose dropped the empty magazine and shoved a fresh one home. He didn't try to think. Everything at this point was nerve and reaction. He was a gun sight just trying to stay alive.

"You've got vehicles headed your way, Alpha Leader," the op tech said. "Evidently somebody's called for backup and let them know someone's still inside the building."

"Affirmative, Base."

Hoping his Kevlar armor and helmet would keep him protected— knowing that if reinforcements arrived before he could secure a car, he probably wouldn't get one—Goose stepped into the garage with an MP5 in each hand.

The guy in the corner had evidently been hit because he didn't even try to move. The 9mm rounds knocked him back against the wall and put him down. Goose targeted the guy behind the steering wheel in the big four-wheel-drive Ford Explorer and squeezed the trigger.

A fist-sized hole appeared in the windshield over the driver's head.

"Am I clear?" Goose asked.

"Clean and green inside, Alpha Leader."

Goose called for Hannah, picking up his speed till he reached the Explorer. The vehicle was expensive and a long way from home, proof that the drug-money profits were considerable. The custom paint job further elaborated on that.

The driver's door was unlocked. He opened it, reached in, and yanked the dead man from behind the steering wheel. He tripped the electronic locks, opening all the doors.

"Get in, belt up, and stay down," Goose ordered. The key was in the ignition and the engine was running. There was no electronic garage-door opener. Evidently not all options were available.

"Alpha Leader, you've got a T-72 parked nearly at your doorstep. Hey, the turret is swiveling. He's targeting the garage."

Goose pulled the gearshift into drive, thanking God that the vehicle was an automatic, and floored the accelerator. The reinforced front end plowed through the tin-and-wood garage door.

Thirty yards out, Goose sideswiped the T-72 main battle tank just as the main gun fired. The collision shivered through the Explorer but the big vehicle held together. Metal screeched in his ears. Then he realized why he hadn't seen the tank: The underground caverns that had held the fuel stores were fiery pits of forty-foot orange flames with serpentine coils of black smoke that looked gray against the night sky.

"Base," Goose called over the headset. He stripped off the NVGs and tossed them on the floor.

"Go, Alpha Leader."

Goose drove through burning hulks of APCs and tanks. Maybe Lieutenant York's team hadn't gotten all of their targets, but they'd gotten most of them. He steered for the airfield.

"Where are the evac birds?"

"Birds are in the air, Alpha Leader," Lieutenant Keller responded. "We tried to hold back but were ordered to move."

Goose thought about that. Remington had to have known he was in motion, had to have known he had the three women with him.

"How far out are the incoming Syrian birds?" Goose asked.

"Less than a minute away," the op tech said. "Closing fast."

"Alpha Leader," Remington said, his voice strong and cold. "Those birds will not sit down. If they do, I'm going to lose twenty-something Rangers while trying to save one."

And three women, Goose thought, but he didn't say anything.

"Understood, Base. We won't need them to land. We'll make a transfer from the vehicle I've commandeered to the helo." He cut the wheel, catching sight of a tank's turret spinning in his direction. A second later the main gun belched flame and the round whistled past them to explode against the ground and leave a huge crater.

"Too risky," Remington said.

"We can do it," Keller said.

"I've got three women with me," Goose said.

"We're not going to leave those women behind, Base," Keller said.

"Affirmative," Remington said, but he didn't sound happy.

"Base," Keller called out, "get me a lock on Alpha Leader."

"Base, Alpha Prime, be advised that I'm running due north." With the four-wheel drive, Goose was able to cross the broken terrain. He kept the accelerator down, mowing over everything that wasn't big enough to stop him.

"Alpha Leader," Keller said, "we have you in sight."

The Explorer bounced and careened over the rough ground.

Glancing up, both hands on the wheel, Goose saw one of the Mi-8s descend on him like a hawk taking a mouse. Four Rangers hung from lines from the helo. The helo pilot matched speeds with the Explorer and seconds later, the Rangers landed on top of the luxury vehicle and grabbed hold of the luggage rack.

Hannah and the others put up only a small argument once they were advised that the Syrian air force was in pursuit. With the Rangers assisting them, they were hauled up on lines into the safety of the Mi-8.

Goose was given his own line. He locked the Explorer into cruise control, opened the door, and stepped off into the loop of the line. For one dizzying second, he spun at the end of the line. Then everything straightened out as the Explorer went airborne and flipped end over end before catching on fire and exploding.

Seconds later, Goose was packed into the belly of the fleeing Mi-8 with the other Rangers, listening to Base's report that the Syrian air force was pulling back in an effort to return to the main camp and help with the attack there that was proving devastating.

Goose gazed down at the battlefield. The fuel would burn for a while, as would the armored cav. As he watched, another T-55 blew up, then broke apart as the ammo touched off as well.

The mission was a success. They'd cost the Syrian army dearly and reminded them who they were facing. Five Rangers, including Fieldstone, had fallen. Six others were wounded.

As Goose sat on the bare metal floor of the helo's cargo area, he watched as two of the medical corpsmen handed the women blankets and water and offered them food. Watching them, Goose remembered who they were fighting for and why.

But was the 75th going to be strong enough to stand up against whatever the Tribulation was going to throw at them?

He settled back against the metal wall and tried to relax, but images of Fieldstone getting killed just inches from him wouldn't go away. Fieldstone had been young, too young to die.

How many young men were going to be required to make those kinds of sacrifices during the next seven years? And in the end, would they be able to make a difference?

Thinking about differences also made Goose think about Captain Cal Remington. He didn't like the thoughts that came to his mind or the knowledge that whatever was going on in Sanliurfa was pulling them apart.

EPILOGUE

Delroy Harte drove the tractor through the dense undergrowth that had filled the acreage behind the Church of the Word. A small stream still ran through it, and he'd uncovered most of it with the brush-hog attachment. Here and there, lines in the earth showed where it had once been tilled. He remembered picking snap beans and sugar peas with his mother, waiting till the strawberries ripened in May and June, digging potatoes and sweet potatoes and onions with his daddy to put into the root cellar.

He found the frayed gray rope of what might have been a tire swing. He'd even found the pitcher's mound his daddy had made almost fifty years ago when he'd taught Delroy how to throw and catch and bat.

While mowing, Delroy imagined the voices and laughter of dozens, maybe even hundreds, of baseball games played in the back of the field as part of the church functions, and—a lot of times—just when a bunch of kids had gathered with their bats and gloves. When someone had gotten a new baseball, all shiny and white, that usually guaranteed a game that day.

Delroy guessed there were at least a million memories of his family and growing up here, and as he mowed, he also mined them. He'd even brought Terrence out to this field a few times to pitch and hit, but it just hadn't been the same. Delroy had kept looking for his daddy, thinking how grand it would have been if they could have all played baseball together.

Maybe some other time, he thought. *God willing, there will be a time when we can all play together.*

He took out more of the undergrowth, pleased with the ripsaw sound of the brush hog as it brought civilization back into the neighborhood. Other members of the congregation had offered to do the work, but Delroy wanted to do it himself, wanted to feel how it was to work the land again. He had accepted the loan of a pair of bib overalls because he didn't have any.

Several members of the congregation still labored on the church, cleaning and painting and retooling woodwork that hadn't been touched in years. A group of them had even started sanding the pews down one by one, then putting new lacquer on them.

As he backed the tractor up, Delroy saw Glenda standing only a short distance away. She carried a big picnic basket under her arm.

Delroy had to smile. The wooden picnic basket had been one of their first extravagances as a married couple.

He switched off the engine, sat with his arms wrapped around the steering wheel, and looked at her. She still had the power to take his breath away.

Glenda shaded her eyes. "Hey, sailor. Looking for a good time?"

"Oh, and listen to you," Delroy said with a grin. "All that brave talk from way over there."

"I'm not walking out there in all those brambles. I don't have to."

"And why not?"

"Because I've got fried chicken, mashed potatoes and gravy, corn on the cob, green beans, and buttermilk rolls in this basket."

"It's tempting," Delroy said.

"Better than that," Glenda said. "It's homemade. So is the deep-dish apple pie I made for dessert. I also made a jug of tea, sweet and dark, with some fresh lemon."

"That'll close the deal." Delroy climbed down from the tractor, surprised at how stiff he'd gotten from just a few hours of work. He crossed over to her and gave her a brief hug.

Even though she'd come to the revival yesterday and stayed late at the church, Delroy spent the night again at the Purcell home. After nearly five years of absence, more than the times they'd been apart while he'd been at sea, Delroy knew they were going to have to move slowly to rekindle everything they'd once had.

If that was even possible.

After five years of being more or less alone, both of them had changed in some ways, grown more independent.

Phyllis, however, had been willing to bet they'd be back together before another six months were gone. But she didn't know that what Delroy planned would put even more strain on an already strained relationship.

"Where do you want to sit?" Glenda asked.

"I found the old stream again," Delroy said.

Together, they walked toward it and found a comfortable shaded spot. Evening was starting to stretch the shadows long and thin.

Glenda wore slacks and a blouse, but she'd brought a sweater against the evening's chill.

Delroy helped her spread out the red-and-white-checked blanket, then put out the food. They ate and talked about the memories they shared, about Terrence, and even a little about the things that had happened in the past five years.

But they stayed away from the topic of the future. That subject was still too unsettling, and that was before any of the threats of the Tribulation were thrown in.

Until Glenda looked at Delroy, while he was taking his time with the deep-dish apple pie, and said, "You're not staying, are you?"

Delroy finished chewing the bite he had, giving himself a little more time to think about how handle that question.

"You don't have to beat around the bush, Delroy," Glenda said. "I knew that you couldn't stay here. Not yet anyway."

"No, ma'am," Delroy said. "I've still got a ship out there that's wrapped up in a war." He hesitated. "I've got to wrap up some things before I try taking on anything new."

Glenda drew her legs up and wrapped her arms around her knees. "I'm not going to act like I'm not disappointed."

"I figured you'd be more relieved to find out," Delroy said.

Glenda laughed. "Maybe there's a little of that too." She looked sad. "It's been such a long time since it's been just you and me."

"I know." Delroy ate another bite of pie. "I've spent five years with those men, Glenda, and I haven't given them everything I was supposed to. I want to go back and do it right."

"That's fine. I understand."

"Then there's the Tribulation. Most people, they're not ready to believe that this is the end, that there's only seven more years left of this world. And so many people aren't going to last that long." Delroy looked at her. "I feel like I'm supposed to be part of this—part of whatever it is, whatever it takes to save what we can of the folks who just don't know what's going on."

"I know. I heard you speak yesterday. I heard your message. It made me think a lot of your daddy. And when I saw you with Clarence Floyd? How you brought even him to Jesus like you did?" Glenda reached out and stroked his face. "You're ready, Delroy. You're a warrior, and this is going to be your fight." She frowned a little. "I'll worry about you, and I'll pray for you, and I'll miss you. But I want you to know that I'm going to wait on you. Till you get back home or we are together again in the hereafter. Whatever it takes."

Delroy captured Glenda's hand in his, seeing how small hers was against his. He kissed her fingers and said, "Thank you." There was nothing else to say. Their hearts knew each other—always had, and always would.

❋   ❋   ❋

United States of America
Fort Benning, Georgia
Local Time 2223 Hours

"I found her," Doug Benbow said on the other end of the phone line.

"Where is she?" Megan juggled her cell phone and the sack of groceries she'd just bought in the commissary to take home to Camp Gander. She crossed the packed parking lot to Goose's pickup truck.

"Saint Francis Hospital," Benbow said.

"They have phones there," Megan pointed out. "She could have called."

"Megan, I know. I tried to put a call through to her father's room, but nobody answers."

"Did you call the floor nurse?"

"Yeah. She says that a young woman who fits Jenny's description is there."

"Did you try to get her to give Jenny a message? Let her know we've been trying to get in touch with her and that we care?" Megan knew she sounded tired.

Yesterday's trial had taken nearly everything out of her. Then returning to Camp Gander without Jenny's help, the additional worrying about Jenny, and fending off media people who wanted to interview the woman who seemed to have set the military on its ear by inspiring them to come forward and declare that there is a God had stranded Megan in a world that seemed too fuzzy and too far away to be real.

"Don't you think sending the nurse in there is a little invasive?" Benbow asked.

"You're right," Megan said. "I can swing by there in twenty minutes and check on her myself. I'll feel better if I can see her." She dug her keys out of her purse. "Did you find out about her dad?"

"Traffic accident. He was drinking. One-car accident." Benbow hesitated. "The nurse I talked to and convinced that I was a family member told me they don't think he's going to pull through."

Megan felt horrible. In spite of everything yesterday, things were still going wrong. She didn't know if she would be allowed to continue her job as counselor for the teens. For the moment she was still providing room and board for many of them, but she was afraid General Braddock would try to phase her out. She didn't know what she would do if that happened.

"You're going out there?" Benbow asked.

"Yes."

"Tonight?"

"Right now."

"Want company?"

"This might be more girl time, Doug. No offense."

"Oh, none taken. Trust me. I can use the sleep. Call me if you need anything. Or if Jenny needs anything."

Megan said she would, then punched End on the cell phone. Only when she was standing beside Goose's pickup did she realize the passenger-side window was broken out. She started to back away.

Then Joey poked his head out of the shadows. He was scared and his face was horribly bruised. "Mom," he said in a quavering voice. "I'm in trouble. I'm in *real* trouble."

❋ ❋ ❋

United States 75th Army Rangers Temporary Post
Sanliurfa, Turkey
Local Time 0623 Hours

Goose stood in front of the foggy mirror in the gym the Rangers used for showers. Few buildings had working power in the city now. He stood with a towel around his hips and used a bar of soap to make a lather, then smeared it across his face. He took another towel and wiped the fog from the mirror.

Captain Cal Remington stood behind Goose.

Turning, Goose snapped to attention and saluted. "Sir."

"As you were, Goose," Remington said. "It's too early in the morning for the dog-and-pony show."

"Yes, sir."

Remington made a show of examining the small razor nicks on Goose's neck. "Are you shaving or attempting suicide here, First Sergeant?"

"Shaving, sir. Haven't been able to get a new blade for a few days. And I like a close shave."

"Remind me and I'll give you some out of my personal kit."

"Yes, sir," Goose said, though he would never ask and they both knew that. But more than likely, Remington would remember and give the blades to him. Goose scraped at the lather with the dull blade and immediately opened up a cut on his chin.

"Those nicks are going to show up on the television cameras," Remington said.

"I don't plan on doing any interviews."

Remington crossed his arms over his chest. "The last couple days, you seem to have done a number of them."

Goose met Remington's gaze full measure in his reflection in the mirror. In a way it was almost like looking back at himself. "I haven't intended to, sir. Your open-arms policy with the media has brought a lot of them my way. If you want, I can start avoiding them or sending them away."

"No." Remington looked like he'd swallowed something unpleasant.

Goose knew that Remington couldn't tell him that. Or wouldn't. It would appear to too many people that Remington was jealous of the attention Goose was getting.

"Rescuing those women seems to have gotten you the most attention," Remington said.

"I didn't plan on it, sir." Goose took a couple swipes along his face, removing beard and lather. Both of them knew that was as close as he'd ever come to pointing out that Remington hadn't let him know the women were there.

On the other hand, Remington had never admitted prior knowledge to their presence.

"Have you talked to the women, sir?" Goose asked.

"No."

"I think you should."

"Why?"

Goose rinsed soap lather from his razor. "When they were kidnapped here in the city by the Bedouin guy—"

"Abu Alam?"

Goose nodded. "They said they thought a guy was there who was an American soldier."

Interest flickered in Remington's eyes. "Why would an American soldier be there?"

"That's what I was wondering, sir."

"Do you believe them?"

"Yes, sir. They're telling that story on CNN right now."

"That an American soldier was present during their kidnapping?"

"Not during the kidnapping, sir," Goose said. "During the trading that went on inside the city."

"Can they prove that?"

"I don't know."

"What's your interest in their story, First Sergeant?"

"If there really was an American soldier involved, somebody who was trading with Abu Alam, I was thinking we might want to check into it."

"Why?"

"You look around this city, sir, and you'll find that most of the American soldiers here are under your command."

Remington bridled. "Are you insinuating something here, First Sergeant?"

"No, sir," Goose answered, though the description he'd gotten put him quickly in mind of Corporal Dean Hardin. He didn't want to get into that. Not yet.

"Then what?"

"Damage control, sir." Goose scraped more whiskers away. "If the media buys into their story, maybe they'll start buying into the story that Abu Alam—who is still missing—was kidnapped by American soldiers. That could bring a lot of unwanted pressure to this command, sir. You get people with cameras out there everywhere, and the Syrians have television and satellite access, we could end up showing more of our defensive and offensive capabilities than we intend or want to."

"That's a good point. I'll take that under advisement."

"Thank you, sir." Goose shaved for a while, knowing something else was on Remington's mind, but the captain hadn't gotten around to it. He opened up yet another nick that streamed scarlet.

"Goose," Remington said, "I want to ask you something."

"Yes, sir."

"In all the years I've known you, you've never lied to me."

"No, sir."

Remington paused. "Do you think you would ever feel compelled to lie to me? Do you think there would ever be anything—or anyone—that you would lie to me about?"

Goose nicked himself again, cutting deeper this time because he was thinking that Remington had found out about Icarus.

"You have to watch out for that razor," Remington cautioned.

Goose washed the blood away, finding that with the addition of water the cut bled even more profusely.

"You didn't answer my question," Remington pointed out.

Goose looked at the captain in the mirror. "I don't know, sir."

Remington was silent for a time. "There was a time when your *immediate* answer would have been no."

Silently Goose concentrated on his shaving. *There was a time, sir, when you wouldn't have sent me into a mission without all the knowledge I needed, or with the intention of leaving me behind at the first sign of trouble.* But he didn't speak any of that.

"You see, I sensed that, Goose. Somehow we've gotten off on the wrong foot. I guess as we progress through this situation we have here in Sanliurfa, I'll have to be careful what I talk to you about."

An explosion suddenly shook the showers, rolling thunder into the room.

Remington was out the door while Goose was grabbing his pants and his M-4A1. He ran out into the street dressed only in his pants, his dog tags thudding against his chest, and his assault rifle in hand.

The showers were right across the street from Baker's church. Where the church had stood, though, only bits and pieces of the tents and the ammo cases remained. A huge crater had opened in the ground, and flames danced in it as if it were some express tube to hell itself.

"It's Baker!" someone yelled. "He's over here!"

Goose ran barefooted, keeping up with Remington.

Baker lay facedown on the ground. Burn splotches showed over his body and smoke curled from his hair.

"What happened?" Remington demanded.

"Don't know, sir," an ashen-faced corporal answered. "Baker asked everyone to leave the tent about twenty minutes ago."

"No one was in there with him?"

"No, sir."

Goose's mind automatically jumped to the fact that Baker had held on to the information Danielle Vinchenzo had gotten from her cryptic source. OneWorld NewsNet had called her away on assignment before Goose had returned from Operation Run Dry.

Gently, Goose turned Baker over. He'd already checked the man's carotid artery and found no pulse. But his fingers had come away crimson with blood.

When Baker was on his back, everyone could see that his throat had been slit from ear to ear.

Shaken, Goose squatted down, ignoring the painful bite of his injured knee, for a closer look. "No," he said. "He couldn't have been in there alone. He didn't cut his own throat. Someone murdered him."

And Goose knew he was going to find out who had done it, even if it was the last thing he ever did.

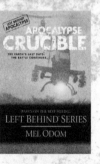